DreamWorks

DRAGONS
RIDERS OF BERK

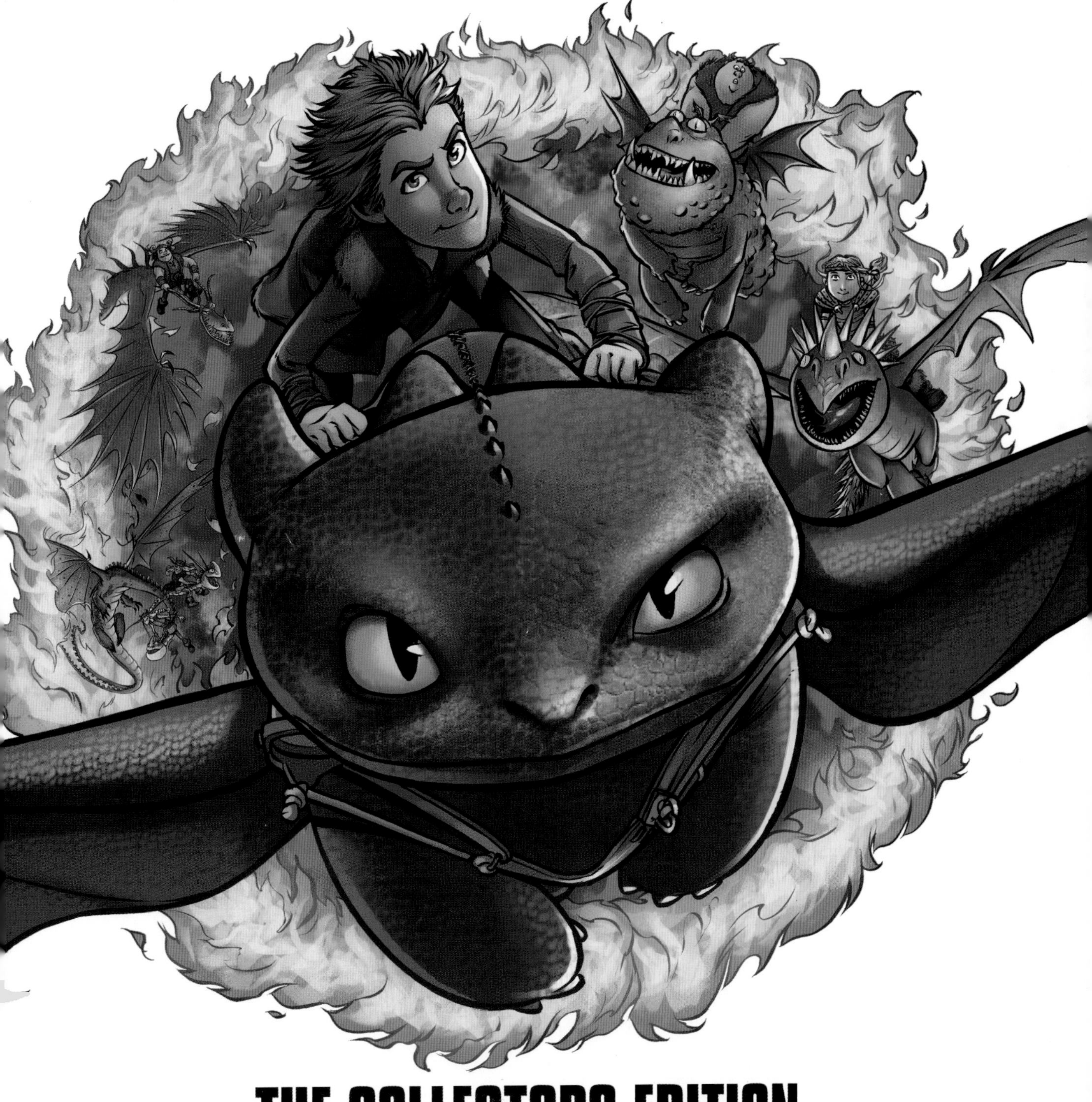

THE COLLECTORS EDITION

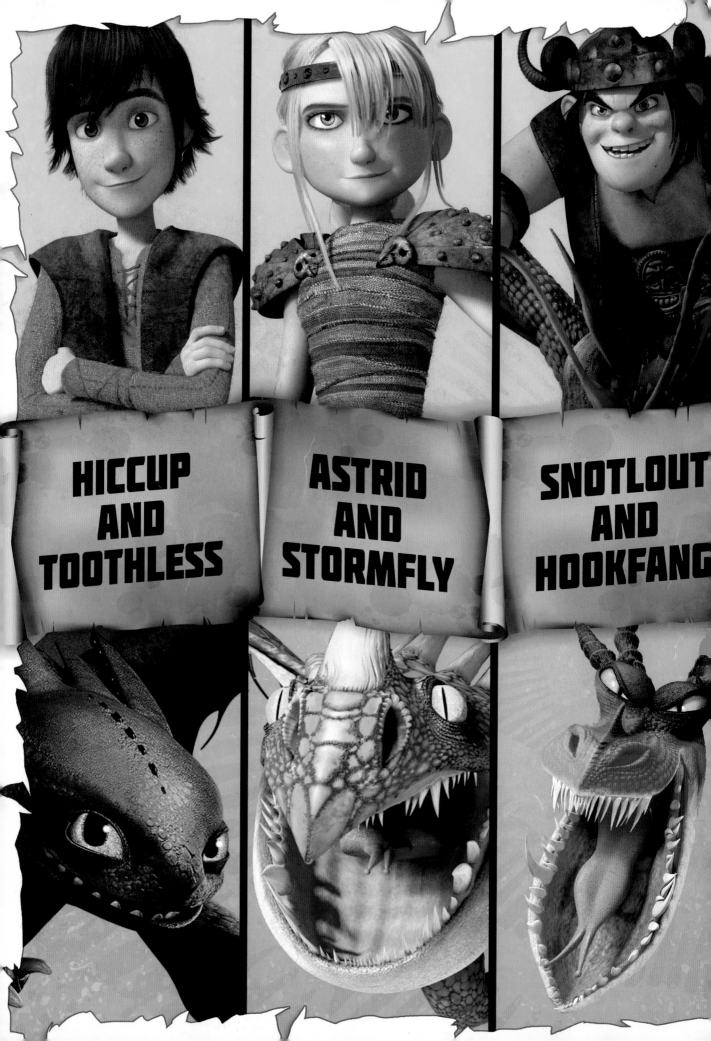

HICCUP AND TOOTHLESS

ASTRID AND STORMFLY

SNOTLOUT AND HOOKFANG

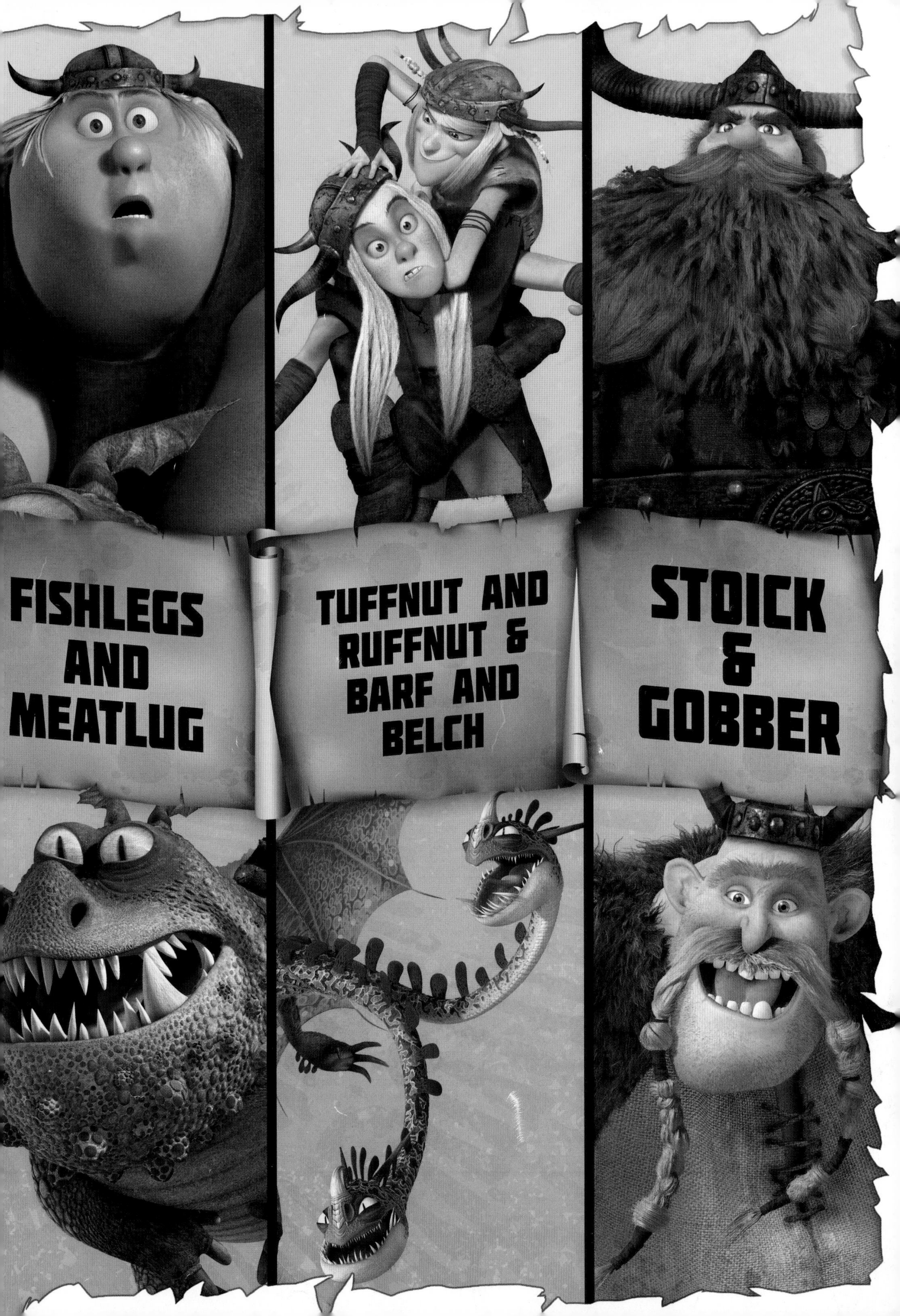
FISHLEGS AND MEATLUG
TUFFNUT AND RUFFNUT & BARF AND BELCH
STOICK & GOBBER

TITAN COMICS

Senior Editor MARTIN EDEN

Production Manager OBI ONUORA

Production Supervisors MARIA PEARSON & JACKIE FLOOK

Production Assistant PETER JAMES

Studio Manager SELINA JUNEJA

Circulation Manager STEVE TOTHILL

Marketing Manager RICKY CLAYDON

Press/Marketing OWEN JOHNSON

Publishing Manager DARRYL TOTHILL

Publishing Director CHRIS TEATHER

Operations Director LEIGH BAULCH

Executive Director VIVIAN CHEUNG

Publisher NICK LANDAU

ISBN: 9781782767664

DreamWorks *Dragons: Riders of Berk* The Collectors Edition, published by Titan Comics, a division of
Titan Publishing Group Ltd. 144 Southwark St. London, SE1 0UP. Contains DreamWorks *Dragons: Riders
of Berk* Volume One: *Dragon Down* and Volume Two: *Dangers of the Deep*. No part of this publication may
be reproduced, stored in a retrieval system, or transmitted, in any form or by any means, without the prior
written permission of the publisher. Names, characters, places and incidents featured in this publication
are either the product of the author's imagination or used fictitiously. Any resemblance to actual persons,
living or dead (except for satirical purposes), is entirely coincidental.

10 9 8 7 6 5 4 3 2 1

First printed in China in October 2015.
A CIP catalogue record for this title is available from the British Library.
Titan Comics. TC0953

Special thanks to Corinne Combs, Alyssa Mauney, Barbara Layman, Lawrence Hamashima, and all at
DreamWorks. Plus Steve White and David Manley-Leach at Titan.

DRAGON DOWN

SCRIPT Simon Furman
PENCILS Iwan Nazif
INKS Iwan Nazif with Bambos Georgiou
COLORS Nestor Pereyra & Digikore
LETTERING David Manley-Leach

CHAPTER ONE

In which the dragons show off some new tricks... Hookfang is sent away... And the town of Berk is hit by a mighty storm...

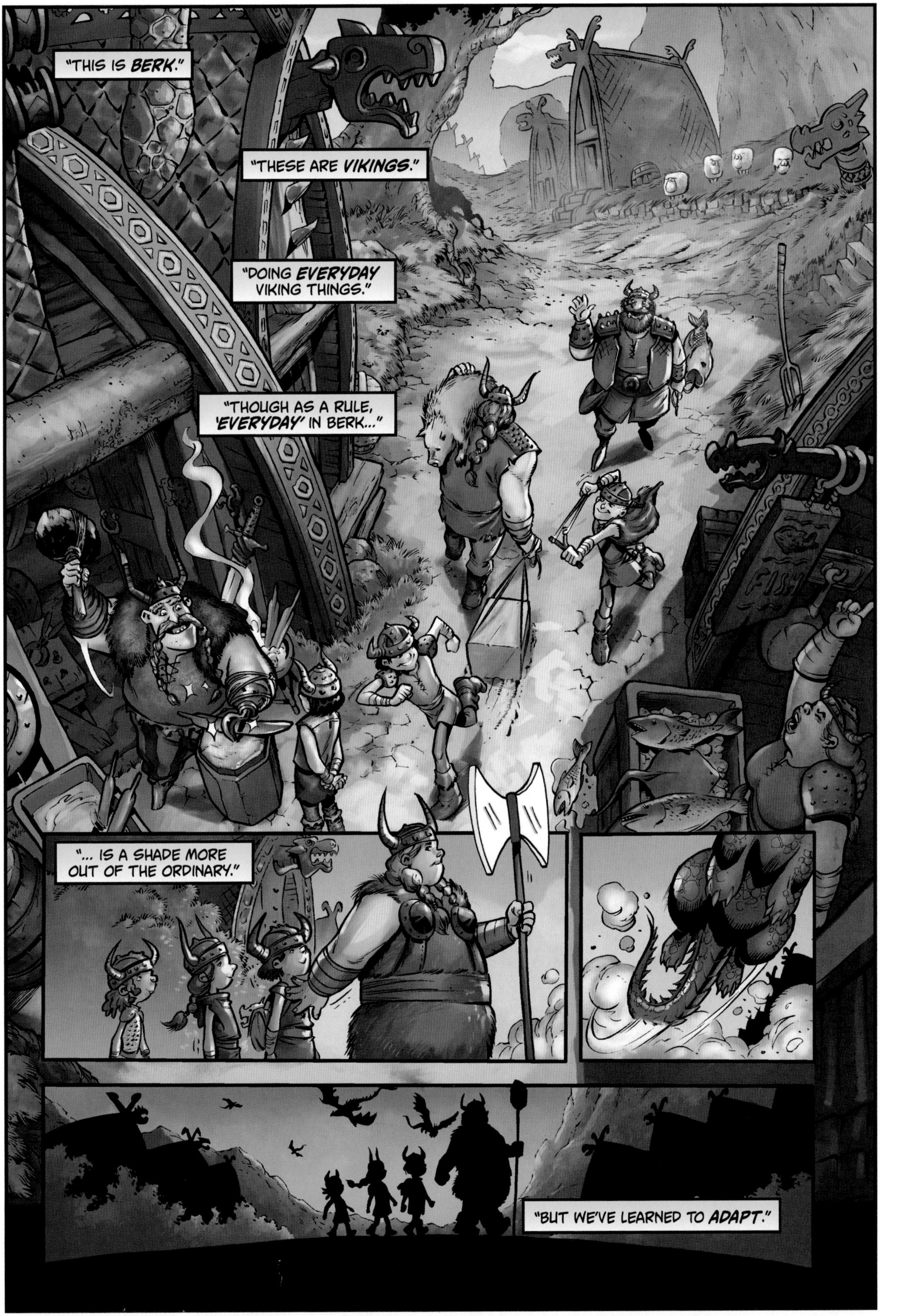
"THIS IS BERK."
"THESE ARE VIKINGS."
"DOING EVERYDAY VIKING THINGS."
"THOUGH AS A RULE, 'EVERYDAY' IN BERK..."
FISH
"... IS A SHADE MORE OUT OF THE ORDINARY."
"BUT WE'VE LEARNED TO ADAPT."

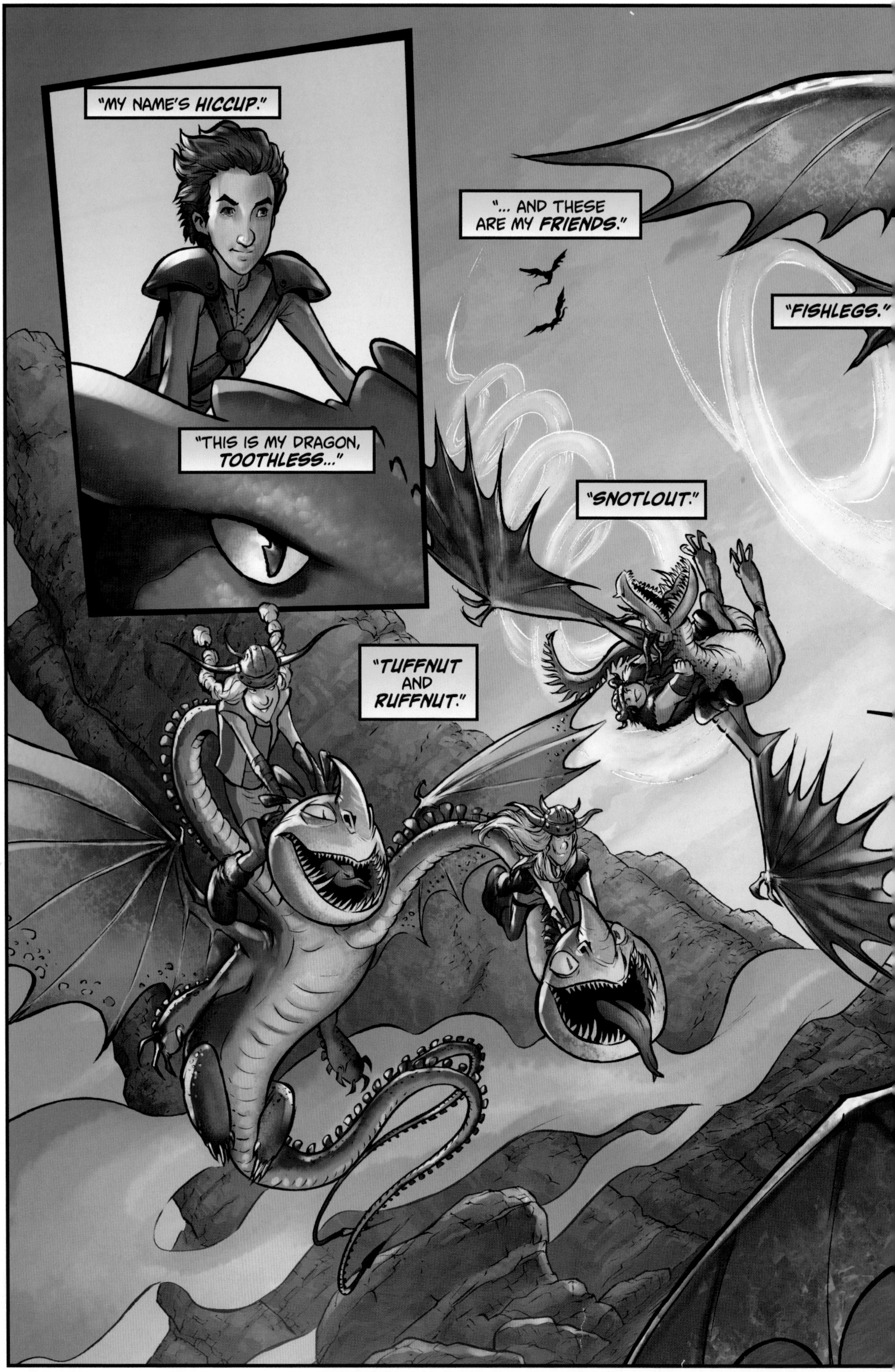
"MY NAME'S HICCUP."
"THIS IS MY DRAGON, TOOTHLESS..."
"... AND THESE ARE MY FRIENDS."
"FISHLEGS."
"SNOTLOUT."
"TUFFNUT AND RUFFNUT."

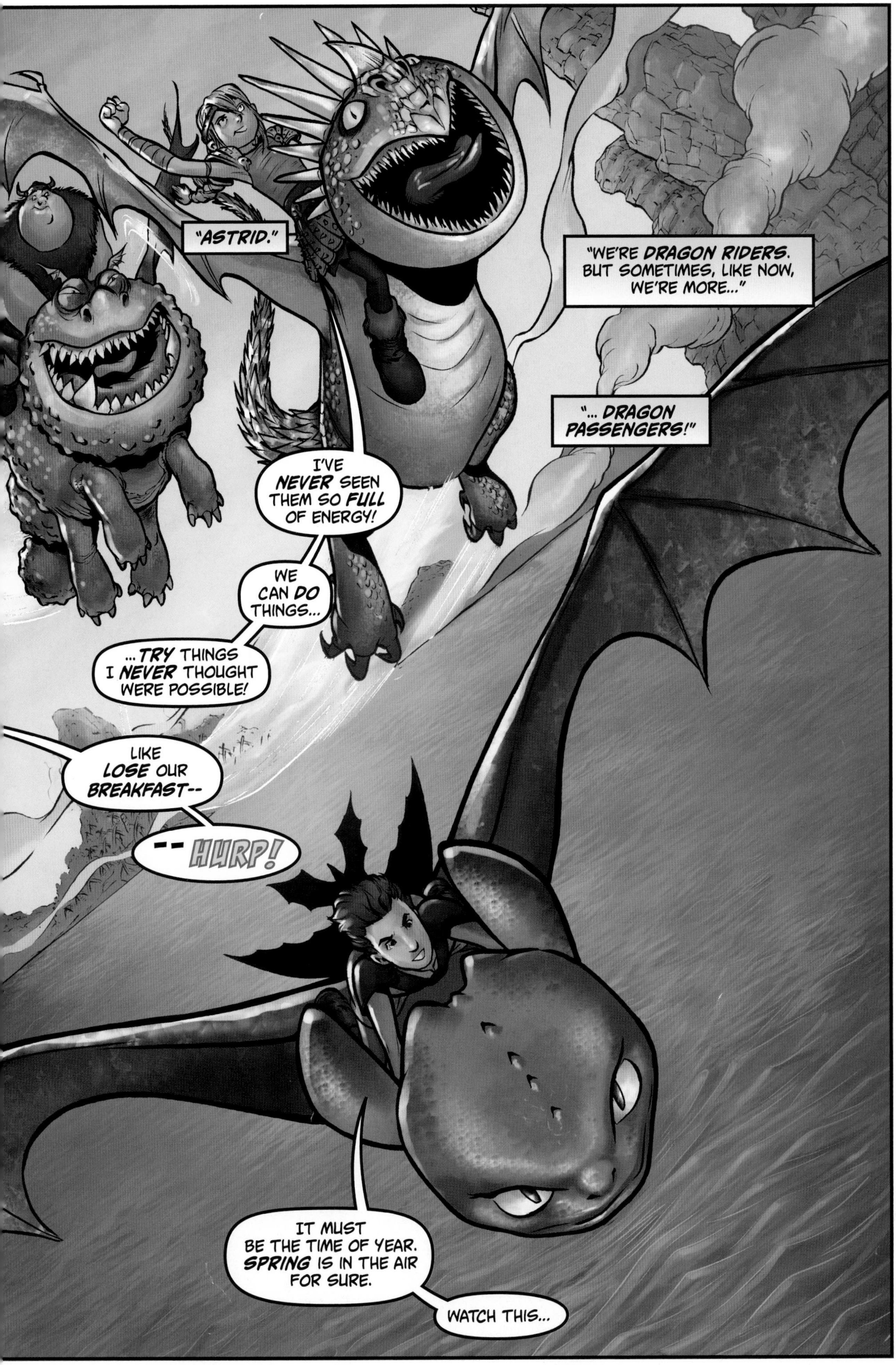
"ASTRID."
"WE'RE DRAGON RIDERS. BUT SOMETIMES, LIKE NOW, WE'RE MORE..."
"... DRAGON PASSENGERS!"
I'VE NEVER SEEN THEM SO FULL OF ENERGY!
WE CAN DO THINGS...
...TRY THINGS I NEVER THOUGHT WERE POSSIBLE!
LIKE LOSE OUR BREAKFAST--
--HURP!
IT MUST BE THE TIME OF YEAR. SPRING IS IN THE AIR FOR SURE.
WATCH THIS...

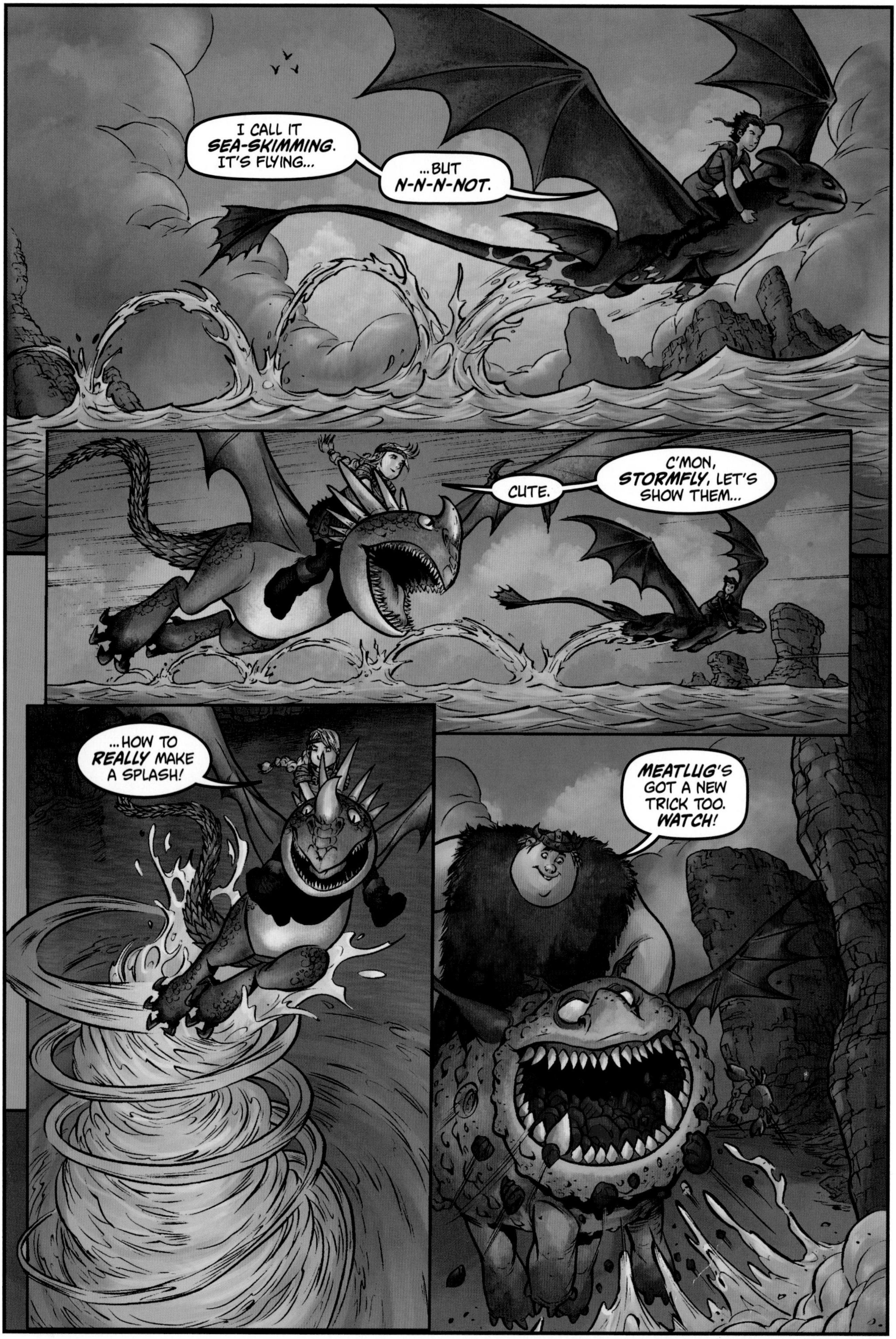

I CALL IT SEA-SKIMMING. IT'S FLYING...
...BUT N-N-N-NOT.
CUTE.
C'MON, STORMFLY, LET'S SHOW THEM...
...HOW TO REALLY MAKE A SPLASH!
MEATLUG'S GOT A NEW TRICK TOO. WATCH!

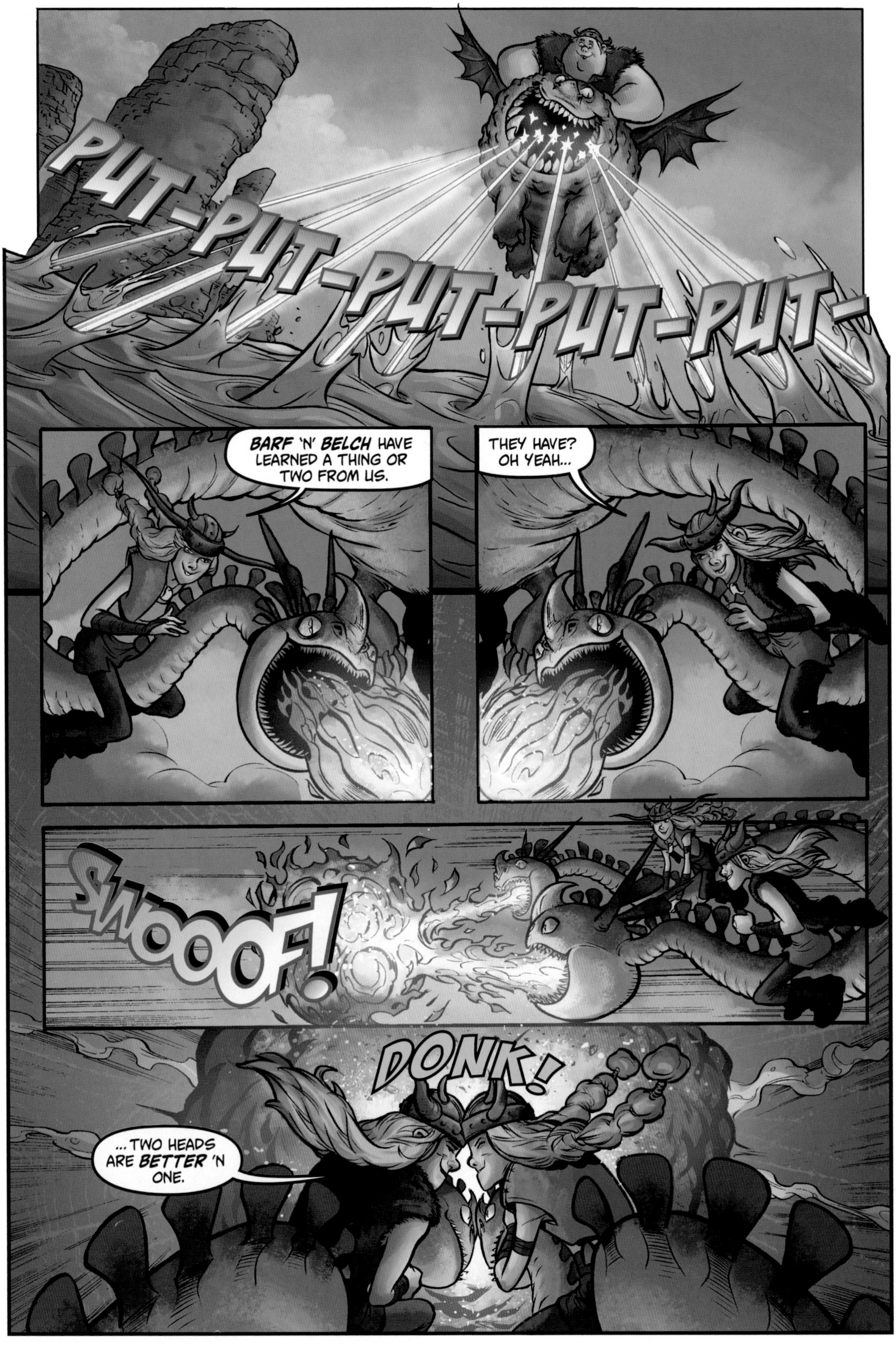
PUT-PUT-PUT-PUT-PUT-
BARF 'N' BELCH HAVE LEARNED A THING OR TWO FROM US.
THEY HAVE? OH YEAH...
SWOOOF!
DONK!
...TWO HEADS ARE BETTER 'N ONE.

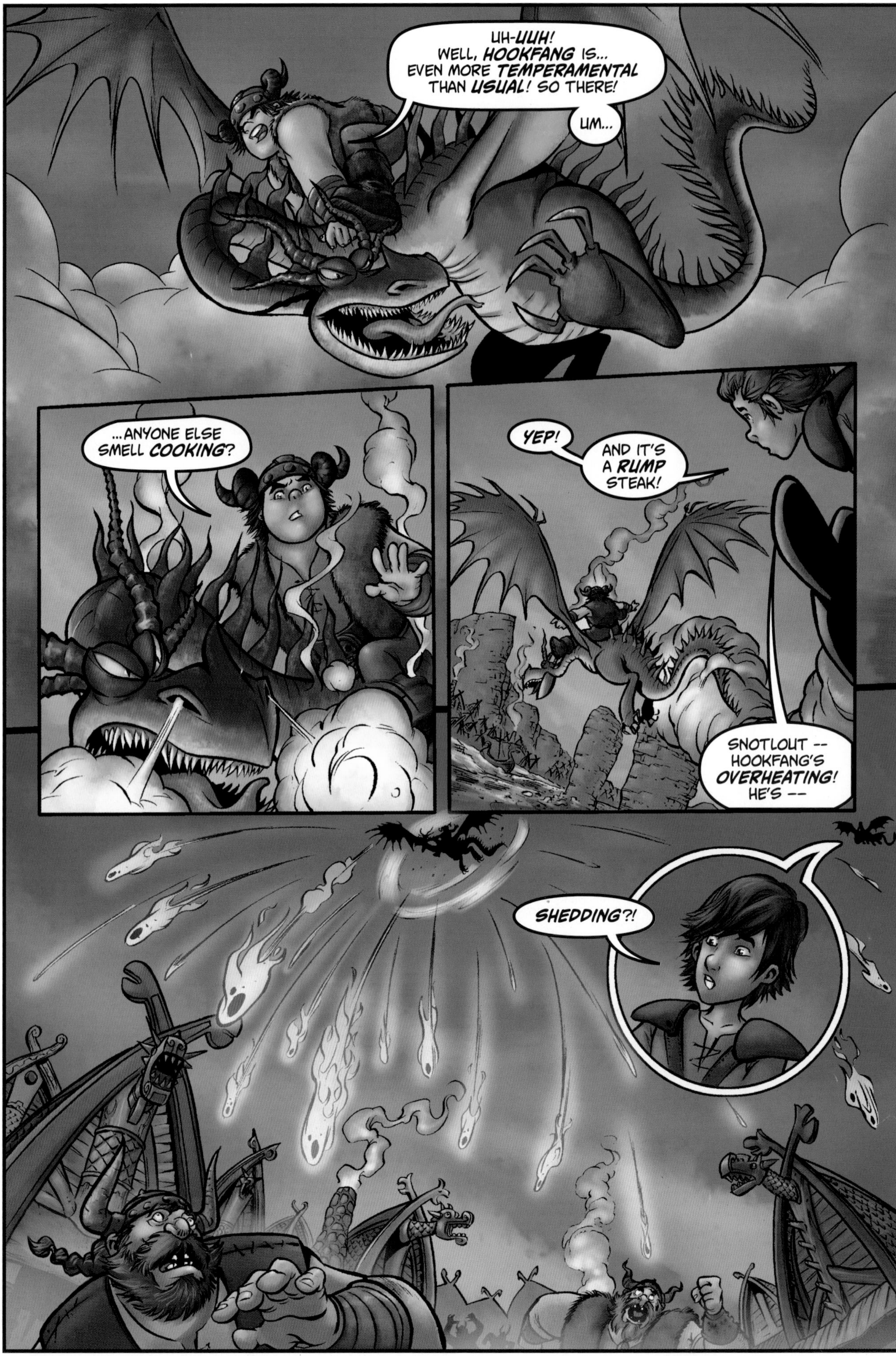
UH-UUH! WELL, HOOKFANG IS... EVEN MORE TEMPERAMENTAL THAN USUAL! SO THERE!
UM...
...ANYONE ELSE SMELL COOKING?
YEP!
AND IT'S A RUMP STEAK!
SNOTLOUT -- HOOKFANG'S OVERHEATING! HE'S --
SHEDDING?!

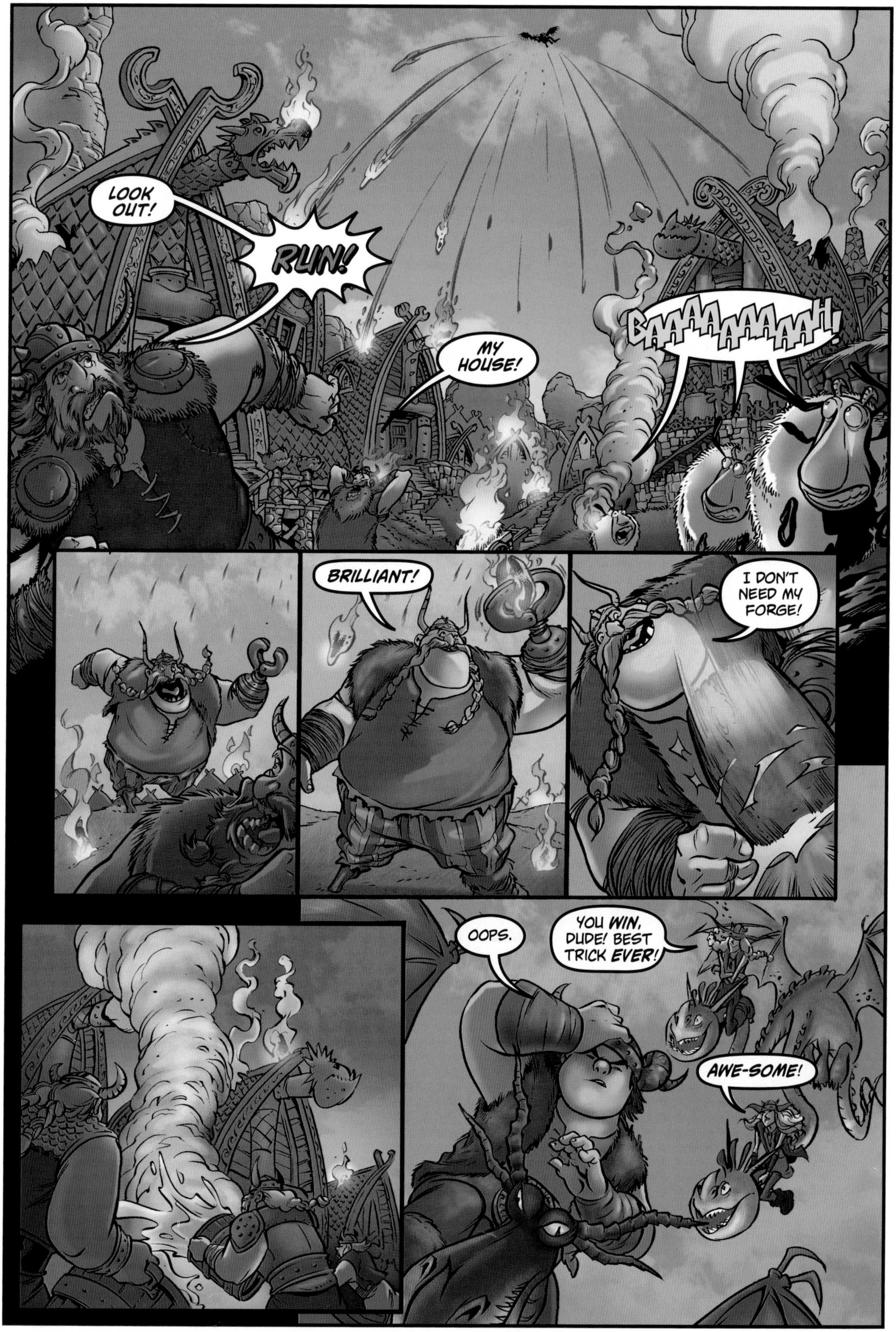

LOOK OUT!
RUN!
MY HOUSE!
BAAAAAAAAAH!
BRILLIANT!
I DON'T NEED MY FORGE!
OOPS.
YOU WIN, DUDE! BEST TRICK EVER!
AWE-SOME!

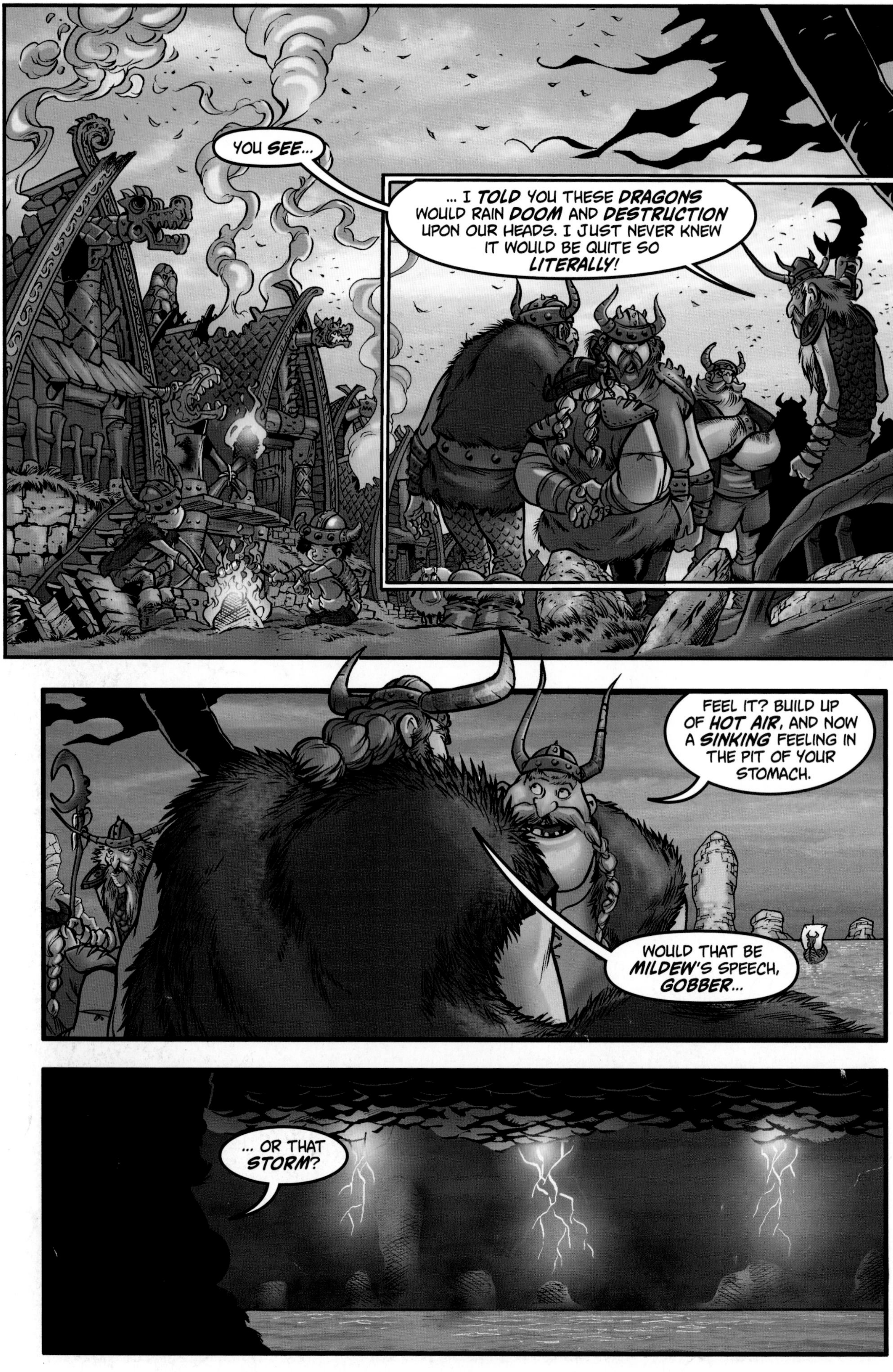
YOU SEE...
... I TOLD YOU THESE DRAGONS WOULD RAIN DOOM AND DESTRUCTION UPON OUR HEADS. I JUST NEVER KNEW IT WOULD BE QUITE SO LITERALLY!
FEEL IT? BUILD UP OF HOT AIR, AND NOW A SINKING FEELING IN THE PIT OF YOUR STOMACH.
WOULD THAT BE MILDEW'S SPEECH, GOBBER...
... OR THAT STORM?

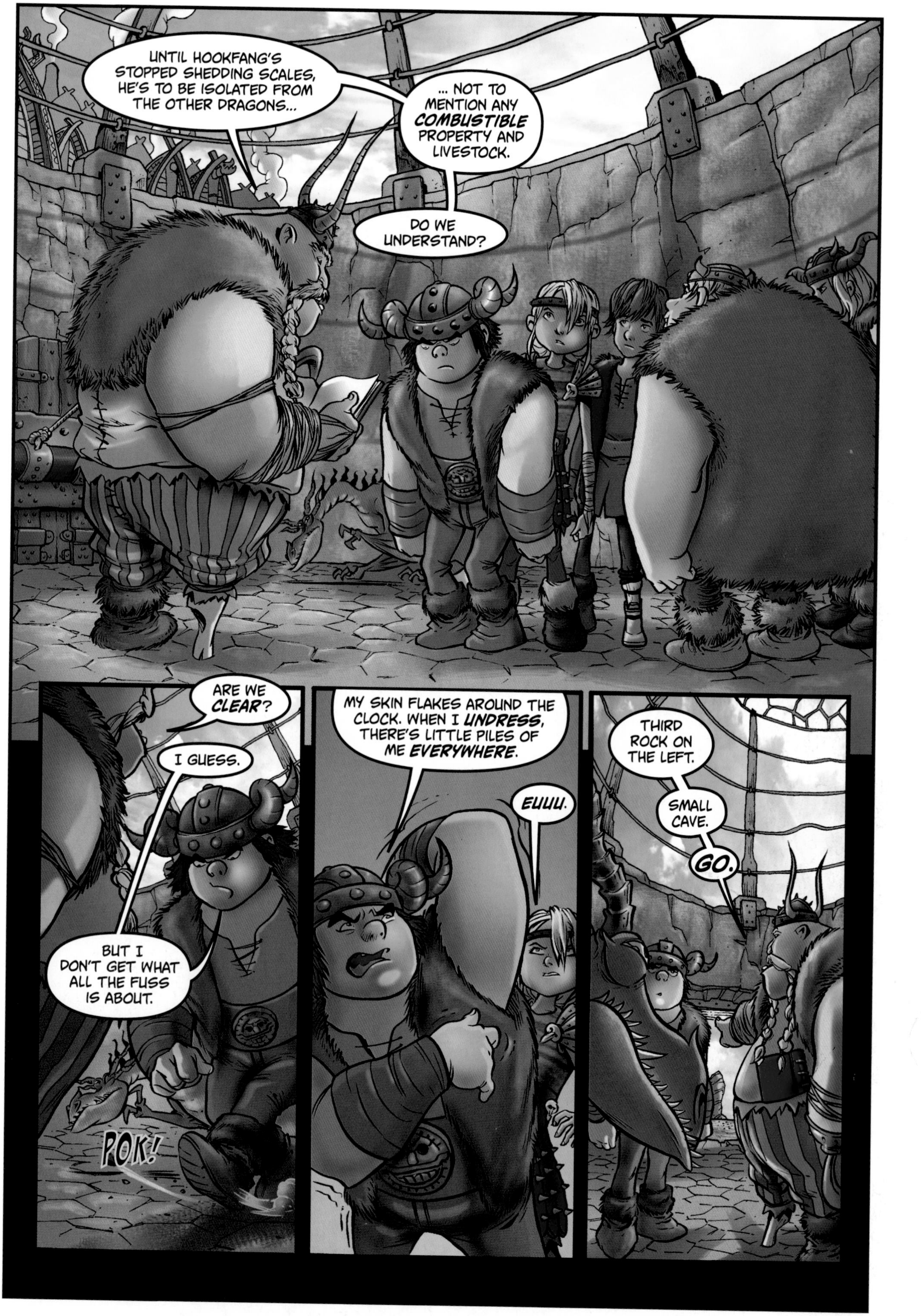
UNTIL HOOKFANG'S STOPPED SHEDDING SCALES, HE'S TO BE ISOLATED FROM THE OTHER DRAGONS...
... NOT TO MENTION ANY *COMBUSTIBLE* PROPERTY AND LIVESTOCK.
DO WE UNDERSTAND?
ARE WE *CLEAR*?
I GUESS.
BUT I DON'T GET WHAT ALL THE FUSS IS ABOUT.
POK!
MY SKIN FLAKES AROUND THE CLOCK. WHEN I *UNDRESS*, THERE'S LITTLE PILES OF ME *EVERYWHERE*.
EUUU.
THIRD ROCK ON THE LEFT.
SMALL CAVE.
GO.

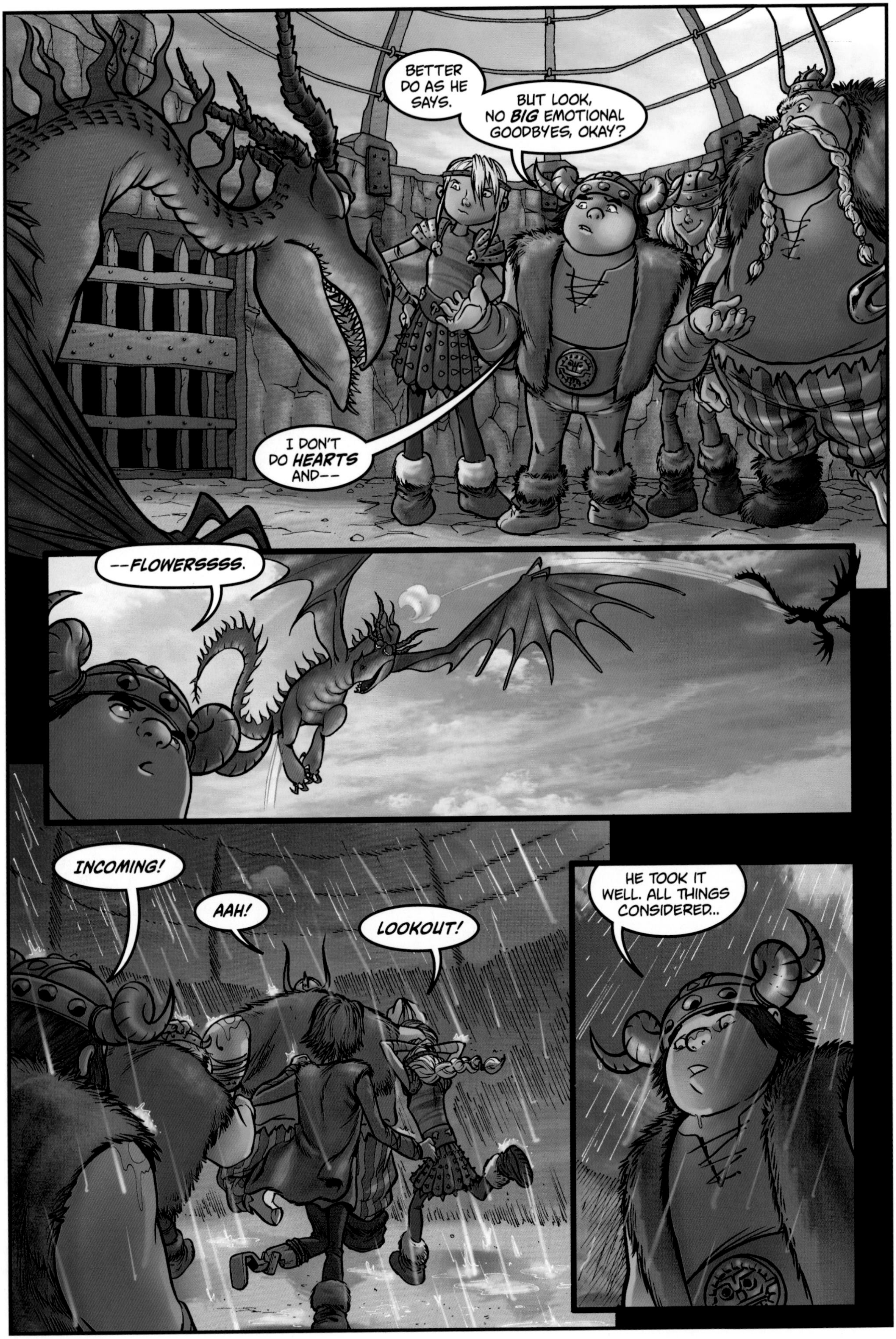
BETTER DO AS HE SAYS.
BUT LOOK, NO BIG EMOTIONAL GOODBYES, OKAY?
I DON'T DO HEARTS AND--
--FLOWERSSSS.
INCOMING!
AAH!
LOOKOUT!
HE TOOK IT WELL. ALL THINGS CONSIDERED...

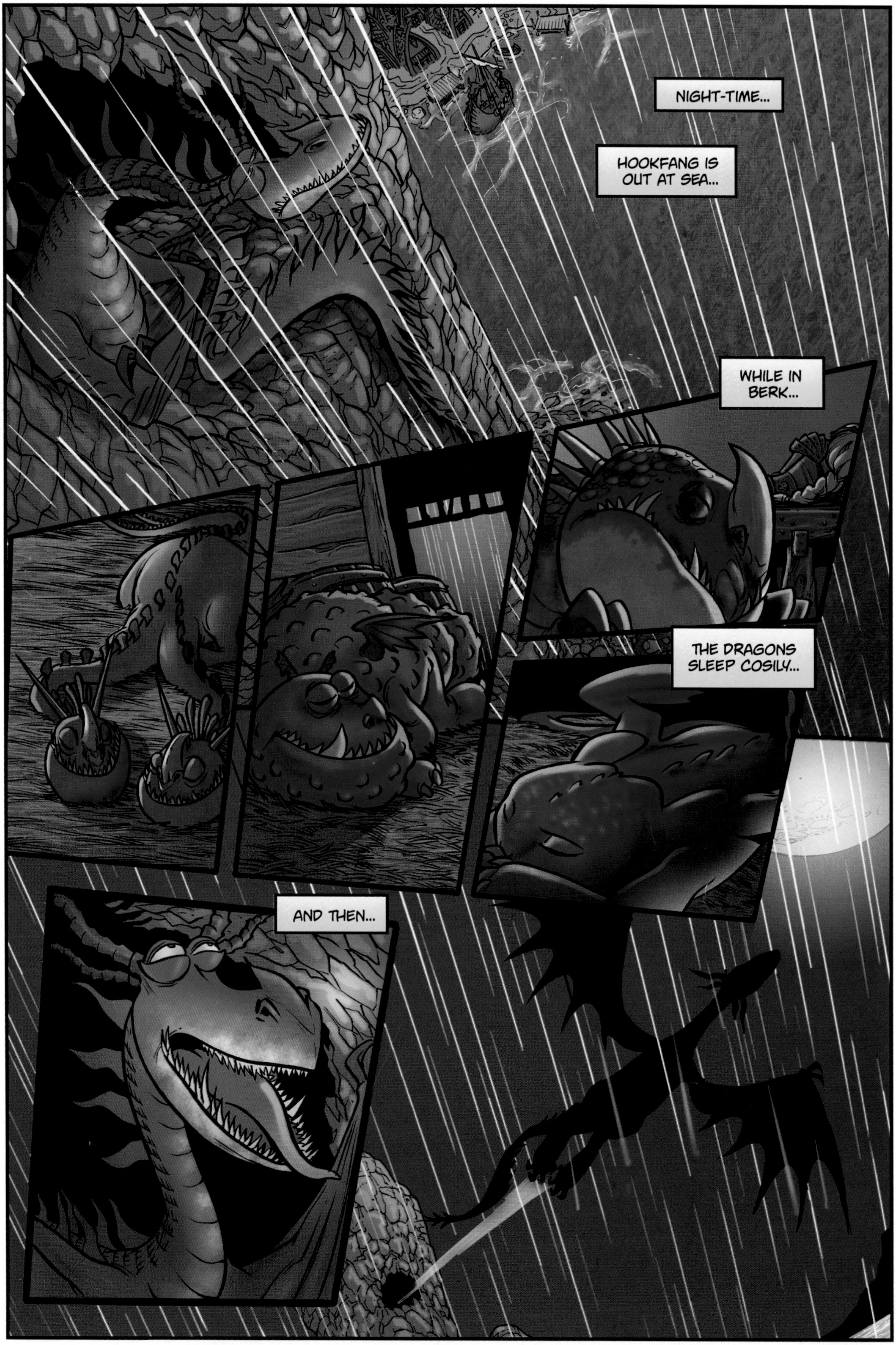
NIGHT-TIME...
HOOKFANG IS OUT AT SEA...
WHILE IN BERK...
THE DRAGONS SLEEP COSILY...
AND THEN...

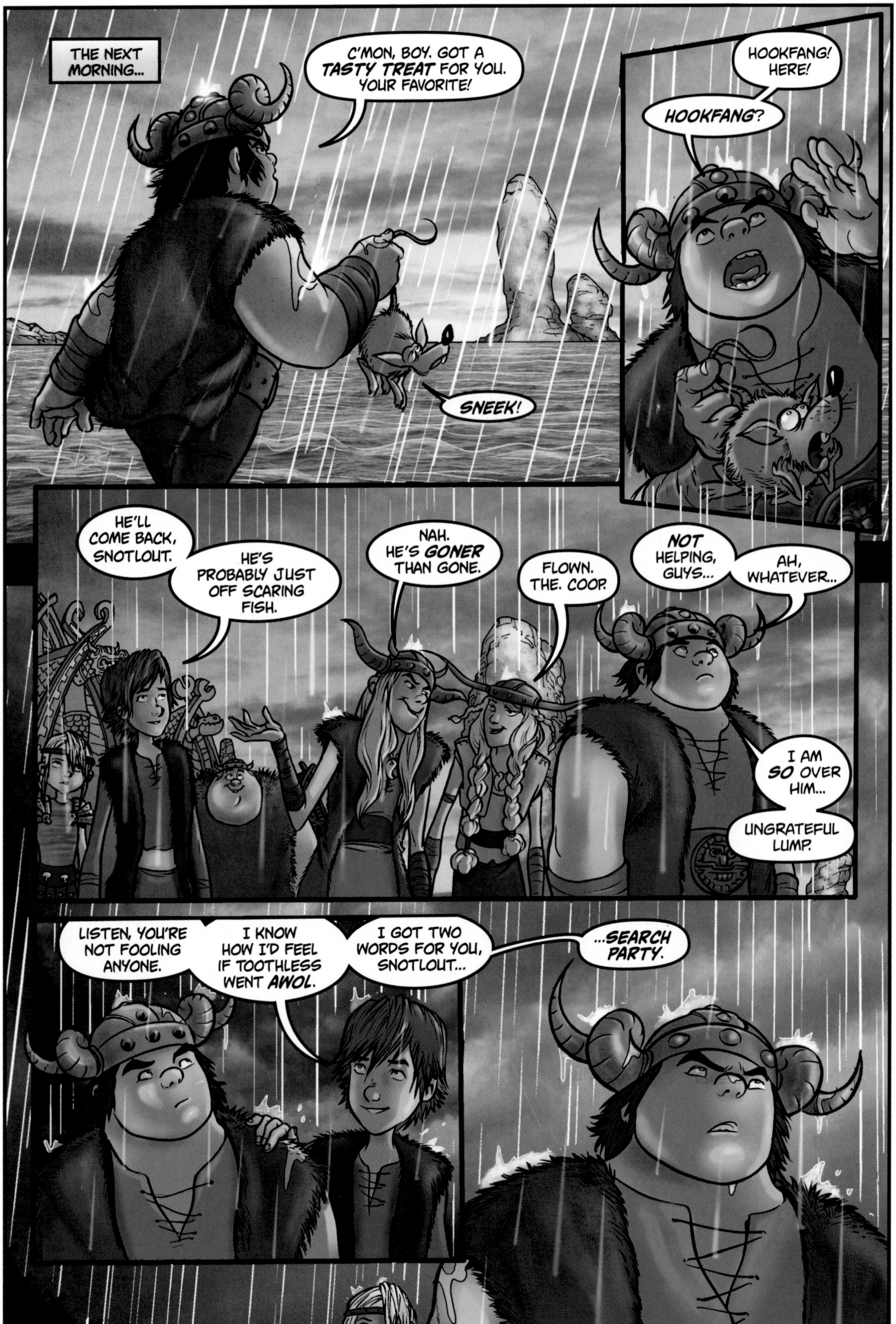
THE NEXT MORNING...
C'MON, BOY. GOT A TASTY TREAT FOR YOU. YOUR FAVORITE!
SNEEK!
HOOKFANG?
HOOKFANG! HERE!
HE'LL COME BACK, SNOTLOUT.
HE'S PROBABLY JUST OFF SCARING FISH.
NAH. HE'S GONER THAN GONE.
FLOWN. THE. COOP.
NOT HELPING, GUYS...
AH, WHATEVER...
I AM SO OVER HIM...
UNGRATEFUL LUMP.
LISTEN, YOU'RE NOT FOOLING ANYONE.
I KNOW HOW I'D FEEL IF TOOTHLESS WENT AWOL.
I GOT TWO WORDS FOR YOU, SNOTLOUT...
...SEARCH PARTY.

CHAPTER TWO

In which Hiccup and his friends search
for Hookfang... Alvin the Treacherous has
a nasty plan... And Hiccup sets out on a
dangerous journey...

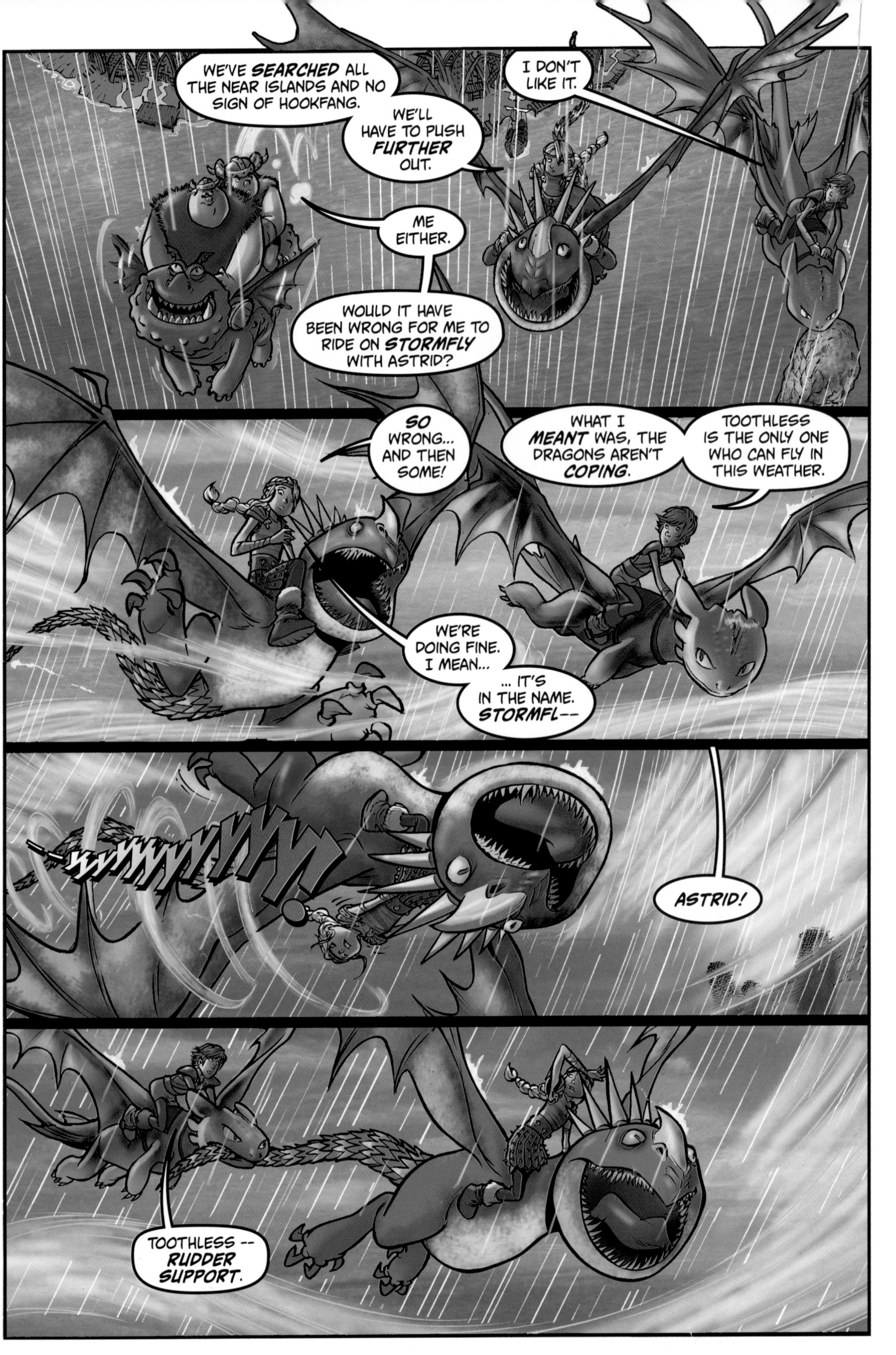

WE'VE SEARCHED ALL THE NEAR ISLANDS AND NO SIGN OF HOOKFANG.
WE'LL HAVE TO PUSH FURTHER OUT.
I DON'T LIKE IT.
ME EITHER.
WOULD IT HAVE BEEN WRONG FOR ME TO RIDE ON STORMFLY WITH ASTRID?
SO WRONG... AND THEN SOME!
WHAT I MEANT WAS, THE DRAGONS AREN'T COPING.
TOOTHLESS IS THE ONLY ONE WHO CAN FLY IN THIS WEATHER.
WE'RE DOING FINE. I MEAN...
... IT'S IN THE NAME. STORMFL--
--VVVVVVVVVVVVN
ASTRID!
TOOTHLESS -- RUDDER SUPPORT.

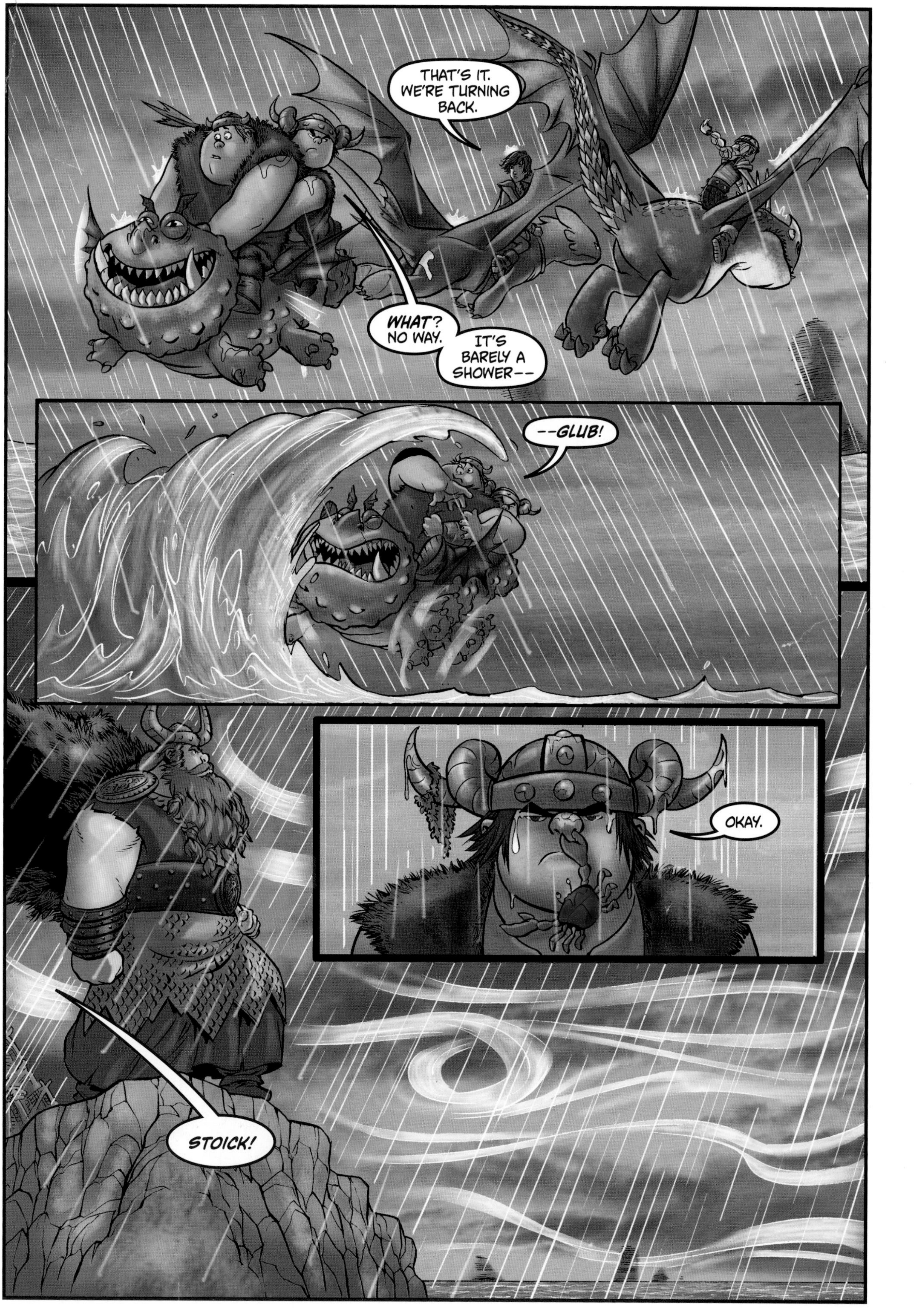
THAT'S IT. WE'RE TURNING BACK.
WHAT? NO WAY.
IT'S BARELY A SHOWER--
--GLUB!
OKAY.
STOICK!

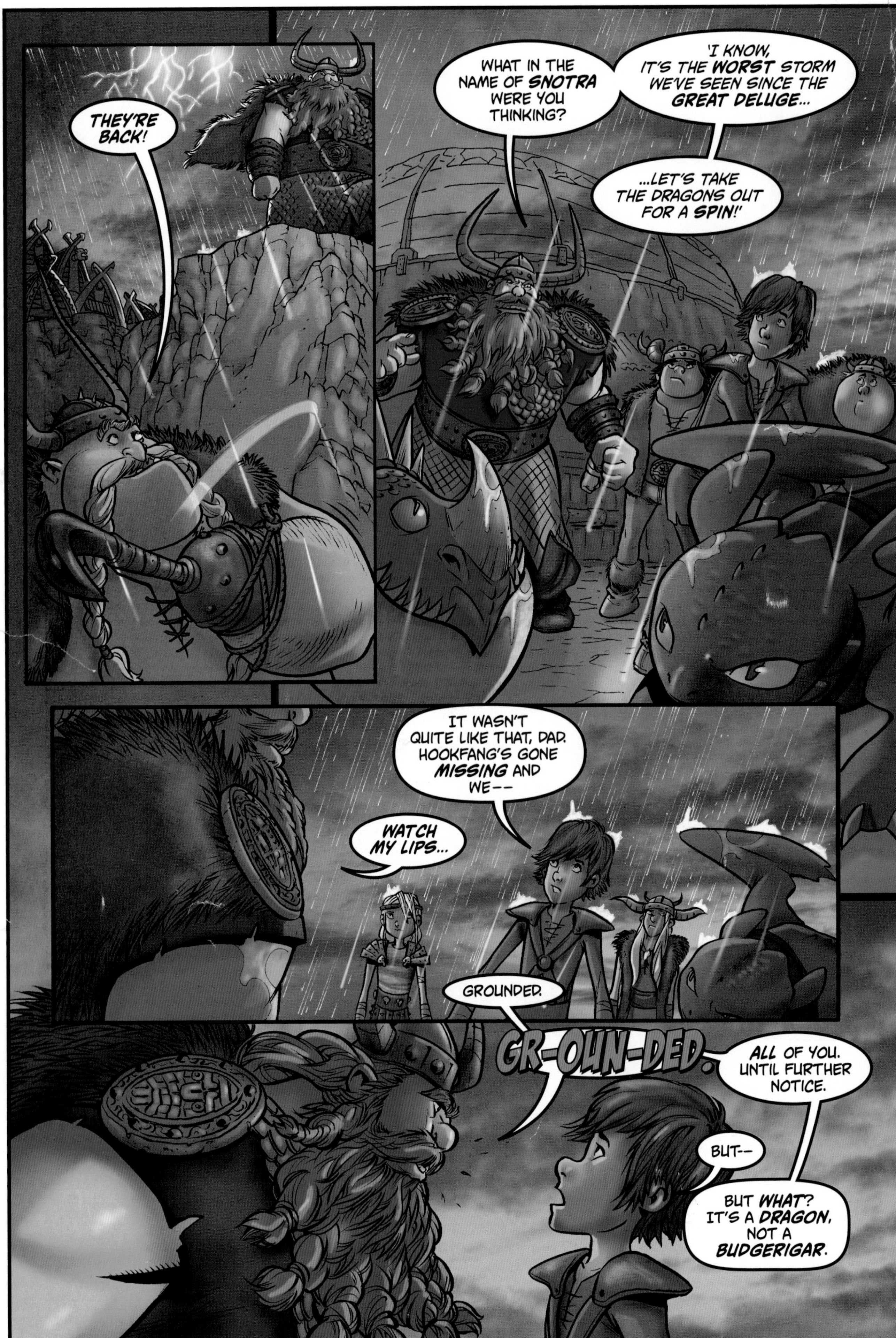
THEY'RE BACK!
WHAT IN THE NAME OF SNOTRA WERE YOU THINKING?
'I KNOW, IT'S THE WORST STORM WE'VE SEEN SINCE THE GREAT DELUGE...
...LET'S TAKE THE DRAGONS OUT FOR A SPIN!'
IT WASN'T QUITE LIKE THAT, DAD. HOOKFANG'S GONE MISSING AND WE--
WATCH MY LIPS...
GROUNDED.
GR-OUN-DED.
ALL OF YOU. UNTIL FURTHER NOTICE.
BUT--
BUT WHAT? IT'S A DRAGON, NOT A BUDGERIGAR.

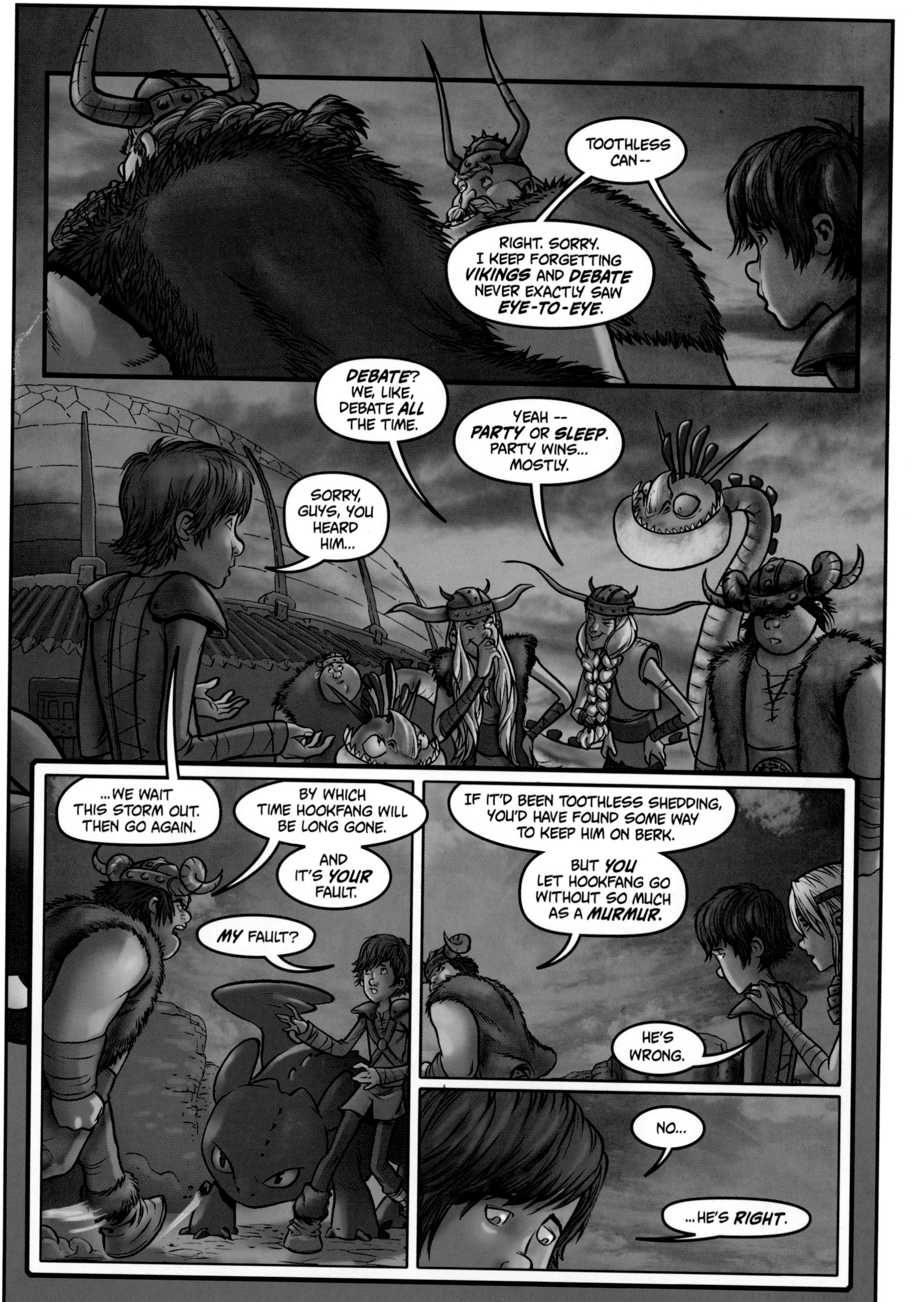
TOOTHLESS CAN--
RIGHT. SORRY. I KEEP FORGETTING **VIKINGS** AND **DEBATE** NEVER EXACTLY SAW **EYE-TO-EYE**.
DEBATE? WE, LIKE, DEBATE **ALL** THE TIME.
YEAH -- **PARTY** OR **SLEEP**. PARTY WINS... MOSTLY.
SORRY, GUYS, YOU HEARD HIM...
...WE WAIT THIS STORM OUT. THEN GO AGAIN.
BY WHICH TIME HOOKFANG WILL BE LONG GONE.
AND IT'S **YOUR** FAULT.
MY FAULT?
IF IT'D BEEN TOOTHLESS SHEDDING, YOU'D HAVE FOUND SOME WAY TO KEEP HIM ON BERK.
BUT **YOU** LET HOOKFANG GO WITHOUT SO MUCH AS A **MURMUR**.
HE'S WRONG.
NO...
...HE'S **RIGHT**.

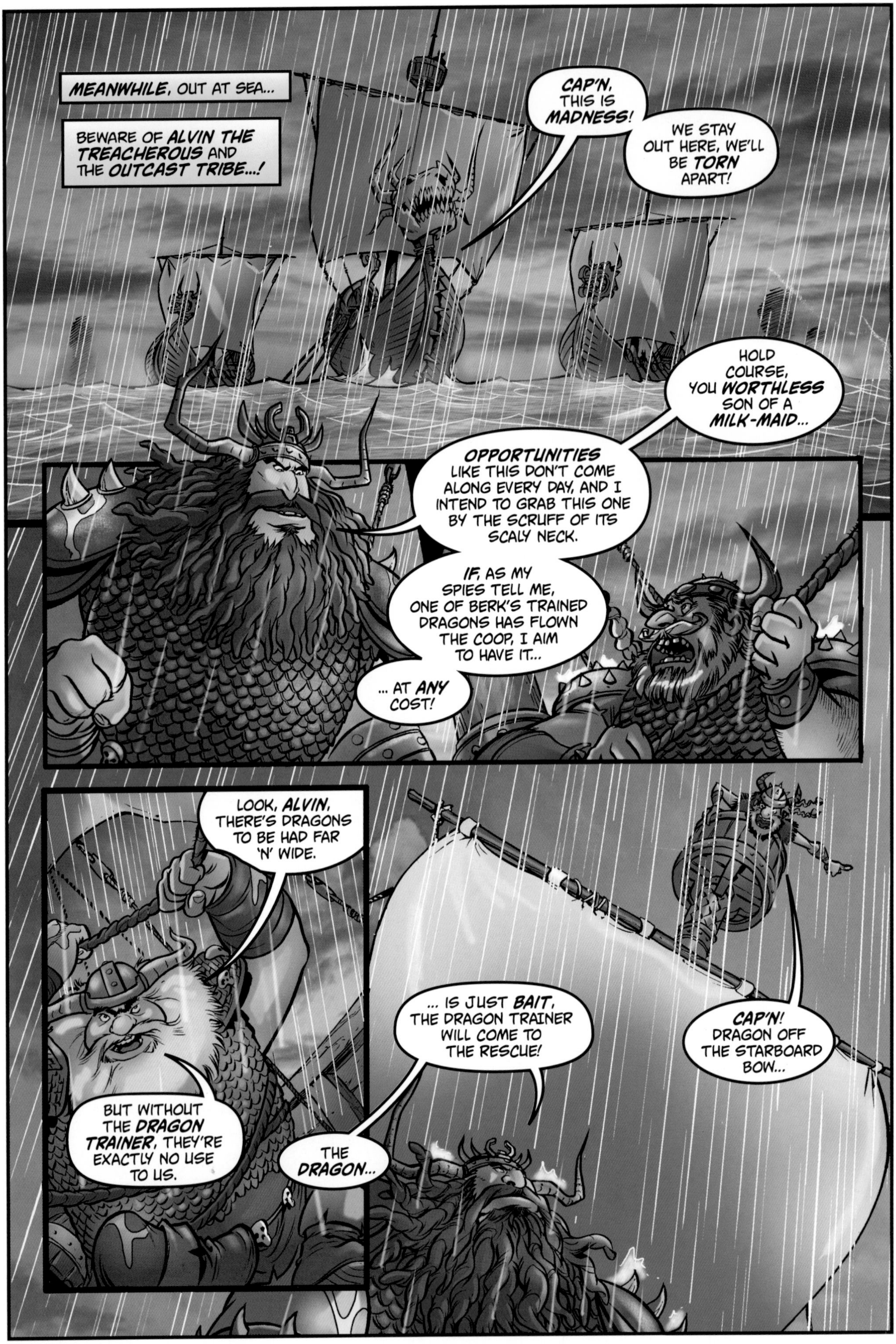
MEANWHILE, OUT AT SEA...
BEWARE OF ALVIN THE TREACHEROUS AND THE OUTCAST TRIBE...!
CAP'N, THIS IS MADNESS!
WE STAY OUT HERE, WE'LL BE TORN APART!
HOLD COURSE, YOU WORTHLESS SON OF A MILK-MAID...
OPPORTUNITIES LIKE THIS DON'T COME ALONG EVERY DAY, AND I INTEND TO GRAB THIS ONE BY THE SCRUFF OF ITS SCALY NECK.
IF, AS MY SPIES TELL ME, ONE OF BERK'S TRAINED DRAGONS HAS FLOWN THE COOP, I AIM TO HAVE IT...
... AT ANY COST!
LOOK, ALVIN, THERE'S DRAGONS TO BE HAD FAR 'N' WIDE.
BUT WITHOUT THE DRAGON TRAINER, THEY'RE EXACTLY NO USE TO US.
THE DRAGON...
... IS JUST BAIT, THE DRAGON TRAINER WILL COME TO THE RESCUE!
CAP'N! DRAGON OFF THE STARBOARD BOW...

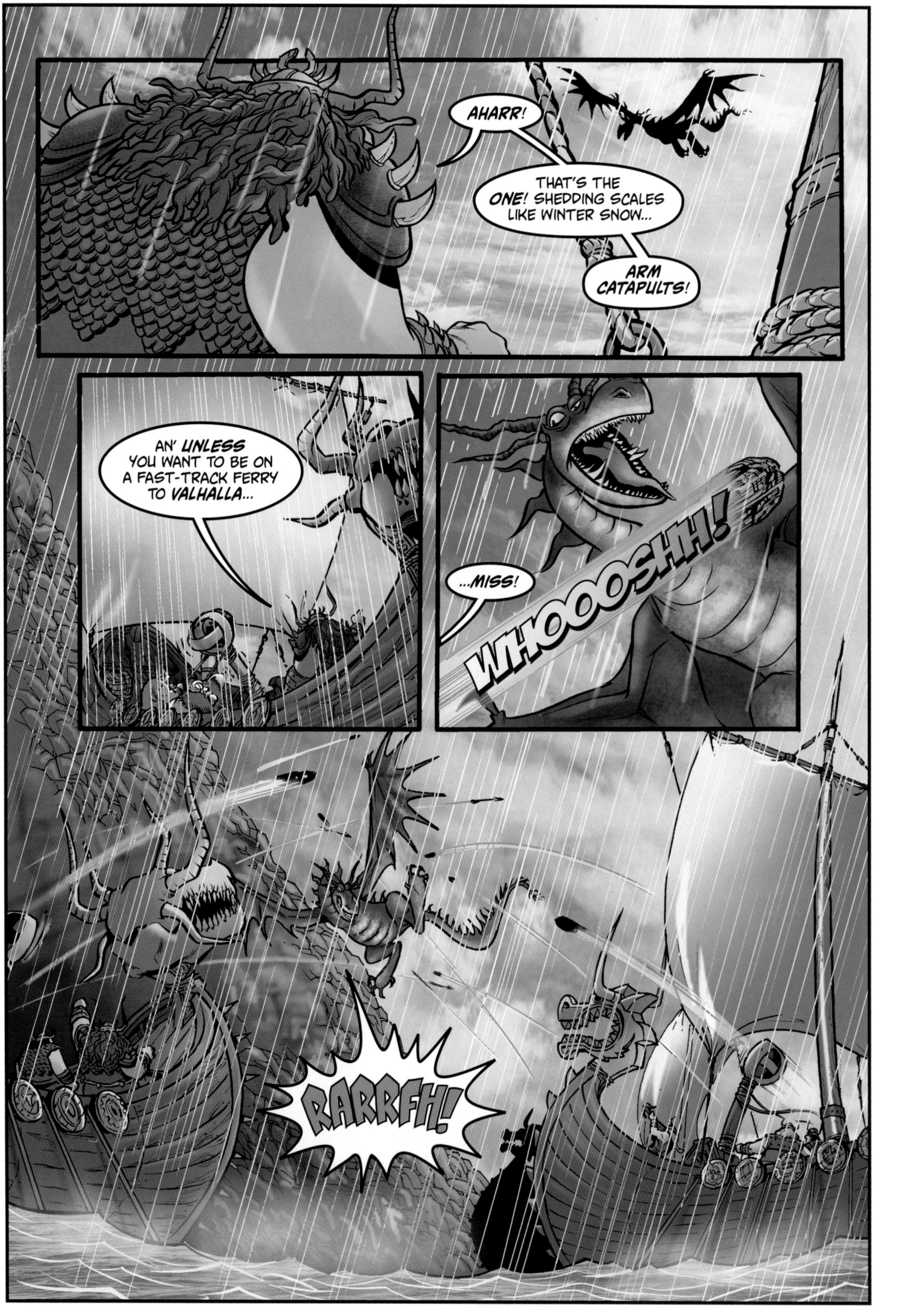
AHARR!
THAT'S THE ONE! SHEDDING SCALES LIKE WINTER SNOW...
ARM CATAPULTS!
AN' UNLESS YOU WANT TO BE ON A FAST-TRACK FERRY TO VALHALLA...
...MISS!
WHOOOOSHH!
RARRFH!

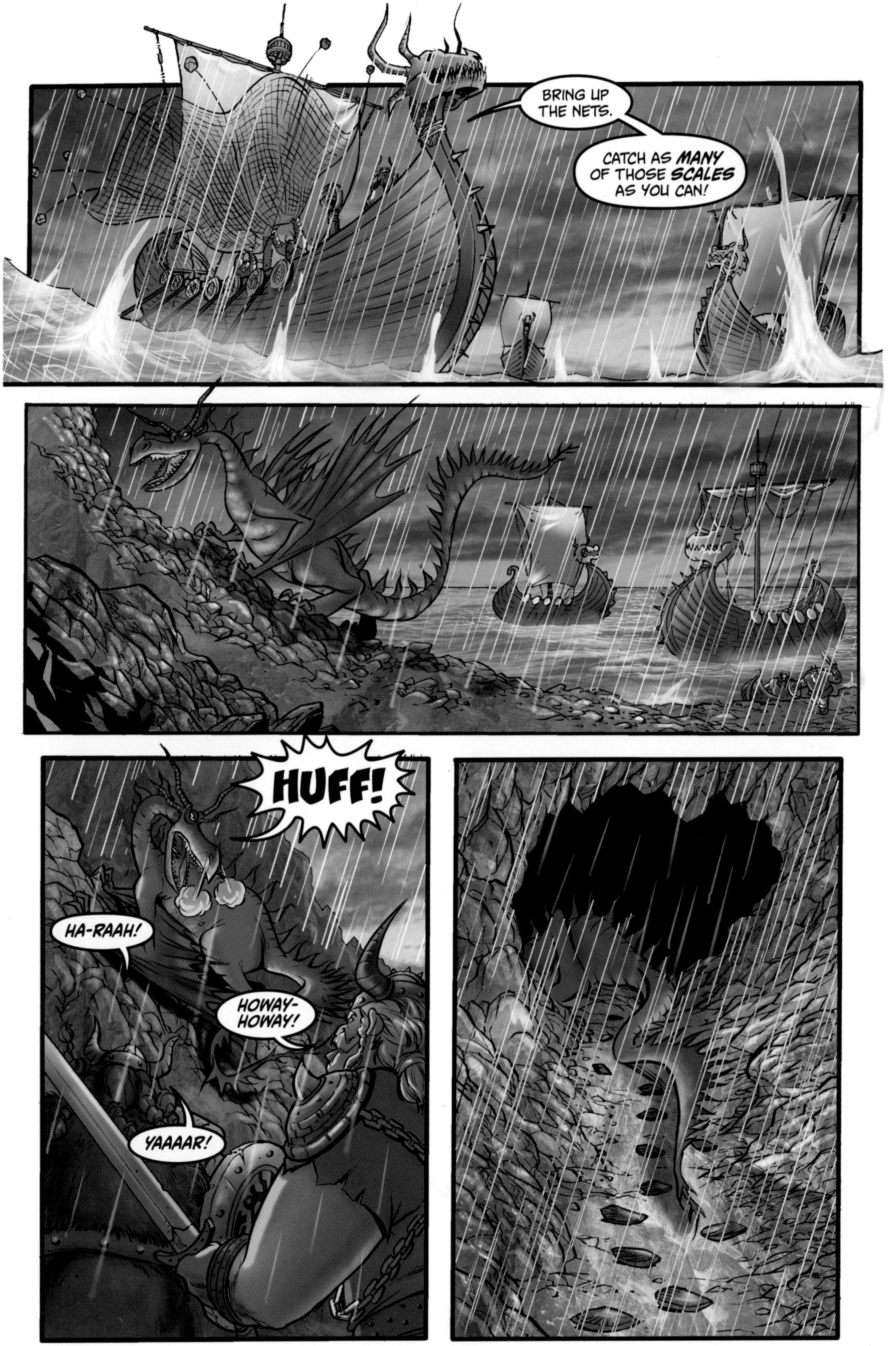
BRING UP THE NETS.
CATCH AS MANY OF THOSE SCALES AS YOU CAN!
HUFF!
HA-RAAH!
HOWAY-HOWAY!
YAAAAR!

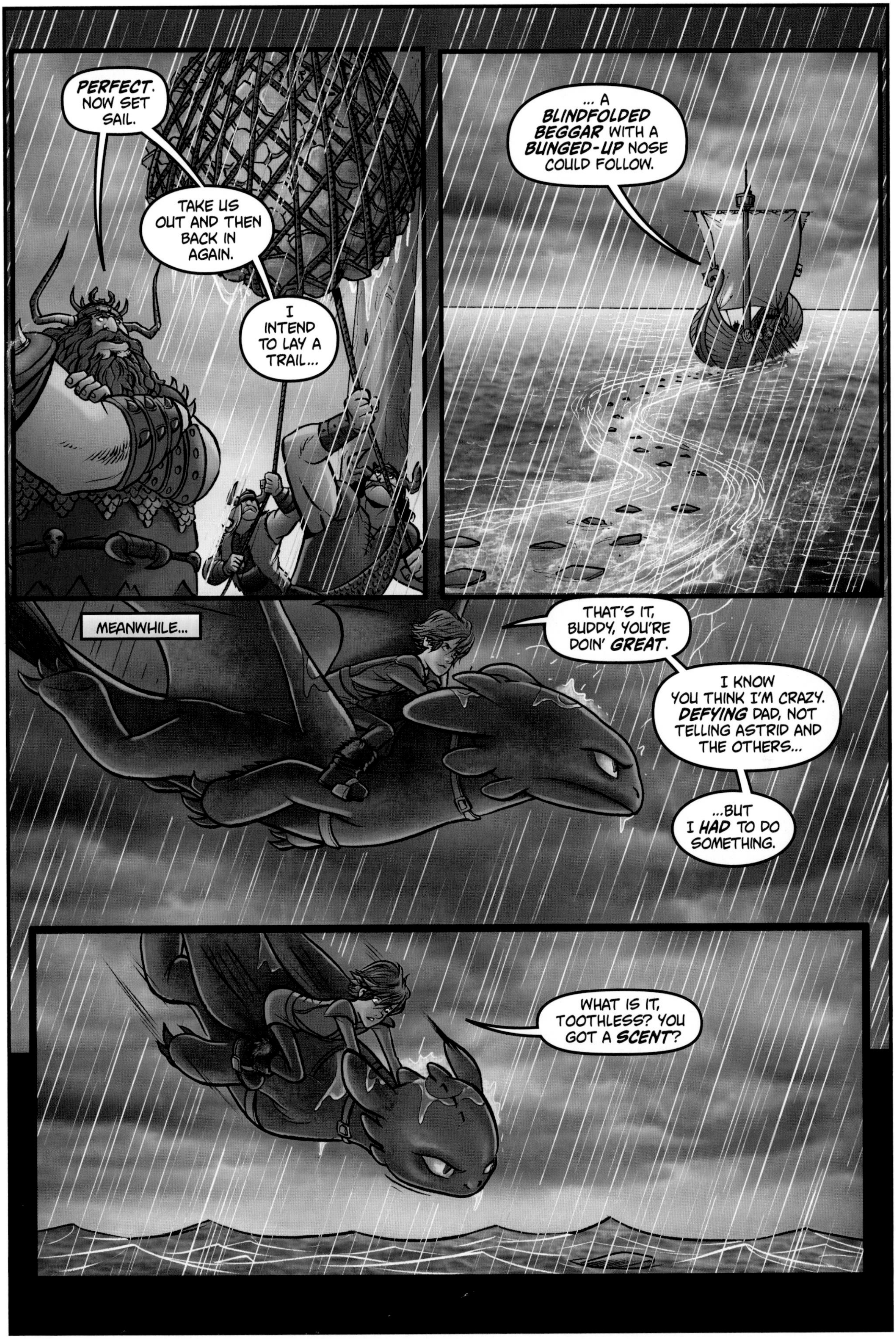
PERFECT. NOW SET SAIL.
TAKE US OUT AND THEN BACK IN AGAIN.
I INTEND TO LAY A TRAIL...
... A BLINDFOLDED BEGGAR WITH A BUNGED-UP NOSE COULD FOLLOW.
MEANWHILE...
THAT'S IT, BUDDY, YOU'RE DOIN' GREAT.
I KNOW YOU THINK I'M CRAZY. DEFYING DAD, NOT TELLING ASTRID AND THE OTHERS...
...BUT I HAD TO DO SOMETHING.
WHAT IS IT, TOOTHLESS? YOU GOT A SCENT?

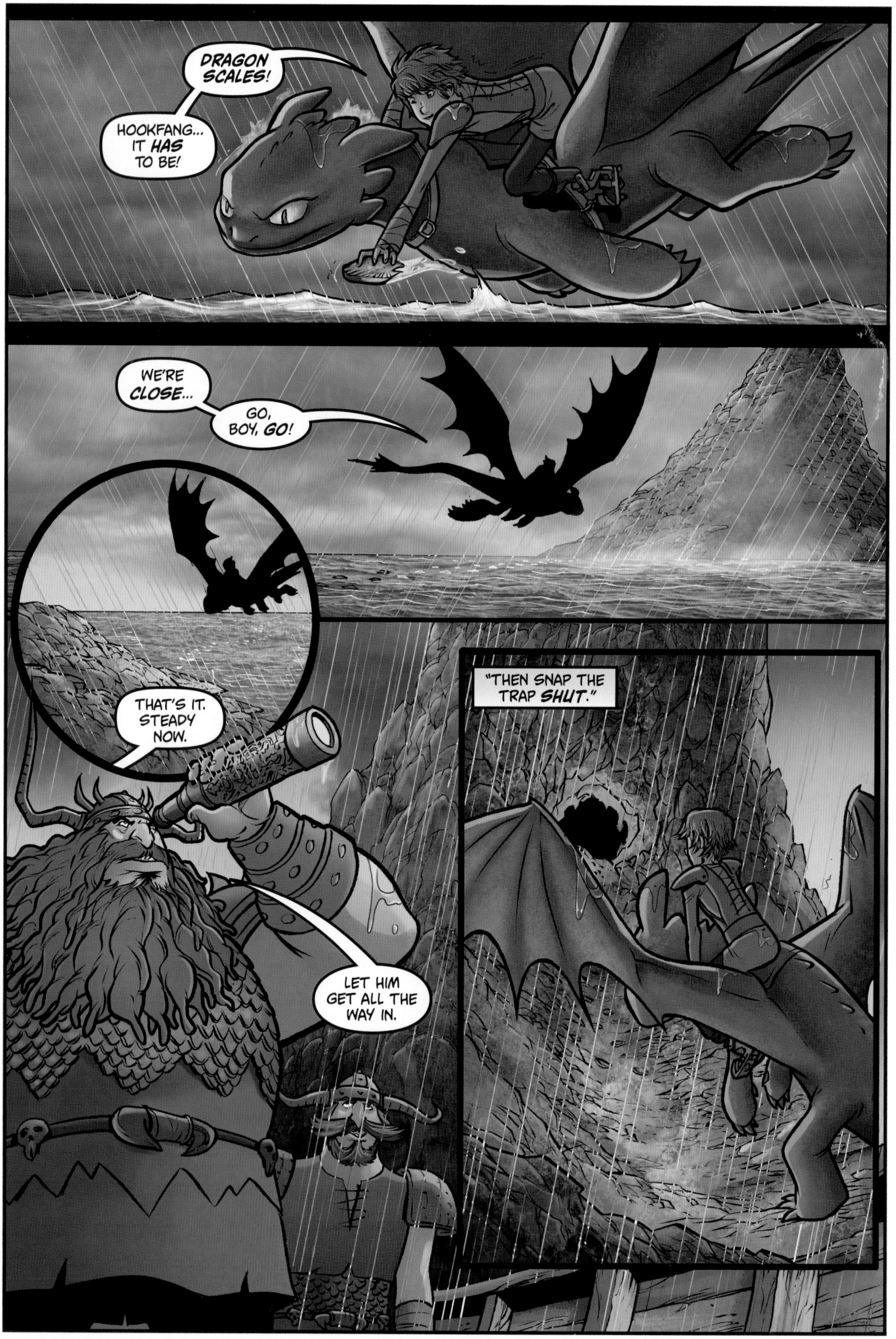
DRAGON SCALES!
HOOKFANG... IT HAS TO BE!
WE'RE CLOSE...
GO, BOY, GO!
THAT'S IT. STEADY NOW.
LET HIM GET ALL THE WAY IN.
"THEN SNAP THE TRAP SHUT."

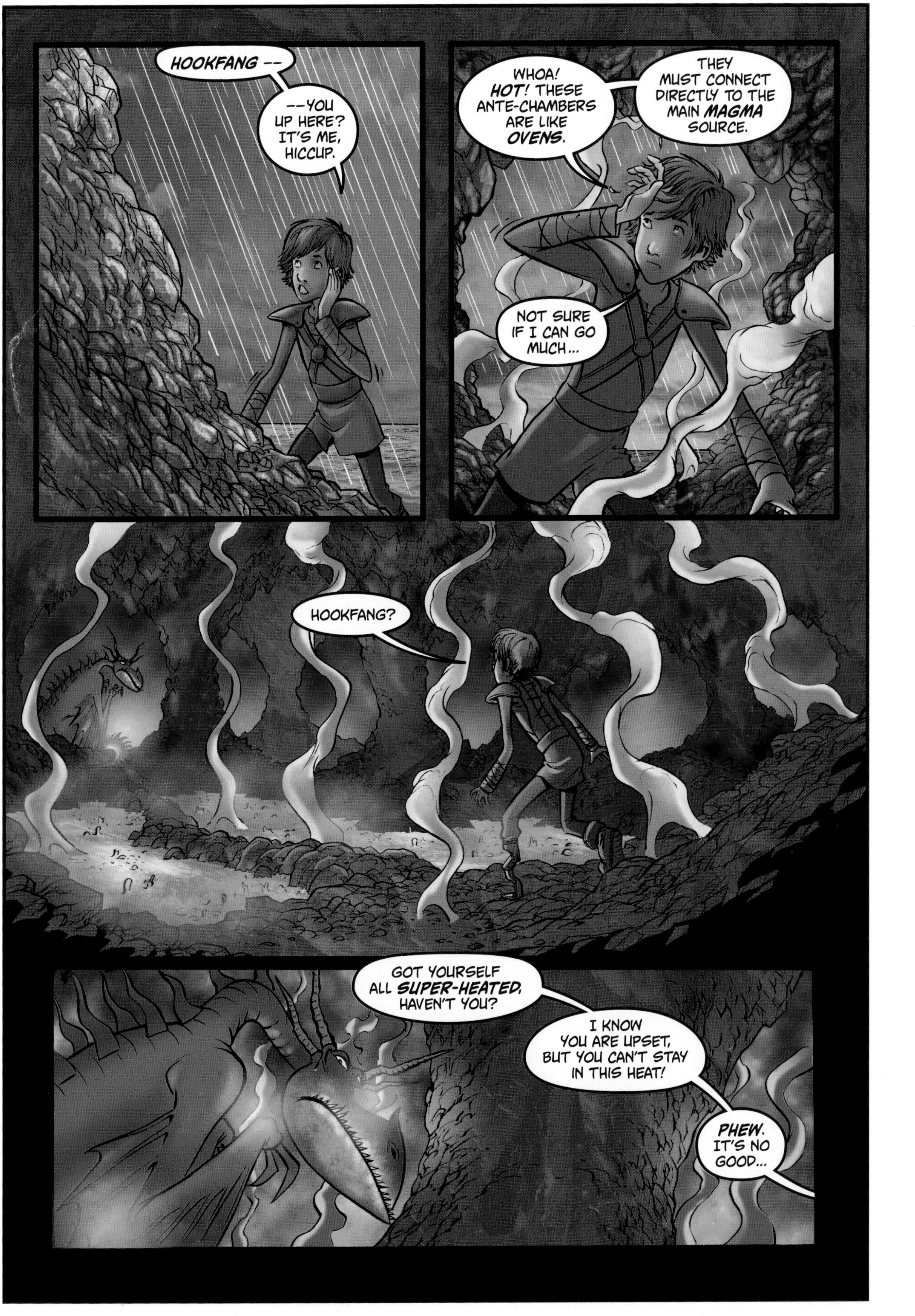
HOOKFANG --
--YOU UP HERE? IT'S ME, HICCUP.
WHOA! HOT! THESE ANTE-CHAMBERS ARE LIKE OVENS.
THEY MUST CONNECT DIRECTLY TO THE MAIN MAGMA SOURCE.
NOT SURE IF I CAN GO MUCH...
HOOKFANG?
GOT YOURSELF ALL SUPER-HEATED, HAVEN'T YOU?
I KNOW YOU ARE UPSET, BUT YOU CAN'T STAY IN THIS HEAT!
PHEW. IT'S NO GOOD...

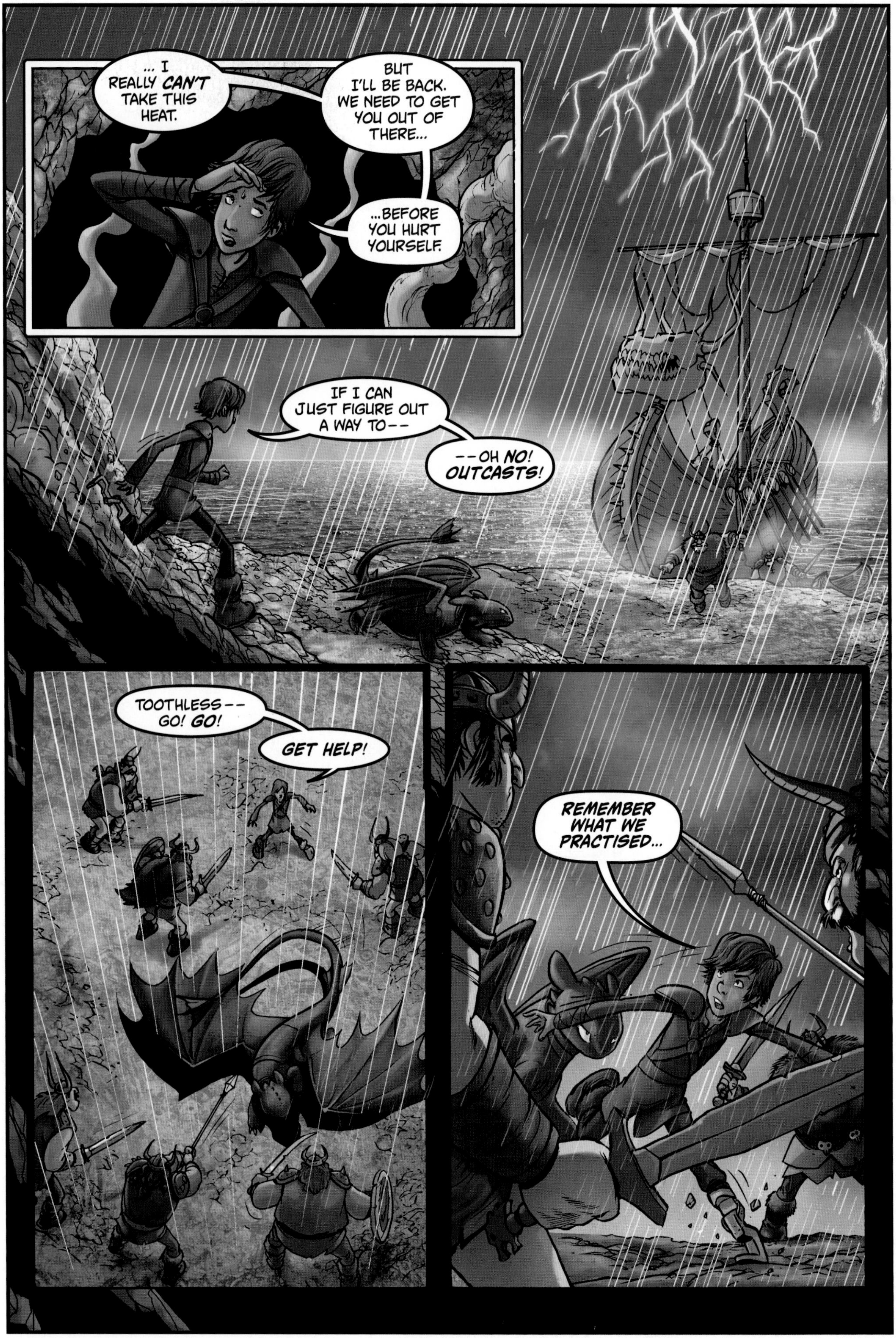
... I REALLY CAN'T TAKE THIS HEAT.
BUT I'LL BE BACK. WE NEED TO GET YOU OUT OF THERE...
...BEFORE YOU HURT YOURSELF.
IF I CAN JUST FIGURE OUT A WAY TO--
--OH NO! OUTCASTS!
TOOTHLESS-- GO! GO!
GET HELP!
REMEMBER WHAT WE PRACTISED...

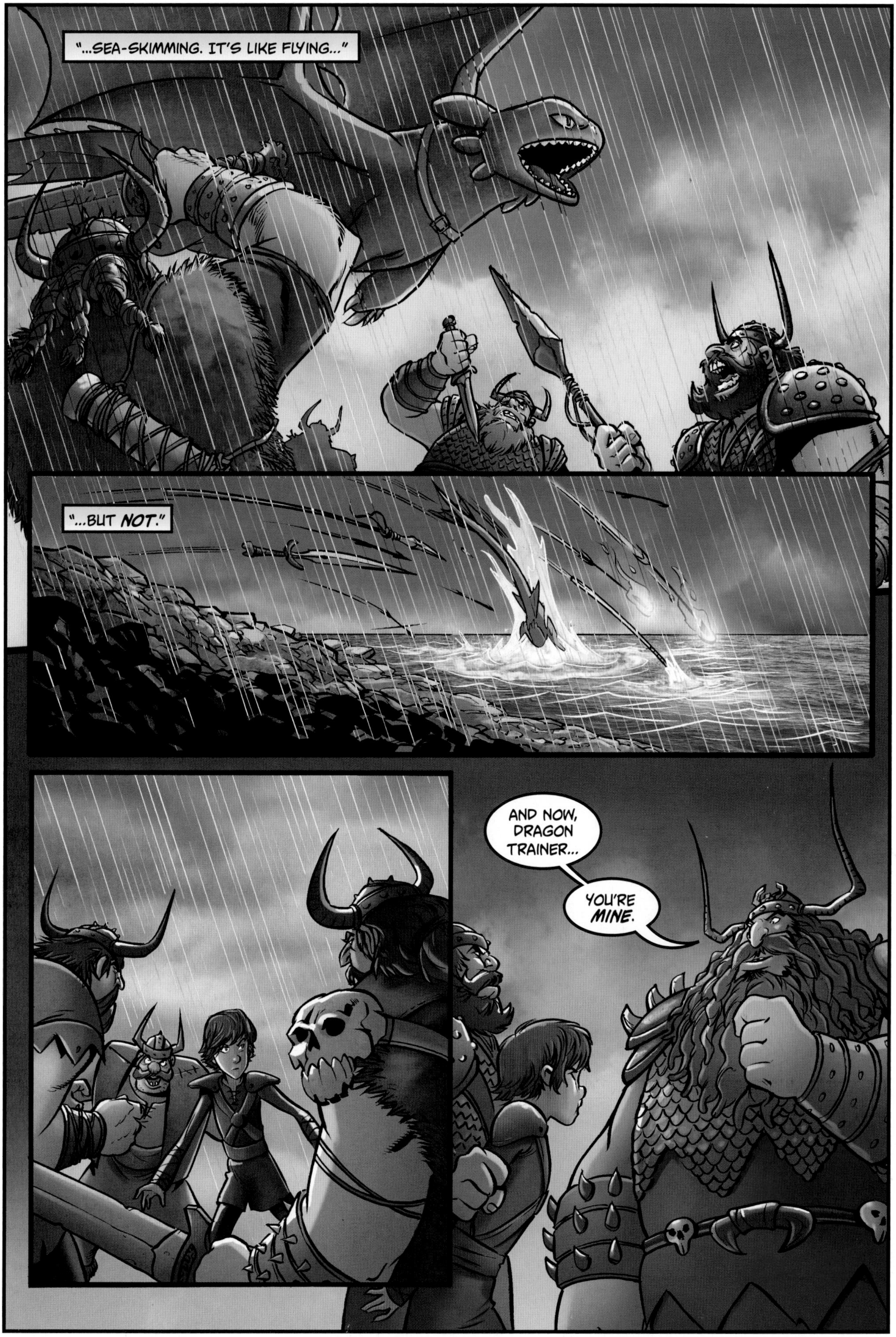
"...SEA-SKIMMING. IT'S LIKE FLYING..."
"...BUT *NOT*."
AND NOW, DRAGON TRAINER...
YOU'RE *MINE*.

CHAPTER THREE

In which Stoick sends out a search party...
Hiccup attempts a daring escape... And the
dragons launch a fiery attack on the
Outcast Tribe...

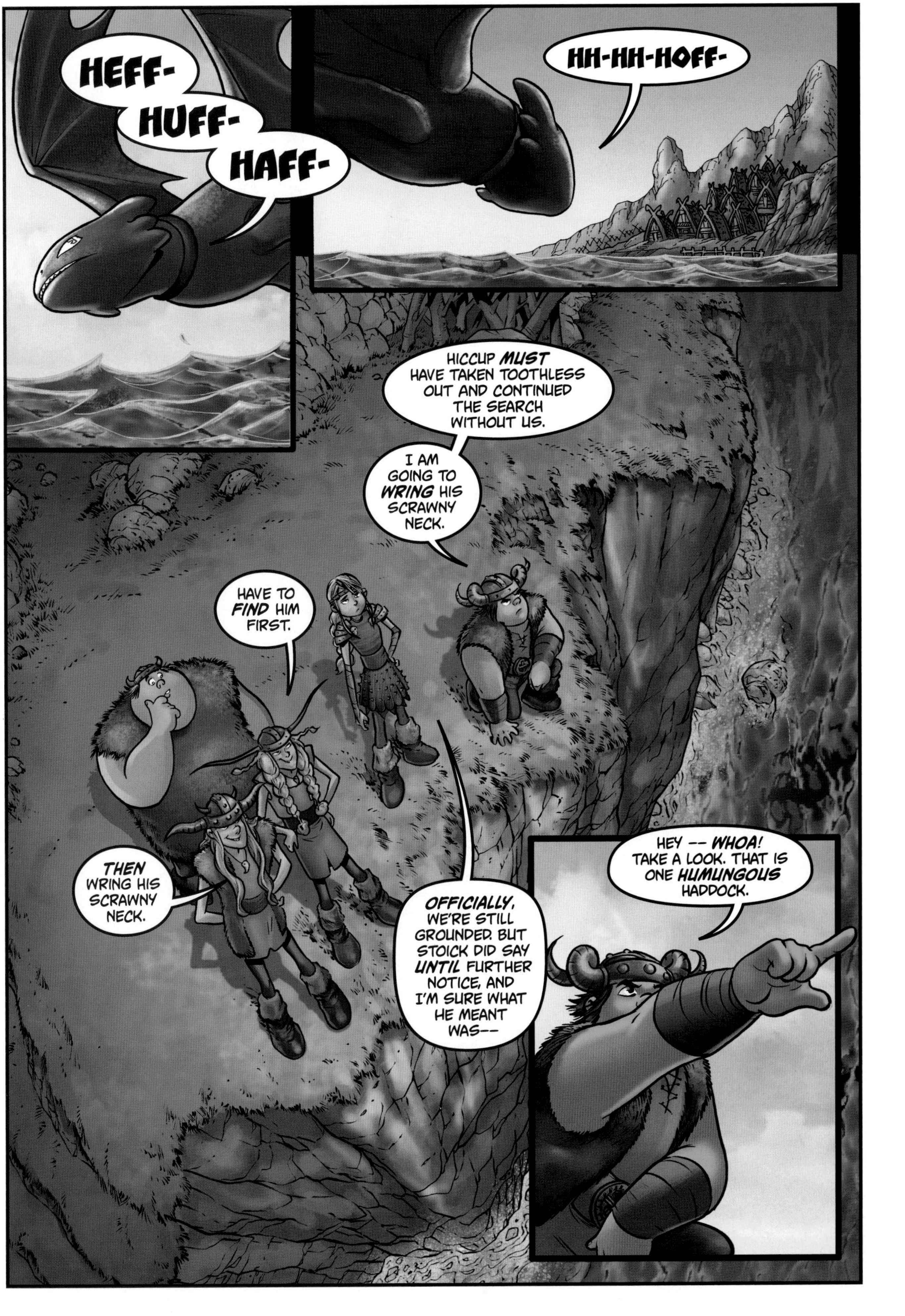
HEFF-
HUFF-
HAFF-
HH-HH-HOFF-
HICCUP MUST HAVE TAKEN TOOTHLESS OUT AND CONTINUED THE SEARCH WITHOUT US.
I AM GOING TO WRING HIS SCRAWNY NECK.
HAVE TO FIND HIM FIRST.
THEN WRING HIS SCRAWNY NECK.
OFFICIALLY, WE'RE STILL GROUNDED. BUT STOICK DID SAY UNTIL FURTHER NOTICE, AND I'M SURE WHAT HE MEANT WAS--
HEY -- WHOA! TAKE A LOOK. THAT IS ONE HUMUNGOUS HADDOCK.

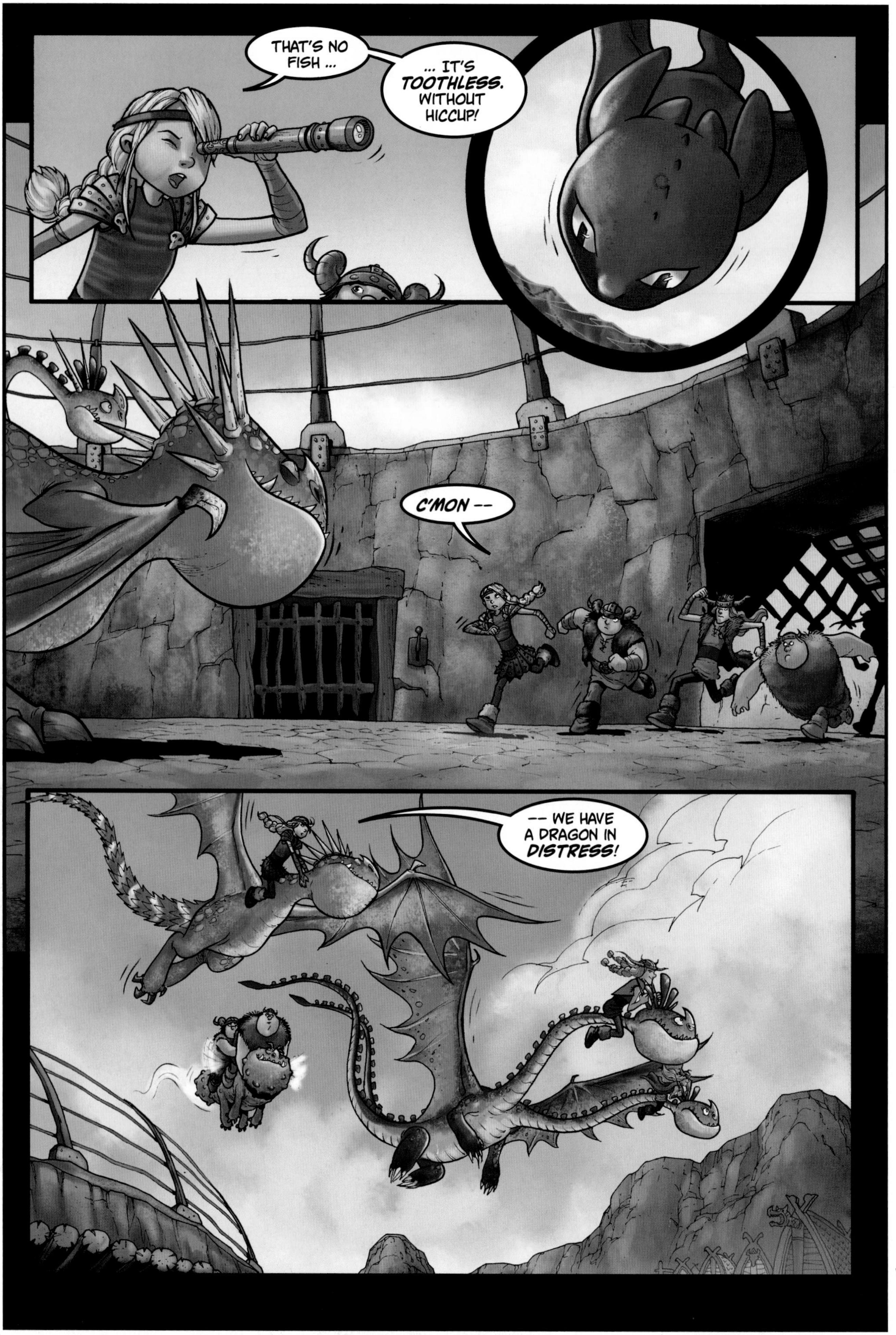

THAT'S NO FISH ...
... IT'S TOOTHLESS. WITHOUT HICCUP!
C'MON --
-- WE HAVE A DRAGON IN DISTRESS!

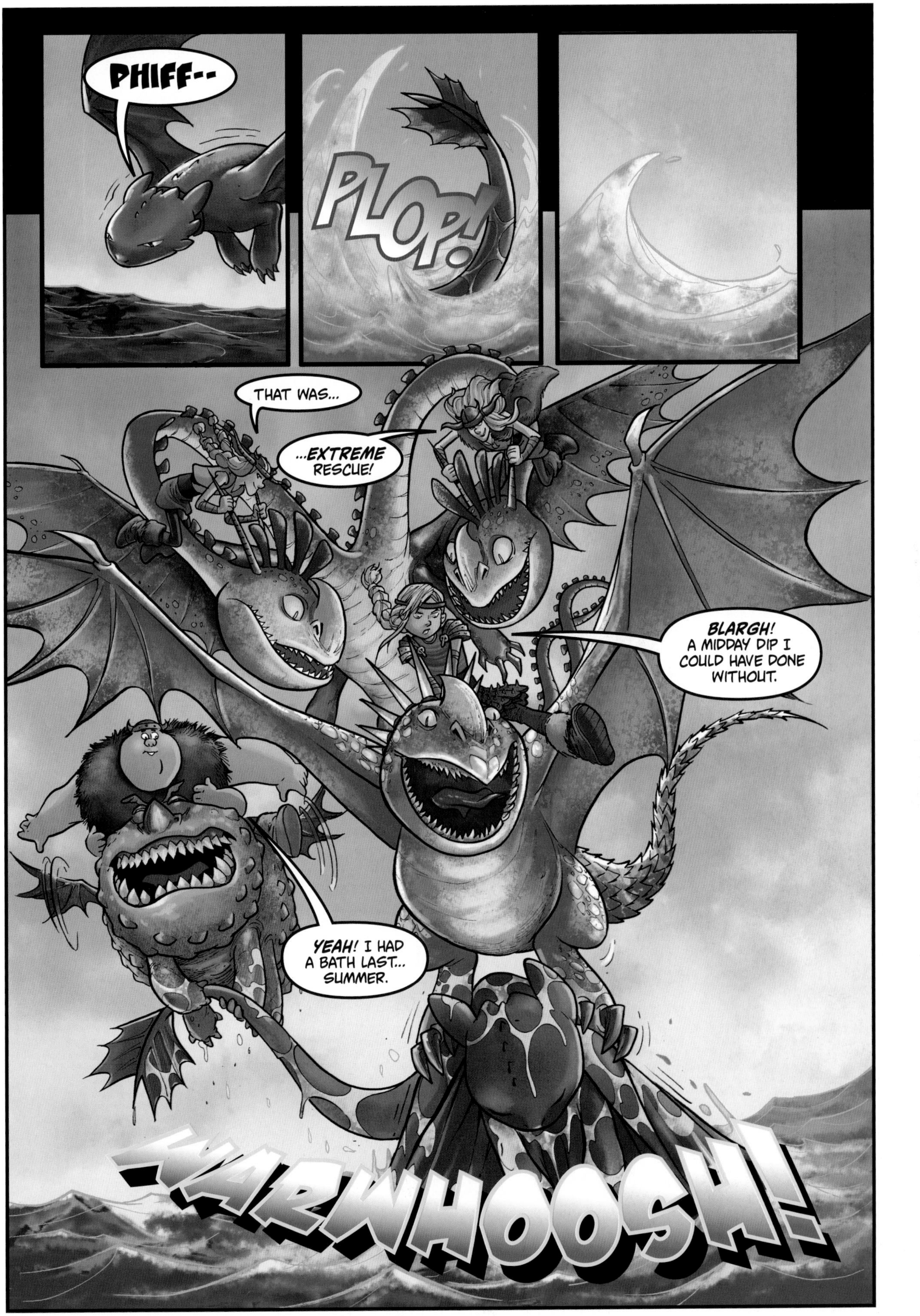
PHIFF--
PLOP!
THAT WAS...
...EXTREME RESCUE!
BLARGH! A MIDDAY DIP I COULD HAVE DONE WITHOUT.
YEAH! I HAD A BATH LAST... SUMMER.
FWARWHOOSH!

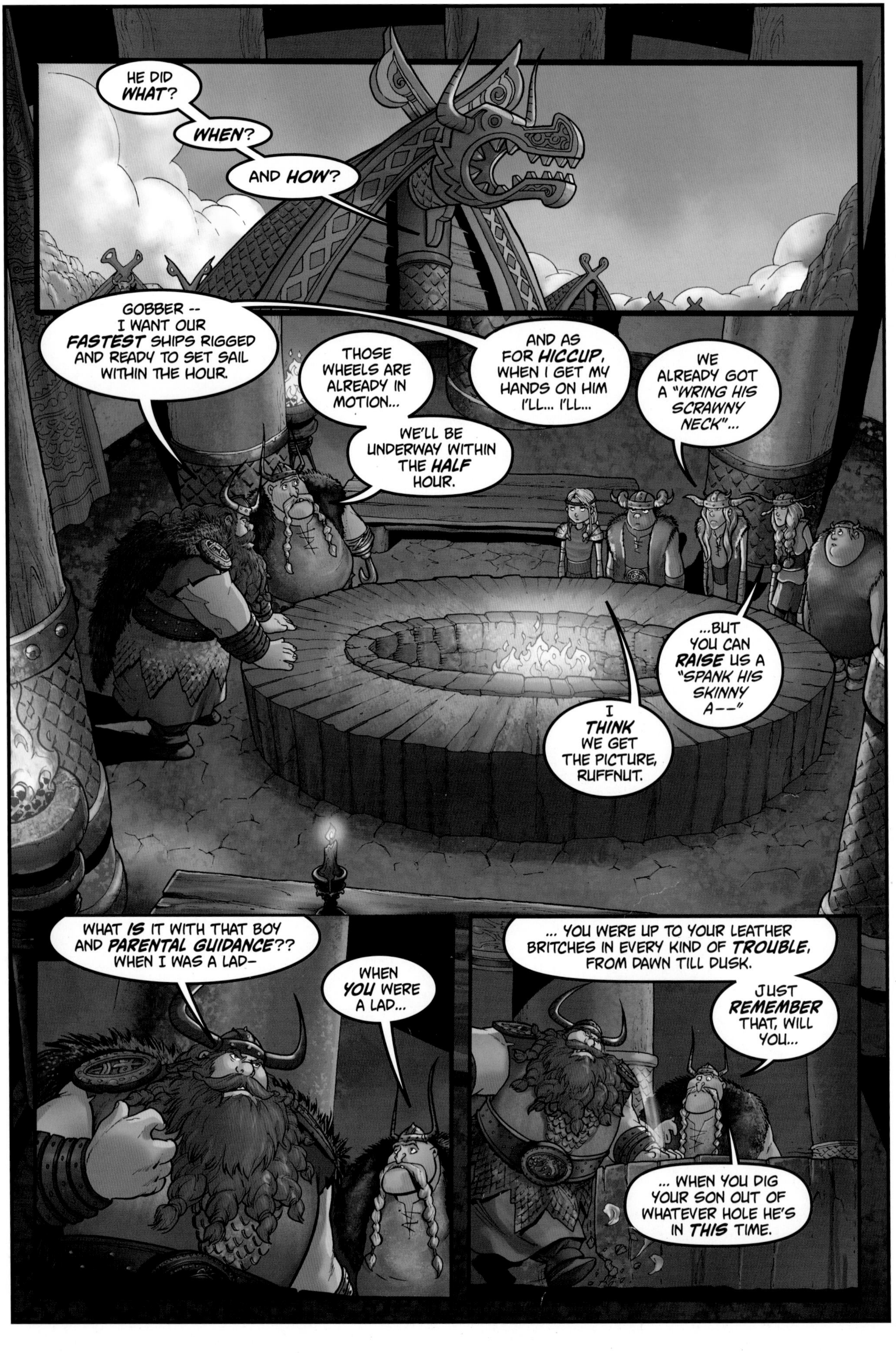
HE DID WHAT?
WHEN?
AND HOW?
GOBBER -- I WANT OUR FASTEST SHIPS RIGGED AND READY TO SET SAIL WITHIN THE HOUR.
THOSE WHEELS ARE ALREADY IN MOTION...
WE'LL BE UNDERWAY WITHIN THE HALF HOUR.
AND AS FOR HICCUP, WHEN I GET MY HANDS ON HIM I'LL... I'LL...
WE ALREADY GOT A "WRING HIS SCRAWNY NECK"...
...BUT YOU CAN RAISE US A "SPANK HIS SKINNY A--"
I THINK WE GET THE PICTURE, RUFFNUT.
WHAT IS IT WITH THAT BOY AND PARENTAL GUIDANCE?? WHEN I WAS A LAD-
WHEN YOU WERE A LAD...
... YOU WERE UP TO YOUR LEATHER BRITCHES IN EVERY KIND OF TROUBLE, FROM DAWN TILL DUSK.
JUST REMEMBER THAT, WILL YOU...
... WHEN YOU DIG YOUR SON OUT OF WHATEVER HOLE HE'S IN THIS TIME.

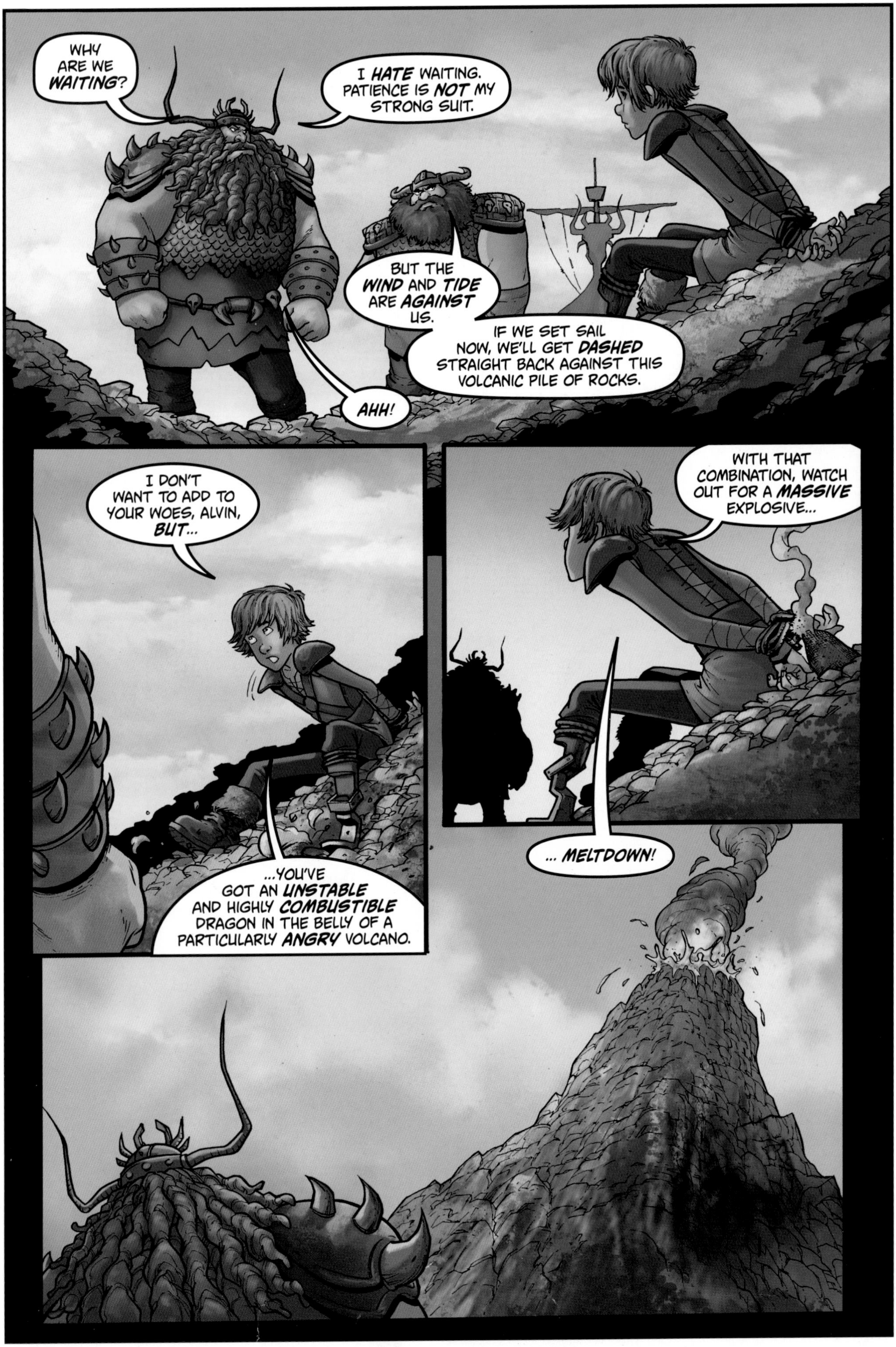

WHY ARE WE WAITING?
I HATE WAITING. PATIENCE IS NOT MY STRONG SUIT.
BUT THE WIND AND TIDE ARE AGAINST US.
IF WE SET SAIL NOW, WE'LL GET DASHED STRAIGHT BACK AGAINST THIS VOLCANIC PILE OF ROCKS.
AHH!
I DON'T WANT TO ADD TO YOUR WOES, ALVIN, BUT...
...YOU'VE GOT AN UNSTABLE AND HIGHLY COMBUSTIBLE DRAGON IN THE BELLY OF A PARTICULARLY ANGRY VOLCANO.
WITH THAT COMBINATION, WATCH OUT FOR A MASSIVE EXPLOSIVE...
... MELTDOWN!

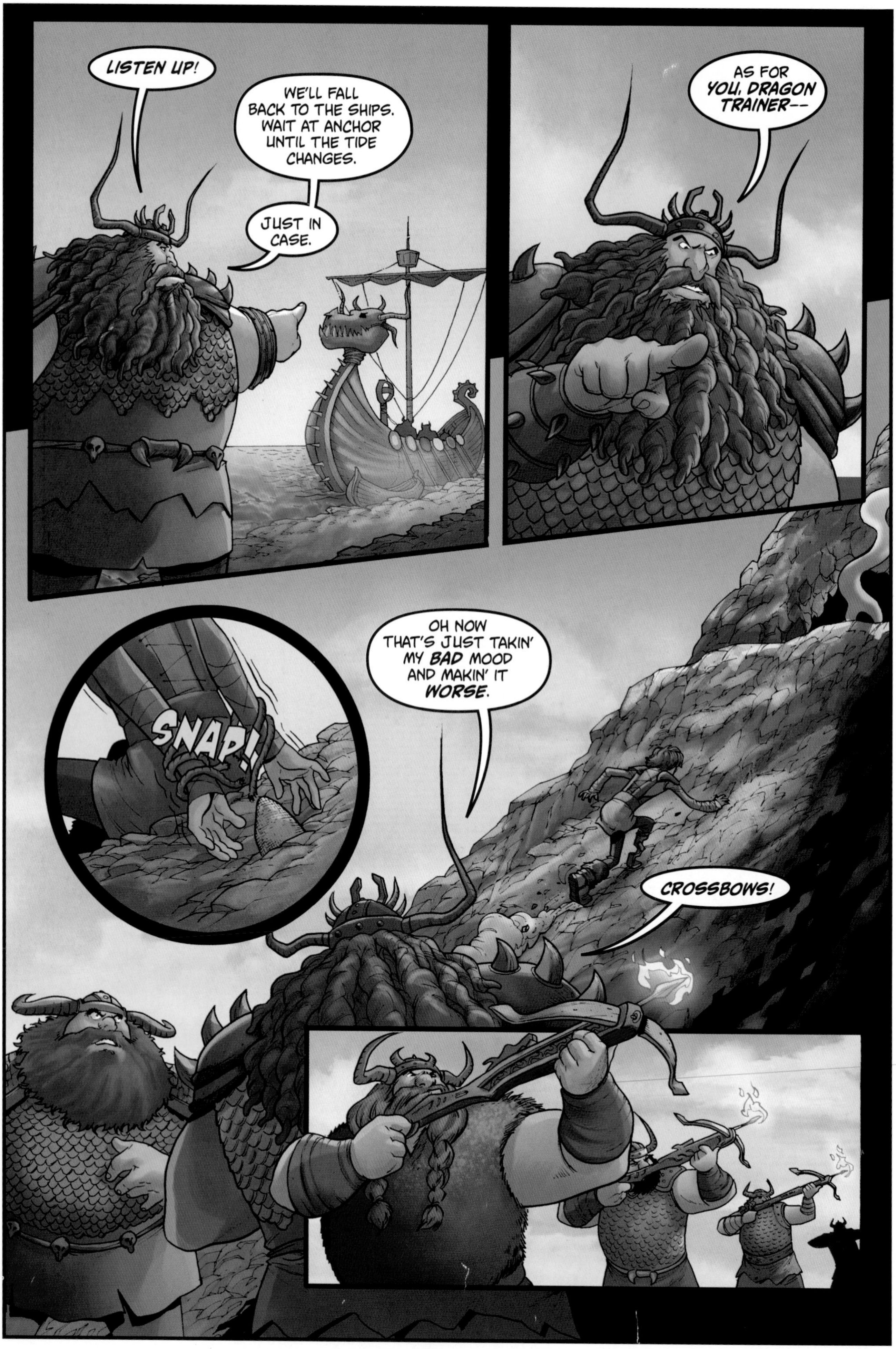
LISTEN UP!
WE'LL FALL BACK TO THE SHIPS. WAIT AT ANCHOR UNTIL THE TIDE CHANGES.
JUST IN CASE.
AS FOR YOU, DRAGON TRAINER--
SNAP!
OH NOW THAT'S JUST TAKIN' MY BAD MOOD AND MAKIN' IT WORSE.
CROSSBOWS!

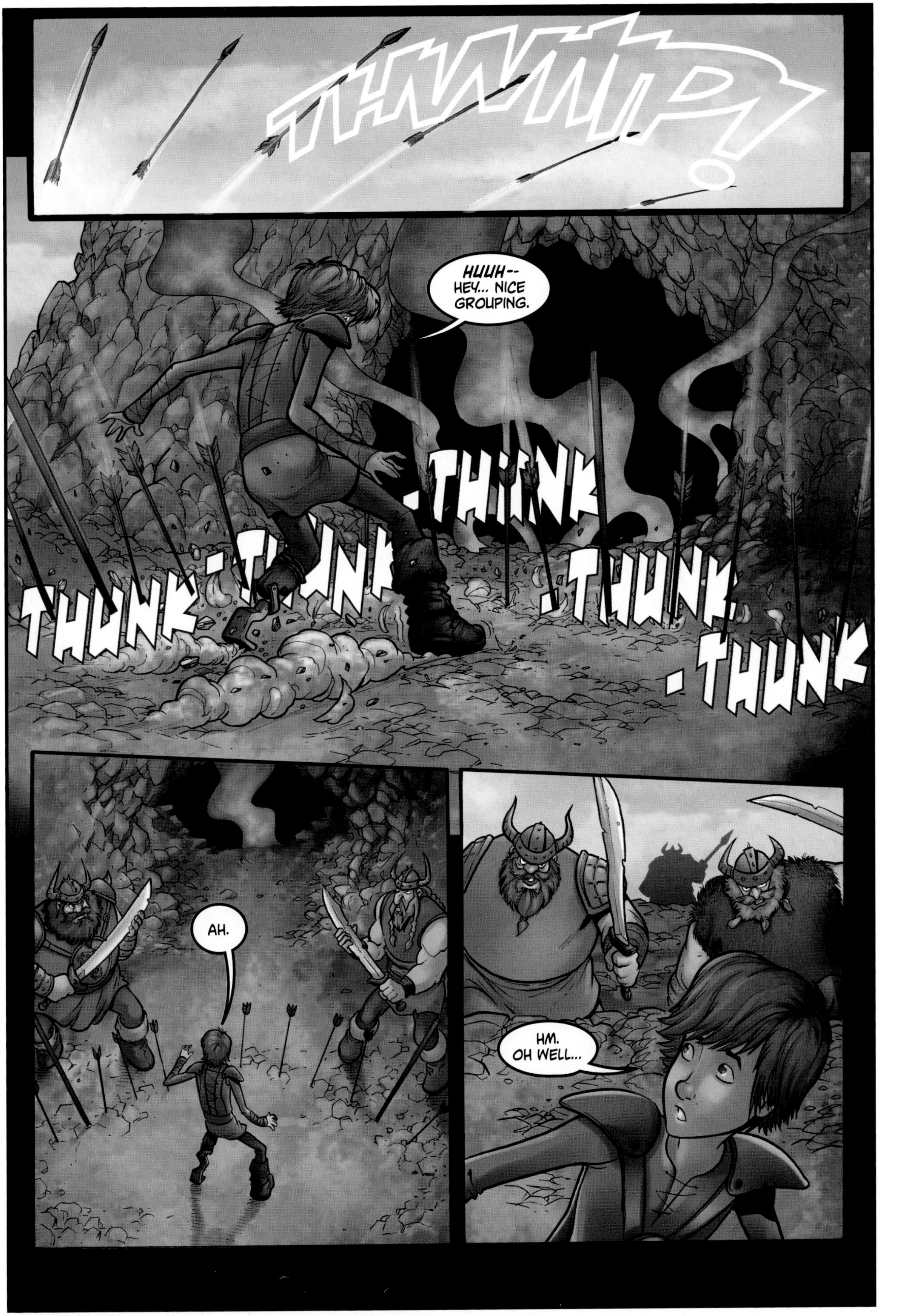
THWWIP!
HUUH--
HEY... NICE
GROUPING.
THUNK-THUNK-THUNK-THUNK-THUNK-THUNK
AH.
HM.
OH WELL...

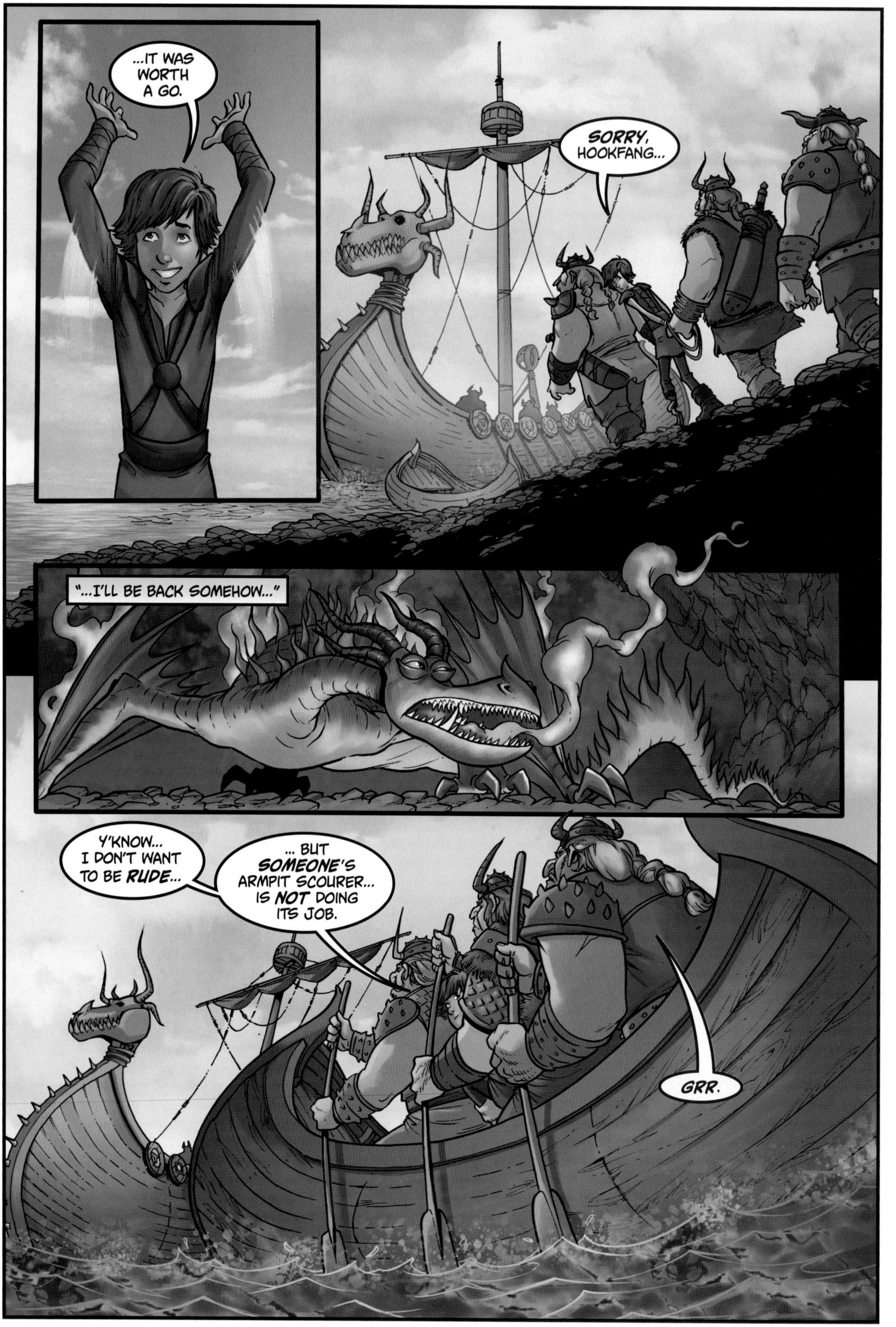
...IT WAS WORTH A GO.
SORRY, HOOKFANG...
"...I'LL BE BACK SOMEHOW..."
Y'KNOW... I DON'T WANT TO BE **RUDE**...
... BUT **SOMEONE**'S ARMPIT SCOURER... IS **NOT** DOING ITS JOB.
GRR.

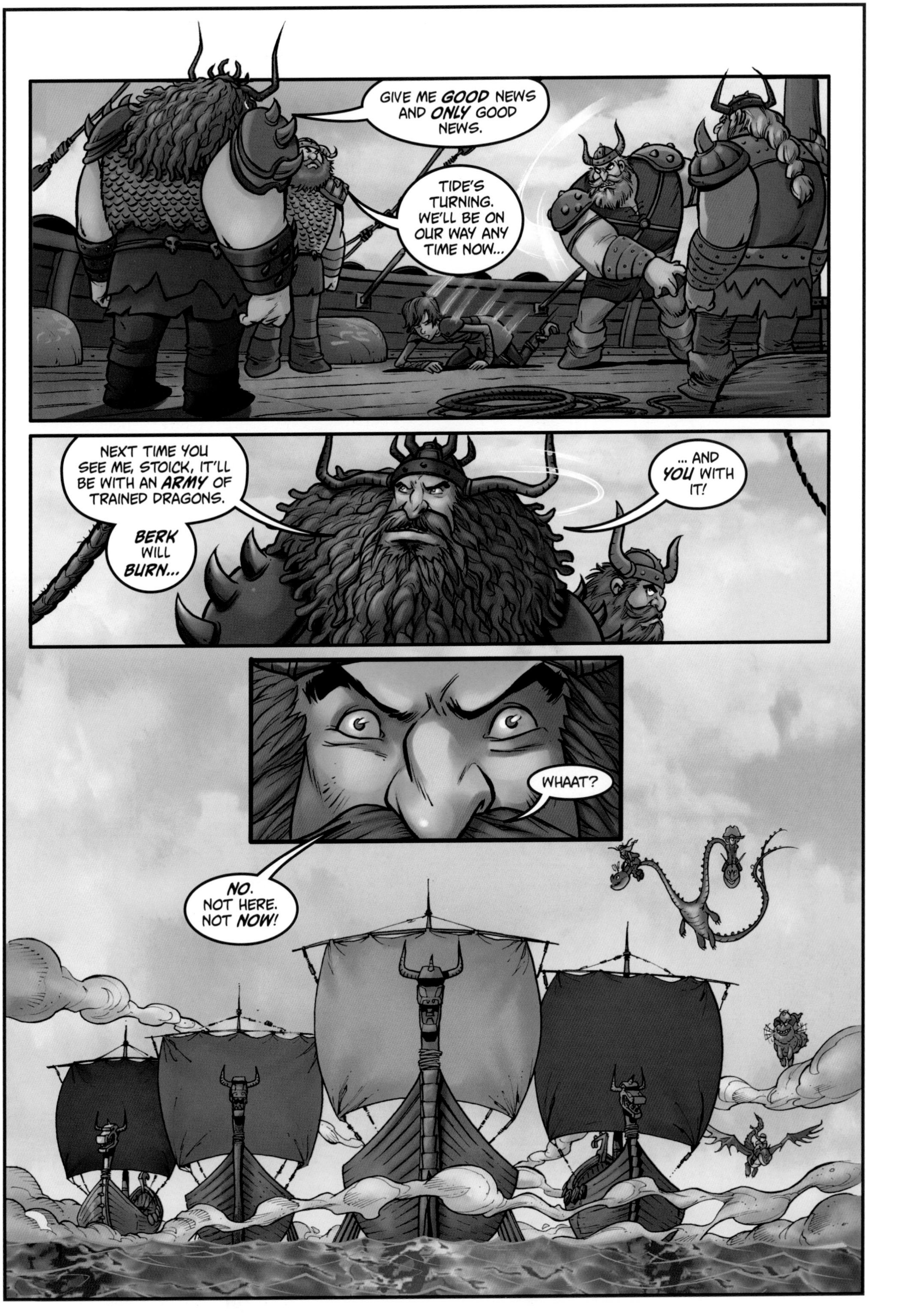
GIVE ME GOOD NEWS AND ONLY GOOD NEWS.
TIDE'S TURNING. WE'LL BE ON OUR WAY ANY TIME NOW...
NEXT TIME YOU SEE ME, STOICK, IT'LL BE WITH AN ARMY OF TRAINED DRAGONS.
BERK WILL BURN...
... AND YOU WITH IT!
WHAAT?
NO. NOT HERE. NOT NOW!

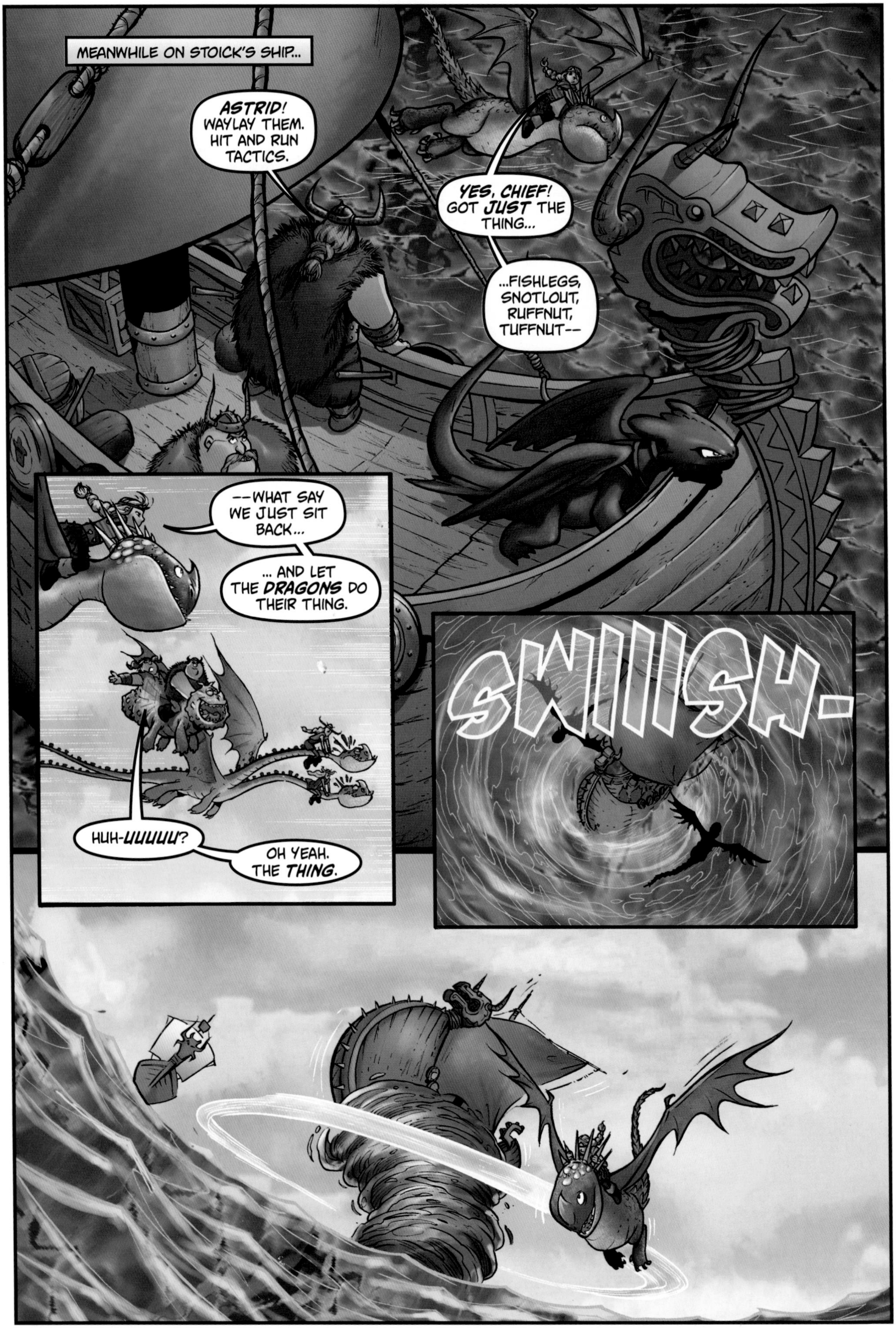
MEANWHILE ON STOICK'S SHIP...
ASTRID! WAYLAY THEM. HIT AND RUN TACTICS.
YES, CHIEF! GOT JUST THE THING...
...FISHLEGS, SNOTLOUT, RUFFNUT, TUFFNUT--
--WHAT SAY WE JUST SIT BACK...
... AND LET THE DRAGONS DO THEIR THING.
HUH-UUUUU?
OH YEAH. THE THING.
SWIIISH-

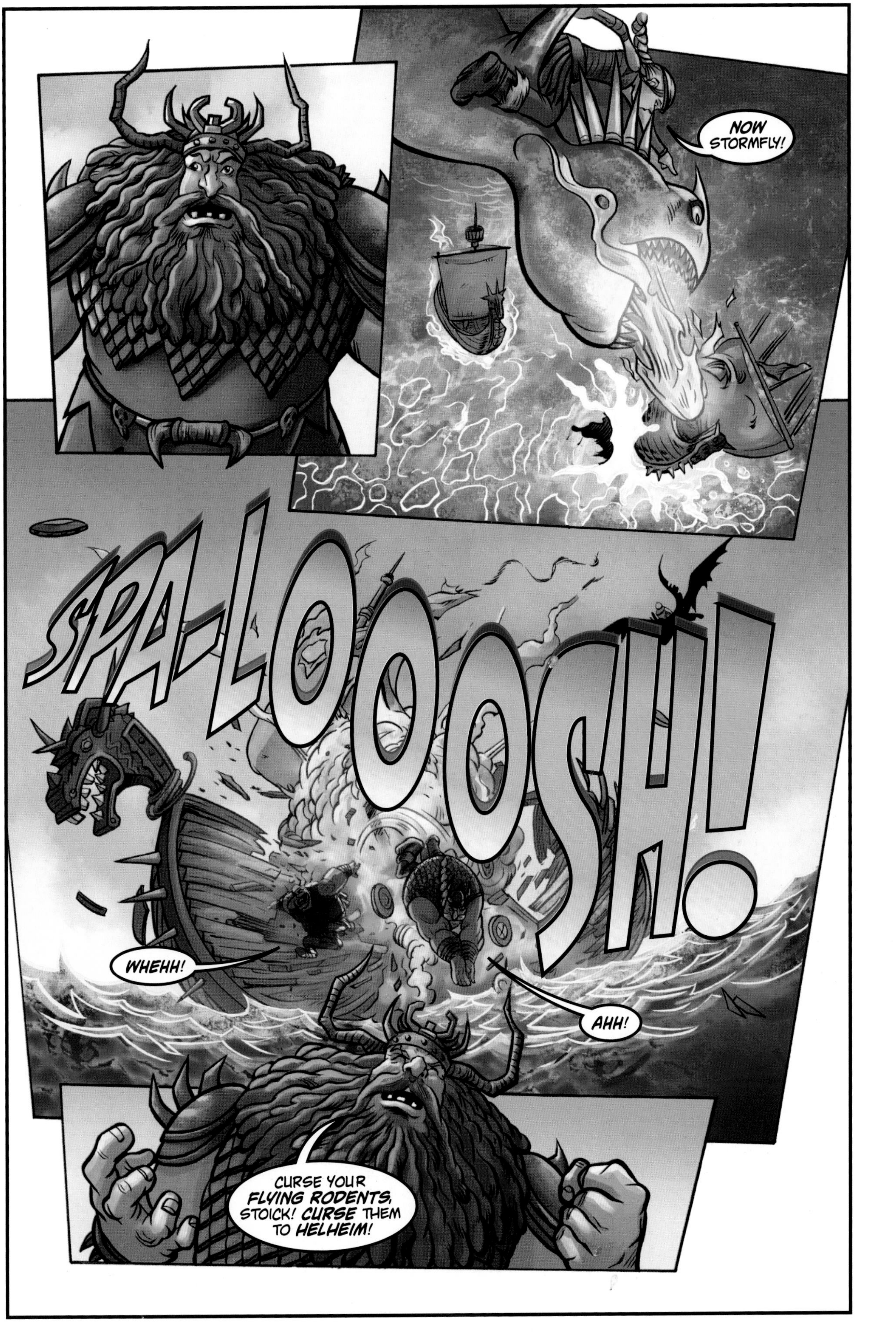
NOW STORMFLY!
SPA-LOOOSH!
WHEHH!
AHH!
CURSE YOUR FLYING RODENTS, STOICK! CURSE THEM TO HELHEIM!

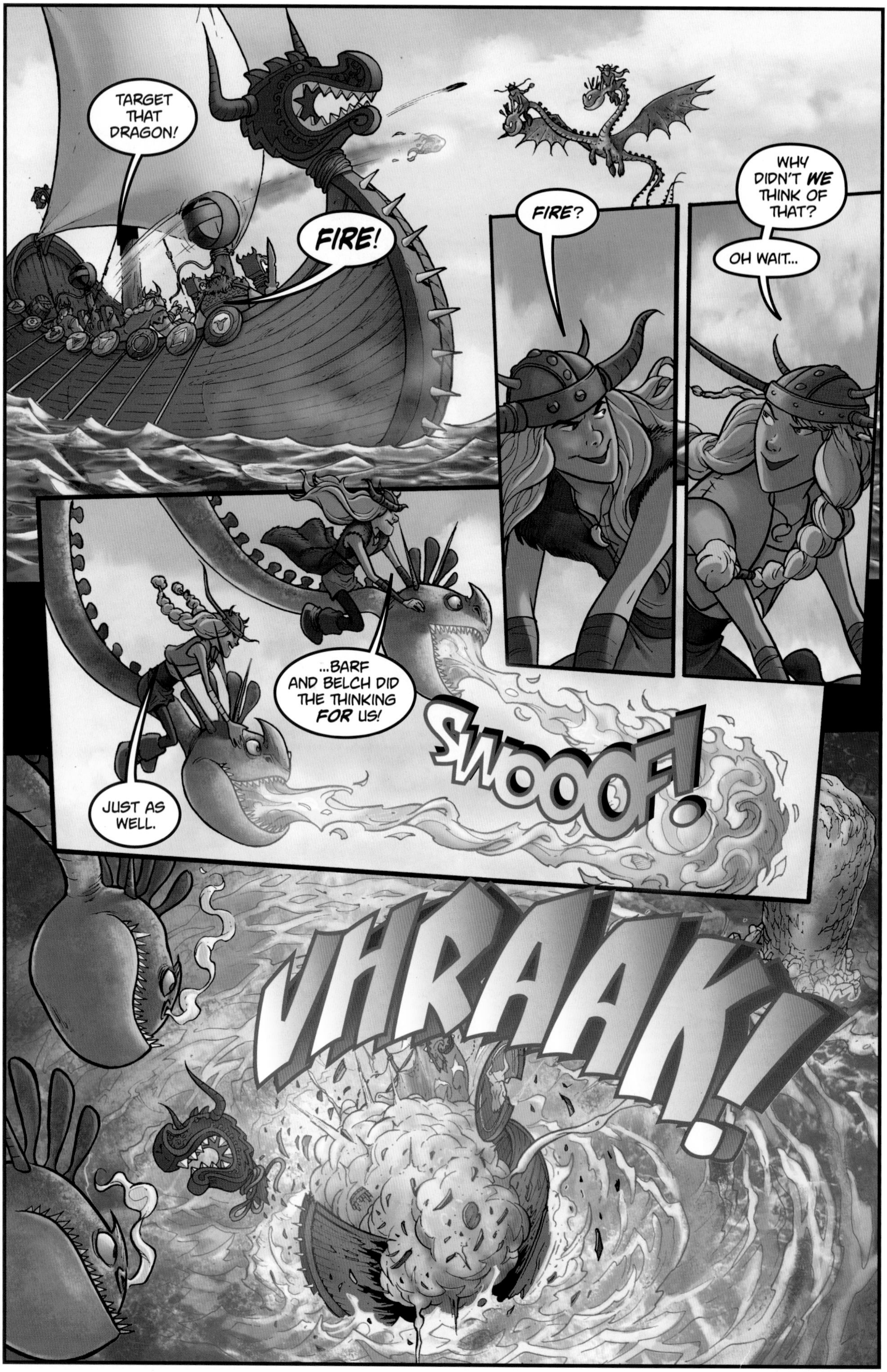
TARGET THAT DRAGON!
FIRE!
FIRE?
WHY DIDN'T WE THINK OF THAT?
OH WAIT...
...BARF AND BELCH DID THE THINKING FOR US!
JUST AS WELL.
SWOOOF!
VHRAAK!

CHAPTER FOUR

In which Hiccup and Snotlout embark on a dangerous rescue mission, and a Viking promise is made...

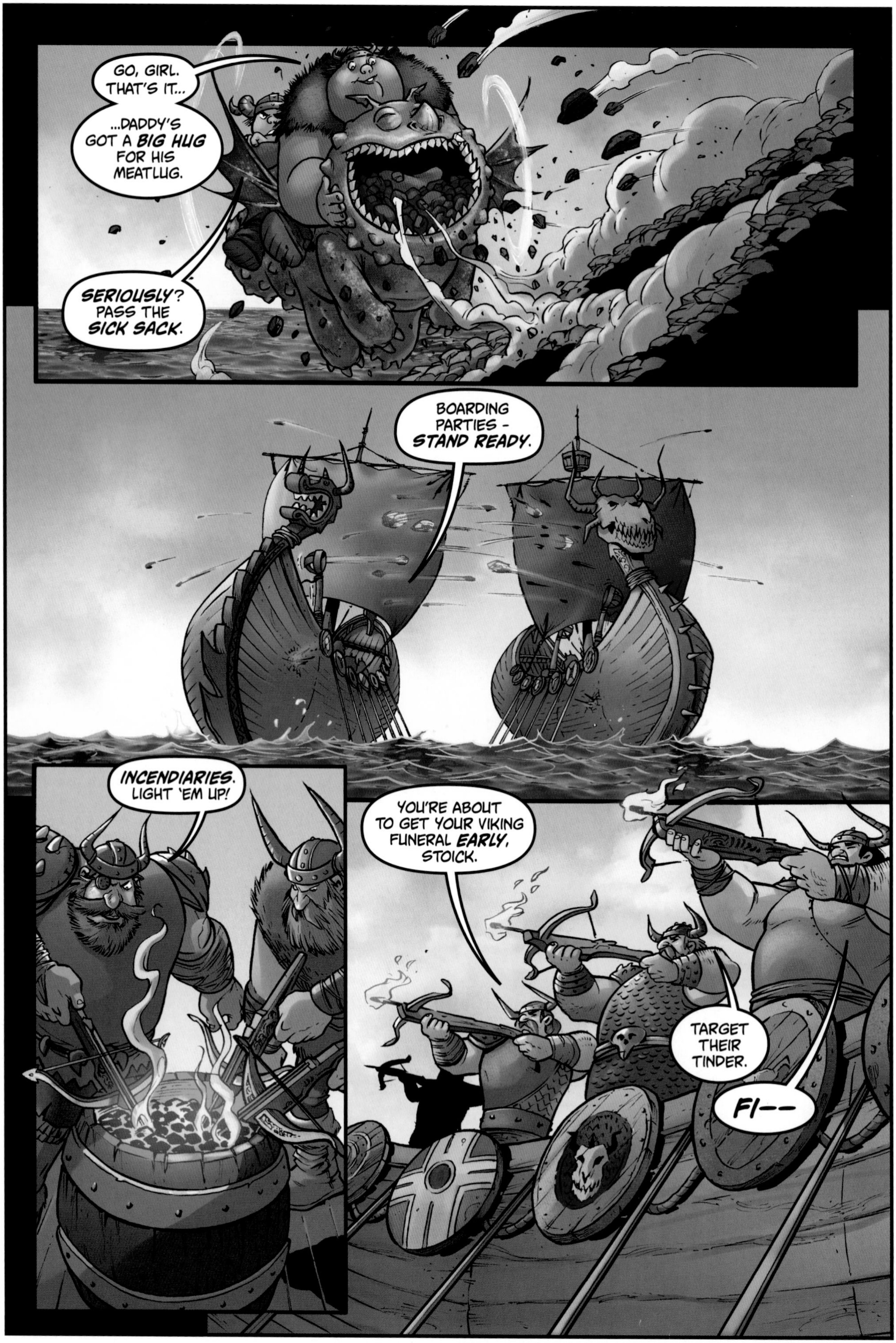
GO, GIRL. THAT'S IT...
...DADDY'S GOT A BIG HUG FOR HIS MEATLUG.
SERIOUSLY? PASS THE SICK SACK.
BOARDING PARTIES - STAND READY.
INCENDIARIES. LIGHT 'EM UP!
YOU'RE ABOUT TO GET YOUR VIKING FUNERAL EARLY, STOICK.
TARGET THEIR TINDER.
FI--

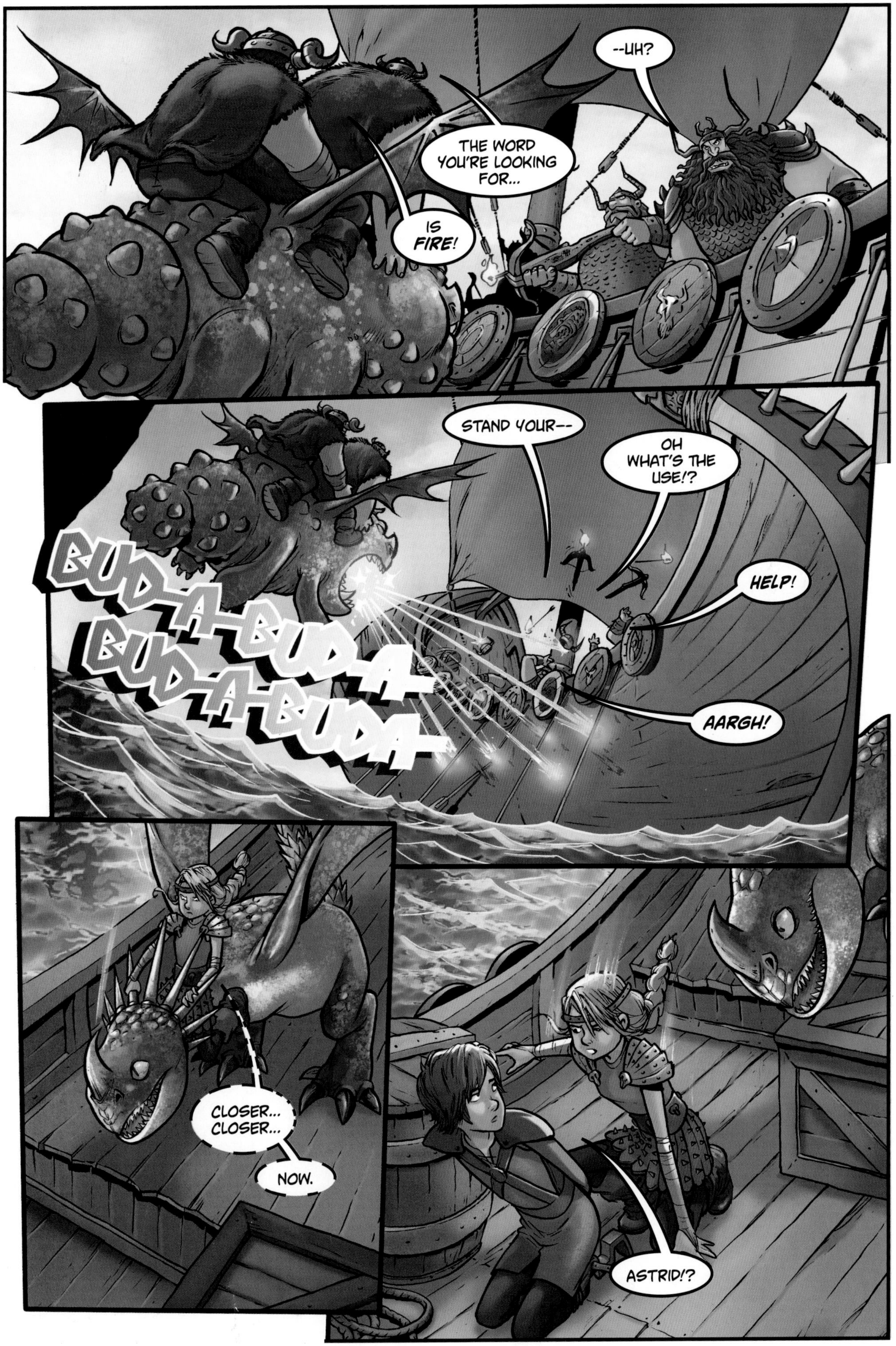
THE WORD YOU'RE LOOKING FOR...
IS FIRE!
--UH?
STAND YOUR--
OH WHAT'S THE USE!?
BUD-A-BUD-A BUD-A-BUD-A BUDA
HELP!
AARGH!
CLOSER... CLOSER...
NOW.
ASTRID!?

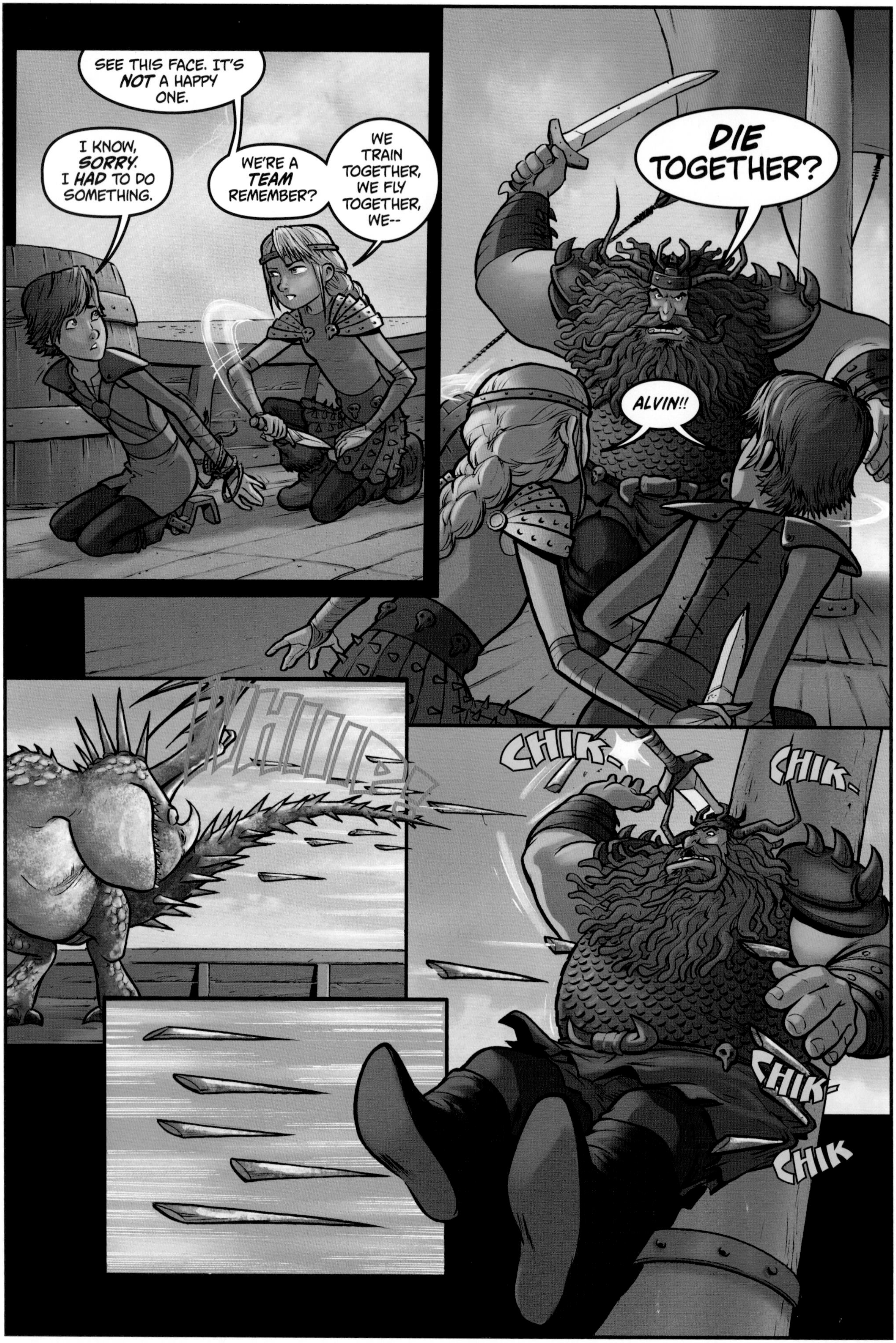
SEE THIS FACE. IT'S NOT A HAPPY ONE.
I KNOW, SORRY. I HAD TO DO SOMETHING.
WE'RE A TEAM REMEMBER?
WE TRAIN TOGETHER, WE FLY TOGETHER, WE--
DIE TOGETHER?
ALVIN!!
CHIK-
CHIK-
CHIK-
CHIK

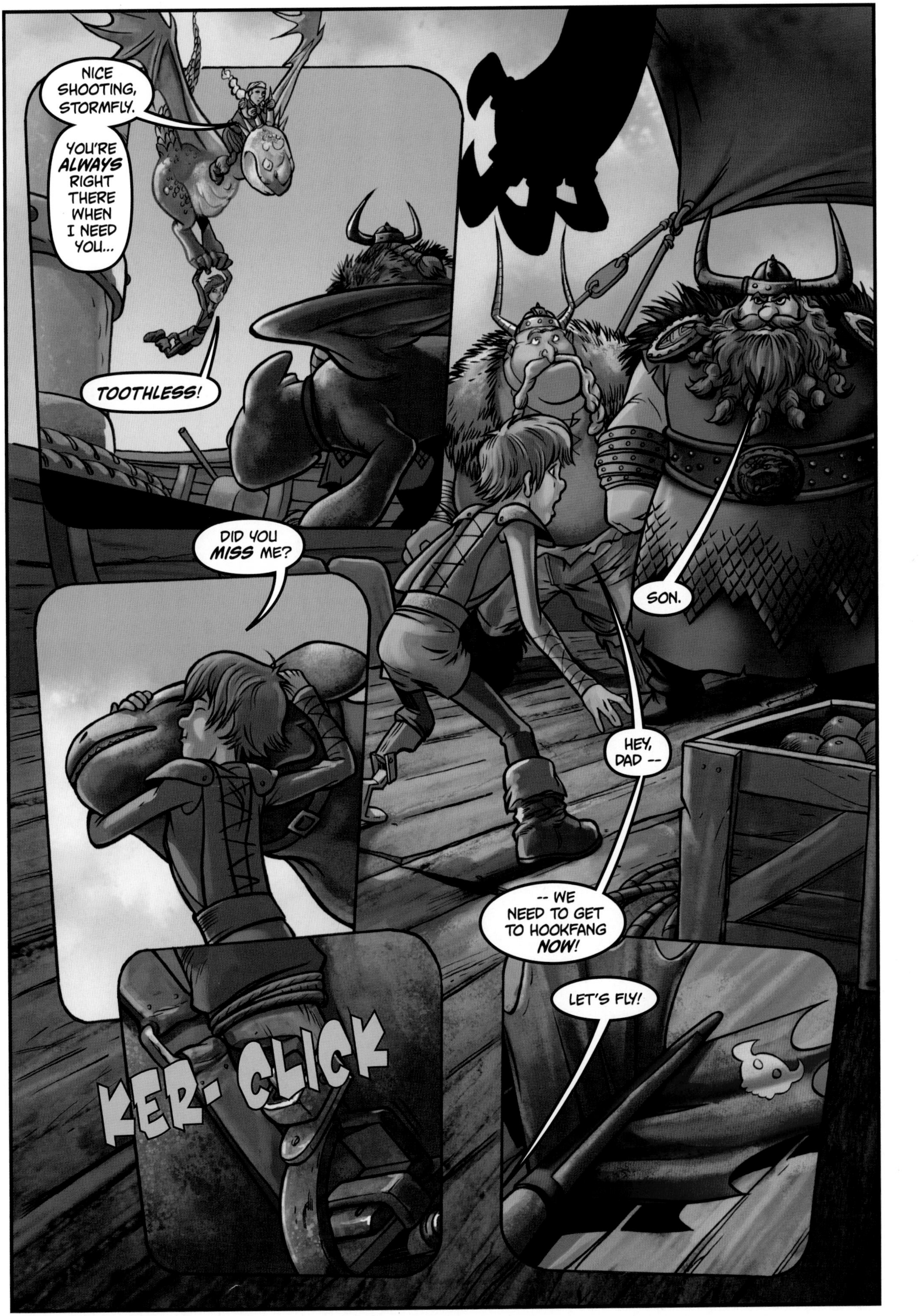
NICE SHOOTING, STORMFLY.
YOU'RE ALWAYS RIGHT THERE WHEN I NEED YOU...
TOOTHLESS!
SON.
DID YOU MISS ME?
HEY, DAD --
-- WE NEED TO GET TO HOOKFANG NOW!
KER- CLICK
LET'S FLY!

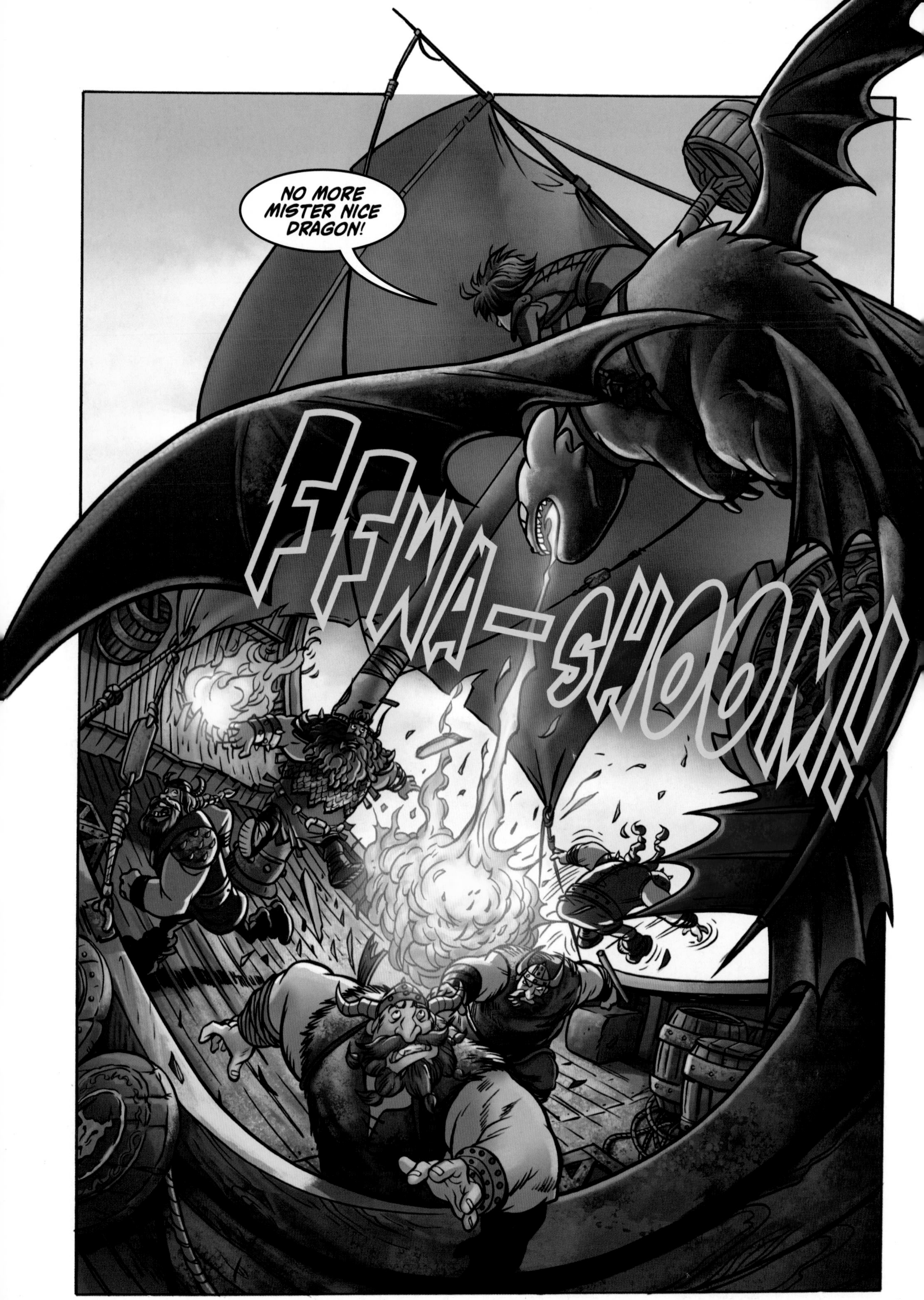
NO MORE MISTER NICE DRAGON!
FFWA-SHOOM!

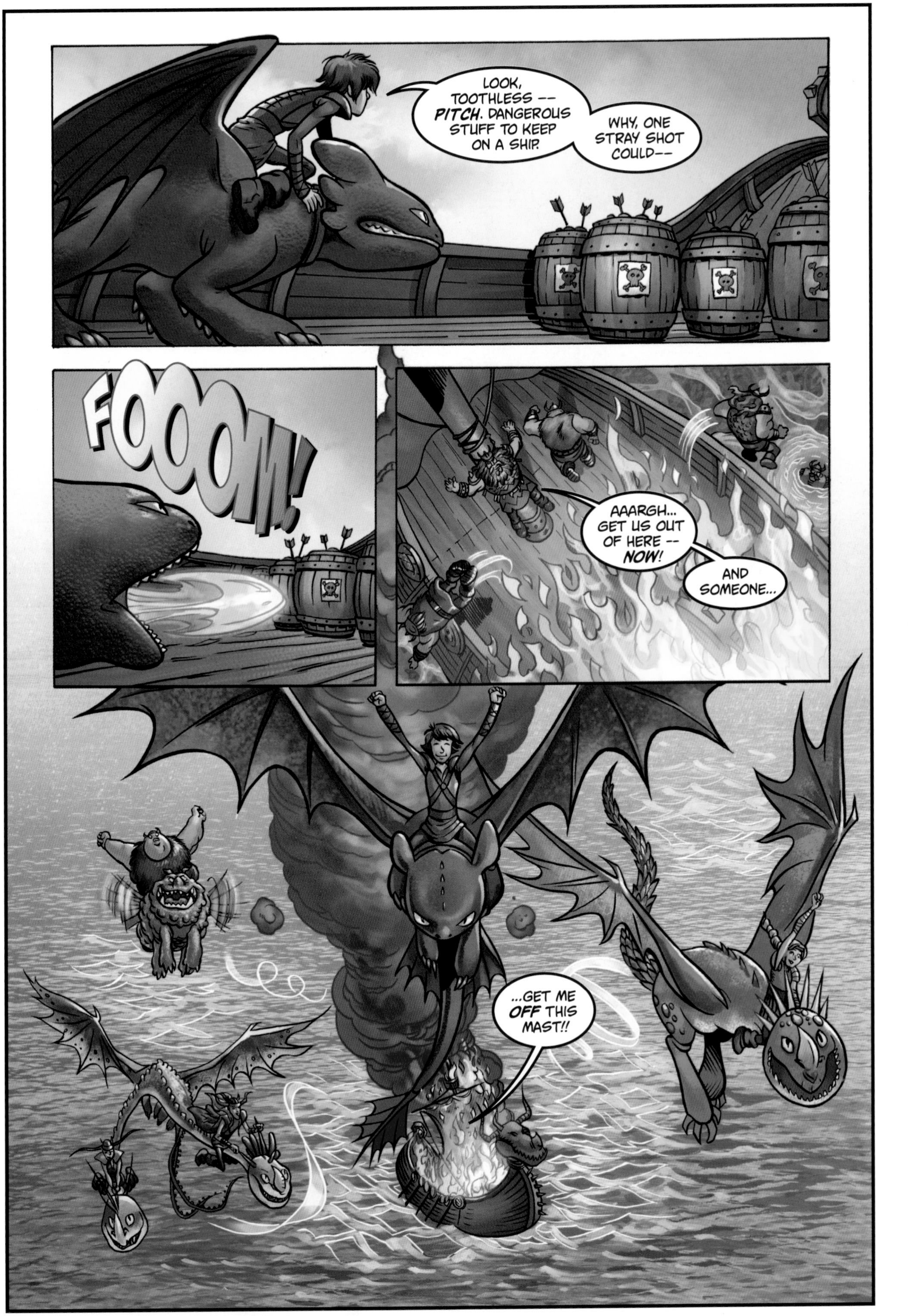
LOOK, TOOTHLESS -- PITCH. DANGEROUS STUFF TO KEEP ON A SHIP.
WHY, ONE STRAY SHOT COULD--
FOOOM!
AAARGH... GET US OUT OF HERE -- NOW!
AND SOMEONE...
...GET ME OFF THIS MAST!!

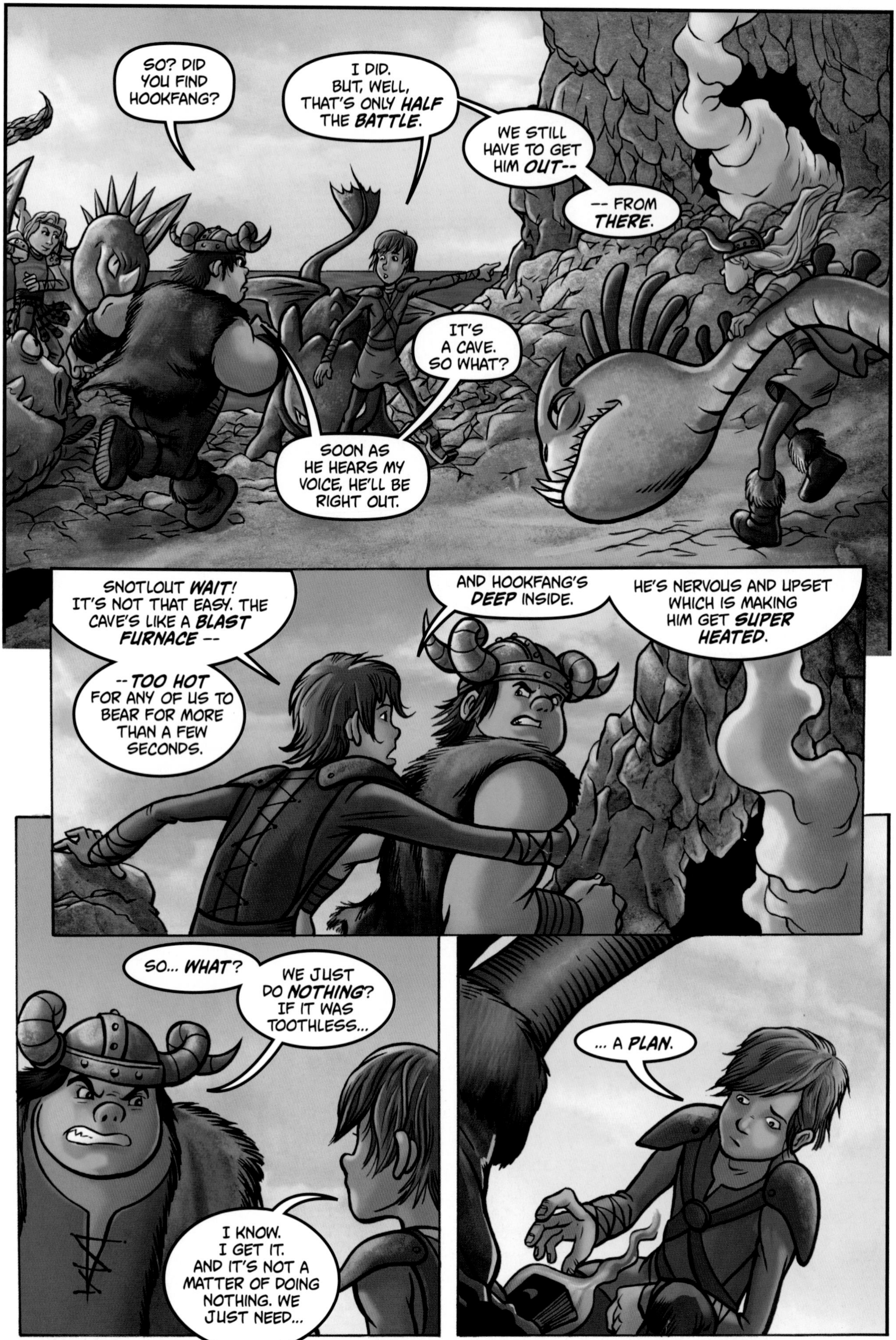
SO? DID YOU FIND HOOKFANG?
I DID. BUT, WELL, THAT'S ONLY HALF THE BATTLE.
WE STILL HAVE TO GET HIM OUT--
-- FROM THERE.
IT'S A CAVE. SO WHAT?
SOON AS HE HEARS MY VOICE, HE'LL BE RIGHT OUT.
SNOTLOUT WAIT! IT'S NOT THAT EASY. THE CAVE'S LIKE A BLAST FURNACE --
--TOO HOT FOR ANY OF US TO BEAR FOR MORE THAN A FEW SECONDS.
AND HOOKFANG'S DEEP INSIDE.
HE'S NERVOUS AND UPSET WHICH IS MAKING HIM GET SUPER HEATED.
SO... WHAT?
WE JUST DO NOTHING? IF IT WAS TOOTHLESS...
I KNOW. I GET IT. AND IT'S NOT A MATTER OF DOING NOTHING. WE JUST NEED...
... A PLAN.

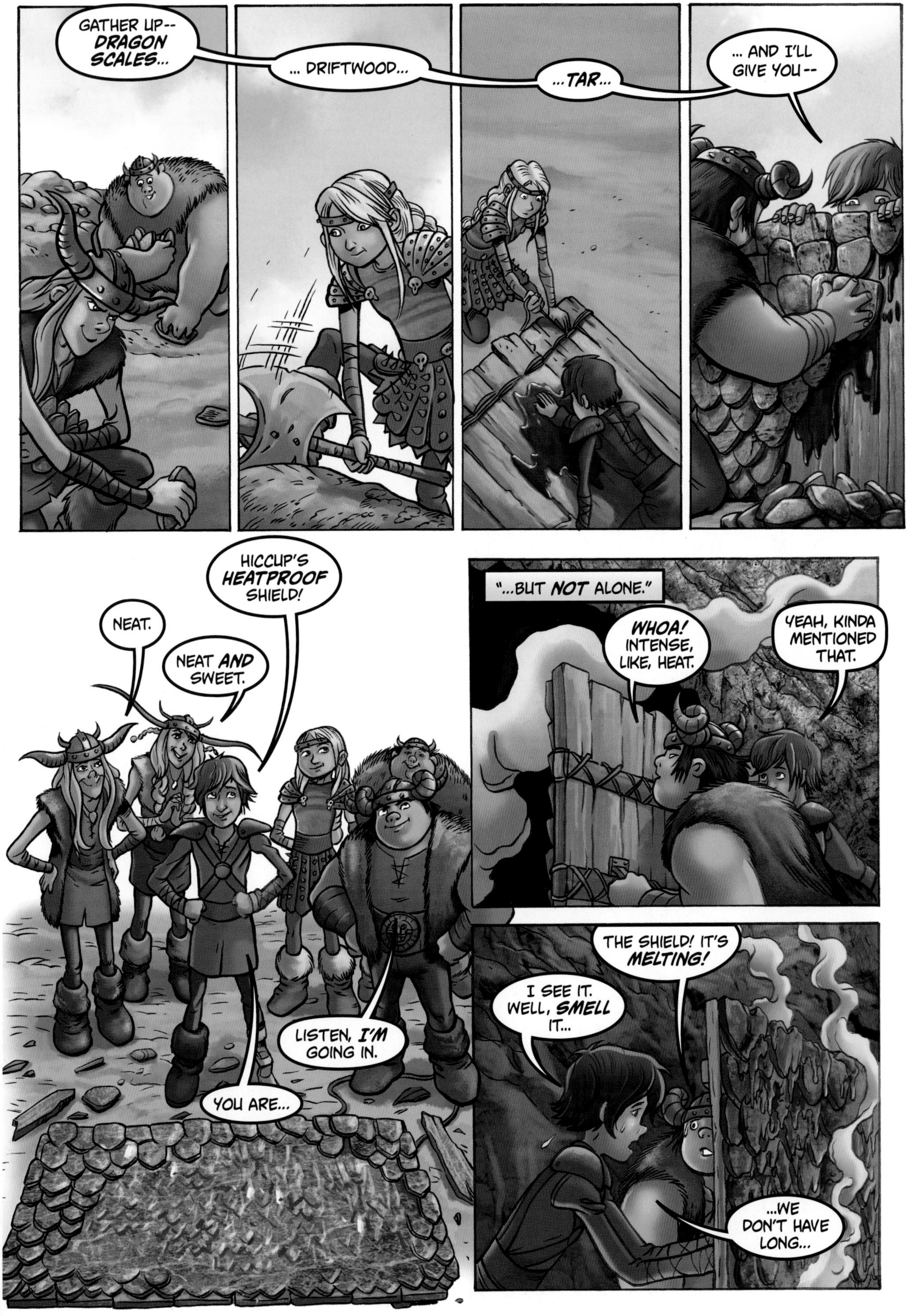
GATHER UP-- DRAGON SCALES...
... DRIFTWOOD...
... TAR...
... AND I'LL GIVE YOU --
HICCUP'S HEATPROOF SHIELD!
NEAT.
NEAT AND SWEET.
LISTEN, I'M GOING IN.
YOU ARE...
"...BUT NOT ALONE."
WHOA! INTENSE, LIKE, HEAT.
YEAH, KINDA MENTIONED THAT.
THE SHIELD! IT'S MELTING!
I SEE IT. WELL, SMELL IT...
...WE DON'T HAVE LONG...

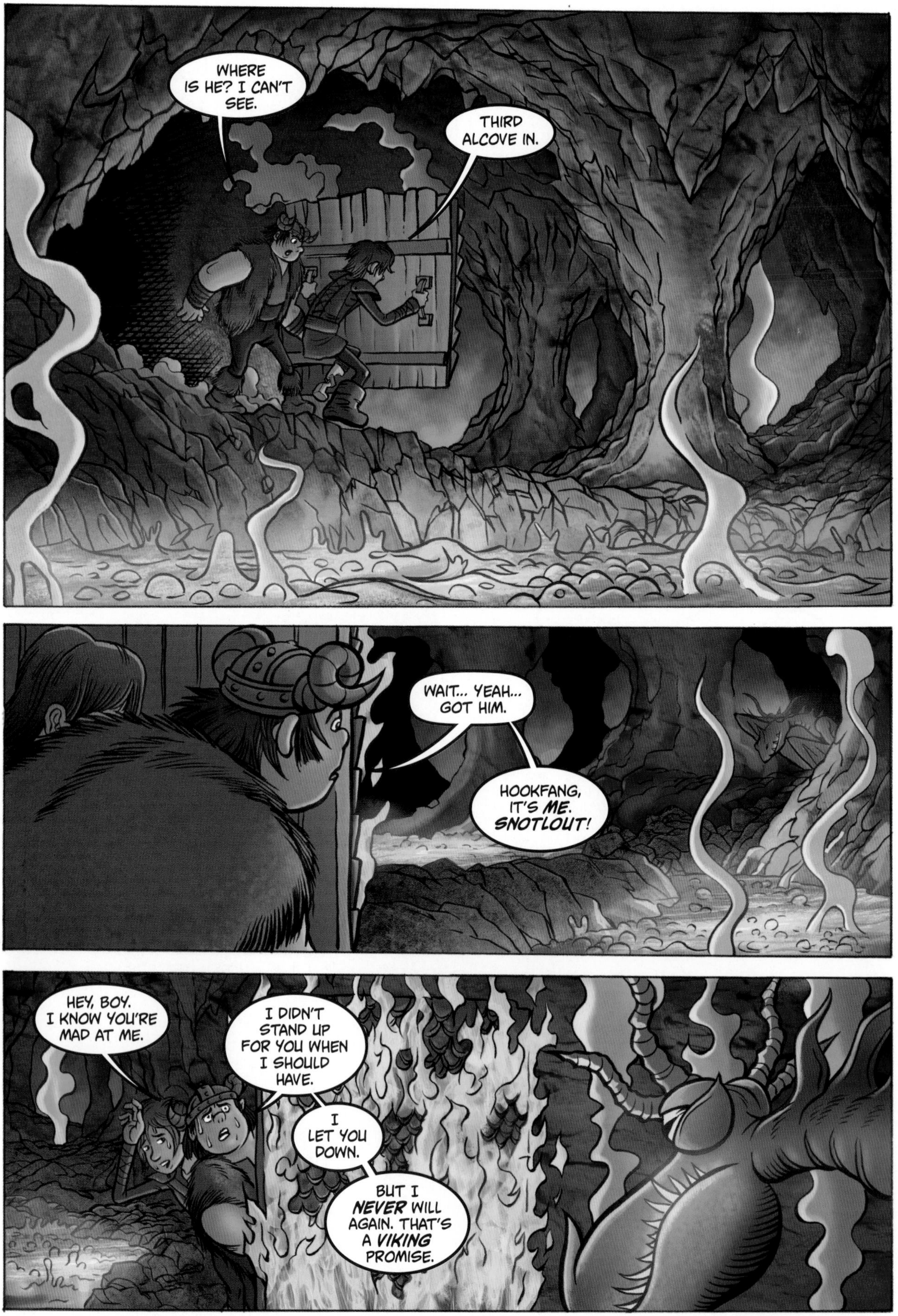
WHERE IS HE? I CAN'T SEE.
THIRD ALCOVE IN.
WAIT... YEAH... GOT HIM.
HOOKFANG, IT'S ME. SNOTLOUT!
HEY, BOY. I KNOW YOU'RE MAD AT ME.
I DIDN'T STAND UP FOR YOU WHEN I SHOULD HAVE.
I LET YOU DOWN.
BUT I NEVER WILL AGAIN. THAT'S A VIKING PROMISE.

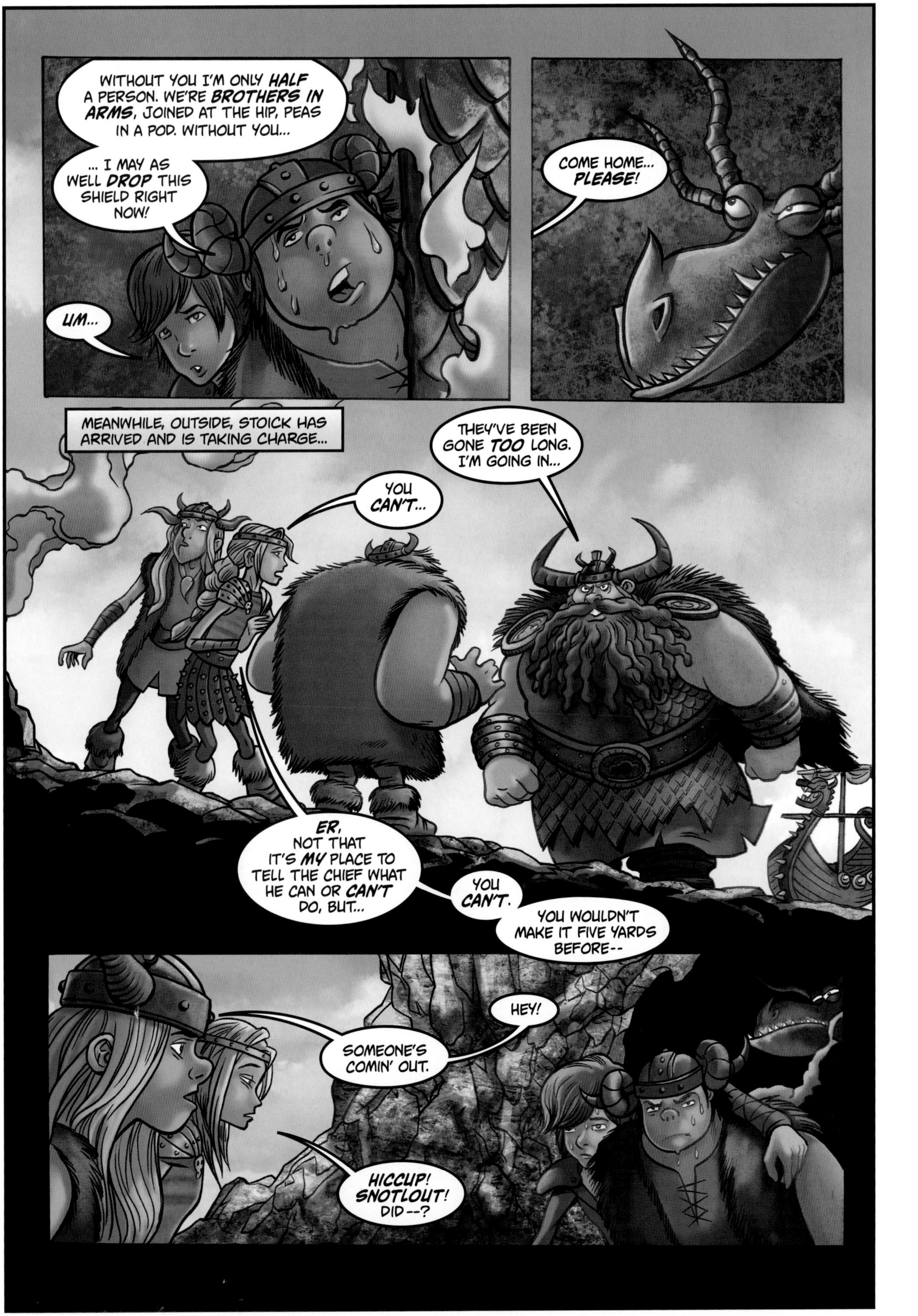
WITHOUT YOU I'M ONLY HALF A PERSON. WE'RE BROTHERS IN ARMS, JOINED AT THE HIP, PEAS IN A POD. WITHOUT YOU...
... I MAY AS WELL DROP THIS SHIELD RIGHT NOW!
UM...
COME HOME... PLEASE!
MEANWHILE, OUTSIDE, STOICK HAS ARRIVED AND IS TAKING CHARGE...
THEY'VE BEEN GONE TOO LONG. I'M GOING IN...
YOU CAN'T...
ER, NOT THAT IT'S MY PLACE TO TELL THE CHIEF WHAT HE CAN OR CAN'T DO, BUT...
YOU CAN'T.
YOU WOULDN'T MAKE IT FIVE YARDS BEFORE--
HEY!
SOMEONE'S COMIN' OUT.
HICCUP! SNOTLOUT! DID--?

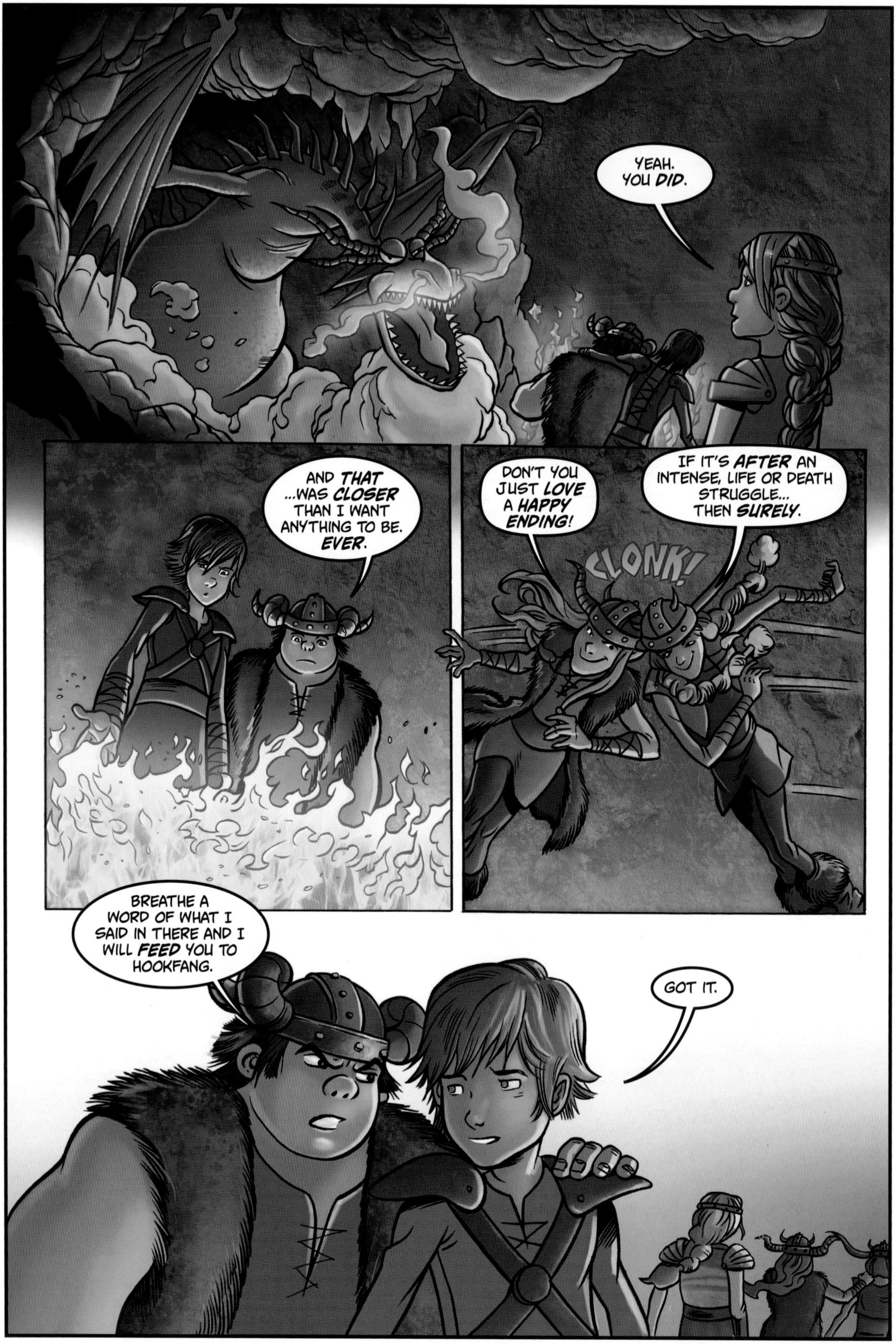

YEAH. YOU DID.
AND THAT ...WAS CLOSER THAN I WANT ANYTHING TO BE. EVER.
DON'T YOU JUST LOVE A HAPPY ENDING!
IF IT'S AFTER AN INTENSE, LIFE OR DEATH STRUGGLE... THEN SURELY.
CLONK!
BREATHE A WORD OF WHAT I SAID IN THERE AND I WILL FEED YOU TO HOOKFANG.
GOT IT.

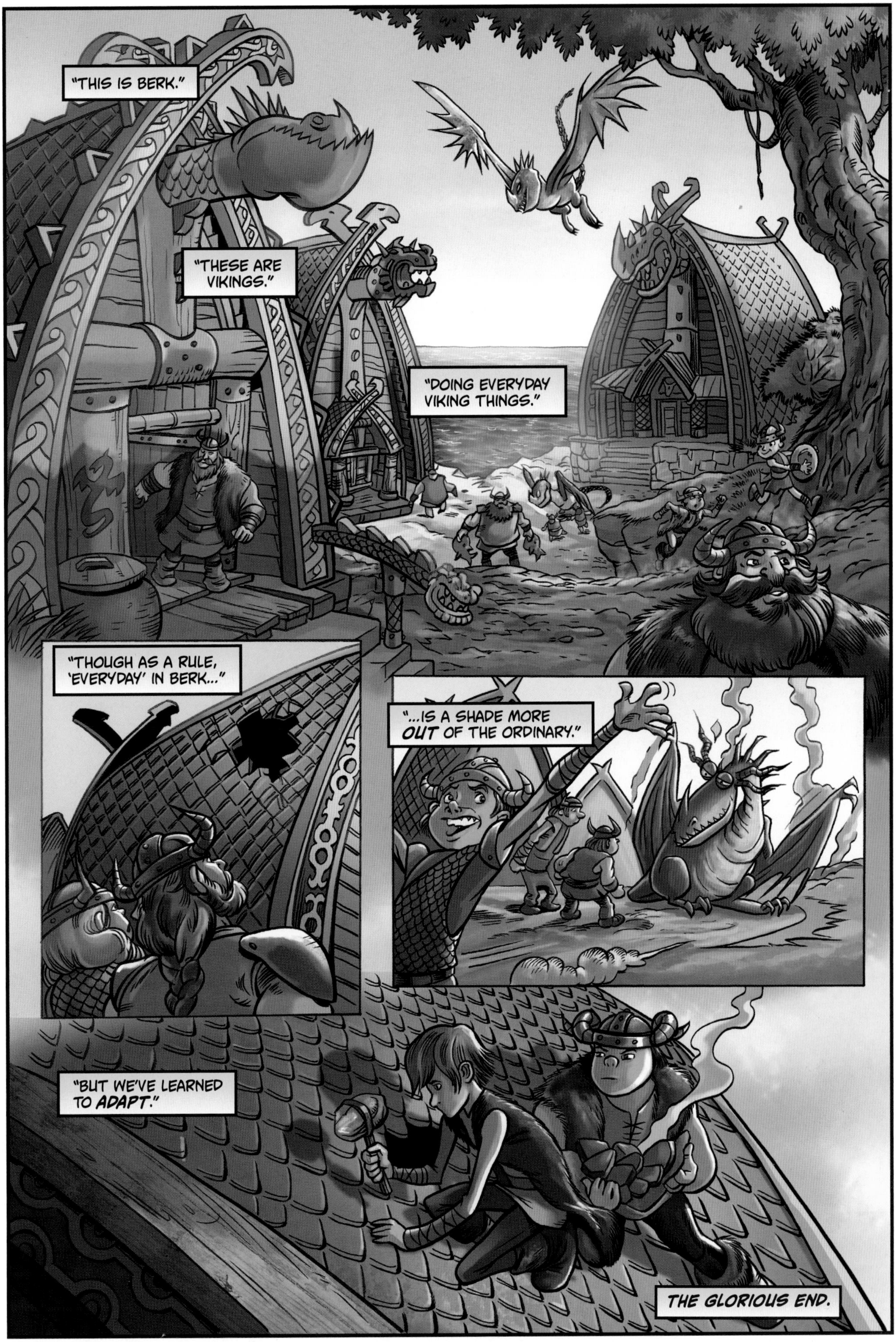
"THIS IS BERK."
"THESE ARE VIKINGS."
"DOING EVERYDAY VIKING THINGS."
"THOUGH AS A RULE, 'EVERYDAY' IN BERK..."
"...IS A SHADE MORE *OUT* OF THE ORDINARY."
"BUT WE'VE LEARNED TO *ADAPT*."
THE GLORIOUS END.

DANGERS OF THE DEEP

SCRIPT Simon Furman
PENCILS Iwan Nazif
INKS Iwan Nazif & Lee Townsend
COLORS Nestor Pereyra, John Charles & Digikore
LETTERING David Manley-Leach

CHAPTER ONE

In which the town of Berk encounters a problem... A meeting is held... And a dangerous decision is made...

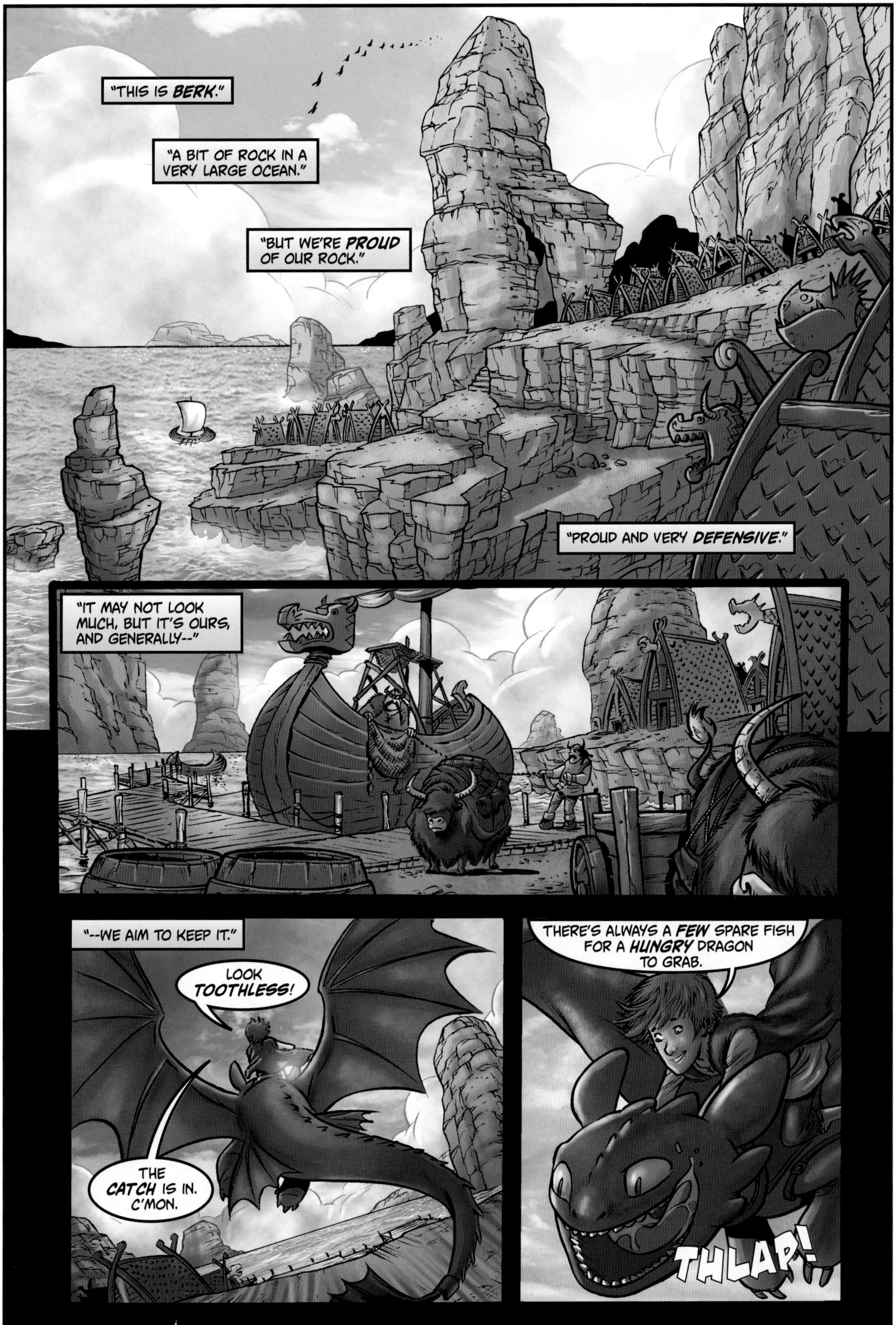
"THIS IS BERK."
"A BIT OF ROCK IN A VERY LARGE OCEAN."
"BUT WE'RE PROUD OF OUR ROCK."
"PROUD AND VERY DEFENSIVE."
"IT MAY NOT LOOK MUCH, BUT IT'S OURS, AND GENERALLY--"
"--WE AIM TO KEEP IT."
LOOK TOOTHLESS!
THE CATCH IS IN. C'MON.
THERE'S ALWAYS A FEW SPARE FISH FOR A HUNGRY DRAGON TO GRAB.
THLAP!

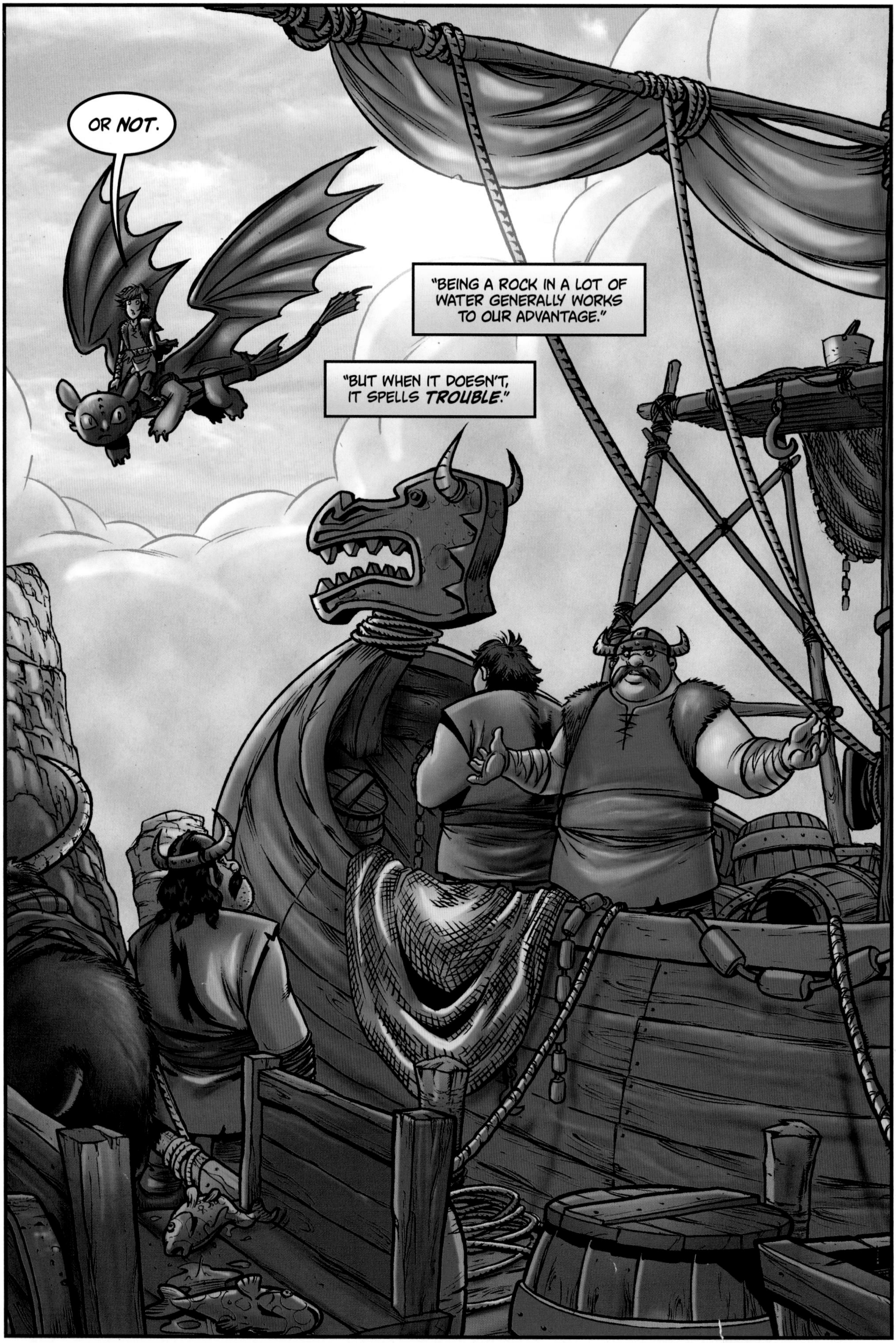
OR NOT.
"BEING A ROCK IN A LOT OF WATER GENERALLY WORKS TO OUR ADVANTAGE."
"BUT WHEN IT DOESN'T, IT SPELLS TROUBLE."

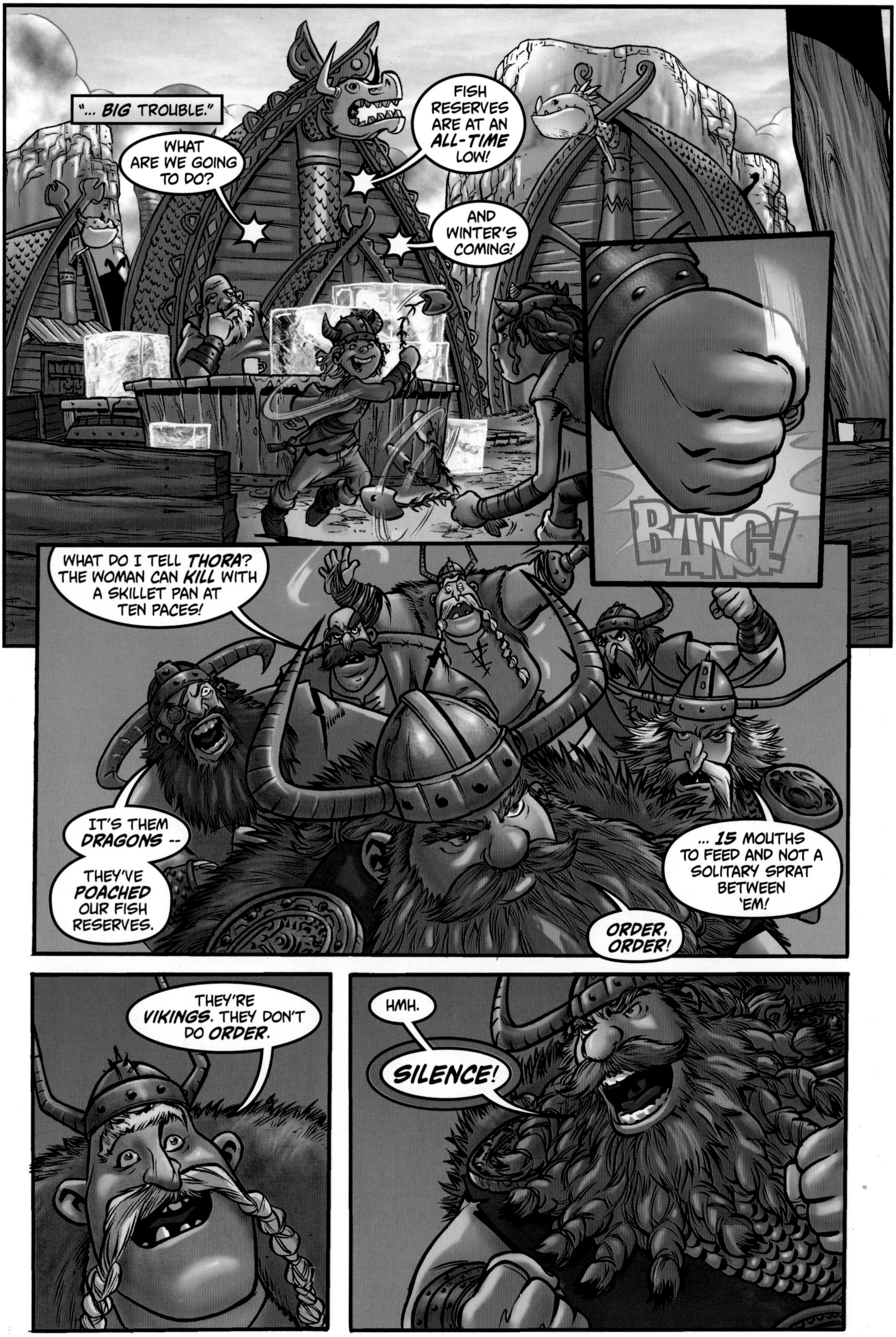
"... BIG TROUBLE."
WHAT ARE WE GOING TO DO?
FISH RESERVES ARE AT AN ALL-TIME LOW!
AND WINTER'S COMING!
BANG!
WHAT DO I TELL THORA? THE WOMAN CAN KILL WITH A SKILLET PAN AT TEN PACES!
IT'S THEM DRAGONS --
THEY'VE POACHED OUR FISH RESERVES.
... 15 MOUTHS TO FEED AND NOT A SOLITARY SPRAT BETWEEN 'EM!
ORDER, ORDER!
THEY'RE VIKINGS. THEY DON'T DO ORDER.
HMH.
SILENCE!

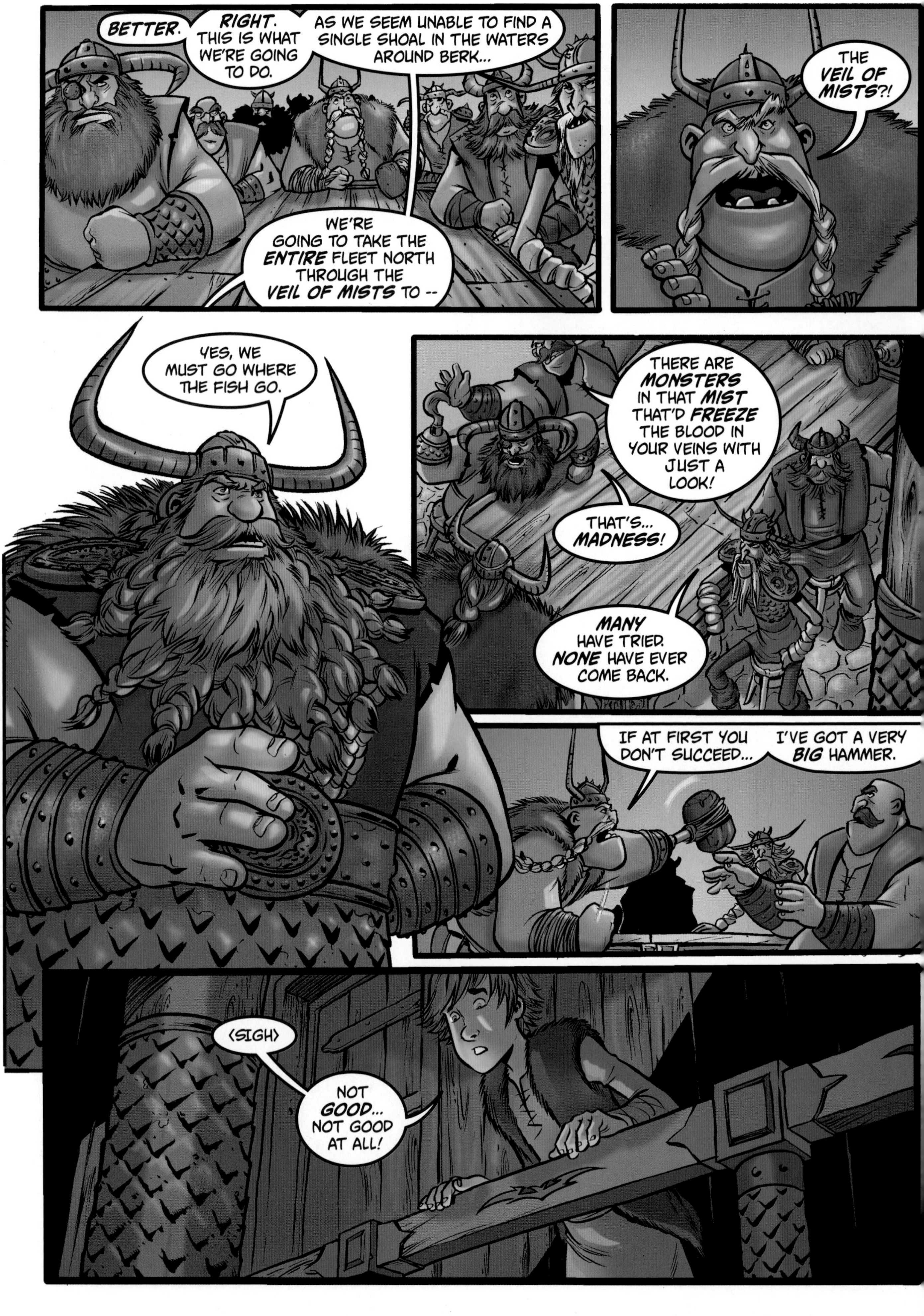
BETTER.
RIGHT. THIS IS WHAT WE'RE GOING TO DO.
AS WE SEEM UNABLE TO FIND A SINGLE SHOAL IN THE WATERS AROUND BERK...
WE'RE GOING TO TAKE THE ENTIRE FLEET NORTH THROUGH THE VEIL OF MISTS TO --
THE VEIL OF MISTS?!
YES, WE MUST GO WHERE THE FISH GO.
THERE ARE MONSTERS IN THAT MIST THAT'D FREEZE THE BLOOD IN YOUR VEINS WITH JUST A LOOK!
THAT'S... MADNESS!
MANY HAVE TRIED. NONE HAVE EVER COME BACK.
IF AT FIRST YOU DON'T SUCCEED...
I'VE GOT A VERY BIG HAMMER.
<SIGH>
NOT GOOD... NOT GOOD AT ALL!

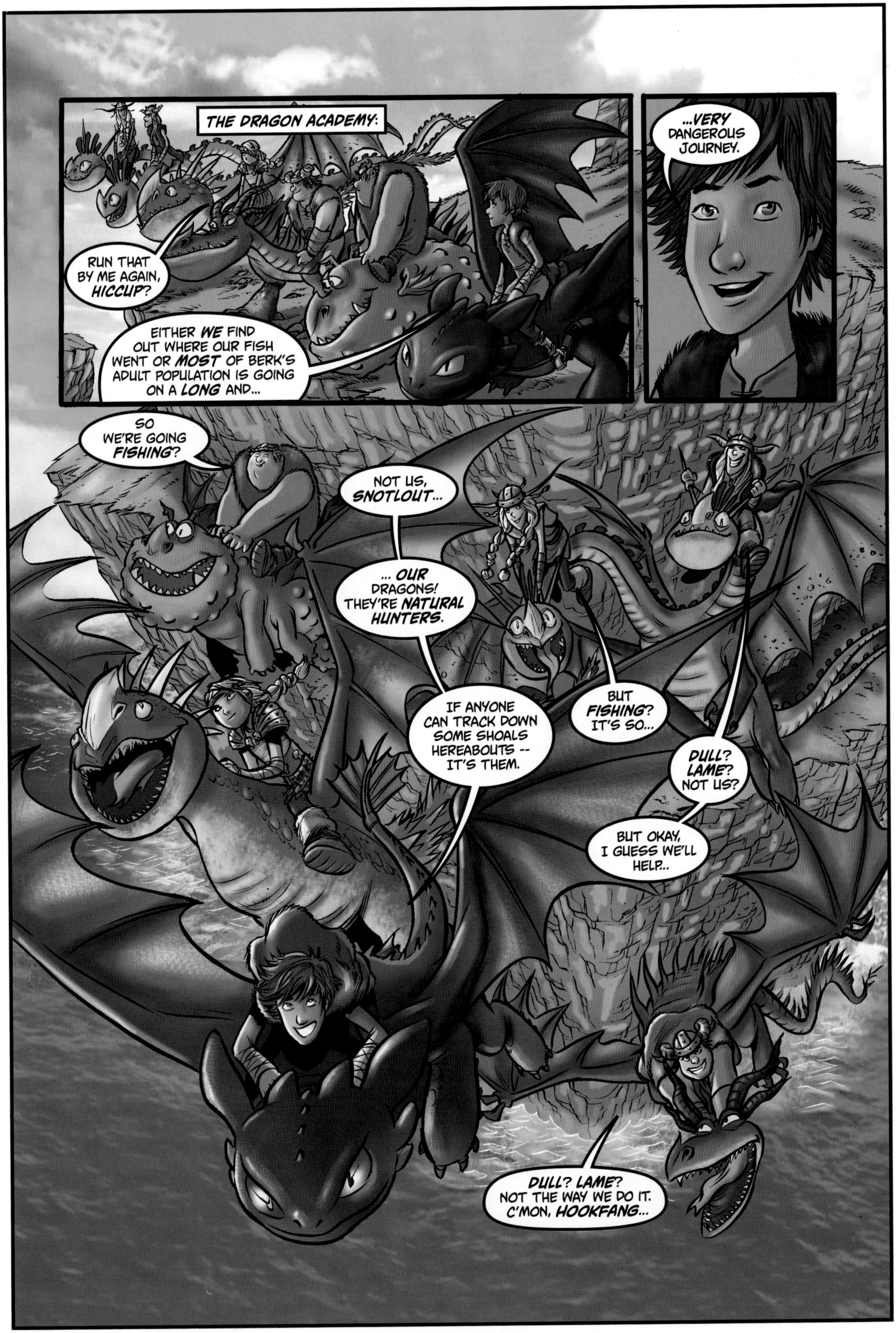
THE DRAGON ACADEMY:
RUN THAT BY ME AGAIN, HICCUP?
EITHER WE FIND OUT WHERE OUR FISH WENT OR MOST OF BERK'S ADULT POPULATION IS GOING ON A LONG AND...
...VERY DANGEROUS JOURNEY.
SO WE'RE GOING FISHING?
NOT US, SNOTLOUT...
... OUR DRAGONS! THEY'RE NATURAL HUNTERS.
IF ANYONE CAN TRACK DOWN SOME SHOALS HEREABOUTS -- IT'S THEM.
BUT FISHING? IT'S SO...
DULL? LAME? NOT US?
BUT OKAY, I GUESS WE'LL HELP...
DULL? LAME? NOT THE WAY WE DO IT. C'MON, HOOKFANG...

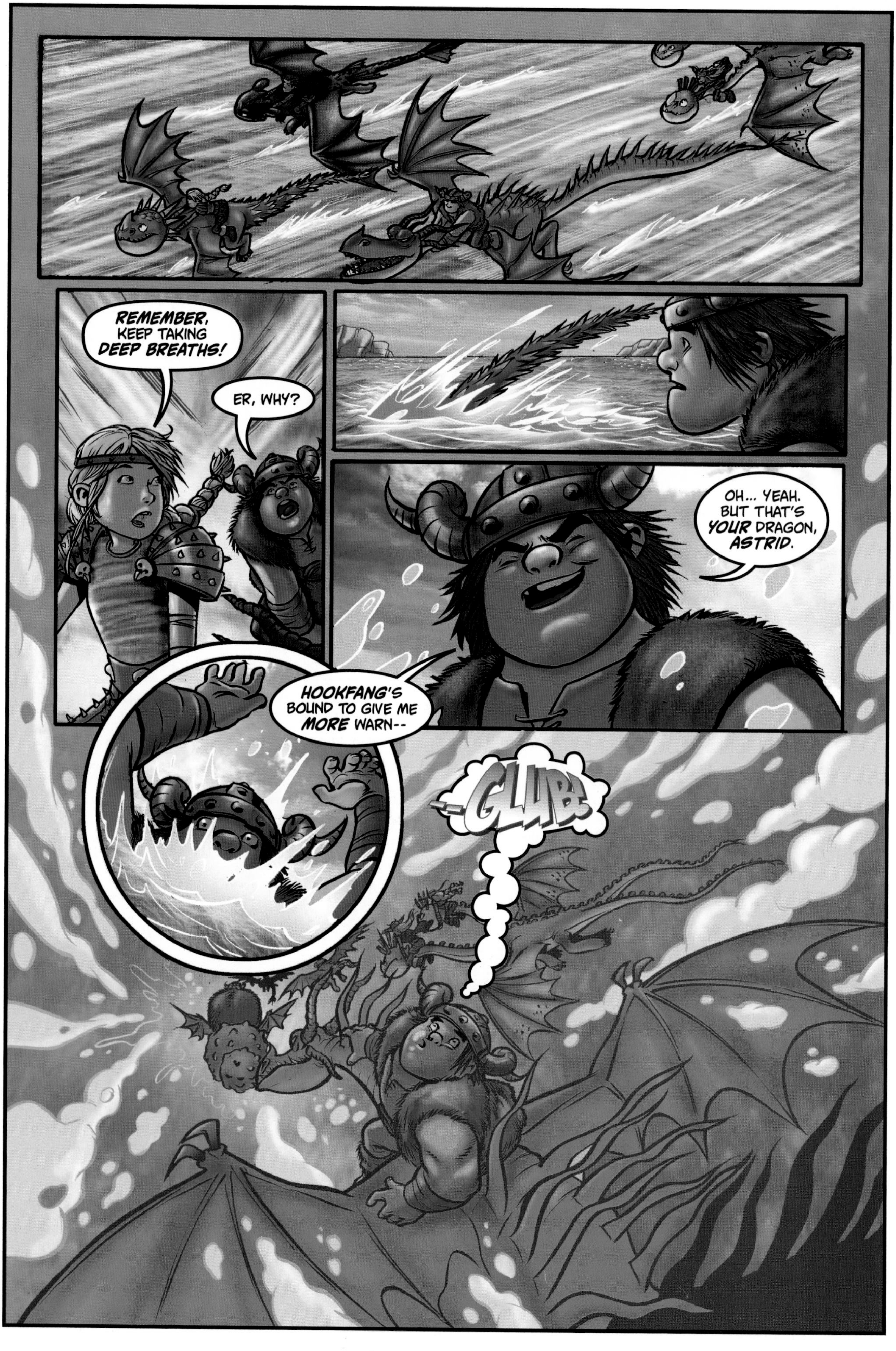
REMEMBER, KEEP TAKING DEEP BREATHS!
ER, WHY?
OH... YEAH. BUT THAT'S YOUR DRAGON, ASTRID.
HOOKFANG'S BOUND TO GIVE ME MORE WARN--
--GLUB!

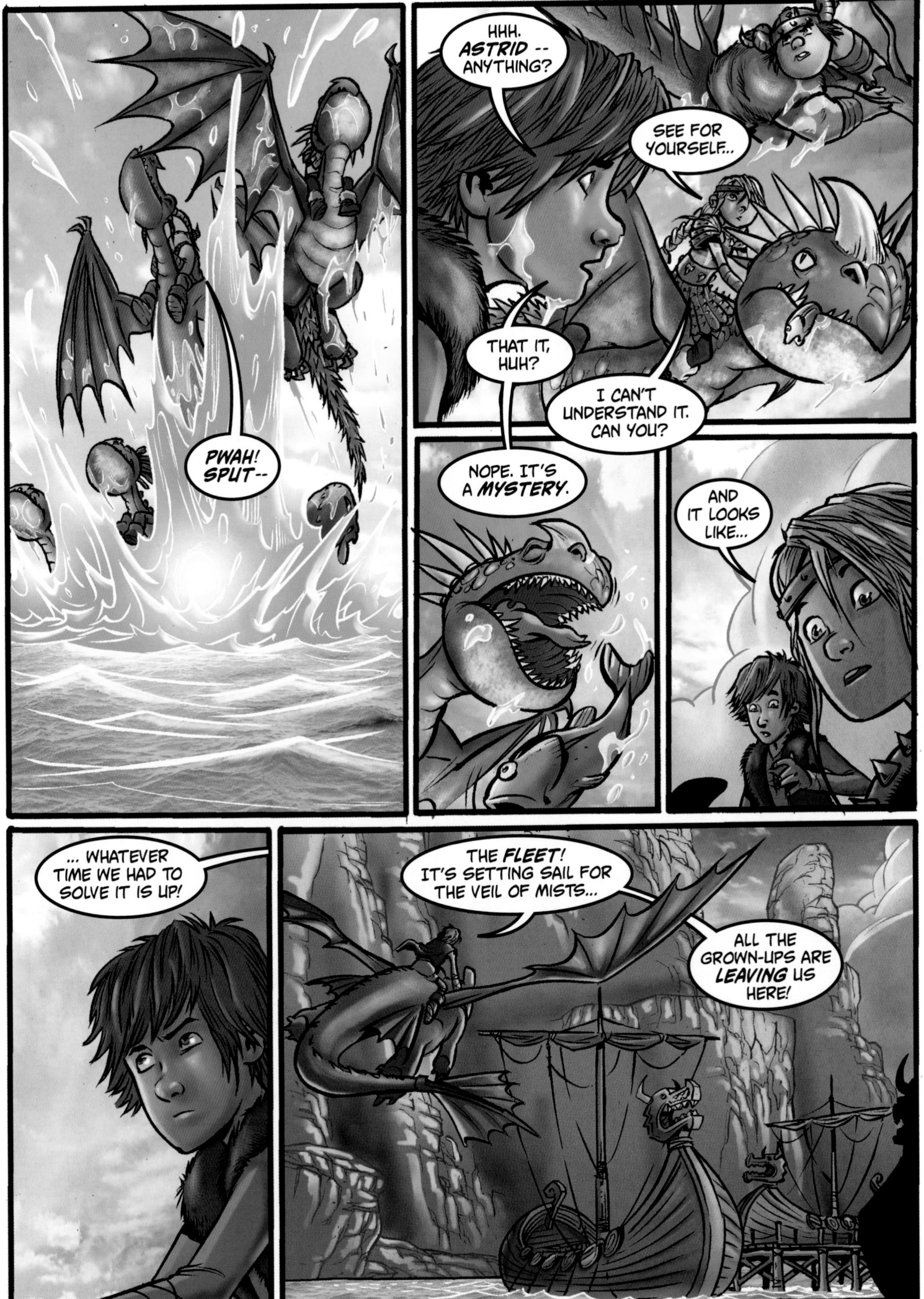
PWAH! SPUT--
HHH. ASTRID -- ANYTHING?
SEE FOR YOURSELF...
THAT IT, HUH?
I CAN'T UNDERSTAND IT. CAN YOU?
NOPE. IT'S A MYSTERY.
AND IT LOOKS LIKE...
... WHATEVER TIME WE HAD TO SOLVE IT IS UP!
THE FLEET! IT'S SETTING SAIL FOR THE VEIL OF MISTS...
ALL THE GROWN-UPS ARE LEAVING US HERE!

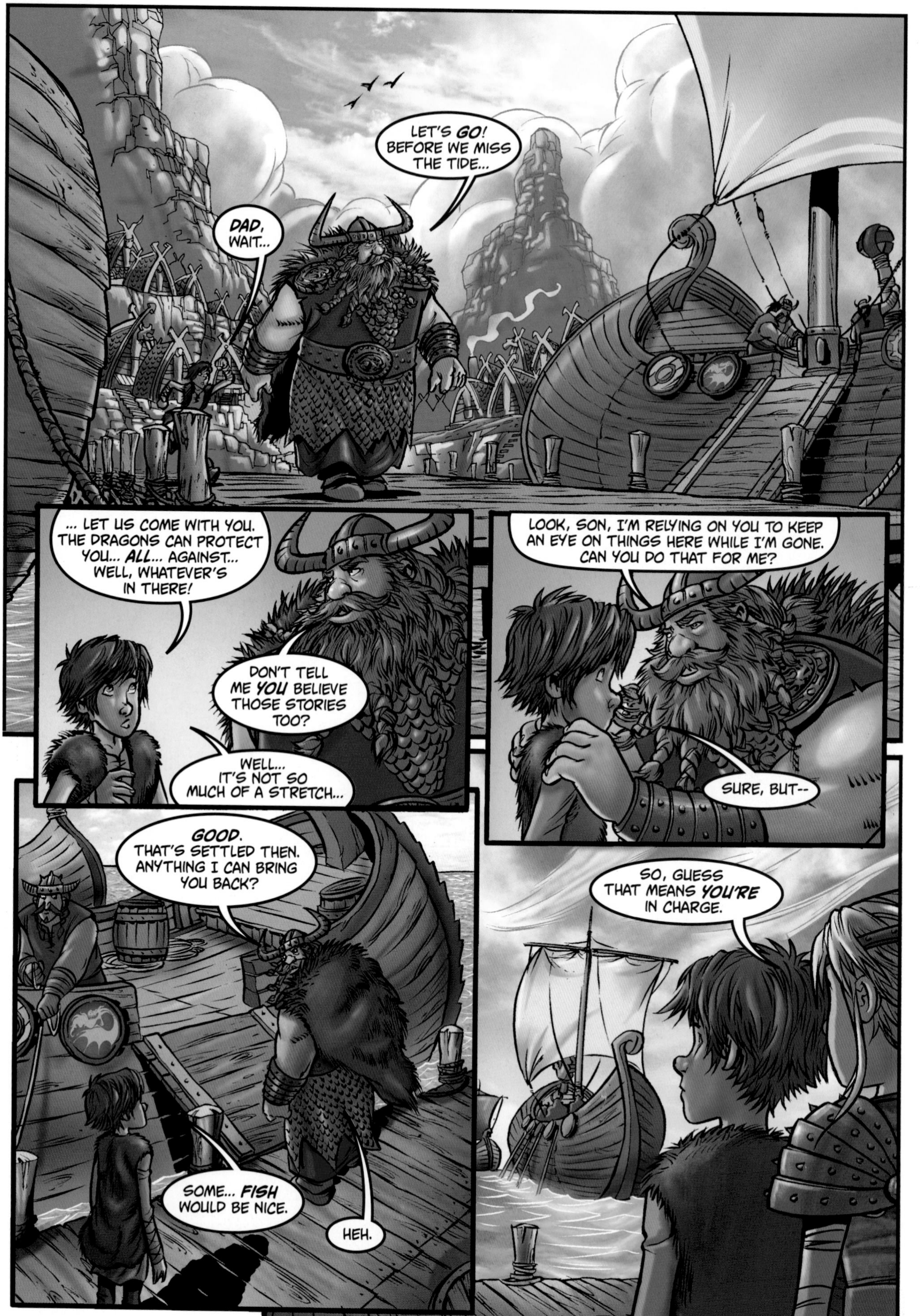
LET'S GO! BEFORE WE MISS THE TIDE...
DAD, WAIT...
... LET US COME WITH YOU. THE DRAGONS CAN PROTECT YOU... ALL... AGAINST... WELL, WHATEVER'S IN THERE!
DON'T TELL ME YOU BELIEVE THOSE STORIES TOO?
WELL... IT'S NOT SO MUCH OF A STRETCH...
LOOK, SON, I'M RELYING ON YOU TO KEEP AN EYE ON THINGS HERE WHILE I'M GONE. CAN YOU DO THAT FOR ME?
SURE, BUT--
GOOD. THAT'S SETTLED THEN. ANYTHING I CAN BRING YOU BACK?
SOME... FISH WOULD BE NICE.
HEH.
SO, GUESS THAT MEANS YOU'RE IN CHARGE.

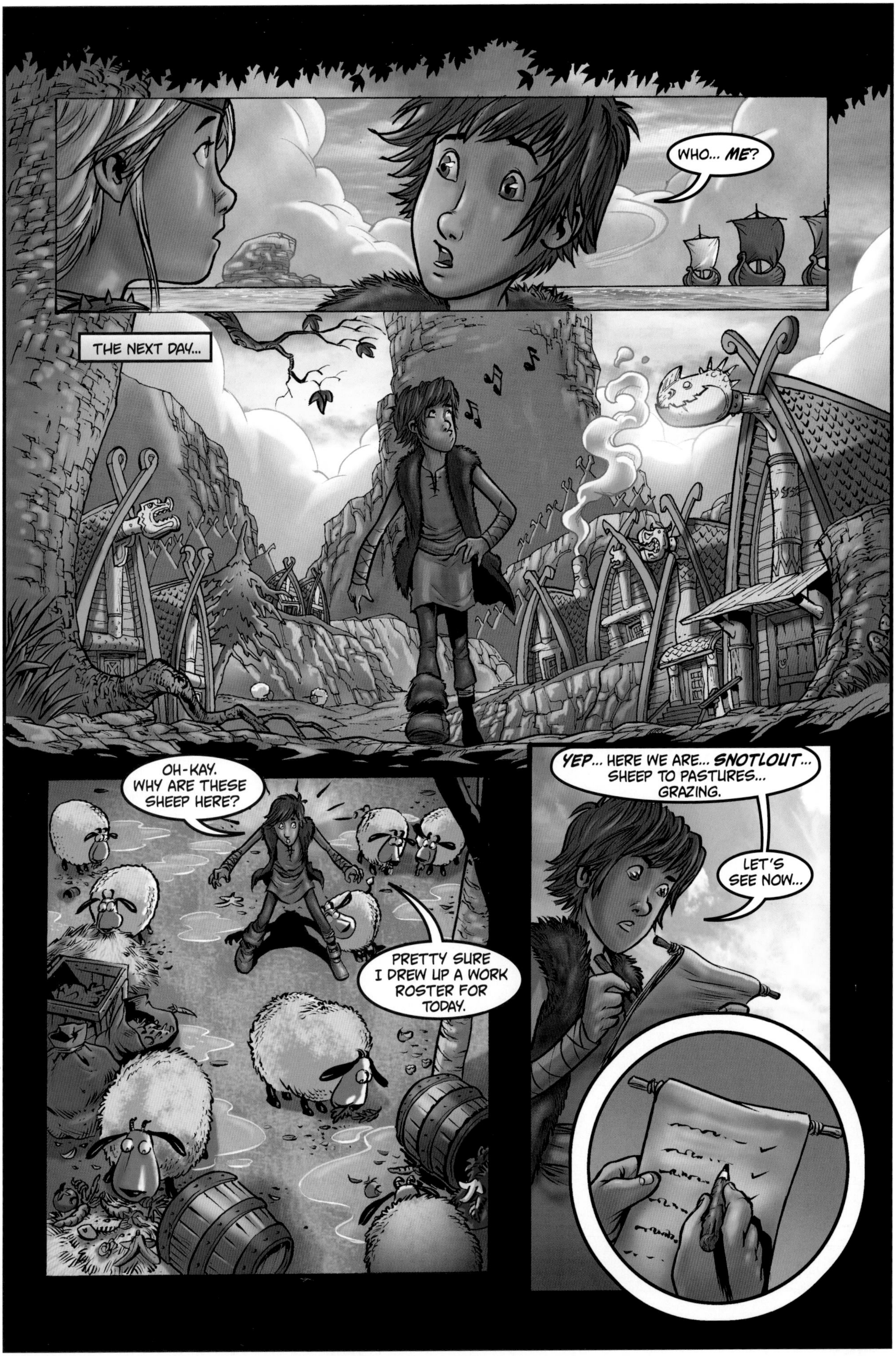
WHO... ME?
THE NEXT DAY...
OH-KAY. WHY ARE THESE SHEEP HERE?
PRETTY SURE I DREW UP A WORK ROSTER FOR TODAY.
YEP... HERE WE ARE... SNOTLOUT... SHEEP TO PASTURES... GRAZING.
LET'S SEE NOW...

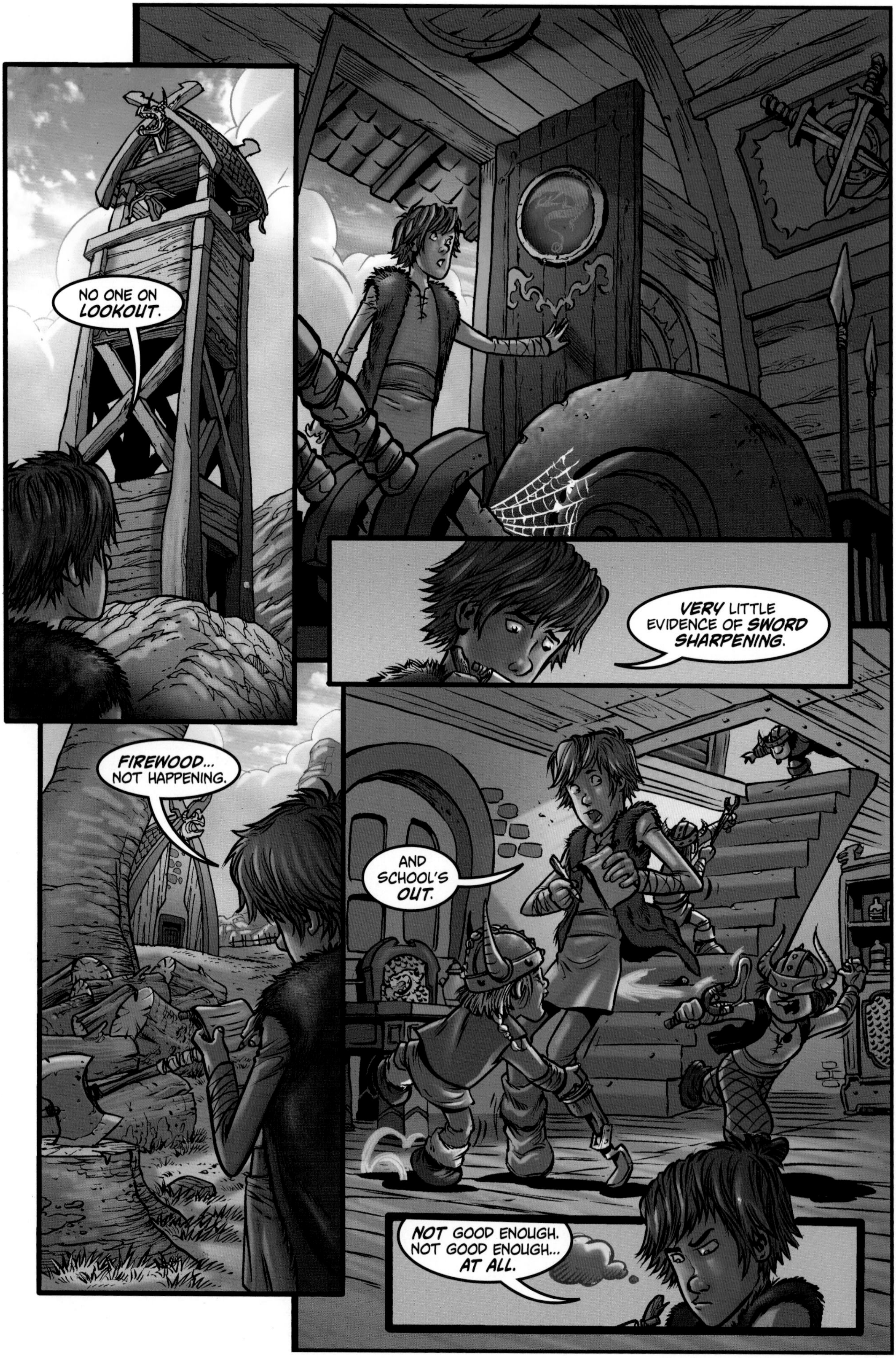
NO ONE ON LOOKOUT.
VERY LITTLE EVIDENCE OF SWORD SHARPENING.
FIREWOOD... NOT HAPPENING.
AND SCHOOL'S OUT.
NOT GOOD ENOUGH. NOT GOOD ENOUGH... AT ALL.

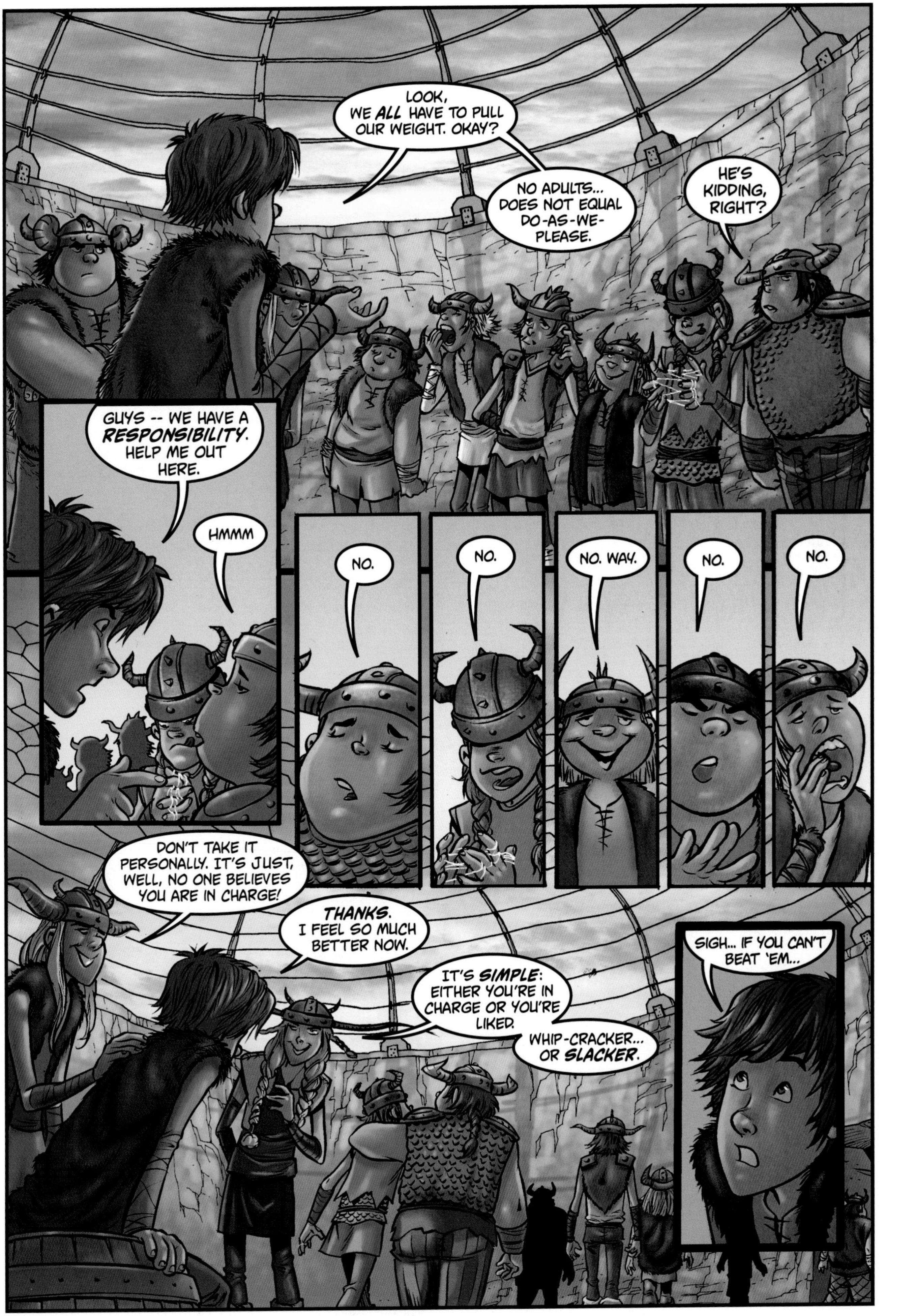
LOOK, WE ALL HAVE TO PULL OUR WEIGHT. OKAY?
NO ADULTS... DOES NOT EQUAL DO-AS-WE-PLEASE.
HE'S KIDDING, RIGHT?
GUYS -- WE HAVE A RESPONSIBILITY. HELP ME OUT HERE.
HMMM
NO.
NO.
NO. WAY.
NO.
NO.
DON'T TAKE IT PERSONALLY. IT'S JUST, WELL, NO ONE BELIEVES YOU ARE IN CHARGE!
THANKS. I FEEL SO MUCH BETTER NOW.
IT'S SIMPLE: EITHER YOU'RE IN CHARGE OR YOU'RE LIKED.
WHIP-CRACKER... OR SLACKER.
SIGH... IF YOU CAN'T BEAT 'EM...

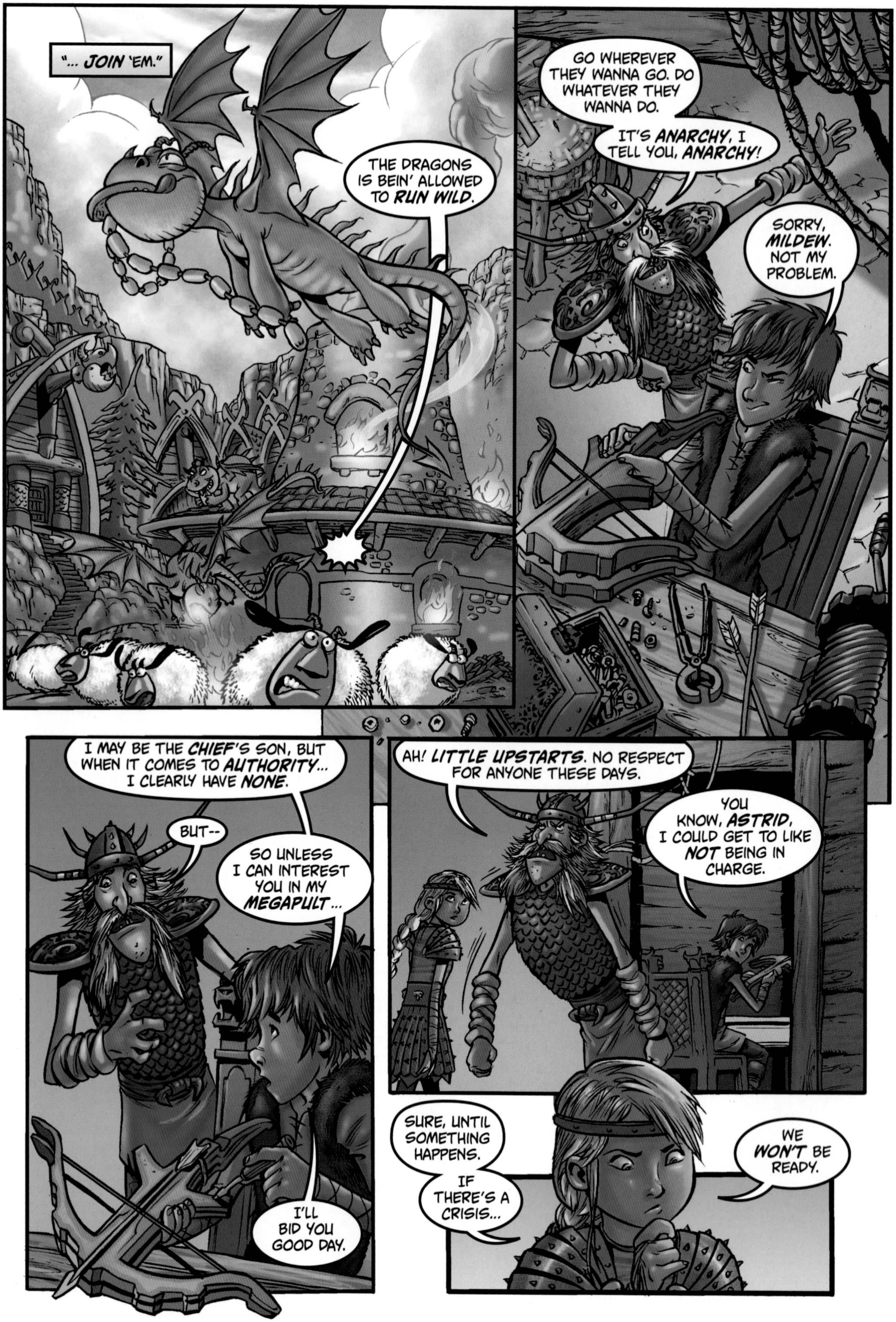
"... JOIN 'EM."
THE DRAGONS IS BEIN' ALLOWED TO RUN WILD.
GO WHEREVER THEY WANNA GO. DO WHATEVER THEY WANNA DO.
IT'S ANARCHY, I TELL YOU, ANARCHY!
SORRY, MILDEW. NOT MY PROBLEM.
I MAY BE THE CHIEF'S SON, BUT WHEN IT COMES TO AUTHORITY... I CLEARLY HAVE NONE.
BUT--
SO UNLESS I CAN INTEREST YOU IN MY MEGAPULT...
I'LL BID YOU GOOD DAY.
AH! LITTLE UPSTARTS. NO RESPECT FOR ANYONE THESE DAYS.
YOU KNOW, ASTRID, I COULD GET TO LIKE NOT BEING IN CHARGE.
SURE, UNTIL SOMETHING HAPPENS.
IF THERE'S A CRISIS...
WE WON'T BE READY.

CHAPTER TWO

In which an old enemy appears...
Hiccup has a problem or two... And the
Veil of Mists is entered...

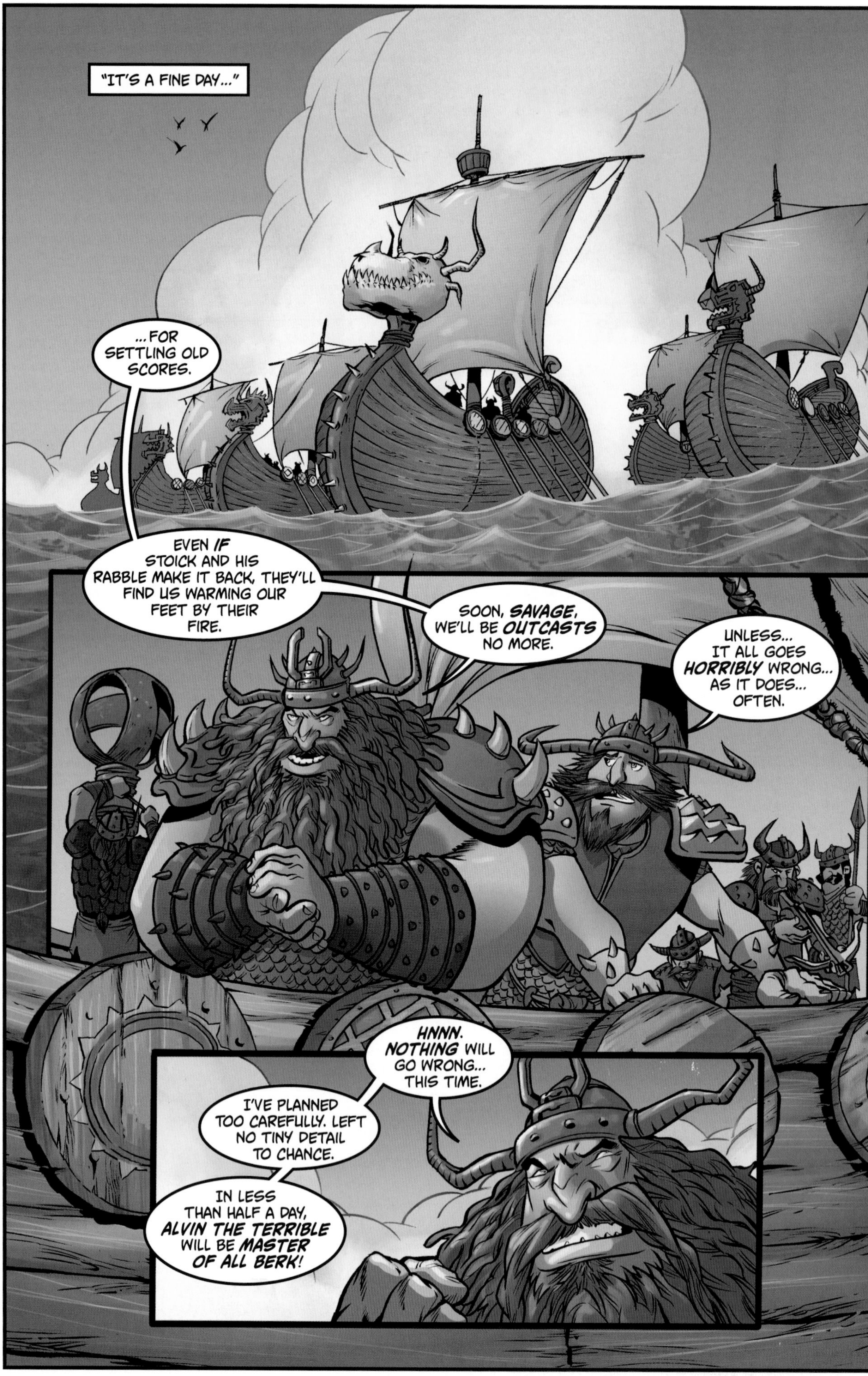
"IT'S A FINE DAY..."
...FOR SETTLING OLD SCORES.
EVEN *IF* STOICK AND HIS RABBLE MAKE IT BACK, THEY'LL FIND US WARMING OUR FEET BY THEIR FIRE.
SOON, *SAVAGE*, WE'LL BE *OUTCASTS* NO MORE.
UNLESS... IT ALL GOES *HORRIBLY* WRONG... AS IT DOES... OFTEN.
HNNN. NOTHING WILL GO WRONG... THIS TIME.
I'VE PLANNED TOO CAREFULLY. LEFT NO TINY DETAIL TO CHANCE.
IN LESS THAN HALF A DAY, *ALVIN THE TERRIBLE* WILL BE *MASTER OF ALL BERK*!

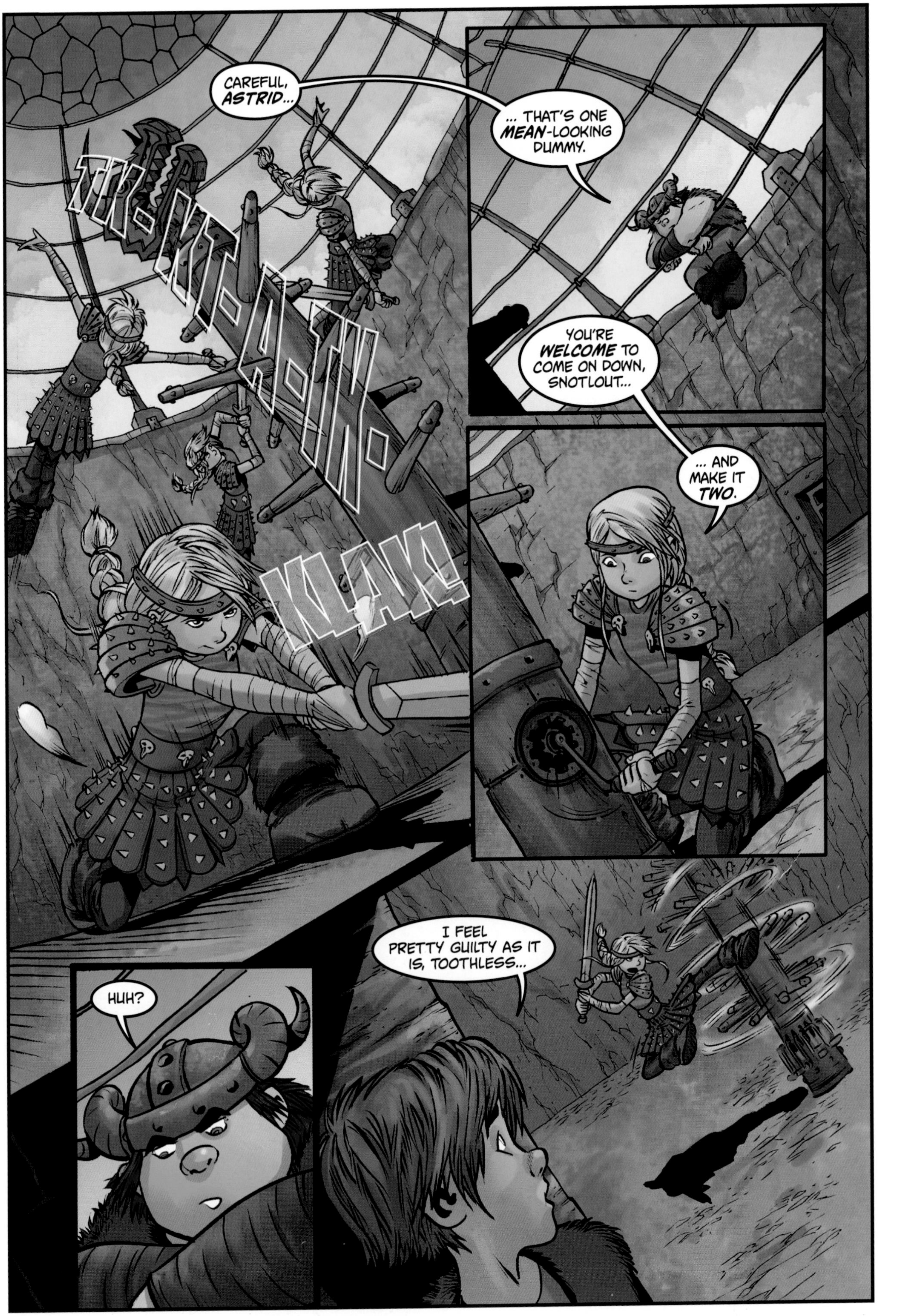
CAREFUL, ASTRID...
... THAT'S ONE MEAN-LOOKING DUMMY.
TK-KT-A-TK-
KLAK!
YOU'RE WELCOME TO COME ON DOWN, SNOTLOUT...
... AND MAKE IT TWO.
I FEEL PRETTY GUILTY AS IT IS, TOOTHLESS...
HUH?

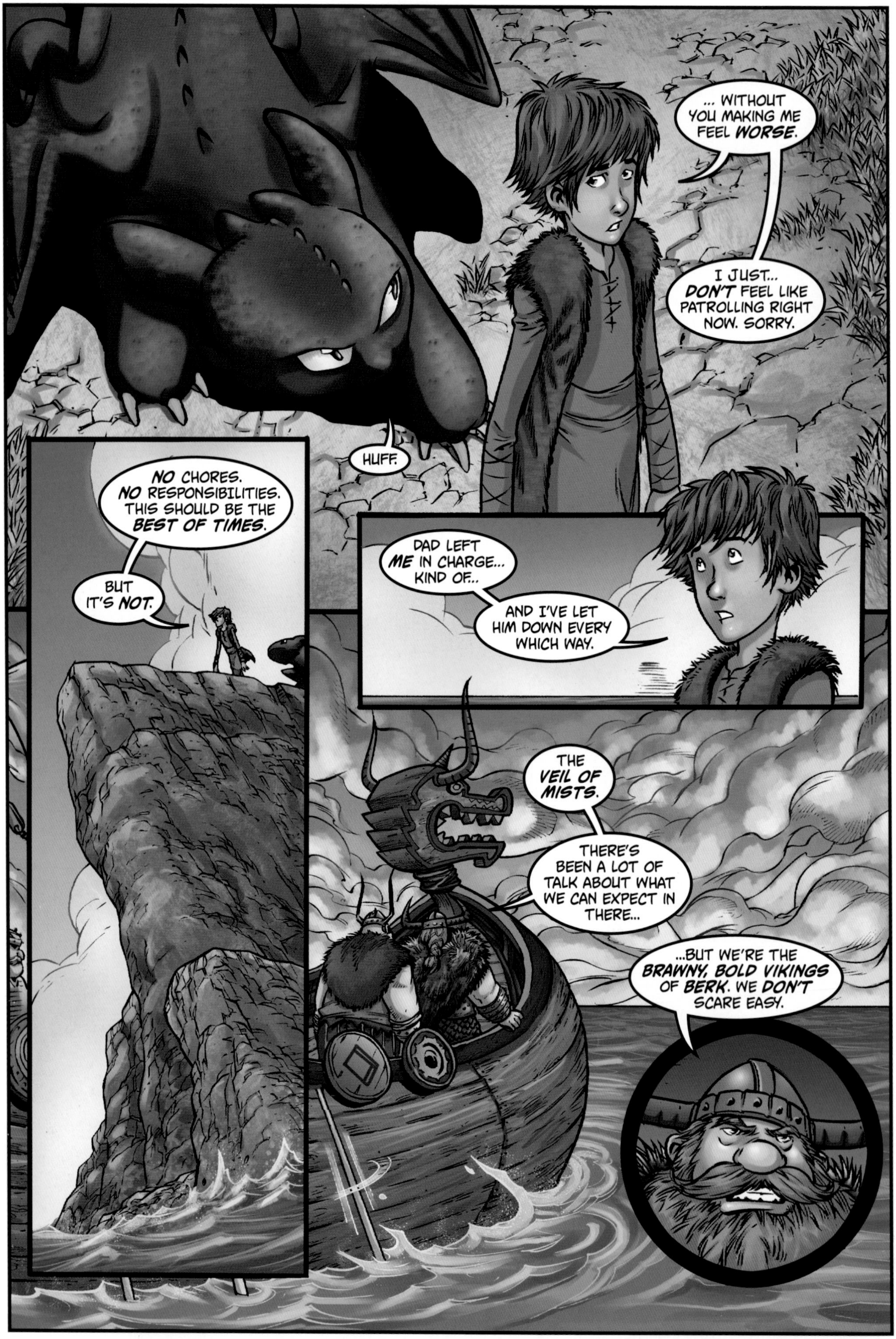
... WITHOUT YOU MAKING ME FEEL *WORSE*.
I JUST... *DON'T* FEEL LIKE PATROLLING RIGHT NOW. SORRY.
HUFF.
NO CHORES. *NO* RESPONSIBILITIES. THIS SHOULD BE THE *BEST OF TIMES*.
BUT IT'S *NOT*.
DAD LEFT *ME* IN CHARGE... KIND OF...
AND I'VE LET HIM DOWN EVERY WHICH WAY.
THE *VEIL OF MISTS*.
THERE'S BEEN A LOT OF TALK ABOUT WHAT WE CAN EXPECT IN THERE...
...BUT WE'RE THE *BRAWNY, BOLD VIKINGS* OF *BERK*. WE *DON'T* SCARE EASY.

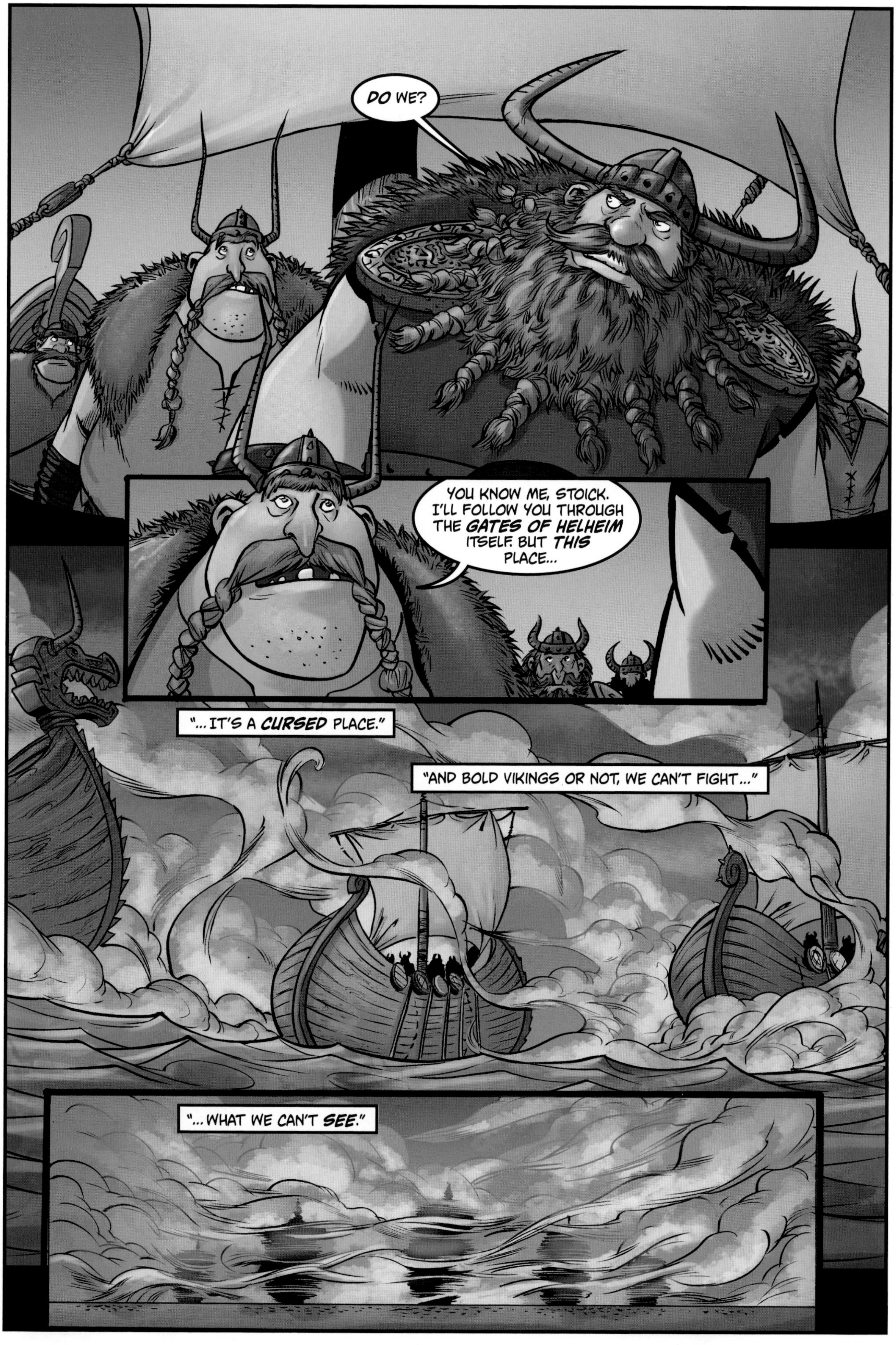
DO WE?
YOU KNOW ME, STOICK. I'LL FOLLOW YOU THROUGH THE GATES OF HELHEIM ITSELF. BUT THIS PLACE...
"... IT'S A CURSED PLACE."
"AND BOLD VIKINGS OR NOT, WE CAN'T FIGHT..."
"... WHAT WE CAN'T SEE."

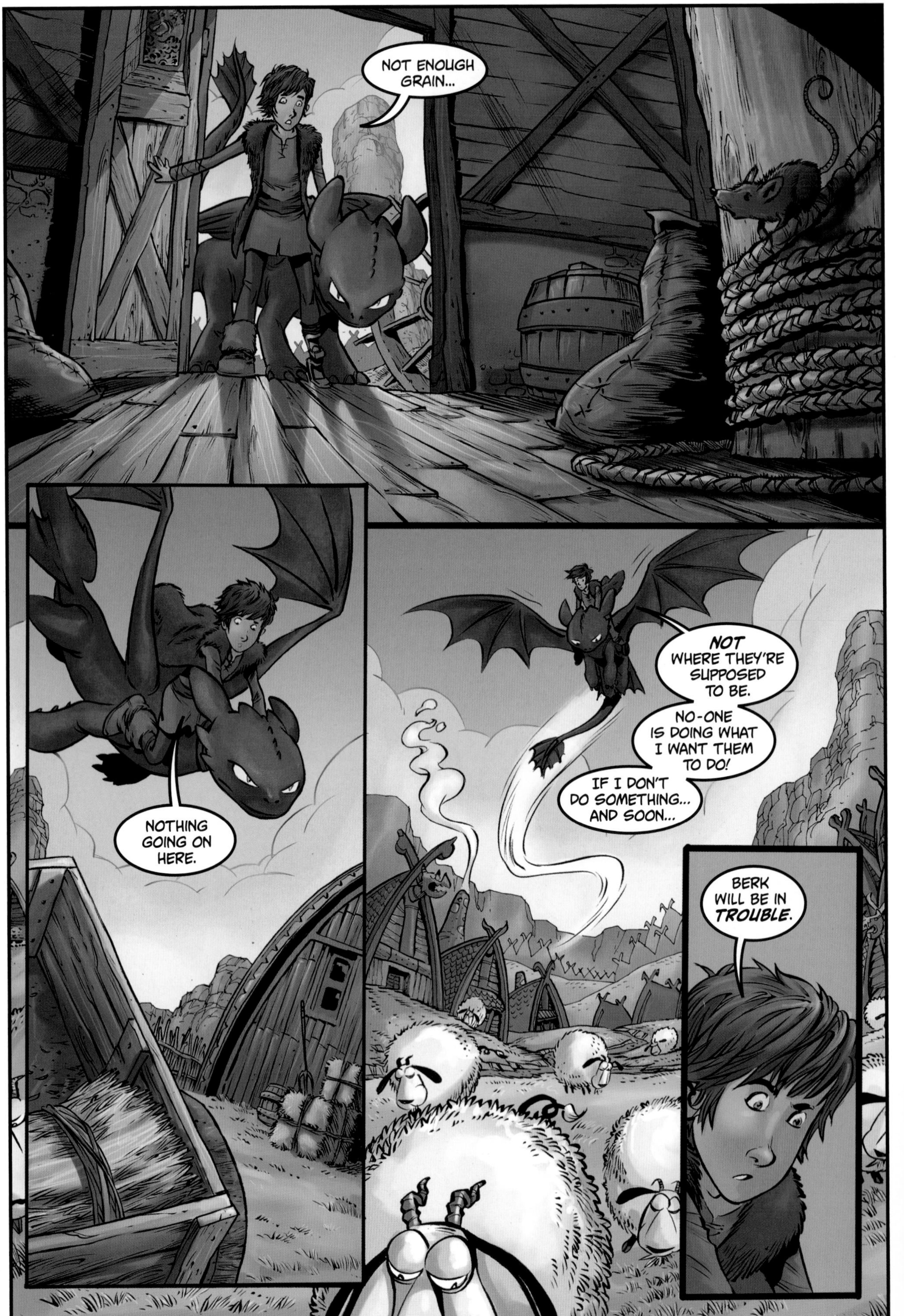

NOT ENOUGH GRAIN...
NOTHING GOING ON HERE.
NOT WHERE THEY'RE SUPPOSED TO BE.
NO-ONE IS DOING WHAT I WANT THEM TO DO!
IF I DON'T DO SOMETHING... AND SOON...
BERK WILL BE IN TROUBLE.

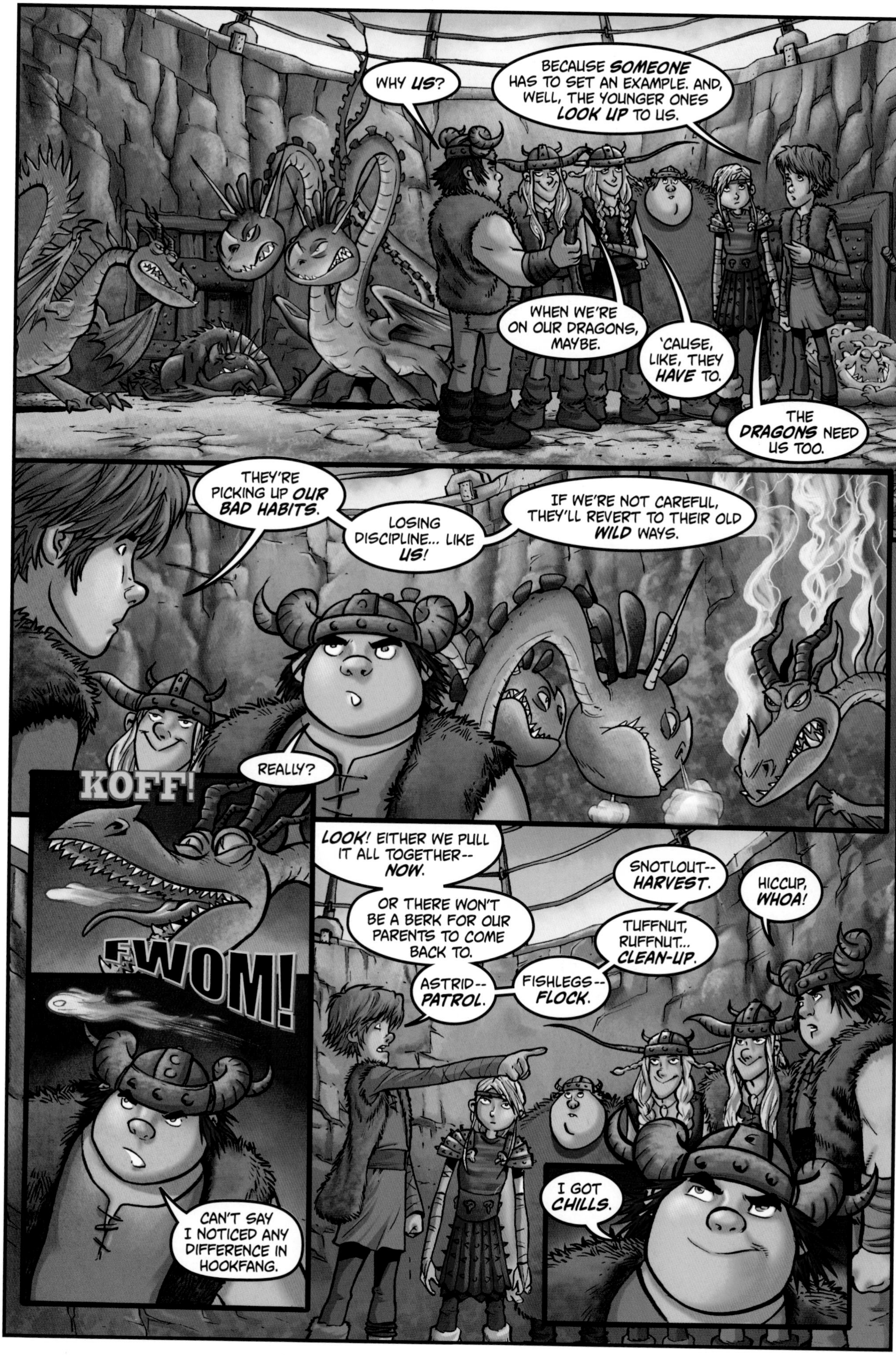
WHY US?
BECAUSE SOMEONE HAS TO SET AN EXAMPLE. AND, WELL, THE YOUNGER ONES LOOK UP TO US.
WHEN WE'RE ON OUR DRAGONS, MAYBE.
'CAUSE, LIKE, THEY HAVE TO.
THE DRAGONS NEED US TOO.
THEY'RE PICKING UP OUR BAD HABITS.
LOSING DISCIPLINE... LIKE US!
IF WE'RE NOT CAREFUL, THEY'LL REVERT TO THEIR OLD WILD WAYS.
REALLY?
KOFF!
FWOM!
CAN'T SAY I NOTICED ANY DIFFERENCE IN HOOKFANG.
LOOK! EITHER WE PULL IT ALL TOGETHER-- NOW.
OR THERE WON'T BE A BERK FOR OUR PARENTS TO COME BACK TO.
ASTRID-- PATROL.
FISHLEGS-- FLOCK.
TUFFNUT, RUFFNUT... CLEAN-UP.
SNOTLOUT-- HARVEST.
HICCUP, WHOA!
I GOT CHILLS.

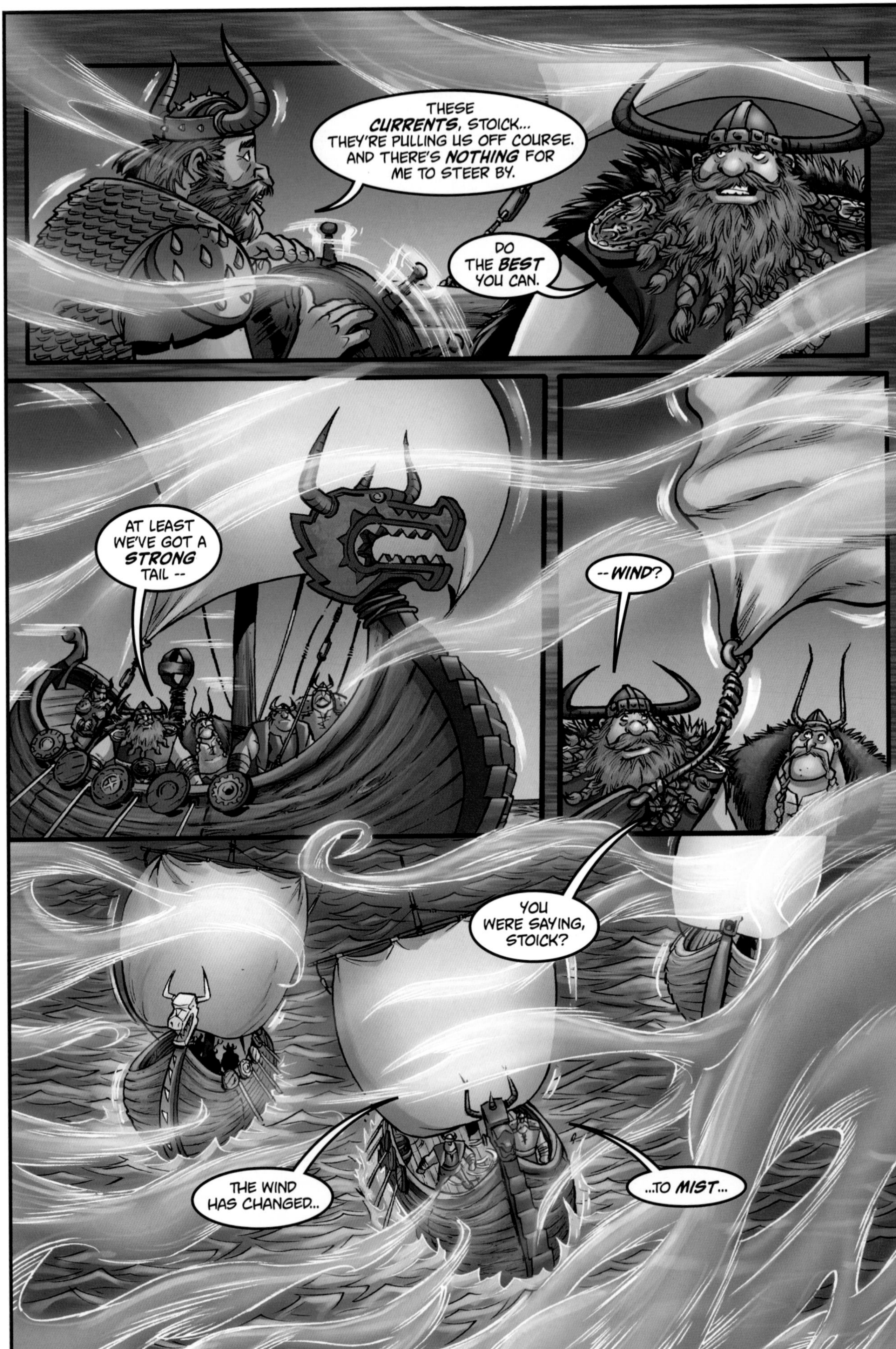
THESE CURRENTS, STOICK... THEY'RE PULLING US OFF COURSE. AND THERE'S NOTHING FOR ME TO STEER BY.
DO THE BEST YOU CAN.
AT LEAST WE'VE GOT A STRONG TAIL --
--WIND?
YOU WERE SAYING, STOICK?
THE WIND HAS CHANGED...
...TO MIST...

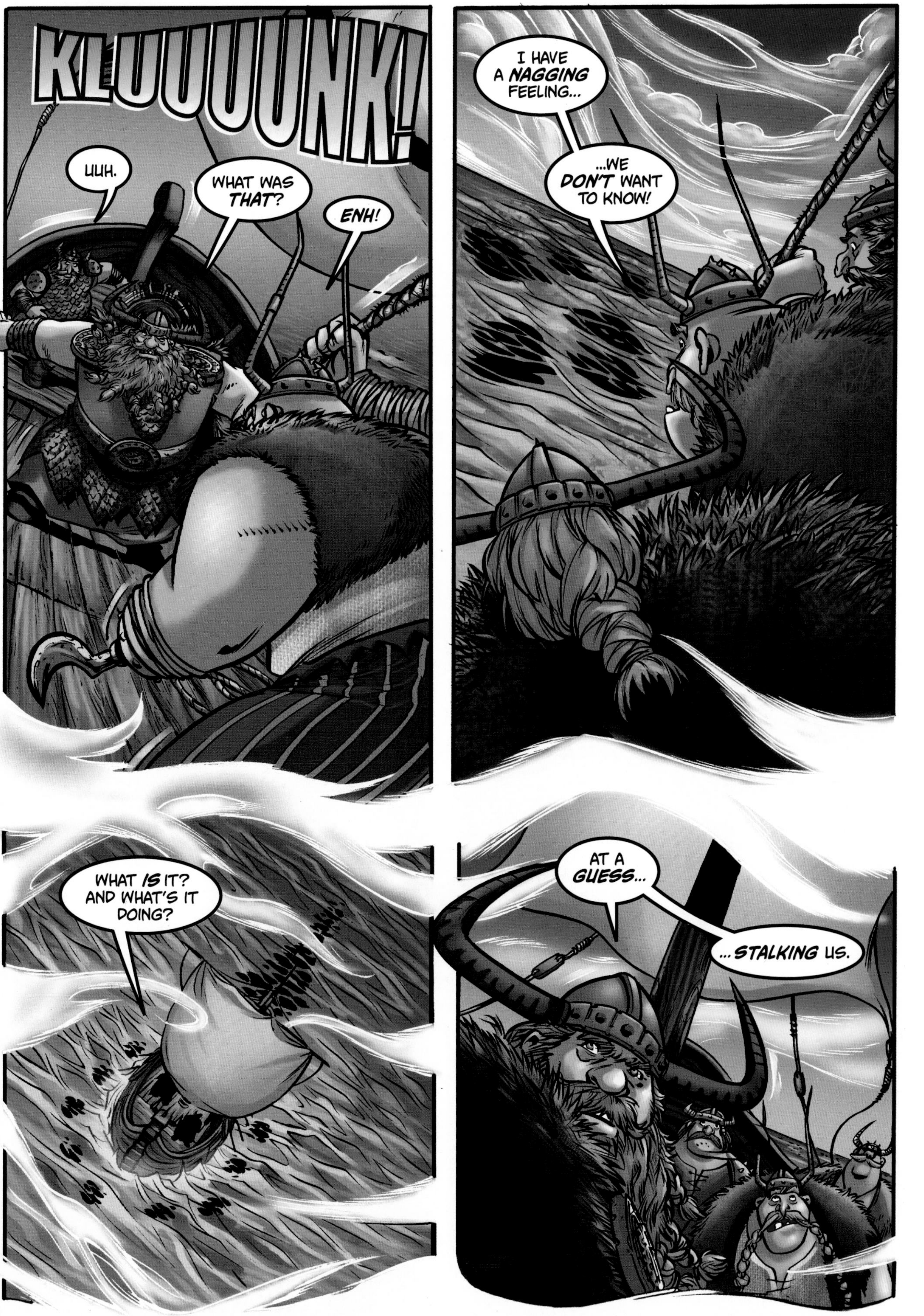
KLUUUUNK!
UUH.
WHAT WAS THAT?
ENH!
I HAVE A NAGGING FEELING...
...WE DON'T WANT TO KNOW!
WHAT IS IT? AND WHAT'S IT DOING?
AT A GUESS...
...STALKING US.

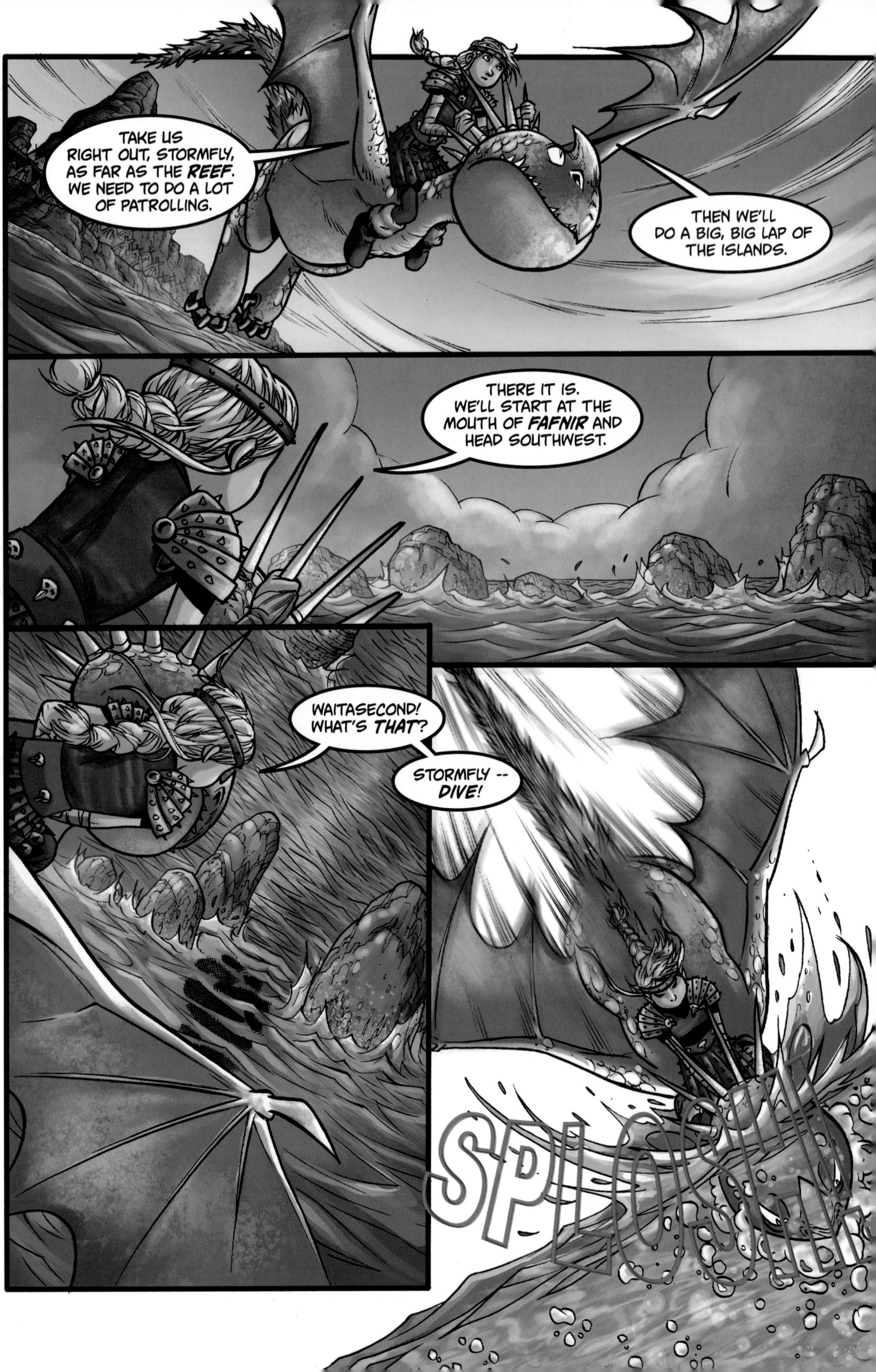
TAKE US RIGHT OUT, STORMFLY, AS FAR AS THE **REEF**. WE NEED TO DO A LOT OF PATROLLING.
THEN WE'LL DO A BIG, BIG LAP OF THE ISLANDS.
THERE IT IS. WE'LL START AT THE MOUTH OF **FAFNIR** AND HEAD SOUTHWEST.
WAITASECOND! WHAT'S **THAT**?
STORMFLY -- **DIVE**!
SPLOSHH!

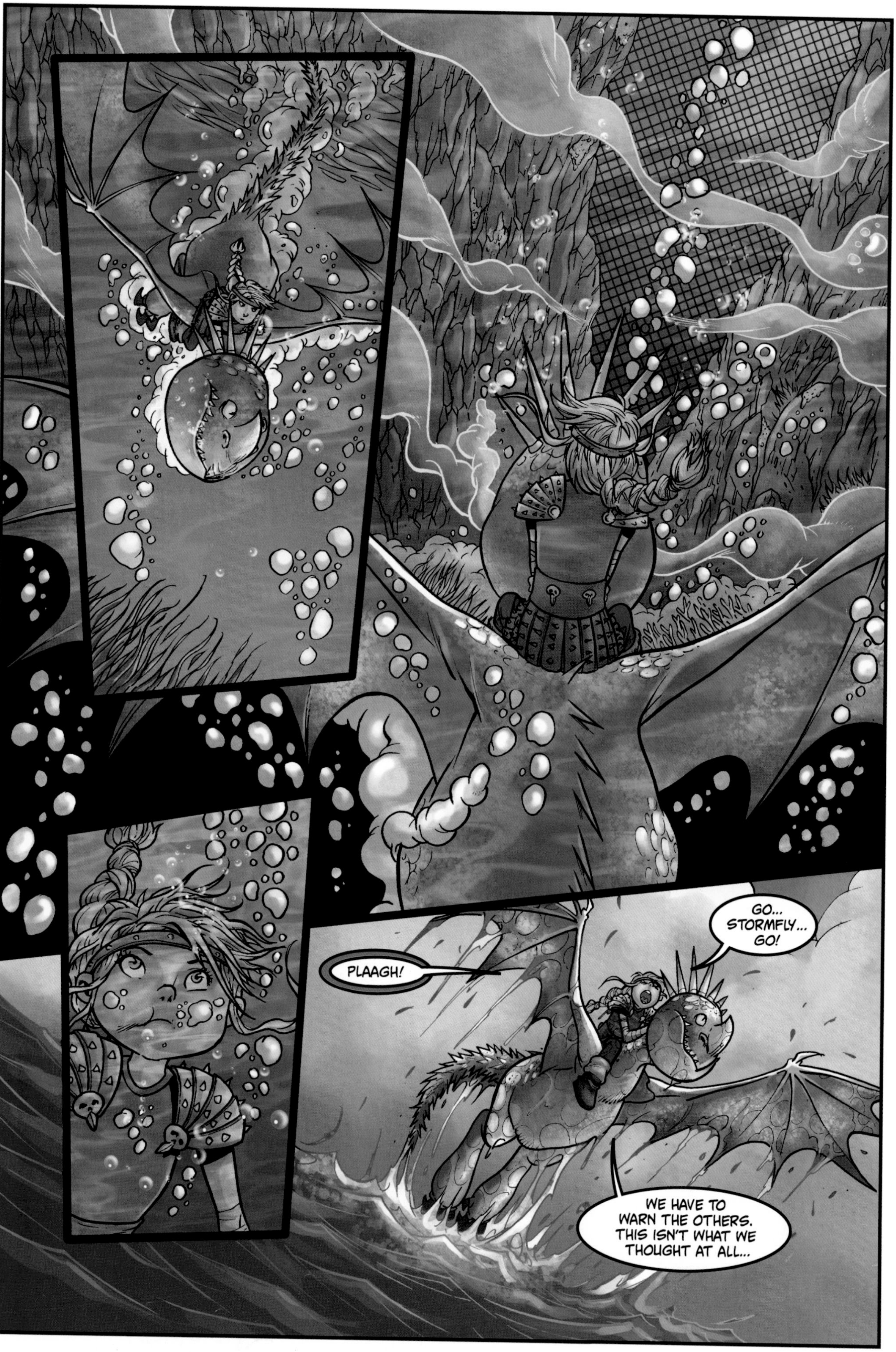

GO... STORMFLY... GO!
PLAAGH!
WE HAVE TO WARN THE OTHERS. THIS ISN'T WHAT WE THOUGHT AT ALL...

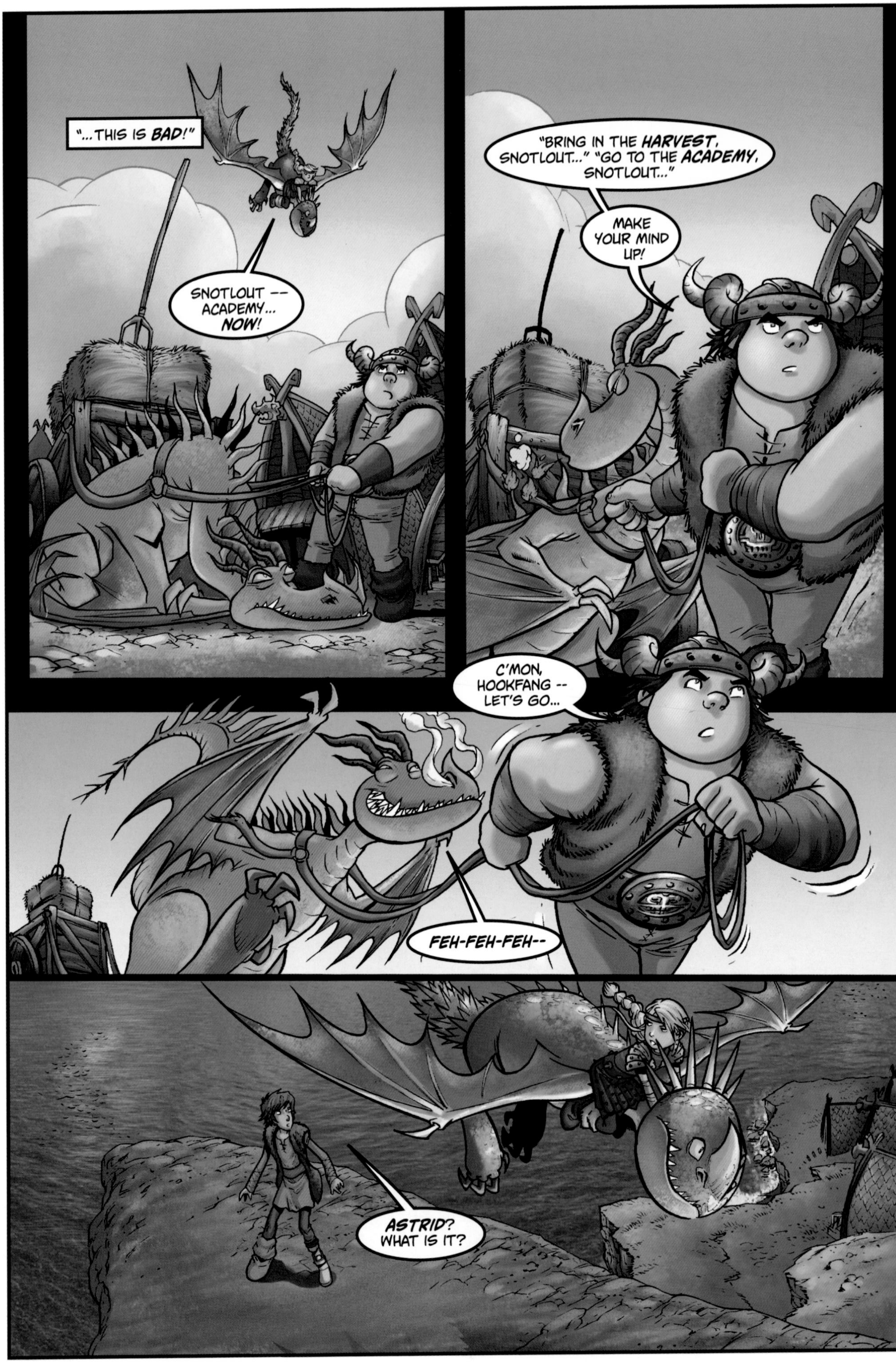
"...THIS IS *BAD!*"
SNOTLOUT -- ACADEMY... *NOW!*
"BRING IN THE *HARVEST*, SNOTLOUT..." "GO TO THE *ACADEMY*, SNOTLOUT..."
MAKE YOUR MIND UP!
C'MON, HOOKFANG -- LET'S GO...
FEH-FEH-FEH--
ASTRID? WHAT IS IT?

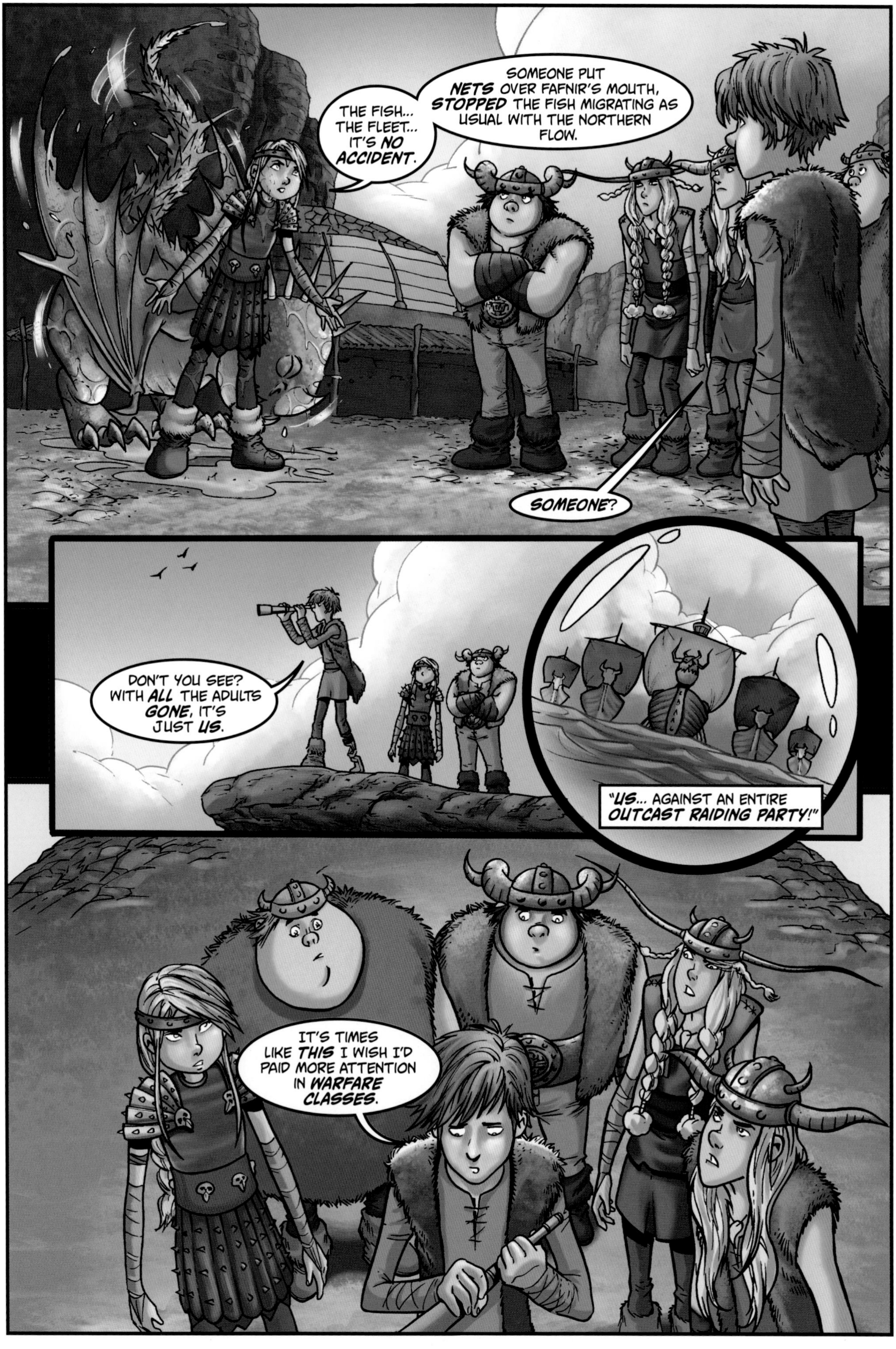
THE FISH... THE FLEET... IT'S **NO ACCIDENT**.
SOMEONE PUT **NETS** OVER FAFNIR'S MOUTH, **STOPPED** THE FISH MIGRATING AS USUAL WITH THE NORTHERN FLOW.
SOMEONE?
DON'T YOU SEE? WITH **ALL** THE ADULTS **GONE**, IT'S JUST **US**.
"**US**... AGAINST AN ENTIRE **OUTCAST RAIDING PARTY**!"
IT'S TIMES LIKE **THIS** I WISH I'D PAID MORE ATTENTION IN **WARFARE CLASSES**.

CHAPTER THREE

In which danger lurks in the Veil of Mists...
Hiccup has a plan... And a ship is attacked by
something very, very big...

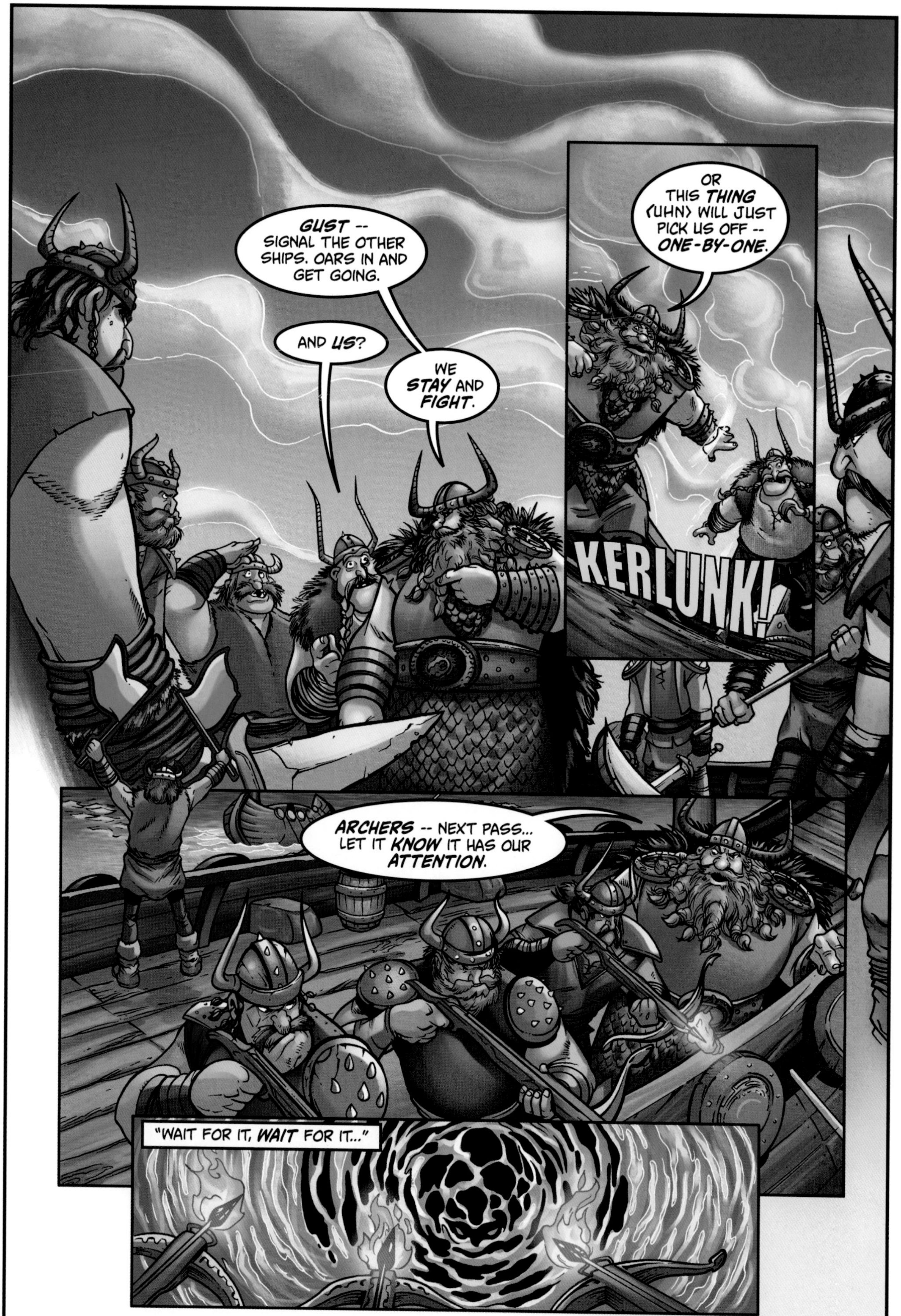

GUST -- SIGNAL THE OTHER SHIPS. OARS IN AND GET GOING.
AND US?
WE STAY AND FIGHT.
OR THIS THING (UHN) WILL JUST PICK US OFF -- ONE-BY-ONE.
KERLUNK!
ARCHERS -- NEXT PASS... LET IT KNOW IT HAS OUR ATTENTION.
"WAIT FOR IT, WAIT FOR IT..."

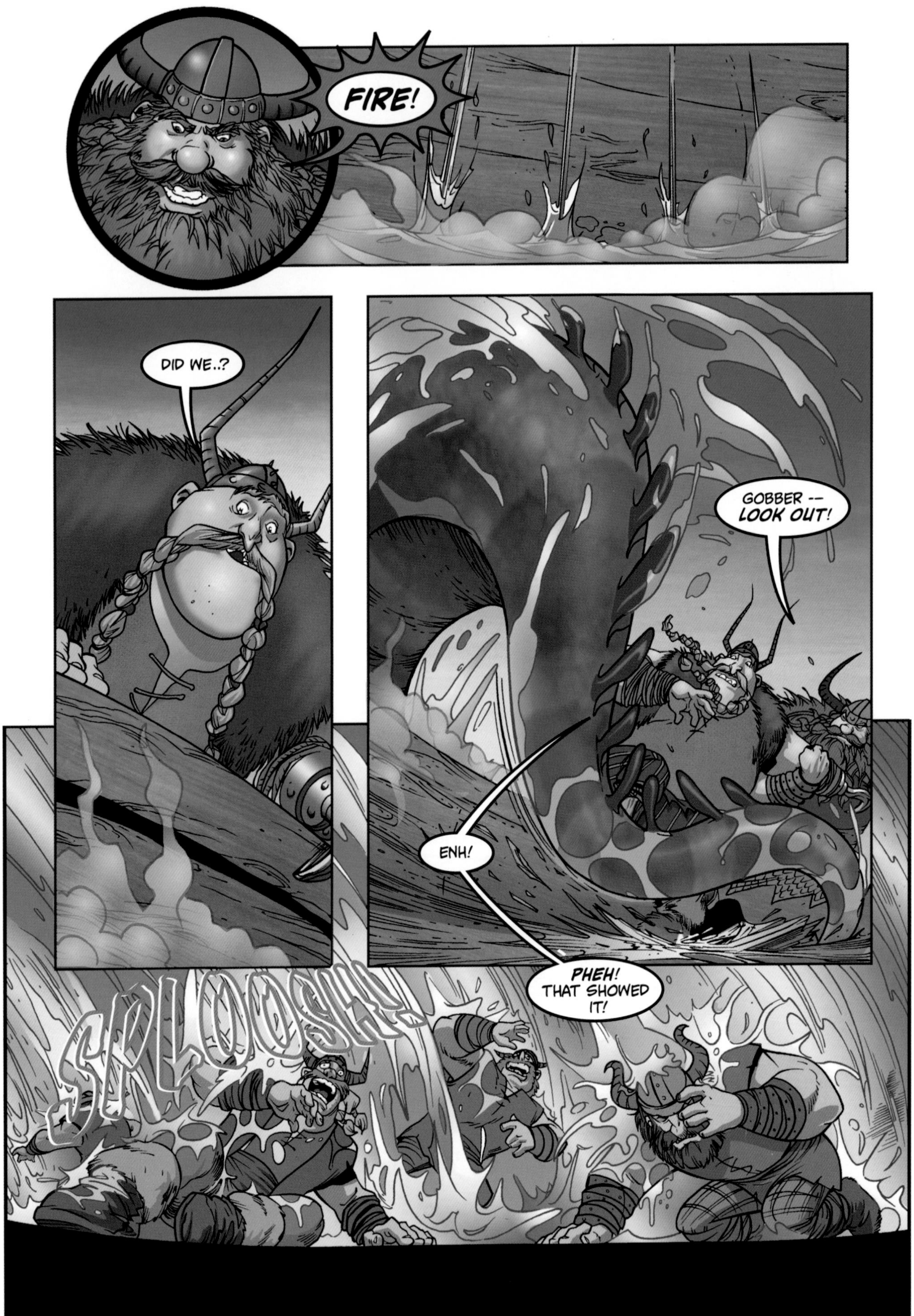
FIRE!
DID WE..?
GOBBER -- LOOK OUT!
ENH!
PHEH! THAT SHOWED IT!
SPLOOSH!

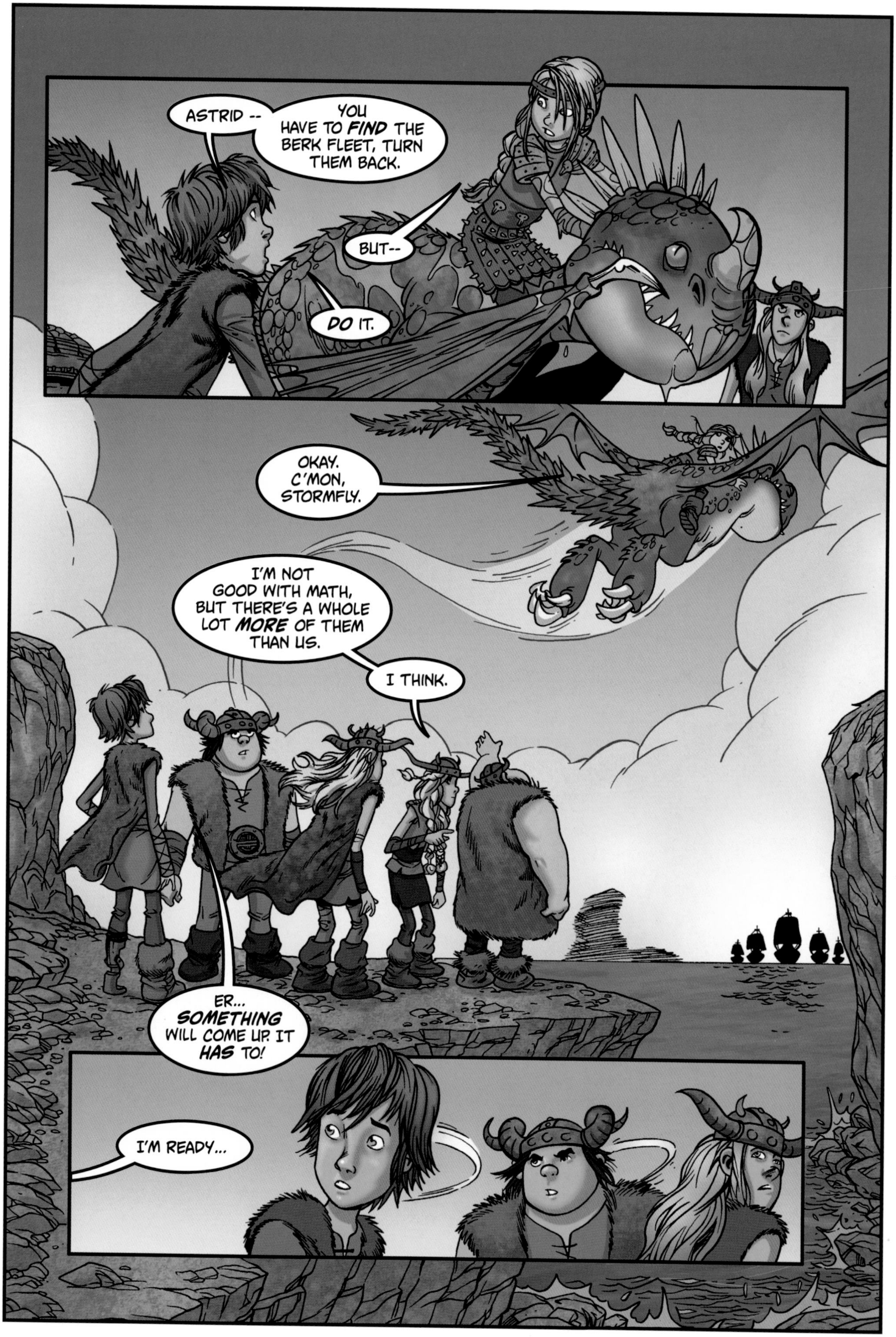
ASTRID --
YOU HAVE TO FIND THE BERK FLEET, TURN THEM BACK.
BUT--
DO IT.
OKAY. C'MON, STORMFLY.
I'M NOT GOOD WITH MATH, BUT THERE'S A WHOLE LOT MORE OF THEM THAN US.
I THINK.
ER... SOMETHING WILL COME UP. IT HAS TO!
I'M READY...

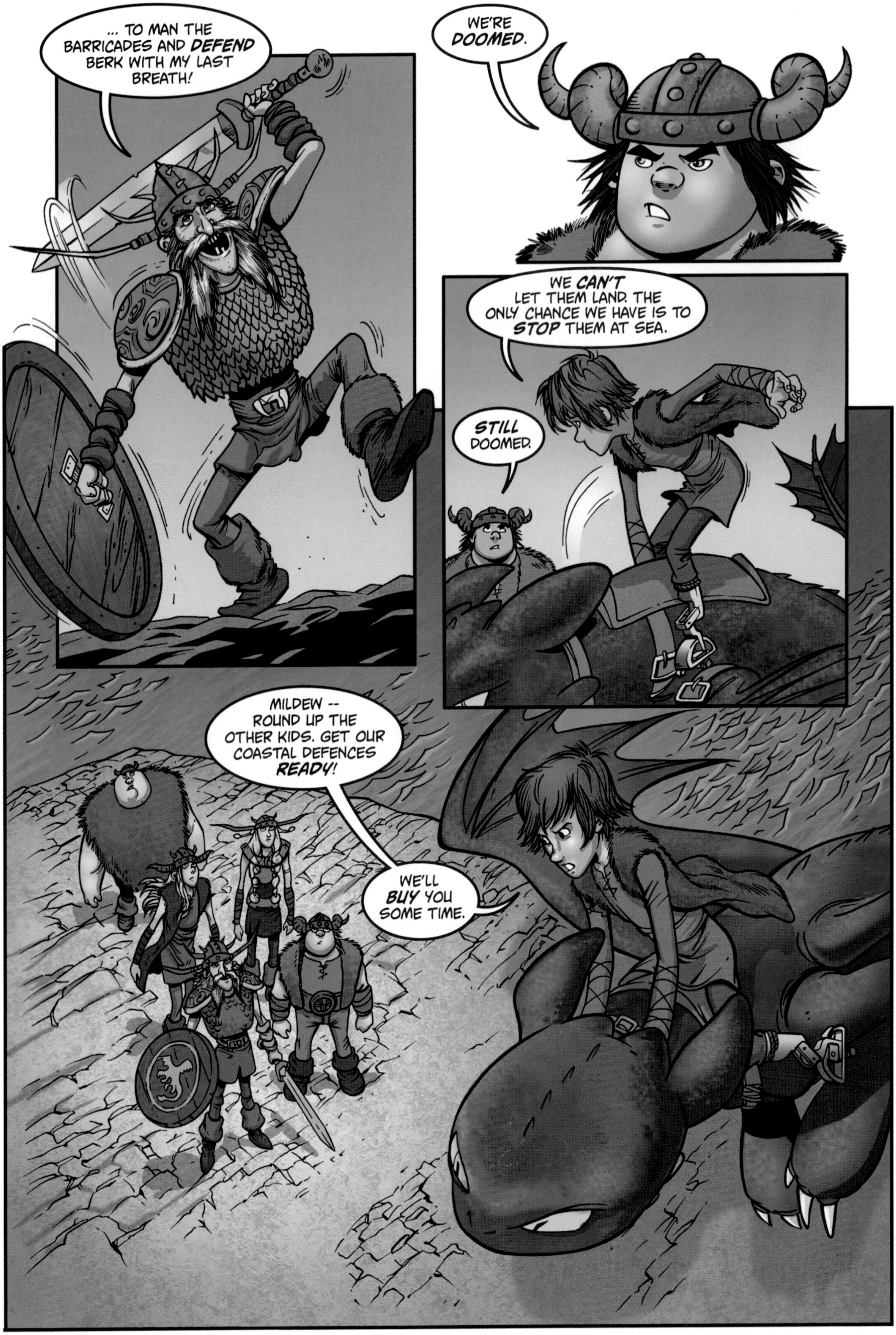
... TO MAN THE BARRICADES AND DEFEND BERK WITH MY LAST BREATH!
WE'RE DOOMED.
WE CAN'T LET THEM LAND. THE ONLY CHANCE WE HAVE IS TO STOP THEM AT SEA.
STILL DOOMED.
MILDEW -- ROUND UP THE OTHER KIDS. GET OUR COASTAL DEFENCES READY!
WE'LL BUY YOU SOME TIME.

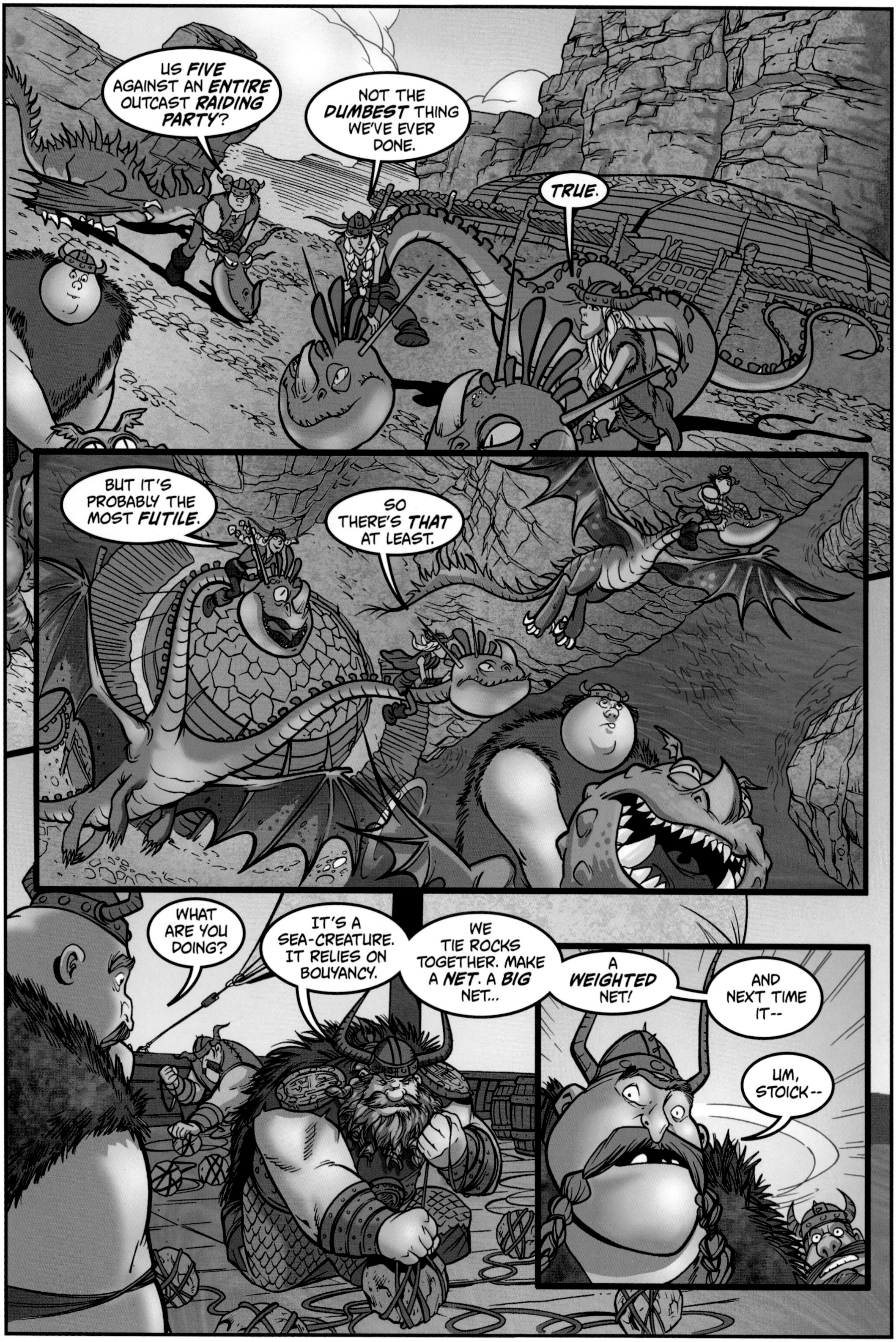
US FIVE AGAINST AN ENTIRE OUTCAST RAIDING PARTY?
NOT THE DUMBEST THING WE'VE EVER DONE.
TRUE.
BUT IT'S PROBABLY THE MOST FUTILE.
SO THERE'S THAT AT LEAST.
WHAT ARE YOU DOING?
IT'S A SEA-CREATURE. IT RELIES ON BOUYANCY.
WE TIE ROCKS TOGETHER. MAKE A NET. A BIG NET...
A WEIGHTED NET!
AND NEXT TIME IT--
UM, STOICK--

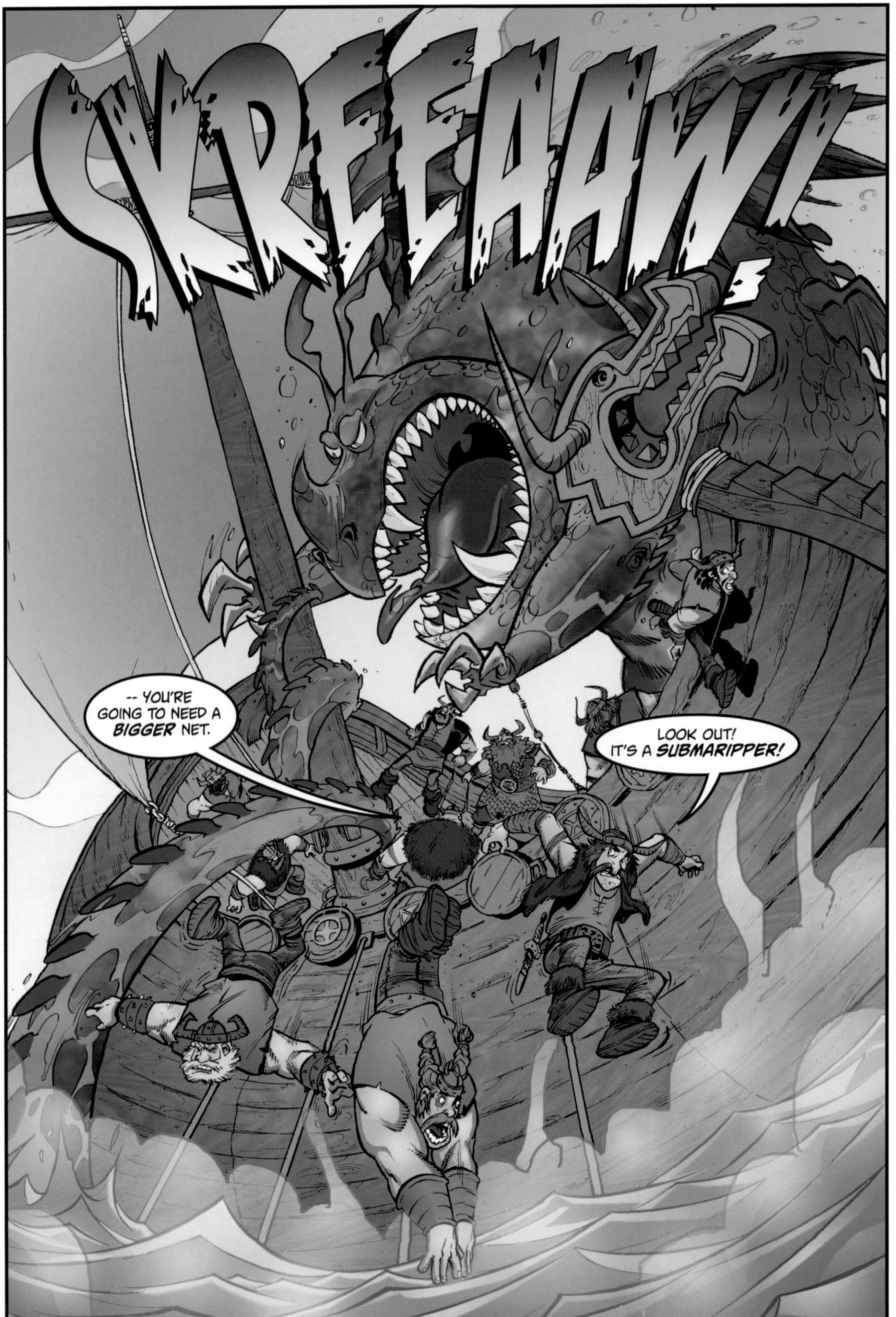
SKREEAAW!
-- YOU'RE GOING TO NEED A BIGGER NET.
LOOK OUT! IT'S A SUBMARIPPER!

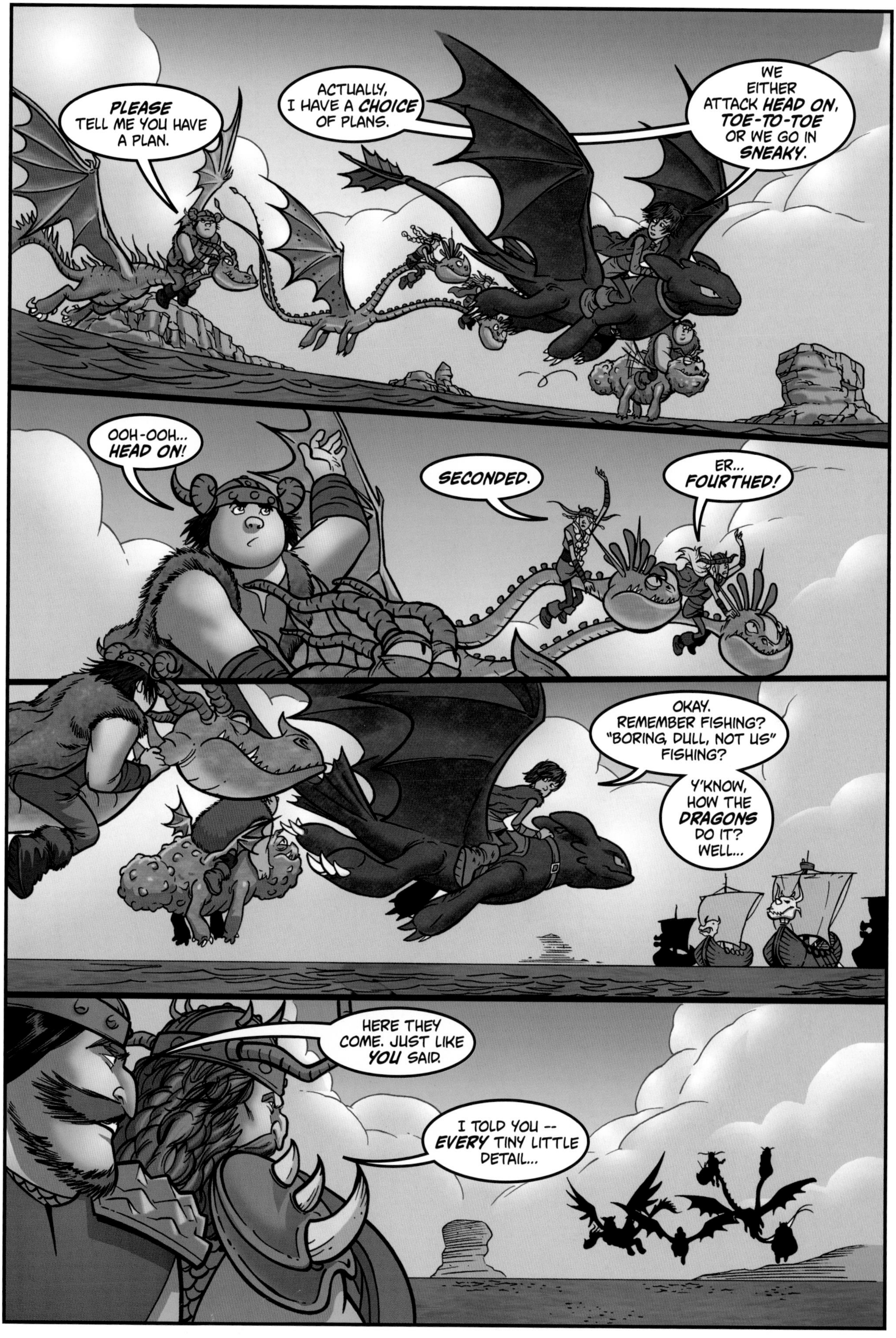
PLEASE TELL ME YOU HAVE A PLAN.
ACTUALLY, I HAVE A CHOICE OF PLANS.
WE EITHER ATTACK HEAD ON, TOE-TO-TOE OR WE GO IN SNEAKY.
OOH-OOH... HEAD ON!
SECONDED.
ER... FOURTHED!
OKAY. REMEMBER FISHING? "BORING, DULL, NOT US" FISHING?
Y'KNOW, HOW THE DRAGONS DO IT? WELL...
HERE THEY COME. JUST LIKE YOU SAID.
I TOLD YOU -- EVERY TINY LITTLE DETAIL...

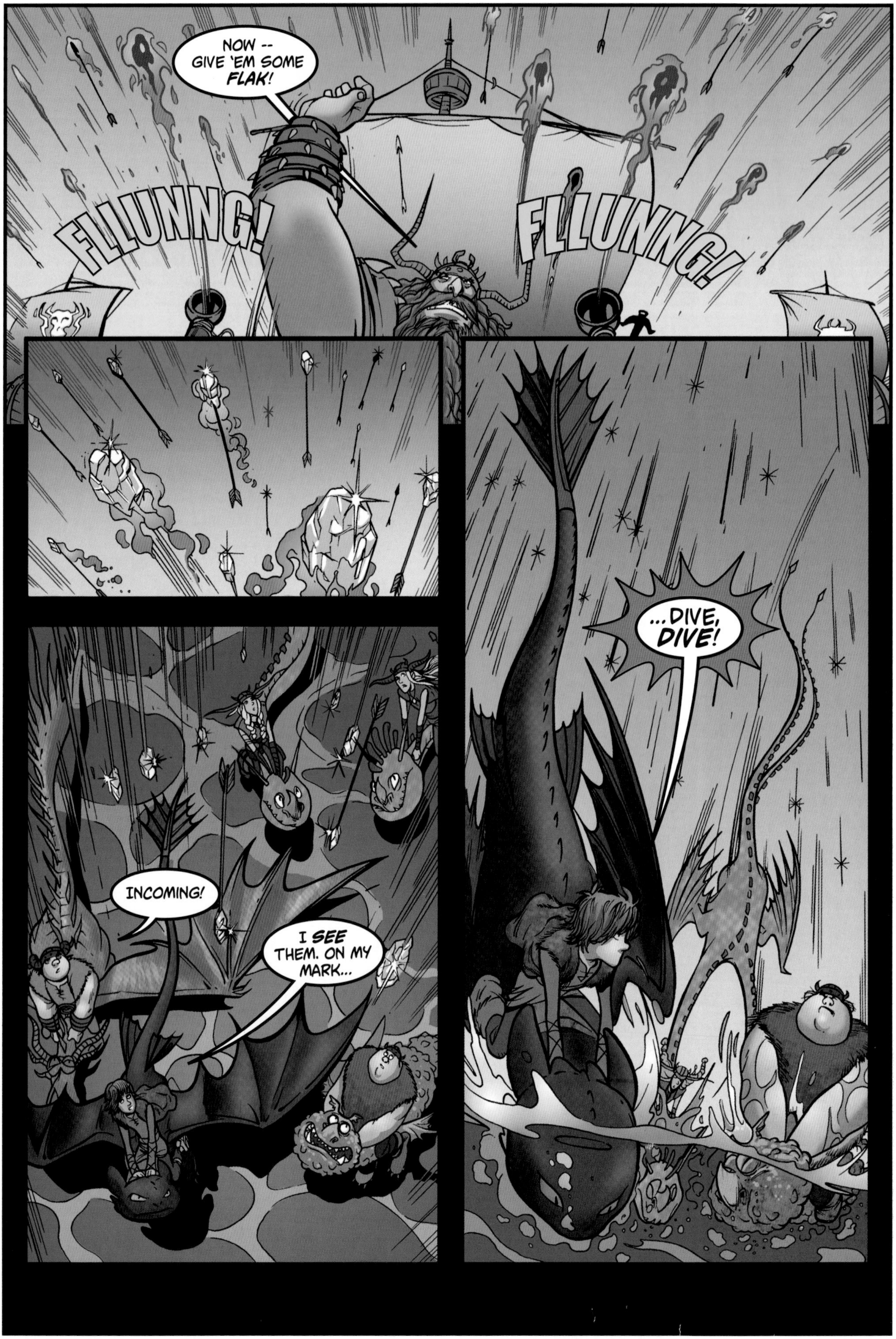
NOW -- GIVE 'EM SOME *FLAK!*
FLLUNNG!
FLLUNNG!
INCOMING!
I *SEE* THEM. ON MY MARK...
...DIVE, *DIVE!*

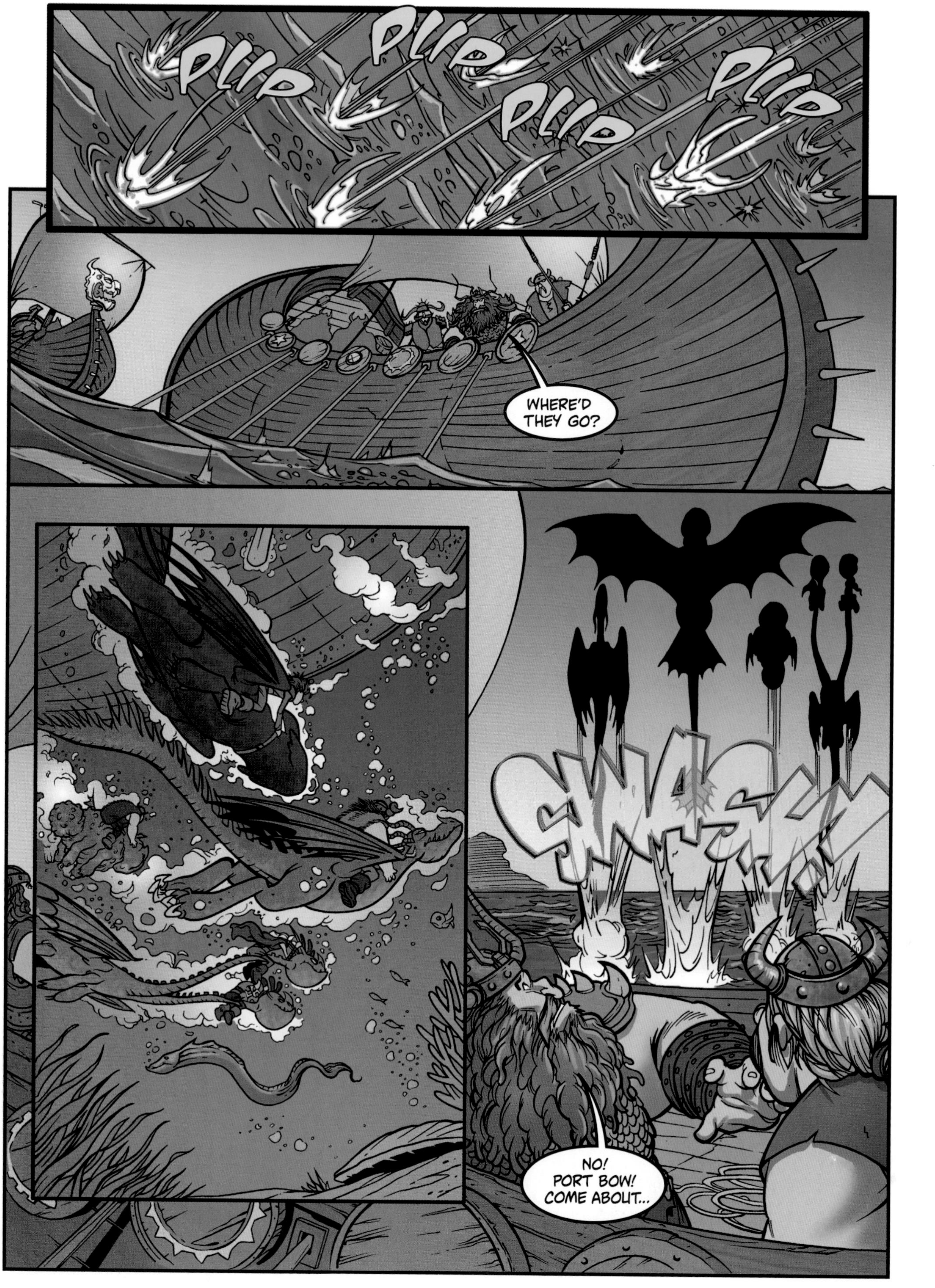
PLIP PLIP PLIP PLIP PLIP PLIP
WHERE'D THEY GO?
SPLASH
NO! PORT BOW! COME ABOUT...

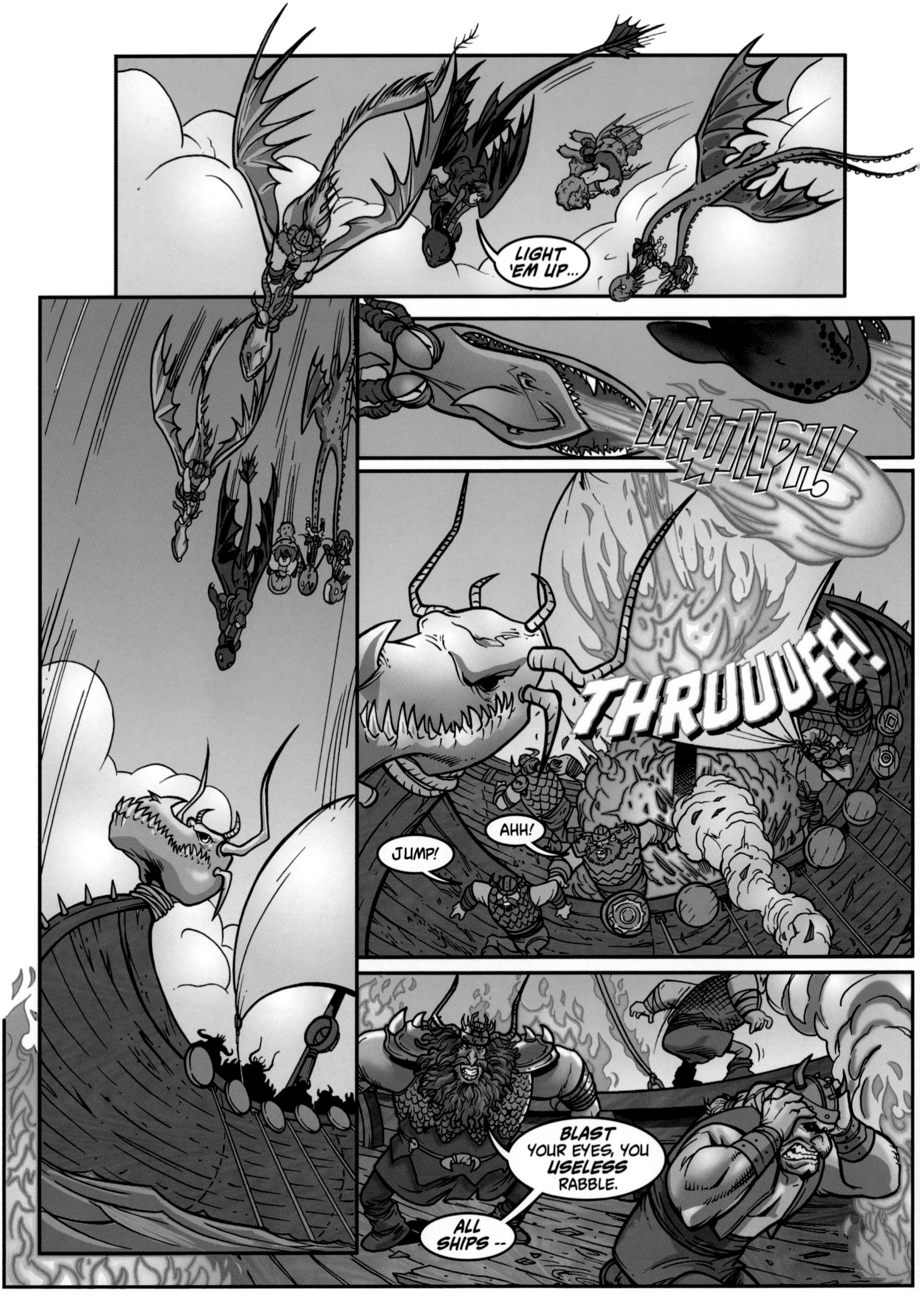
LIGHT 'EM UP...
WHUUMPH!
THRUUUFF!
JUMP!
AHH!
BLAST YOUR EYES, YOU USELESS RABBLE.
ALL SHIPS --

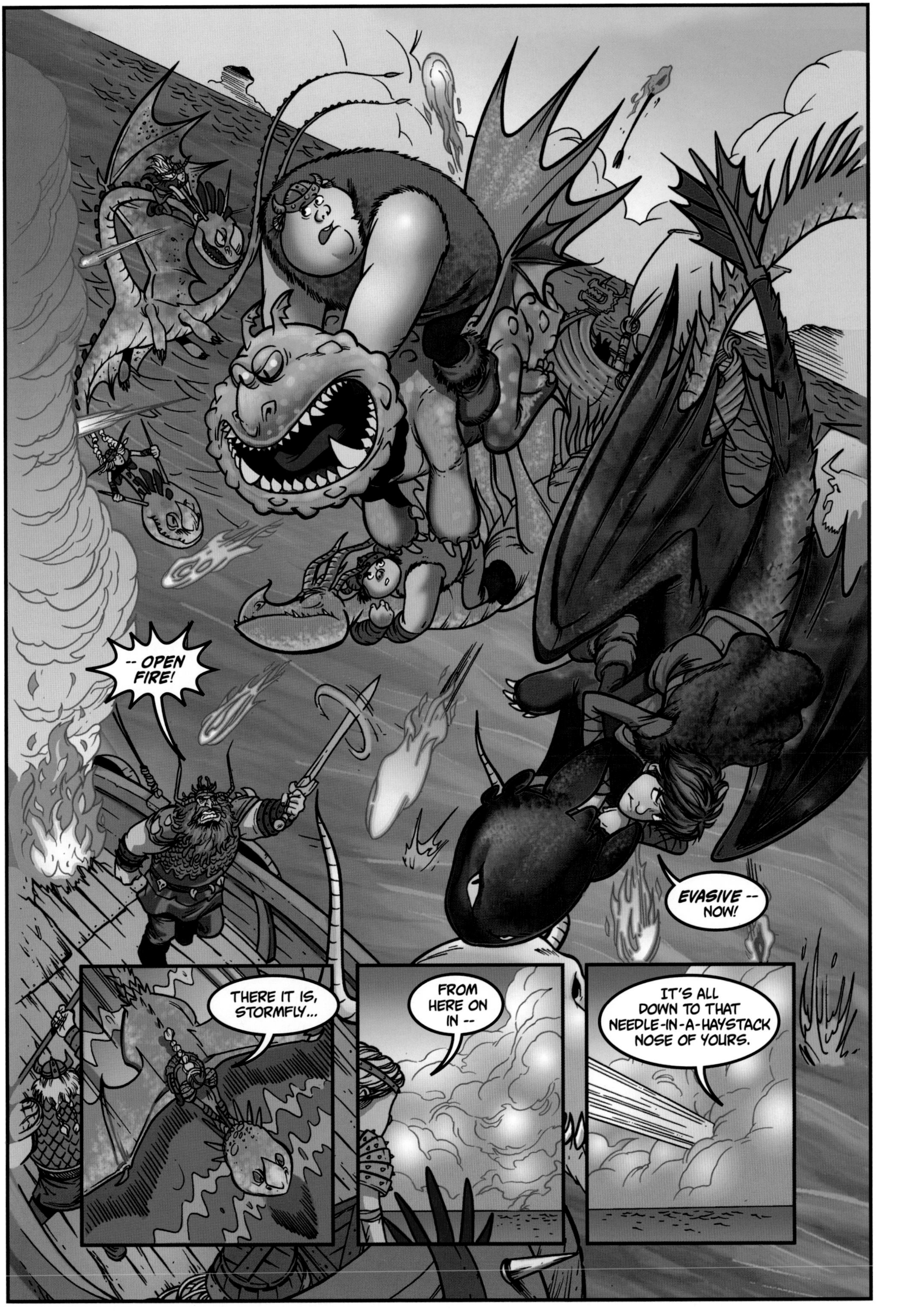
-- OPEN FIRE!
EVASIVE -- NOW!
THERE IT IS, STORMFLY...
FROM HERE ON IN --
IT'S ALL DOWN TO THAT NEEDLE-IN-A-HAYSTACK NOSE OF YOURS.

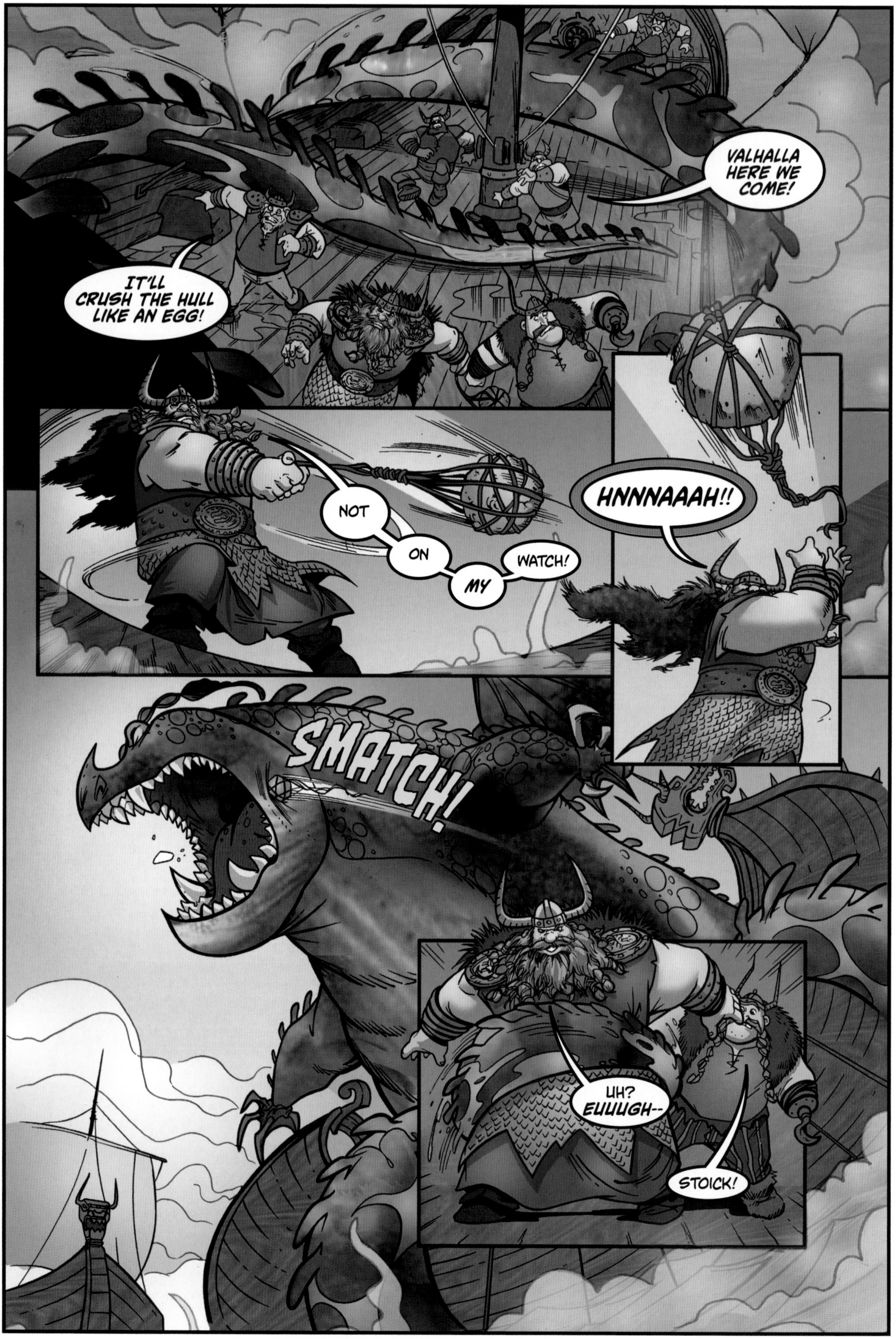
VALHALLA HERE WE COME!
IT'LL CRUSH THE HULL LIKE AN EGG!
NOT ON MY WATCH!
HNNNAAAH!!
SMATCH!
UH? EUUUGH--
STOICK!

CHAPTER FOUR

In which Stoick and his companions must
defeat a giant sea monster, and Hiccup must defeat
the nasty Outcast Tribe...

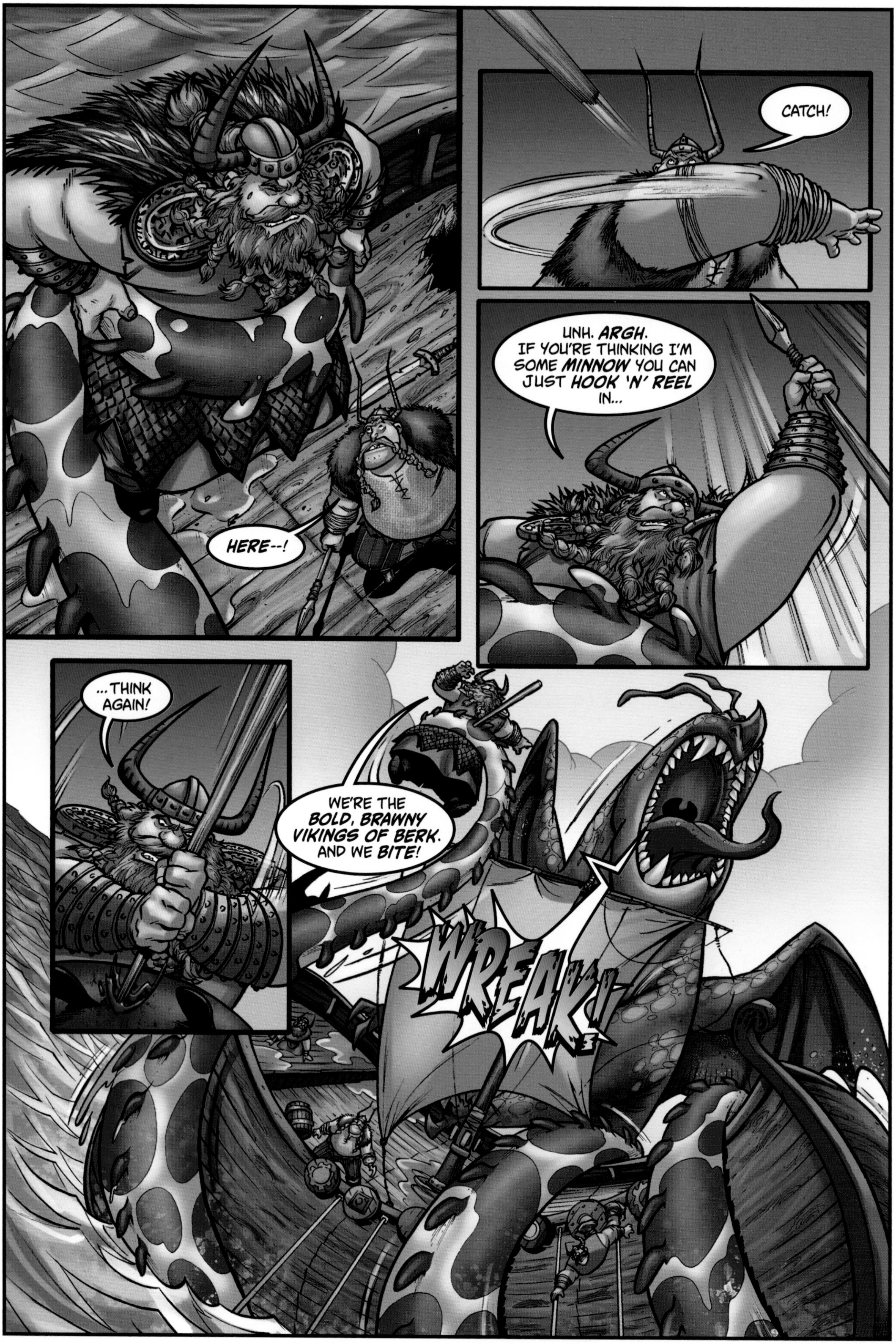
HERE--!
CATCH!
UNH. ARGH. IF YOU'RE THINKING I'M SOME MINNOW YOU CAN JUST HOOK 'N' REEL IN...
...THINK AGAIN!
WE'RE THE BOLD, BRAWNY VIKINGS OF BERK. AND WE BITE!
WREAK!!

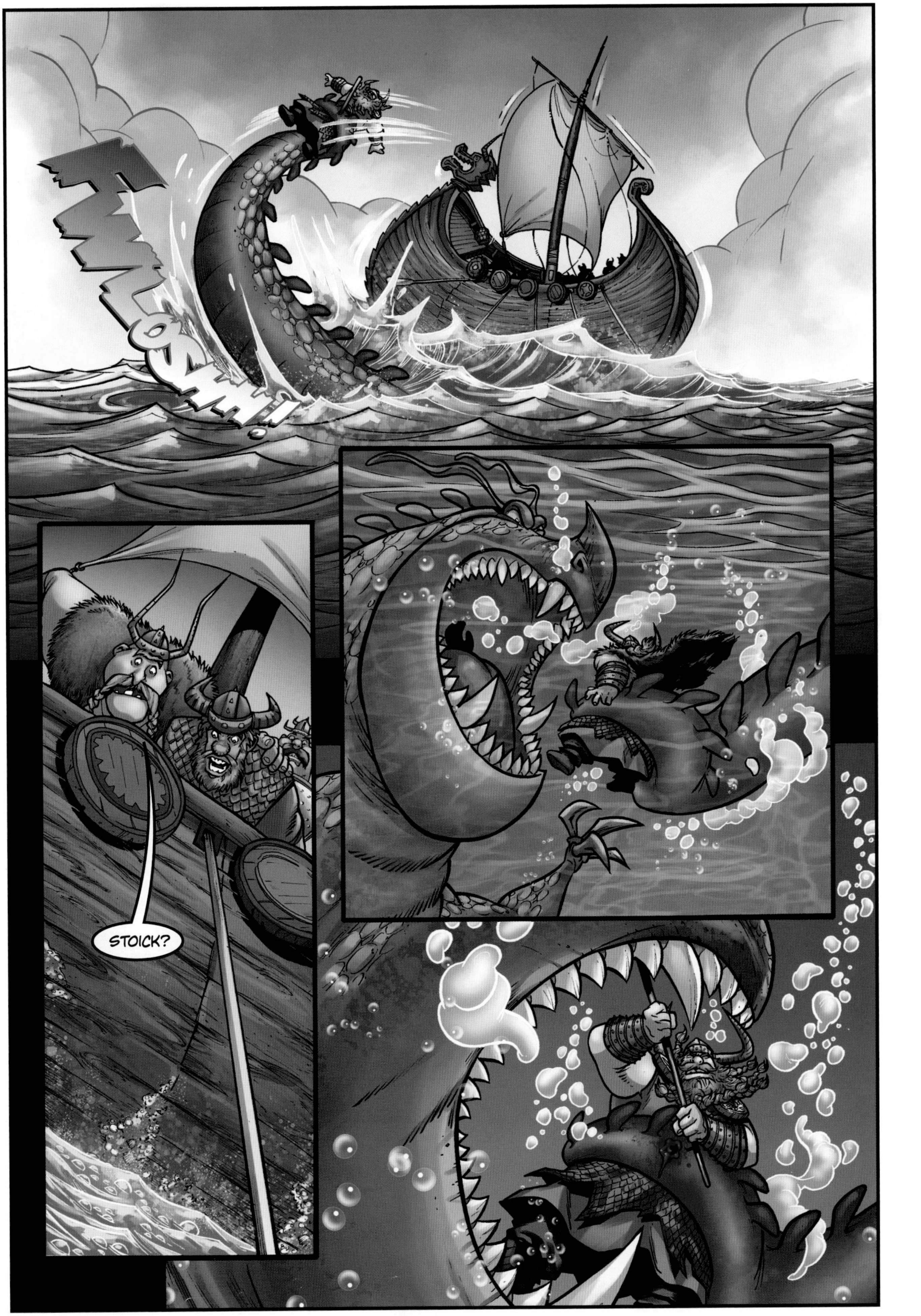
FWLOSH!!
STOICK?

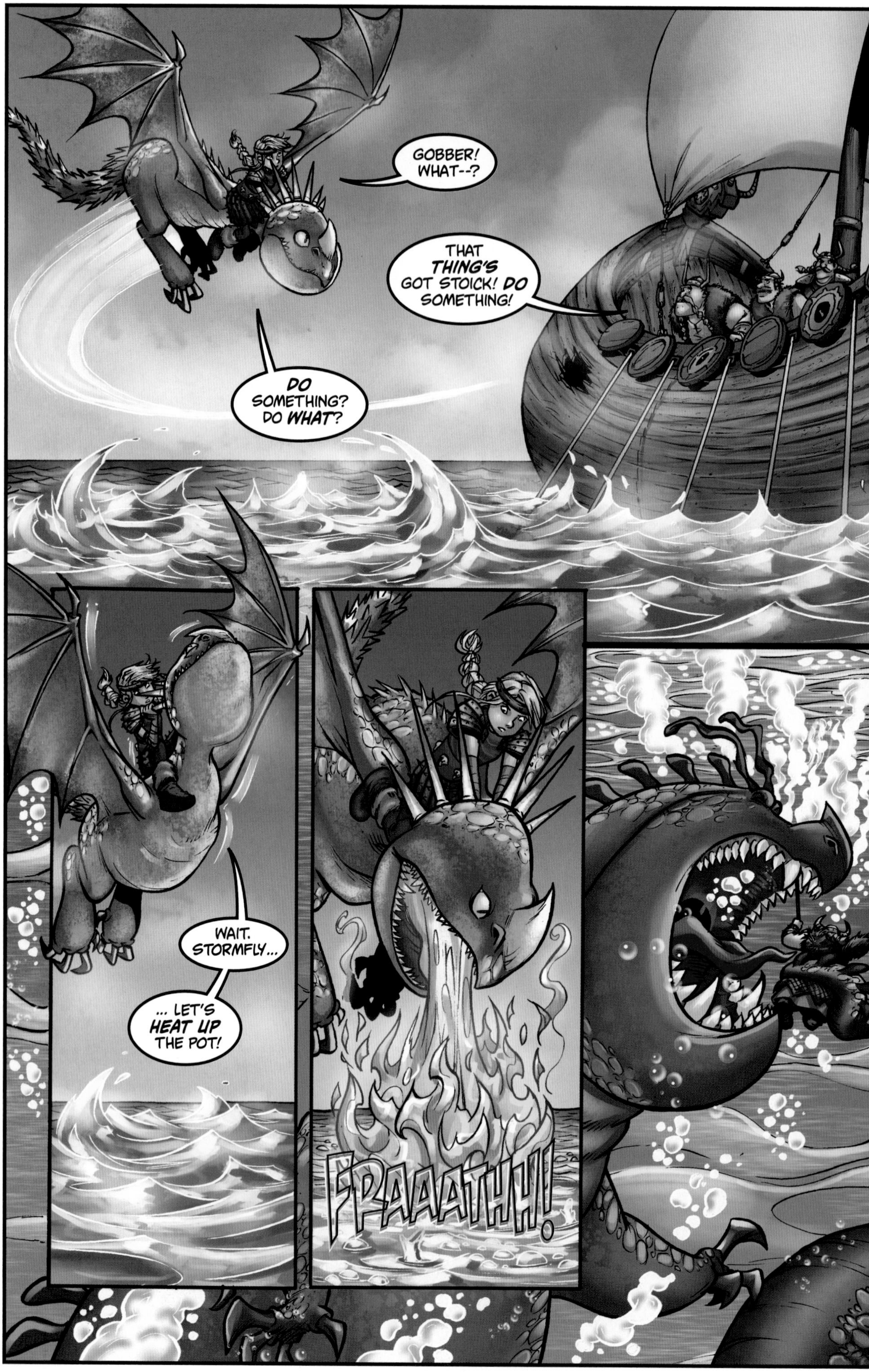
GOBBER! WHAT--?
THAT *THING'S* GOT STOICK! *DO* SOMETHING!
DO SOMETHING? DO *WHAT*?
WAIT. STORMFLY...
... LET'S *HEAT UP* THE POT!
FRAAATHH!

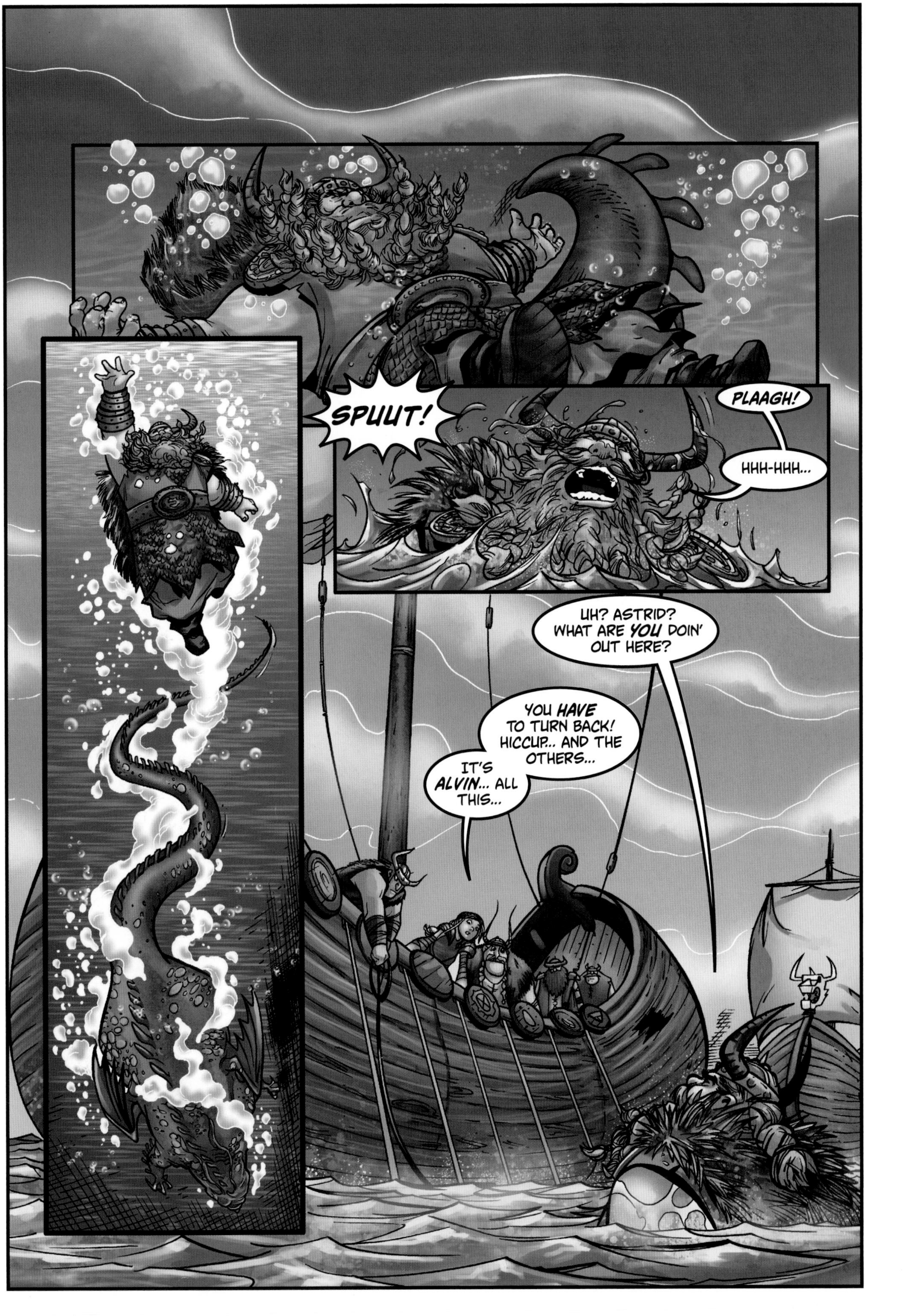
SPUUT!
PLAAGH!
HHH-HHH...
UH? ASTRID? WHAT ARE YOU DOIN' OUT HERE?
YOU HAVE TO TURN BACK! HICCUP... AND THE OTHERS...
IT'S ALVIN... ALL THIS...

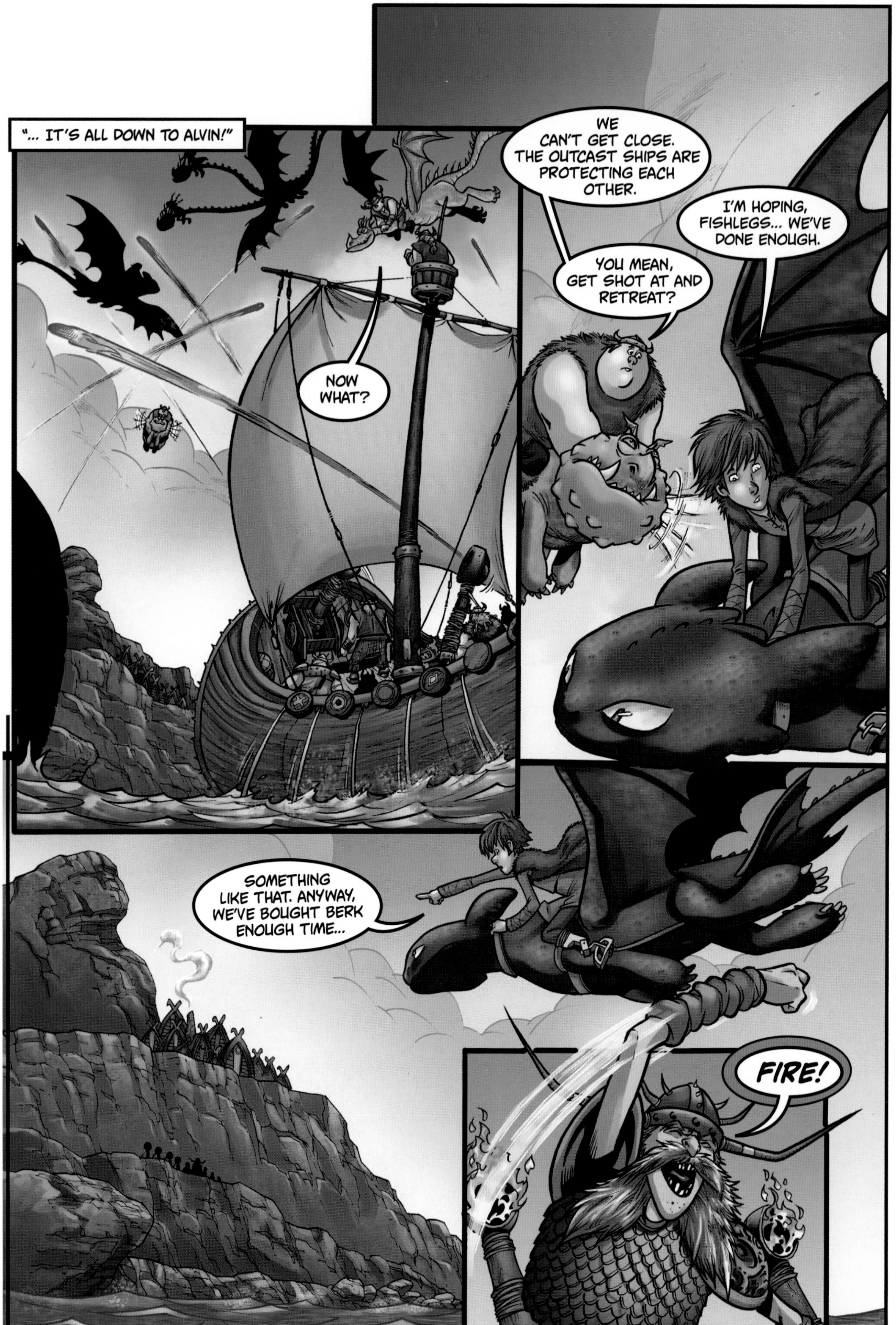
"... IT'S ALL DOWN TO ALVIN!"
NOW WHAT?
WE CAN'T GET CLOSE. THE OUTCAST SHIPS ARE PROTECTING EACH OTHER.
YOU MEAN, GET SHOT AT AND RETREAT?
I'M HOPING, FISHLEGS... WE'VE DONE ENOUGH.
SOMETHING LIKE THAT. ANYWAY, WE'VE BOUGHT BERK ENOUGH TIME...
FIRE!

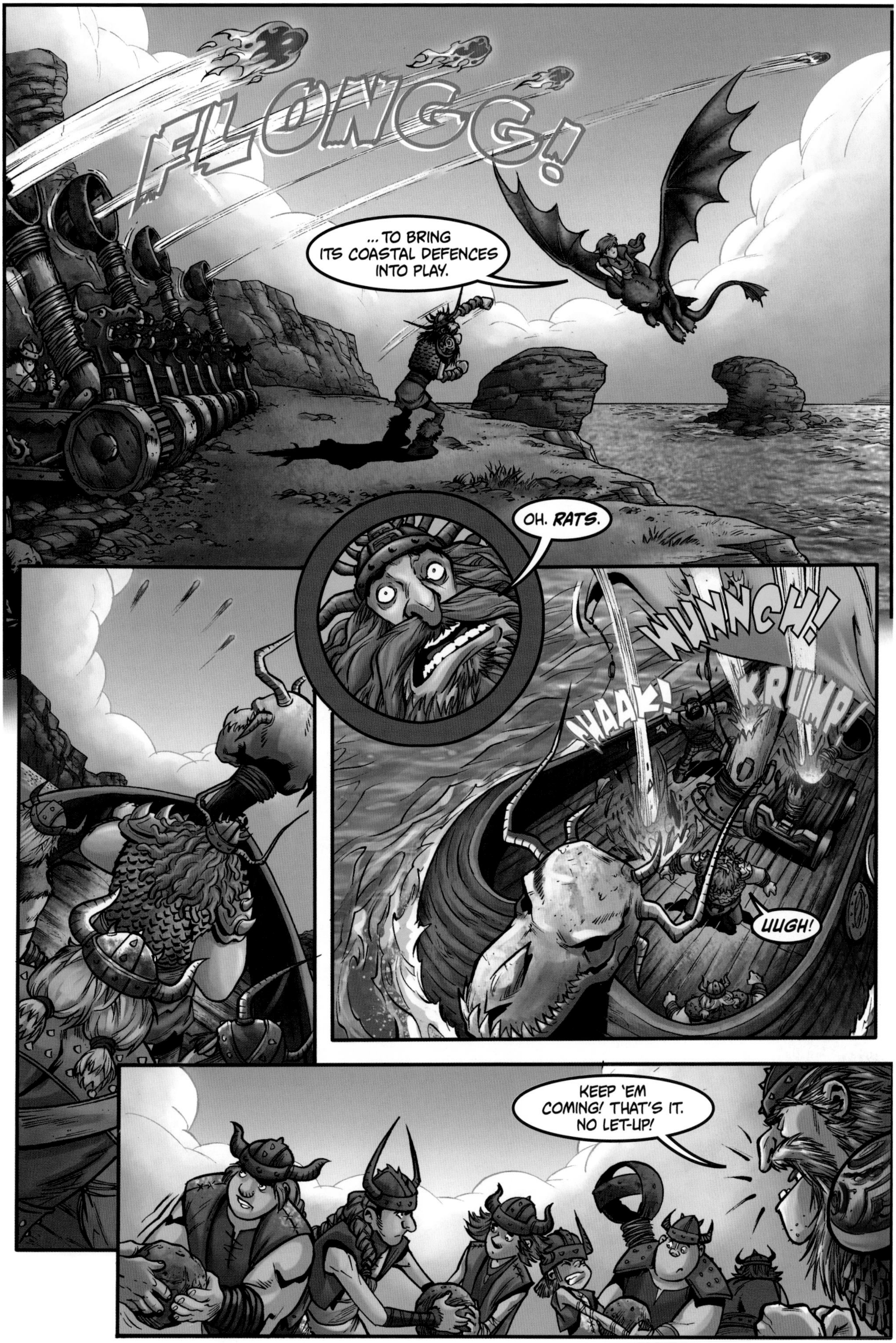
FLONGG!
...TO BRING ITS COASTAL DEFENCES INTO PLAY.
OH. RATS.
WUNNCH!
KRUMP!
WHAAK!
UUGH!
KEEP 'EM COMING! THAT'S IT. NO LET-UP!

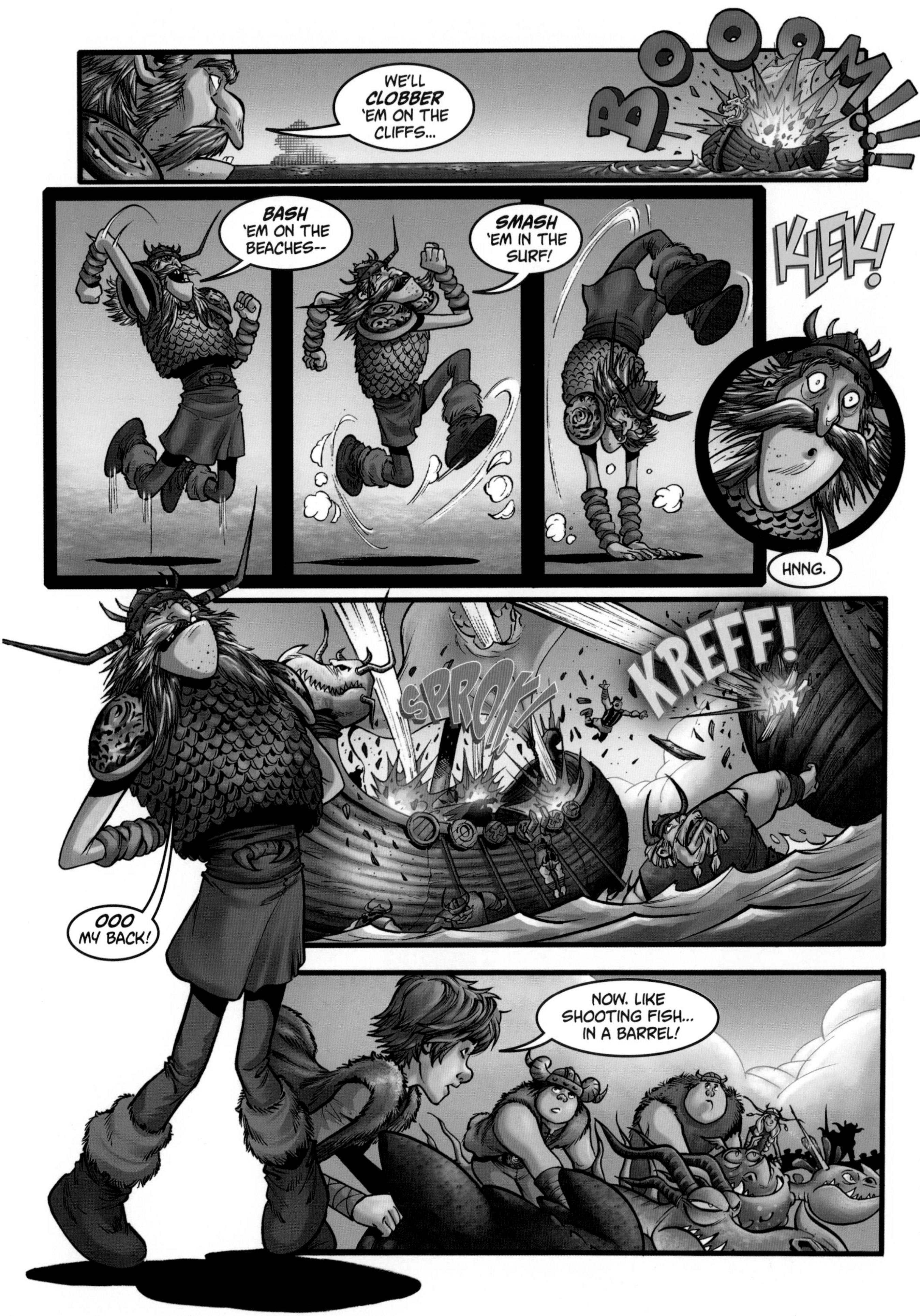
WE'LL CLOBBER 'EM ON THE CLIFFS...
BOOOOM!!!!
BASH 'EM ON THE BEACHES--
SMASH 'EM IN THE SURF!
KLEK!
HNNG.
SPROK!
KREFF!
OOO MY BACK!
NOW. LIKE SHOOTING FISH... IN A BARREL!

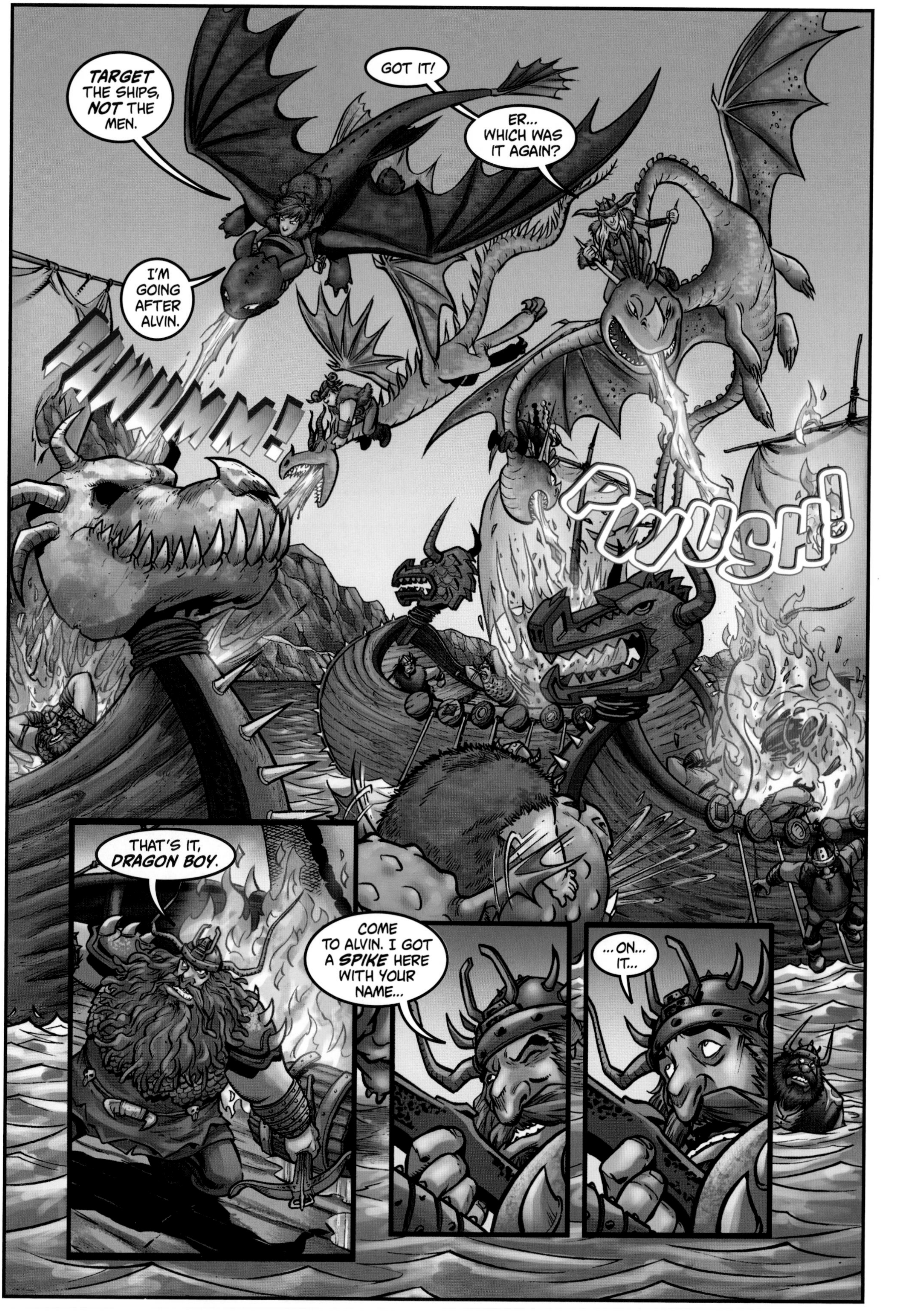
TARGET THE SHIPS, NOT THE MEN.
GOT IT!
ER... WHICH WAS IT AGAIN?
I'M GOING AFTER ALVIN.
FWWUMM!
FWUSH!
THAT'S IT, DRAGON BOY.
COME TO ALVIN. I GOT A SPIKE HERE WITH YOUR NAME...
...ON... IT...

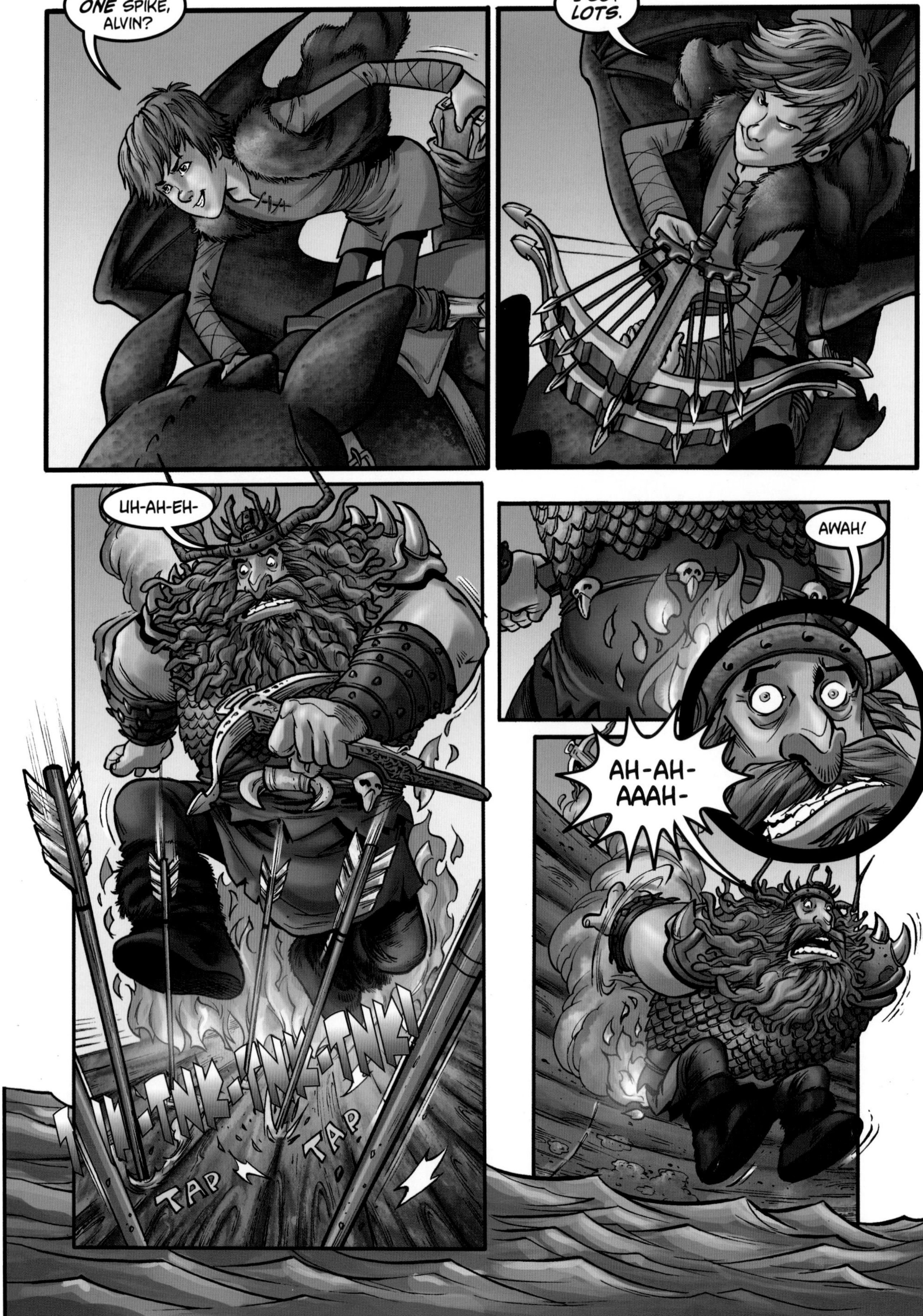
JUST ONE SPIKE, ALVIN?
I GOT LOTS.
UH-AH-EH-
TNK-TNK-TNK-TNK!
TAP
TAP
AWAH!
AH-AH-AAAH-

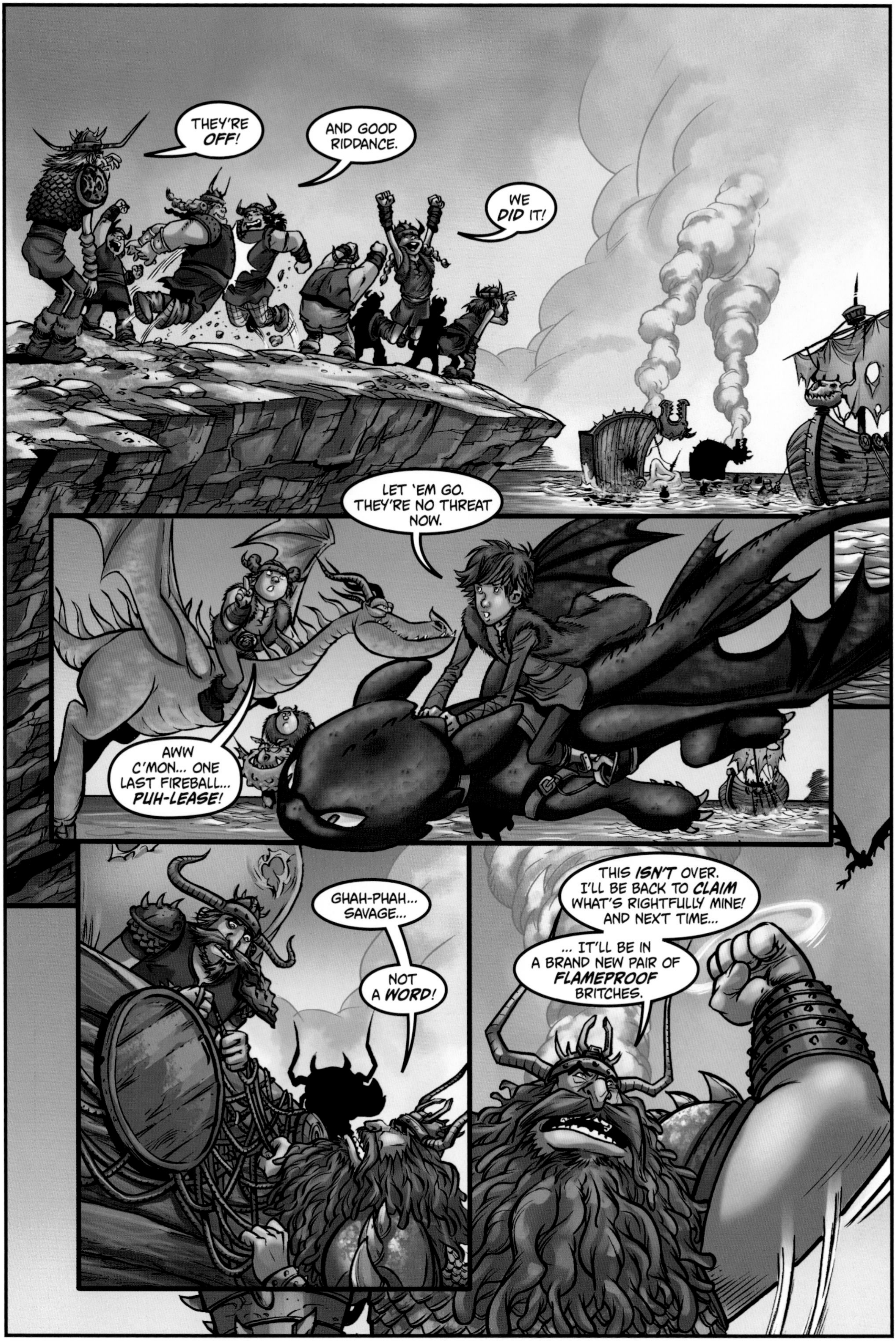
THEY'RE *OFF*!
AND GOOD RIDDANCE.
WE *DID* IT!
LET 'EM GO. THEY'RE NO THREAT NOW.
AWW C'MON... ONE LAST FIREBALL... ***PUH-LEASE***!
GHAH-PHAH... SAVAGE...
NOT A ***WORD***!
THIS ***ISN'T*** OVER. I'LL BE BACK TO ***CLAIM*** WHAT'S RIGHTFULLY MINE! AND NEXT TIME...
... IT'LL BE IN A BRAND NEW PAIR OF ***FLAMEPROOF*** BRITCHES.

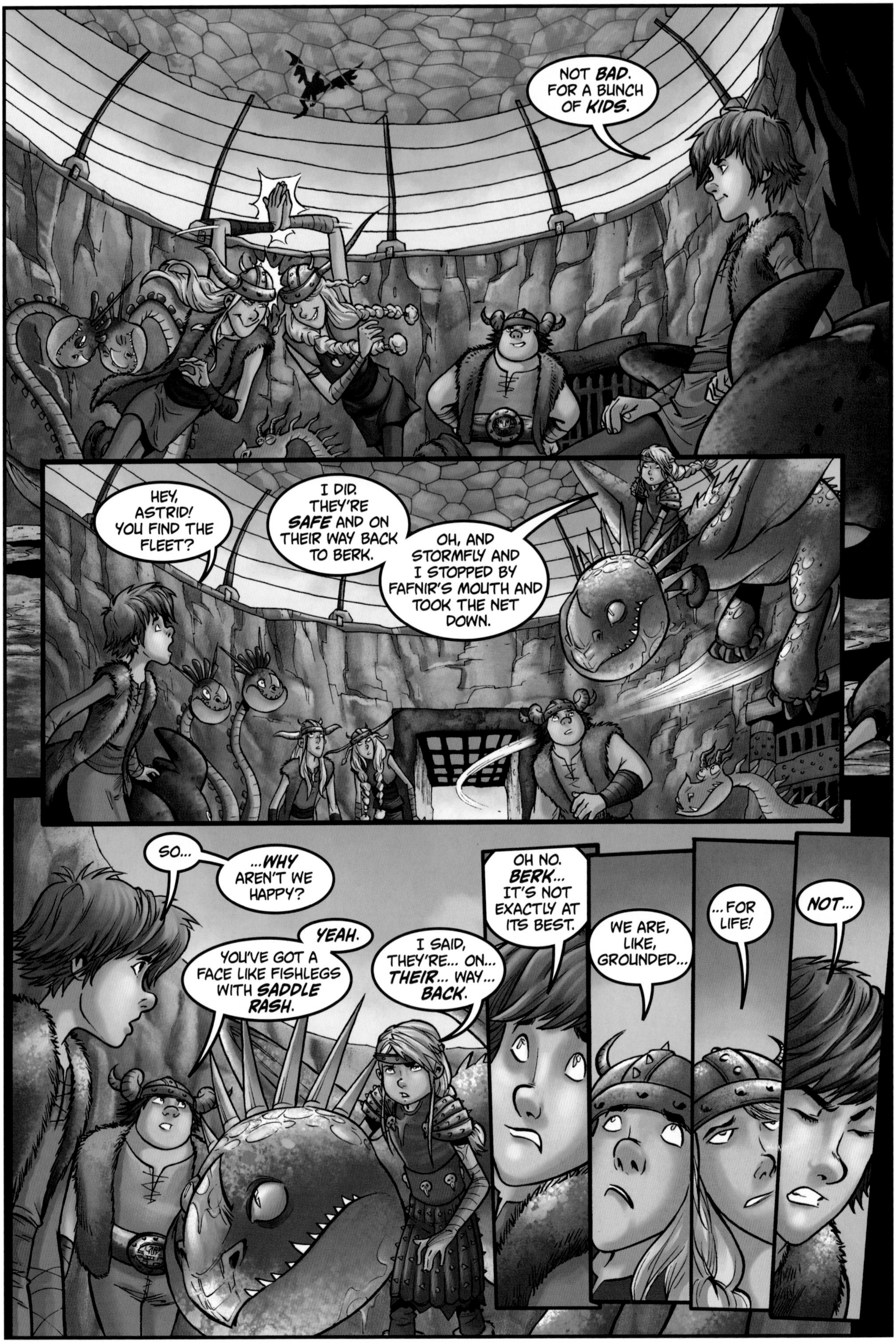
NOT BAD. FOR A BUNCH OF KIDS.
HEY, ASTRID! YOU FIND THE FLEET?
I DID. THEY'RE SAFE AND ON THEIR WAY BACK TO BERK.
OH, AND STORMFLY AND I STOPPED BY FAFNIR'S MOUTH AND TOOK THE NET DOWN.
SO...
...WHY AREN'T WE HAPPY?
YEAH.
YOU'VE GOT A FACE LIKE FISHLEGS WITH SADDLE RASH.
I SAID, THEY'RE... ON... THEIR... WAY... BACK.
OH NO. BERK... IT'S NOT EXACTLY AT ITS BEST.
WE ARE, LIKE, GROUNDED...
...FOR LIFE!
NOT...

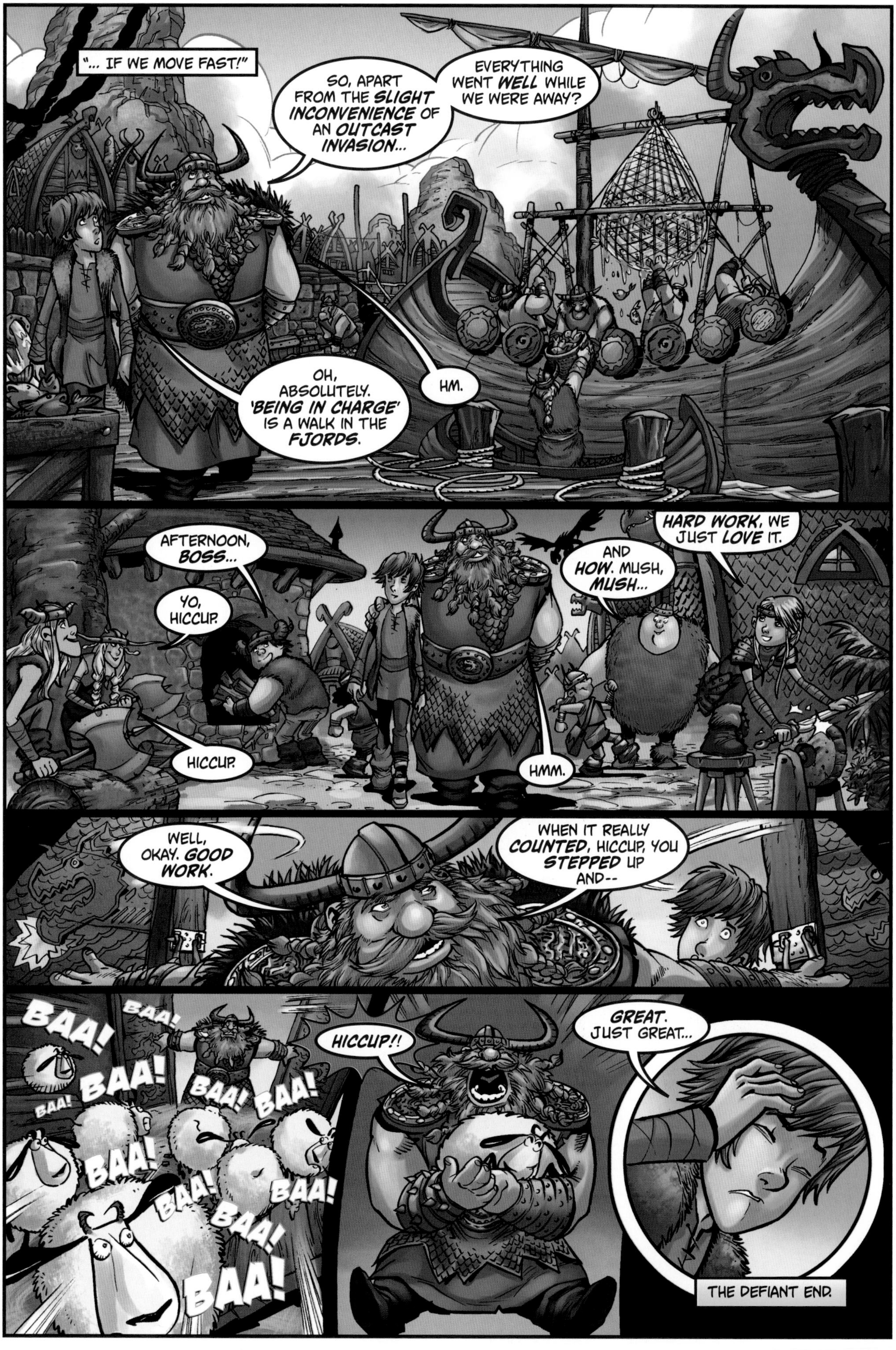
"... IF WE MOVE FAST!"
SO, APART FROM THE SLIGHT INCONVENIENCE OF AN OUTCAST INVASION...
EVERYTHING WENT WELL WHILE WE WERE AWAY?
OH, ABSOLUTELY. 'BEING IN CHARGE' IS A WALK IN THE FJORDS.
HM.
AFTERNOON, BOSS...
YO, HICCUP.
HICCUP.
AND HOW. MUSH, MUSH...
HARD WORK, WE JUST LOVE IT.
HMM.
WELL, OKAY. GOOD WORK.
WHEN IT REALLY COUNTED, HICCUP, YOU STEPPED UP AND--
BAA! BAA! BAA! BAA! BAA! BAA! BAA! BAA! BAA! BAA! BAA!
HICCUP!!
GREAT. JUST GREAT...
THE DEFIANT END.

BONUS MATERIAL

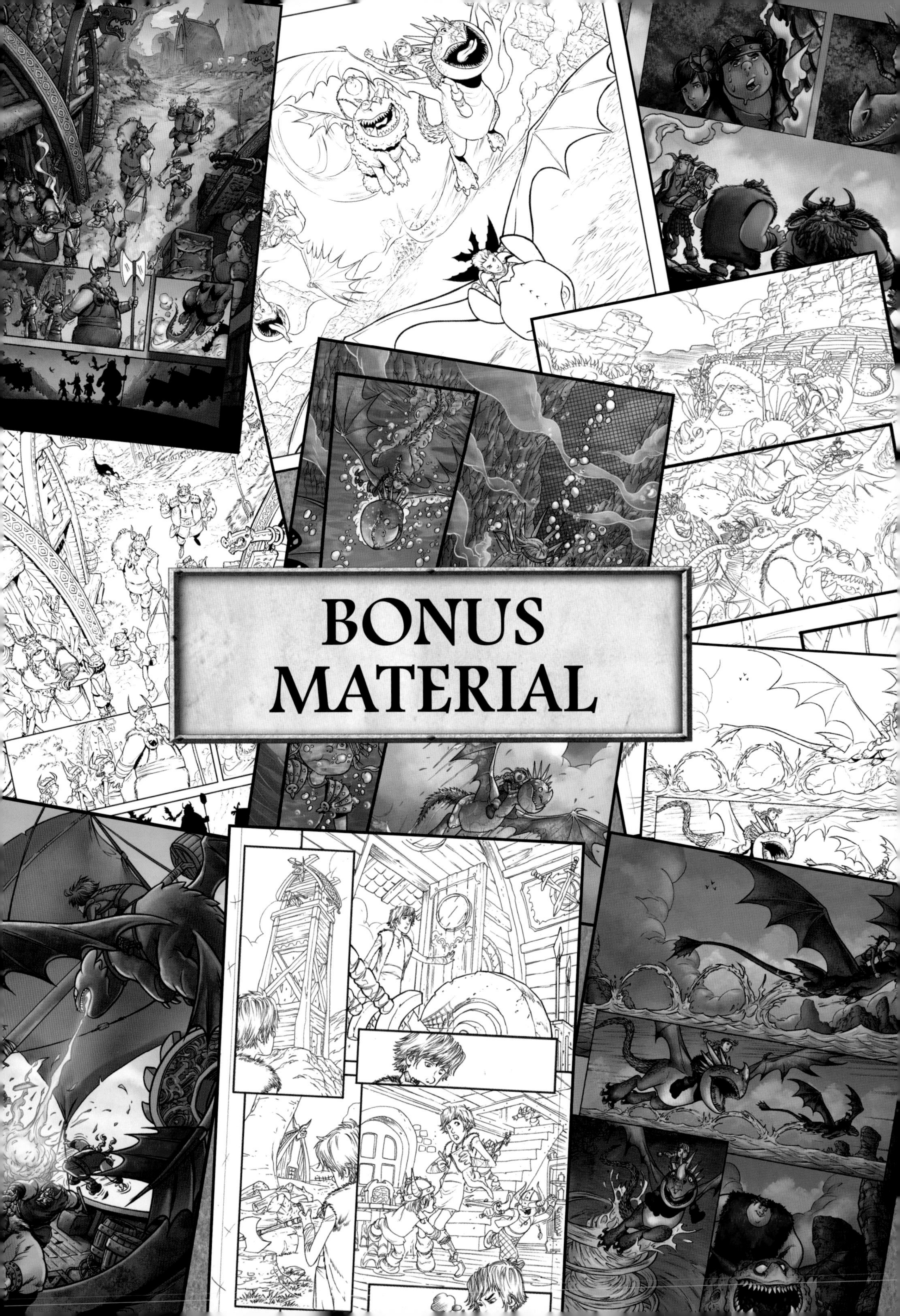

An interview with
IWAN NAZIF,
the talented artist of this collection's two *Dragons: Riders of Berk* stories

For how long have you been drawing?
Since I was a little kid. My parents told me that the first time I knew how to hold a pencil, I started to draw all over the place – on the wall, floor, the back of my school book, basically everywhere!

Are you a big comics fan?
Absolutely! I love every kind of comic. From the all-American super heroes, to European all-ages *Tintin/Asterix*, Japanese manga, and many more.

Which are your favorite *How To Train Your Dragon* characters – human and dragon – to draw, and why?
My favorites are Hiccup and Meatlug. Hiccup because he's the central character and I've loved him since the first time I saw the movie. Meatlug because he is chubby and cute, and easy to draw – his wings are small! ;-)

What is the most challenging aspect of drawing for the *Dragons* graphic novels?
Drawing them consistently and as similar as possible to the original animated characters. That's hard and very challenging. And next to that is to put soul into each panel on the comic so the reader can experience it like they do with the animation.

Were there any particularly difficult pages to draw in *Dragons* Volumes 1 and 2?
Actually there were no difficult pages once I had all the reference materials I needed. I didn't have many references for this comic but I had the animations. So I Googled, watched the movie again and again, screen-captured lots of things. It took the most time in the process. Luckily for me, the editor and staff at Titan were very fast and co-operative on helping me gather those materials. Thanks, guys!

Which page (in Vols 1 and 2) are you most proud of?
Page 1 for book 1, because the page really pictures everyday life on Berk, and I think it's the best page I've ever made during my comic artist career. Next to it is page 44 on book 2, because it's all about an epic colossal battle, and it took me so long to draw.

What advice would you give to aspiring artists?
Never be too lazy to gather materials! It's very important. Also never forget to draw thumbnails (small page layouts). With the small thumbnail, you (and your client) can see the whole idea and find what's missing before you draw the bigger version of it, and even quick-draw some alternatives. Once you work on the big canvas, editing it will be very annoying and time-consuming.

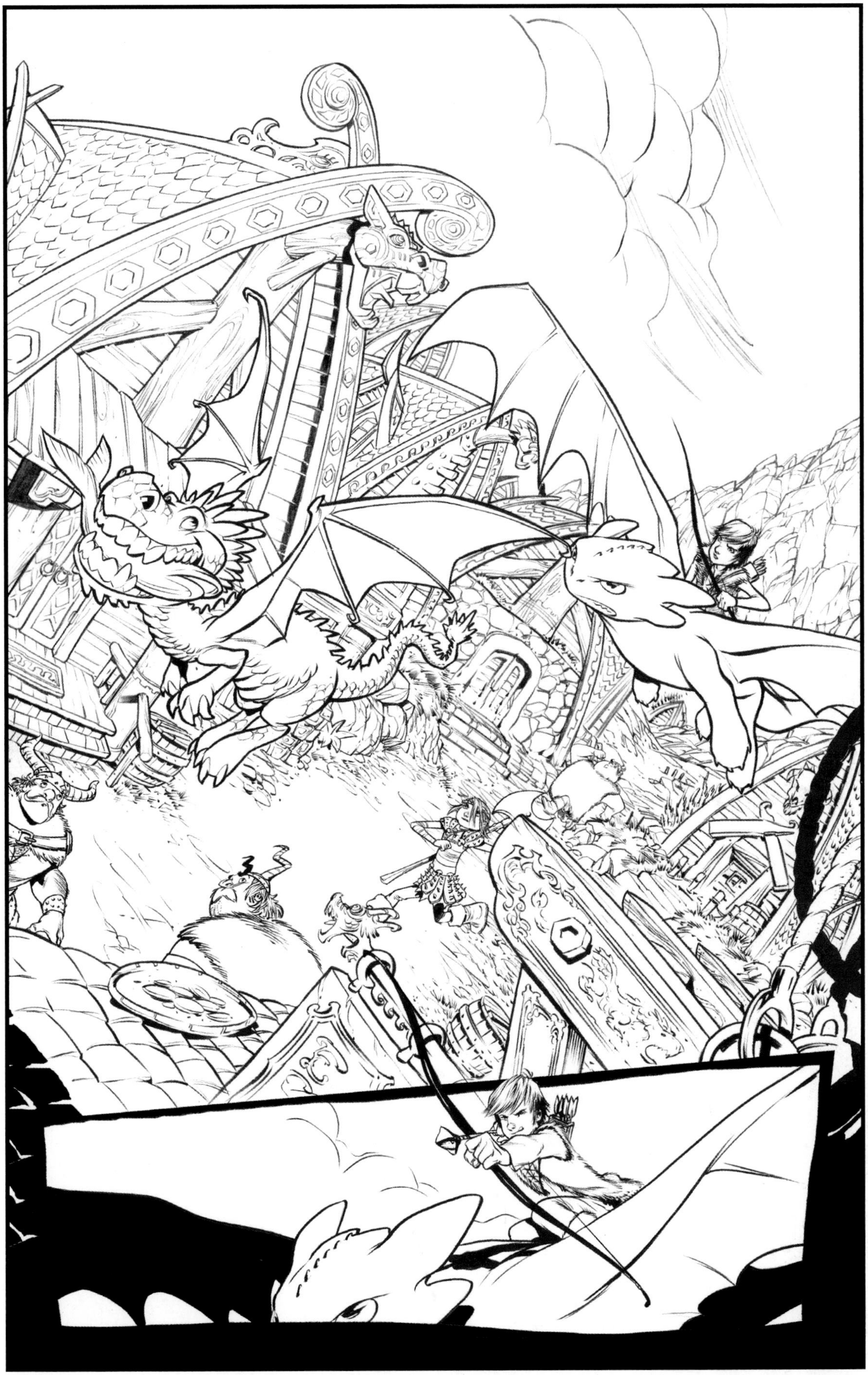

Iwan's trial page for *Dragons*. This pretty much sealed the deal for Iwan to become one of the main artists on the *Dragons* graphic novels.

Please note, this is preliminary artwork, and not fully approved by DreamWorks Animation.

During cover meetings, Titan's *Dragons* Team came up with several ideas for the cover to this Collectors Edition book. We liked one particular version and then someone suggested: "Why not get this image drawn up?" And the rest is history!

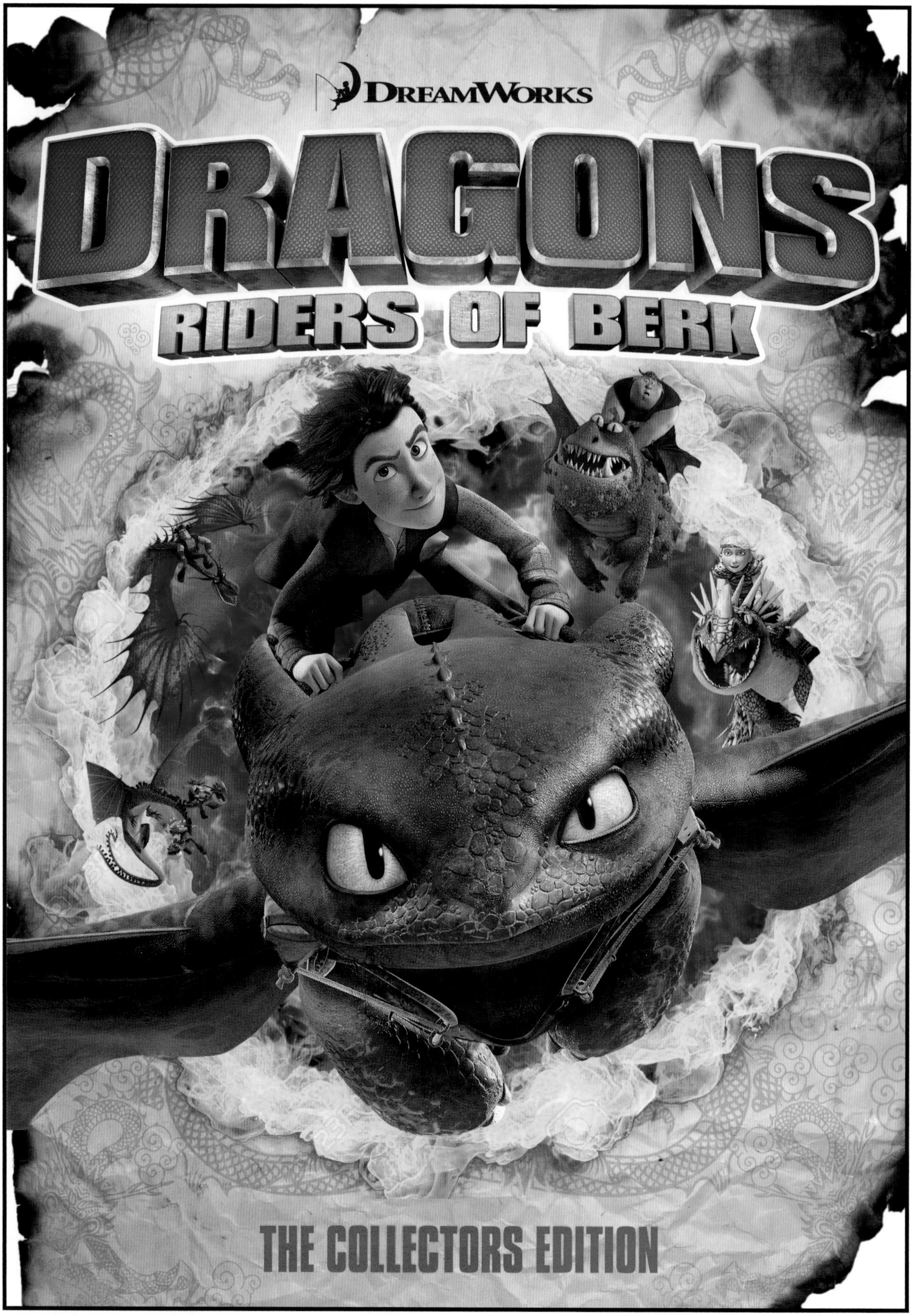
DreamWorks
DRAGONS
RIDERS OF BERK
THE COLLECTORS EDITION

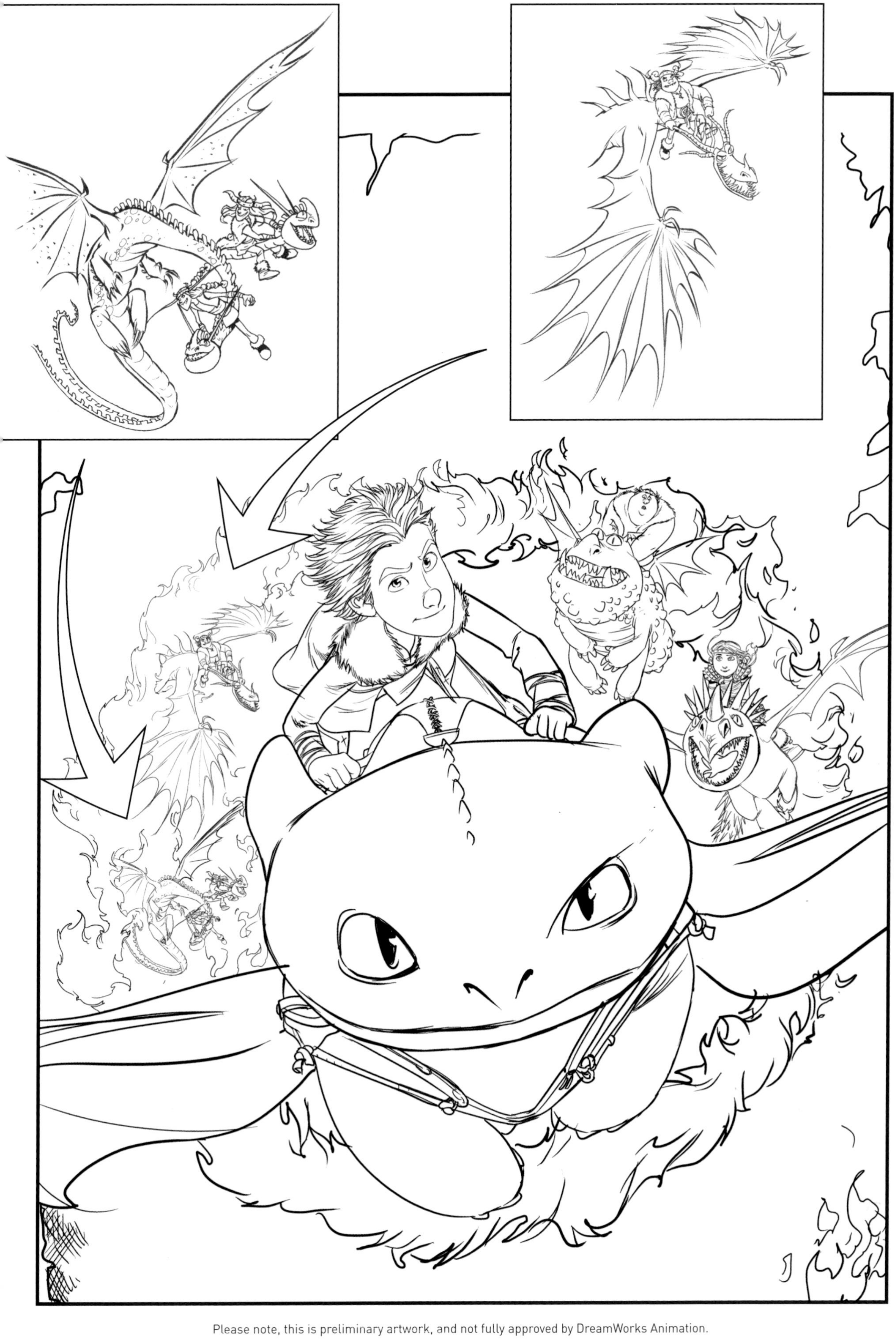

Please note, this is preliminary artwork, and not fully approved by DreamWorks Animation.

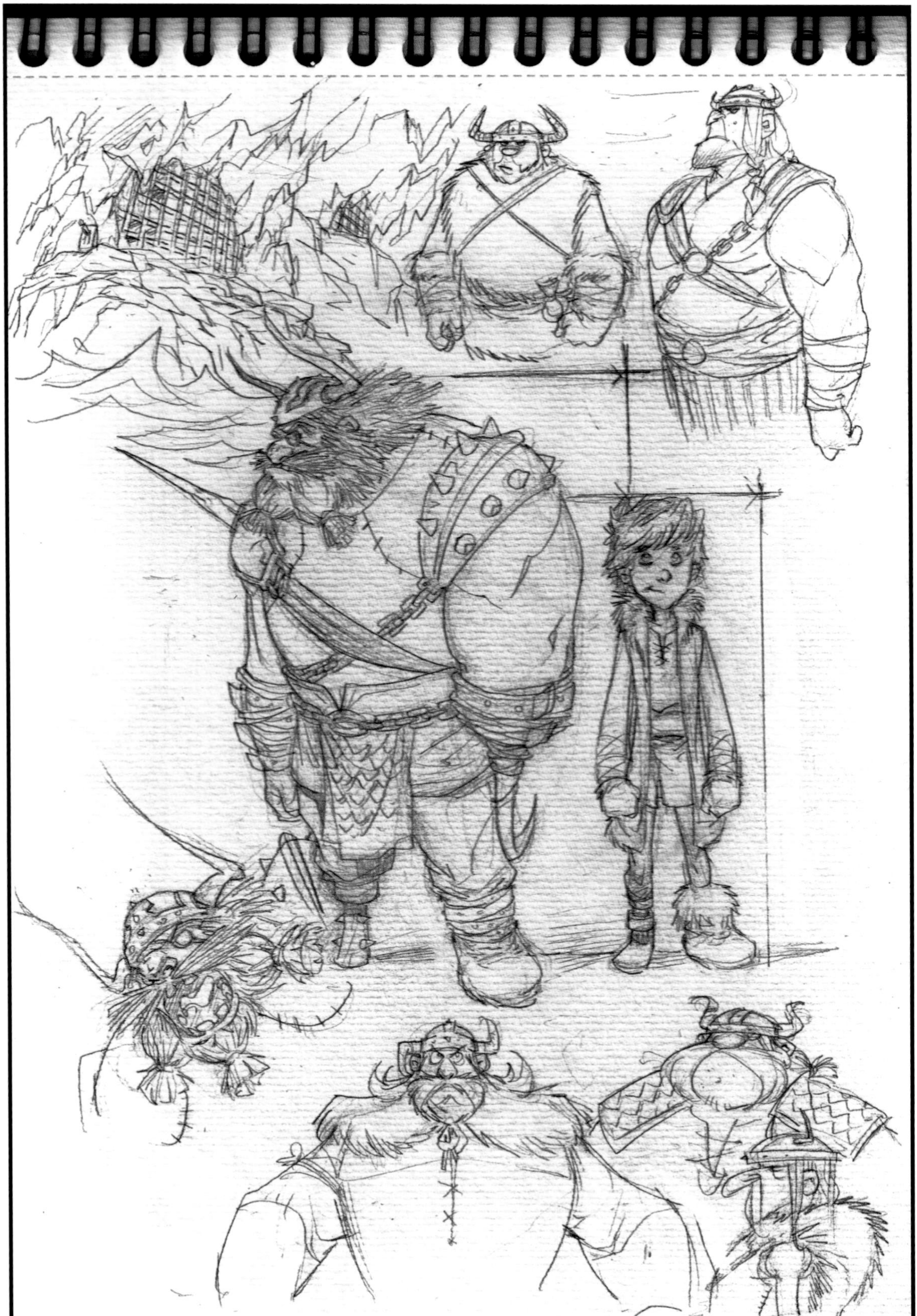

Dragons sketches from Iwan's notepad.

Please note, this is preliminary artwork, and not fully approved by DreamWorks Animation.

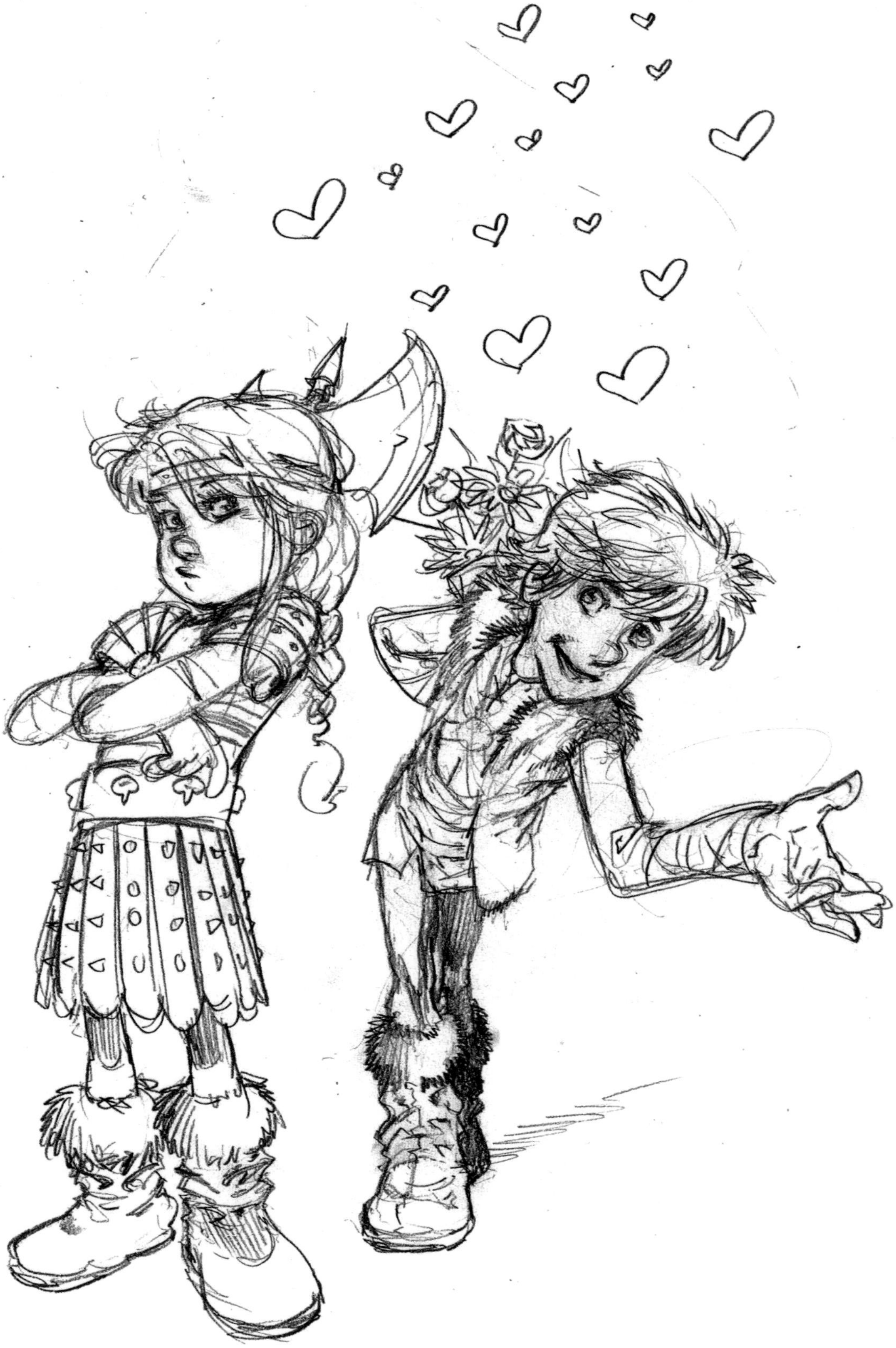

A cute sketch of Hiccup and Astrid by Iwan.

Please note, this is preliminary artwork, and not fully approved by DreamWorks Animation.

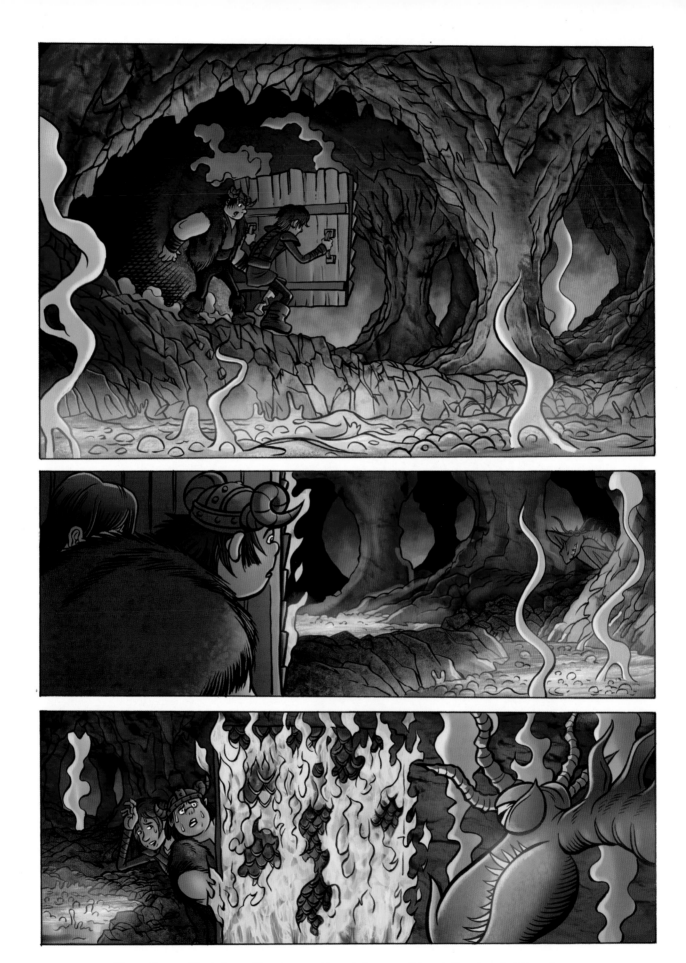

Sometimes it's interesting to see the pictures without the words! Here's an absolutely beautiful page before the lettering was added.

An interview with
SIMON FURMAN,
writer of the *DreamWorks Dragons: Riders of Berk* graphic novels

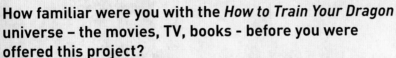

How familiar were you with the *How to Train Your Dragon* universe – the movies, TV, books - before you were offered this project?

I loved the first film, so I was very pumped to be invited to add to this amazing universe, but it was only once I really started delving into the short films, the TV show and the sheer amount of amazing background 'world' detail, that I started to see how much love and thought had gone into *HTTYD*.

It's been a ton of fun immersing myself in the world and then spinning stories that I hope echo that heart and integrity (and fun!) of the first film, and now the sequel, etc. I now consider myself something of a Fishlegs-level *HTTYD* nerd! In other words, I know my Skrills from my Scauldrons.

Which character do you enjoy writing for the most?

It's not actually Hiccup – as you might expect, even though he's a verrrry close second – it's Astrid. I love her no-nonsense and in-your-face attitude. She's great fun to write, and I got a chance to do a little solo Astrid story in Volume Five, *King of the Hill*, which I enjoyed writing immensely. My favorite story (of those I've written) is the Snotlout solo outing in Volume Three, *Litter Sitter*. I thought that one came together really well.

Titan has published six *DreamWorks Dragons: Riders of Berk* graphic novels so far, but there are more in the pipeline and you'll be writing many of them! Can you give us any hints about what to expect?

You can expect action, adventure and monstrous dragons... plus a few new foes as well. I love the idea of pushing further out from Berk, and showing what (and who) else is out there in the Viking world. Volume Three: *The Ice Castle* did a bit of that world mapping and I'd like to do more, introduce other tribes, other chiefs and show how Berk interacts with the wider world.

Oh, and the massive Submaripper may well make another comeback. Watch this space...

If you were a Dragon Rider, which Dragon would be your choice?

I would kill for my very own Toothless, so it'd have to be a Night Fury. But failing that, something really, really big. Like a Submaripper!

What advice would you give to aspiring comic writers?

Just write. Let your imagination have free rein. Tell stories you want to tell. Don't think about doing it – get it down on (virtual) paper and invite constructive criticism.

When I started out, I had imagination but not the discipline and skill. That came through practise and listening when people gave me feedback, good or bad. And mistakes. Make 'em, and learn from them.

From script to pencils! Page 4 of *Dragons* Volume 1.

Script:

Page 4:

1. At speed, Toothless glances off the waves, bouncing (like skimming a stone). Hiccup hangs on for dear life.

HICCUP: I CALL IT SEA-SKIMMING. IT'S FLYING… BUT N-N-N-NOT.

2. Astrid (on Stormfly) accelerates past the skimming Toothless.

ASTRID: CUTE. C'MON, **STORMFLY**, LET'S SHOW THEM…

3. Stormfly circles rapidly over the water, whipping up a tall waterspout funnel (like a tornado).

ASTRID: …HOW TO **REALLY** MAKE A SPLASH!

4. Hovering, Meatlug inhales – vacuuming up small pebbles from a few feet of beach at the foot of a cliff…

FISHLEGS: MEATLUG'S GOT A NEW TRICK TOO. WATCH!

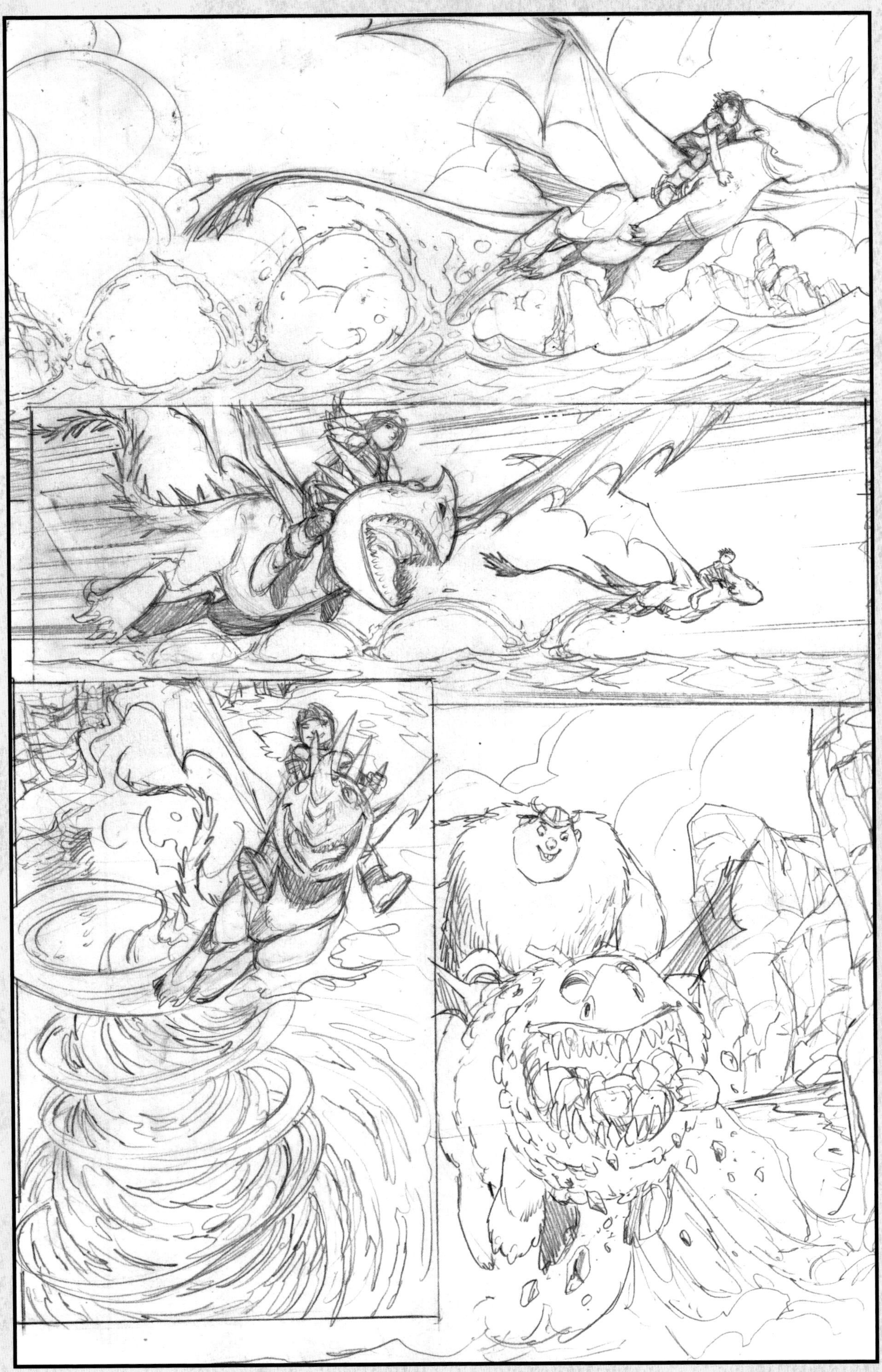

This preliminary artwork is not fully approved by DreamWorks Animation.

From script to pencils! Page 1 of Dragons Volume 2.

DRAGONS VOL2:'DANGERS OF THE DEEP'

48pp Script
– By Simon Furman –

CHAPTER 1

Page 1:

1. Angle on Berk. Enough distance to clearly show it's surrounded on all sides by sea. A large Viking fishing/trawling vessel is manoeuvring itself --

DIALOG CAP: "THIS IS **BERK.**"
DIALOG CAP: "A BIT OF ROCK IN A VERY LARGE OCEAN."
DIALOG CAP: "BUT WE'RE PROUD OF OUR ROCK."
DIALOG CAP: "PROUD AND VERY DEFENSIVE."

2. -- into dock. Where burly Vikings have hold of the Trawler's ropes, heaving it the last few feet up to the wooden jetty. Yak-drawn carts have been reversed up to the edge, ready.

DIALOG CAP: "IT MAY NOT LOOK MUCH, BUT IT'S OURS, AND GENERALLY--"

3. Hiccup (on Toothless) swoops down into shot, heading towards the jetty.

DIALOG CAP: "--WE AIM TO **KEEP** IT."
HICCUP (off): LOOK **TOOTHLESS!**
HICCUP: THE **CATCH** IS IN. C'MON.

4. Reverse angle on Hiccup and Toothless as they descend. Toothless flicks his tongue out the side of his mouth, hungrily.

HICCUP: THERE'S ALWAYS A FEW SPARE FISH FOR A HUNGRY DRAGON TO GRAB.
TOOTHLESS: **THLAP!**

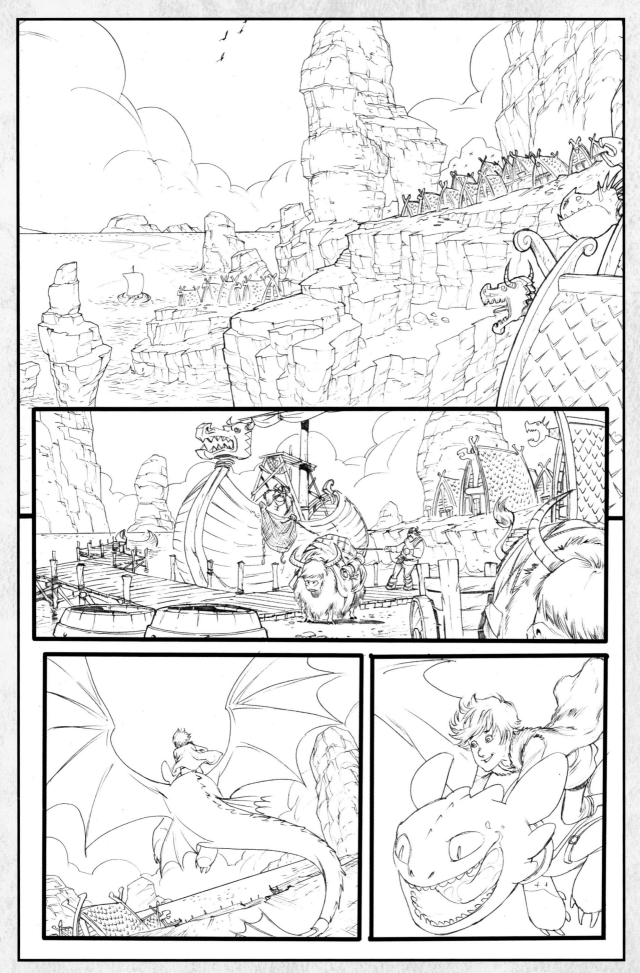

AVAILABLE NOW

DREAMWORKS
DRAGONS
RIDERS OF BERK
DRAGON DOWN

VOLUME ONE

Snotlout's dragon, Hookfang, flies off and goes missing, and a search party is organized... Unfortunately, Alvin the Treacherous is also on the hunt for Hookfang...

On sale now!

DREAMWORKS
DRAGONS
RIDERS OF BERK
DANGERS OF THE DEEP

VOLUME TWO

Berk is attacked while Hiccup is in charge... And in the scary Veil of Mists, Stoick and his crew are being stalked by something huge – and deadly...

On sale now!

DREAMWORKS
DRAGONS
RIDERS OF BERK
FROM THE WORLD OF
DRAGON
THE ICE CASTLE

VOLUME THREE

Astrid's dragon, Stormfly, goes missing, and the whole of Berk tries to track her down! What dangers will they ultimately face at... the Ice Castle? Plus, Snotlout babysits some infant Monstrous Nightmares!

On sale now!

DREAMWORKS
DRAGONS
RIDERS OF BERK
FROM THE WORLD OF
DRAGON
THE STOWAWAY

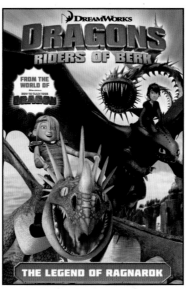

VOLUME FOUR

The Dragon Training Academy gets a new student – a handsome, brave young man named Hroar. And as Hroar becomes more and more popular by impressing Hiccup's friends (especially Astrid), Hiccup grows increasingly suspicious of him...

On sale now!

DREAMWORKS
DRAGONS
RIDERS OF BERK
FROM THE WORLD OF
DRAGON
THE LEGEND OF RAGNAROK

VOLUME FIVE

There is a scary prophecy in Berk that one day a huge monster will rise from the sea and the world will end... And then Hiccup and his friends encounter something huge and scary in the sea... Could this be the end of Berk?!

On sale now!

DREAMWORKS
DRAGONS
RIDERS OF BERK
FROM THE WORLD OF
DRAGON
UNDERWORLD

VOLUME SIX

Hiccup and his friends discover a huge and mysterious cave in the middle of a forest – and they decide to investigate... What dangers will they discover? Meanwhile, out at sea, Stoick faces a gigantic threat from his past...

On sale now!

COMING IN MARCH 2016... DREAMWORKS DRAGONS: DEFENDERS OF BERK VOLUME ONE: 'ENDLESS NIGHT'!

DREAMWORKS CLASSICS GRAPHIC NOVEL COLLECTION

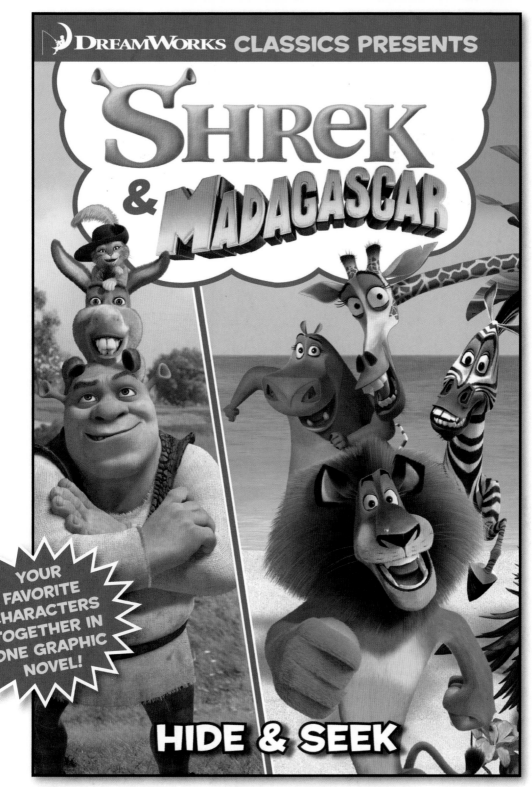

DreamWorks CLASSICS PRESENTS

SHREK & MADAGASCAR

YOUR FAVORITE CHARACTERS TOGETHER IN ONE GRAPHIC NOVEL!

HIDE & SEEK

VOLUME 1 SEPTEMBER 2015!

WWW.TITAN-COMICS.COM

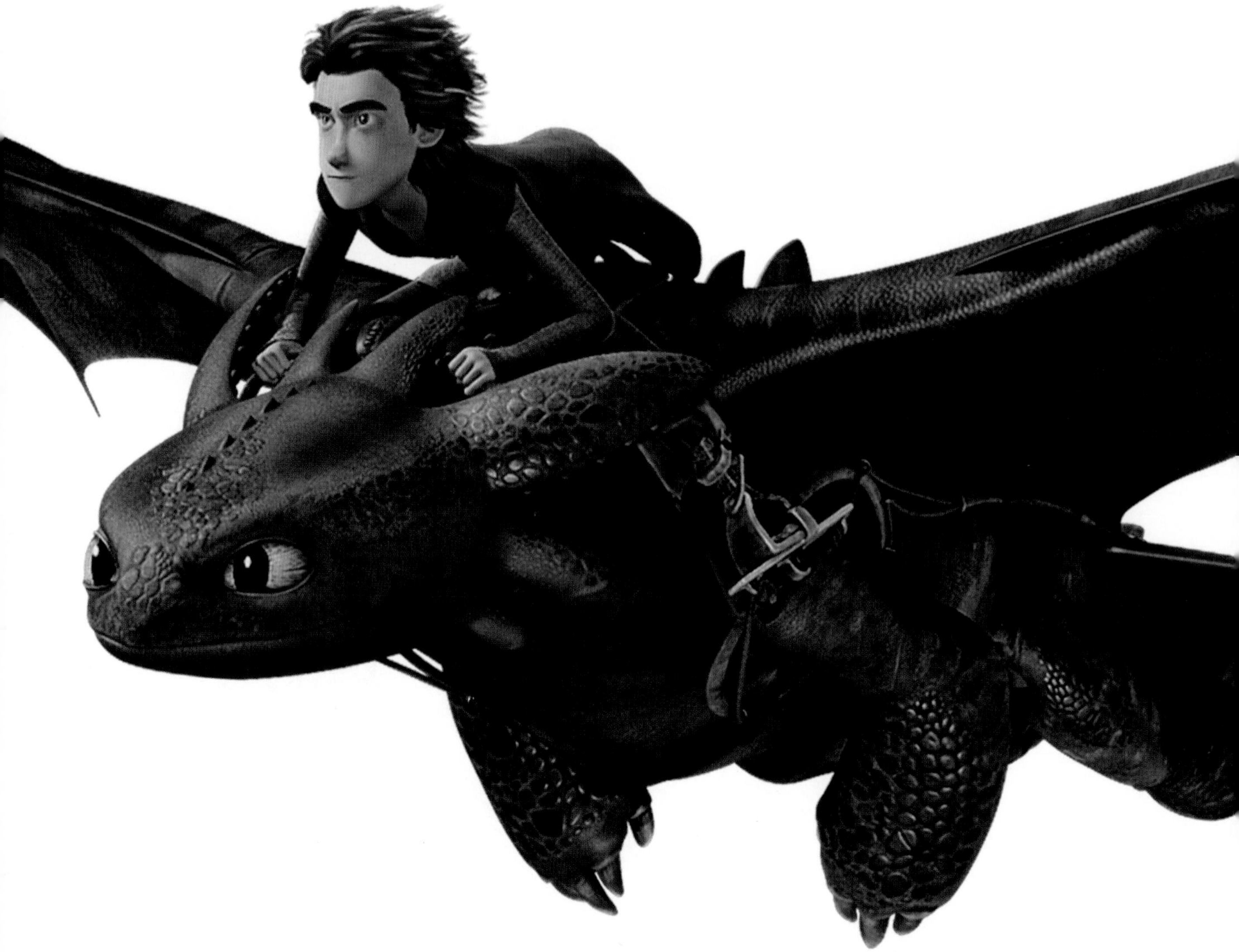